THE GIRL FROM THE SAVOY

Center Point
Large Print

Also by Hazel Gaynor and available from
Center Point Large Print:

A Memory of Violets

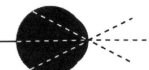

**This Large Print Book carries the
Seal of Approval of N.A.V.H.**

THE GIRL FROM THE SAVOY

Hazel Gaynor

CENTER POINT LARGE PRINT
THORNDIKE, MAINE

This Center Point Large Print edition
is published in the year 2016 by arrangement with
William Morrow, an imprint of HarperCollins Publishers.

The text of this Large Print edition is unabridged.
In other aspects, this book may vary
from the original edition.
Printed in the United States of America
on permanent paper.
Set in 16-point Times New Roman type.

ISBN: 978-1-68324-022-8

Library of Congress Cataloging-in-Publication Data

Names: Gaynor, Hazel, author.
Title: The girl from the Savoy / Hazel Gaynor.
Description: Center Point Large Print edition. | Thorndike, Maine :
Center Point Large Print, 2016.
Identifiers: LCCN 2016017858 | ISBN 9781683240228
     (hardcover : alk. paper)
Subjects: LCSH: Hotel cleaning personnel—Fiction. | Savoy Hotel
(London, England)—Fiction. | Large type books. | GSAFD: Love
stories.
Classification: LCC PR6107.A974 G568 2016 | DDC 823/.92—dc23
LC record available at https://lccn.loc.gov/2016017858

For my sister, Helen.
With love, and a large G&T.

THE GIRL FROM THE SAVOY

. . . men and girls came and went like moths among the whisperings and the champagne and the stars.

—F. Scott Fitzgerald, *The Great Gatsby*

Prologue

In my heart, I always knew he would go; that they would all go, in the end. Now the dreaded day has arrived. Teddy is going to war and there is nothing I can do to prevent it.

Everything is a blur. I don't remember eating breakfast. I don't remember laying the fires or doing any of my usual chores. I don't remember hanging up my apron or putting on my coat and hat. I'm not even sure I closed the door behind me as I set off for the station, but I must have done all these things because somehow I am here, standing on the platform, and he is pressing a bunch of daffodils into my hands. Somehow, he is really leaving.

"I'll be back before you know it," he says, brushing a tear from my cheek. "They won't know what's hit them when we arrive. Look at us. Tough as old boots!" I glance along the platform. The assembled conscripts look like frightened young boys. Not soldiers. Not tough at all. "I'll be back for your birthday and I'll take you to the village dance, just like last year. You'll hardly notice I'm gone before I'm back."

11

I want to believe him, but we all know the truth. Nobody comes back. The thought breaks my heart and I gasp to catch my breath through my tears.

Mam had warned me not to be getting all maudlin and sobbing on his shoulder. "You're to be strong, Dorothy. Tell him how brave he is and how proud you are. No sniveling and wailing." And here I am, doing everything she told me not to. I can't help it. I don't want to be proud. I don't want to tell him how brave he is. I want to sink to my knees and wrap my arms around his ankles so that he can't go anywhere. Not without me.

"We'll be married in the summer and we'll have little 'uns running around our feet and everything will be back to normal, Dolly. Just you and me and a quiet simple life. Just like we've always wanted."

I nod and press my cheek to the thick fabric of his coat. *A quiet simple life. Just like we've always wanted.* I try to ignore the voice in my head that whispers to me of more than a quiet simple life, the voice that speaks of rowdy adventures waiting far away from here. "Head full of nonsense." That's what our Sarah says. She's probably right. She usually is.

A loud hiss of steam pierces the subdued quiet of the platform, drowning out the muffled sobs. Doors start to slam as the men step into the carriages. Embraces end. Hands are prized agonizingly apart. It is time to let go.

I reach up onto my tiptoes and our lips meet in a last kiss. It isn't lingering and passionate as I've imagined, but rushed and interrupted by my wretched sobs and the urgency of others telling Teddy to hurry along now. We part too soon and he is walking away from me. I can hardly see his face through the blur of my tears.

The shrill blast of the stationmaster's whistle makes me jump. Mothers and daughters cling to each other. Wives clutch their children to their chests as they bravely wave their daddy good-bye. Great clouds of smoke billow around us and I cover my mouth with my handkerchief as the pistons yawn into life and begin turning on their cranks. The carriages jolt to attention, and he is going.

I start to move, my feet falling in time with the motion of the train, slow at first, and then a brisk walk. All along the platform, women and children reach out, clinging for all they are worth to prolong the very last touch of a coat sleeve, a fingertip, the last flutter of a white handkerchief. And I am jogging and then running, faster and faster, until I can't keep up and he is gone.

He is gone.

He is gone.

I slow to a walk and stand among the suffocating smoke as my heart cracks into a thousand shards of helpless despair. Everything has changed. Everything will be different now.

I put my hands in my coat pockets, my fingers finding the piece of folded paper in each. I glance at the hastily scribbled note from Teddy in my right hand: *Darling Little Thing, Don't be sad. When the war is over, I'll come back to you, back to Mawdesley. With you beside me, this is all the world I will ever need.* I glance at the page in my left hand, ripped from the morning paper as I lay the fire in Madam's bedroom. SOCIETY DARLING AND BRAVE NURSE VIRGINIA CLEMENTS REVEALED AS WEST END STAR LORETTA MAY! I look at her beautiful face and elegant clothes, the perfect image to accompany the glowing report of Cochran's latest dazzling production and the enchanting new star of his chorus. I stare at the two pieces of paper. The life I know in one hand. The life I dream of in the other.

The church bells chime the hour. Time to go back to the Monday wash and the predictable routines that carve out the hours of a maid-of-all-work like me. Wiping the tears from my eyes, I fold the pages and return them to my pockets. I turn my back on the distant puffs of smoke from Teddy's train and walk along the platform. The surface is icy and I go cautiously, my footing unsure. I slip a little, steady myself, and keep going. Crossing the tracks, I step onto the frosted grass verge that crunches satisfyingly beneath my boots. On firmer ground, my strides lengthen and

I walk faster, and all the while the question nags and nags in my mind: Am I walking away from my future, or walking toward it?

I don't have an answer. It is not mine to give.

War holds all the answers now.

ACT I

⋇ Hope ⋈

LONDON
1923

To the question, "Are stars worthwhile?"
I must give the elusive reply,
"There are stars *and* stars."

—C. B. Cochran,
the *Weekly Dispatch*, 1924

1
DOLLY

"That's the fascinating thing about life, Miss Lane. All its wonderful unpredictability."

"It is as simple as this: a person can be unpunctual or untidy, but if they intend to get on in life they certainly cannot be both." I'll never forget these words, nor the housekeeper who barked them at me as I skulked back to the house—late and disheveled—from my afternoon off. I'd been walking with Teddy in the summer rain and completely lost track of time. It was worth being scolded for. "You, Dorothy Lane, are a prime example of someone who will *never* get on in life. *You* will never become anything." It was the first time I was told I wasn't good enough. It wasn't the last.

I was in my first position in service at the time. Maid-of-all-work. "Maid-of-all-fingers-and-thumbs, more like," the housekeeper groused. Peggy Griffin was her name—"Piggy" as I called her in private, on account of her stubby nose and hands like trotters. Piggy didn't take to me, and I didn't take to her. I didn't take to domestic work either for that matter. I suppose it didn't help that my thoughts were usually anywhere else other than the task in hand.

"Dolly Daydream" was the nickname I earned from the maids at Mawdesley Hall. Open windows and doors left ajar are a gift to a girl with keen ears and a head full of dreams. Music from the gramophone player set my feet itching to dance as I mangled the Monday wash. Snatched fragments of conversations drifted along the corridors as I swept and polished, filling my head with thoughts of the stars of the West End stage, the Ziegfeld Follies, Broadway—all of it a distraction from the dreary routine of work, from war, from my fears of Teddy being called up. I may have lost many things in the years since I first felt those naïve desires, but I held on to my dreams with a stubborn determination worthy of a Lancashire lass. The longing for something more has never left me. I feel it like a fluttering of wings in my heart.

I feel it now, as I shelter from the rain, huddled in the doorway of a watchmaker's shop on the Strand. My attention is drawn to the posters on the passing omnibuses: Tallulah Bankhead, Gertrude Lawrence, Loretta May. The stars whose photographs and first-night notices I cut from newspapers and stick into my scrapbooks; the women I admire from high up in the theater gallery, stamping my feet and shouting my appreciation and wishing I was on the stage with them, dressed in silver chiffon. They call us gallery girls: domestics and shopgirls who buy the cheap tickets and faithfully follow our favorite stars with something like a hysteria. We long for the glamorous life of the chorus girls and principal actresses; for a life that offers more than petticoats to mend and bootlaces to iron and steps to scrub. But I don't just want to escape a life of drudgery. I want to soar. So I care for this restless fluttering in my heart as if it were a bird with a broken wing, in the hope that it will one day heal and fly.

I jump at the sound of a sharp rap on the window beside me. I turn around to see a hard-featured gentleman scowling at me from inside the shop, mean-looking eyes glowering behind black-rimmed spectacles. He says something I can't hear and flaps his hands, shooing me away as if I were a dog salivating outside the butcher's shop. I stick my tongue out at him and leave the doorway, hurrying along, hopping over puddles, my toes drowning like unwanted kittens inside my sodden stockings.

I pass bicycle shops and tobacconists, wine merchants, drapers and milliners, the rain falling in great curtains around me as I catch my reflection in the shop windows. Straggly curls hang limply beneath my cloche, all my efforts with curling irons and spirit lamps ruined by the rain. My new cotton stockings are splashed with dirt and sag at my ankles like folds of pastry, the rubber bands I've used as makeshift garter rolls clearly not up to the job. My borrowed coat is two sizes too big. My thirdhand shoes squeak an apology for their shabby existence with every step. Piggy Griffin was right. I am an unpunctual untidy girl. A girl who will never get on in life.

I dodge newspaper vendors and sidestep a huddle of gentlemen in bowler hats as tramcars and motorcars rattle along the road beside me, clanging their bells and tooting their horns. Cries of the street sellers and the pounding hooves of a dray horse add to the jumble of noise. My stomach tumbles like a butter churn, excited and terrified by the prospect of my new position as a maid at The Savoy hotel.

The Savoy. I like the sound of it.

With my head bent down against the slanting rain, I take the final turn down Carting Lane, where I collide spectacularly with a gentleman hurrying in the opposite direction. I stagger backward, dropping my travel bag as he takes a dramatic tumble to the ground. It reminds me of a scene from a Buster Keaton picture. I clap my hand over my mouth to stop myself laughing.

"I'm so sorry! Are you all right?" I raise my voice above the noise of the rain and the hiss of motorcar tires through puddles. "My fault. I wasn't looking where I was going."

Dozens of sheets of paper are scattered around him, plastered to the sodden street like a child's hopscotch markings. He attempts to stand up, slipping and sliding on the wet paving stones. I offer my hand and an arm for him to balance on. He grasps hold of both and I pull him upright. He is surprisingly tall when he's vertical. And handsome. Rusted stubble peppers his chin. His lips are crowned with a slim sandy mustache, a shade lighter than his russet hair; the color of fox fur. I really want to touch it, and clench my fists to make sure I don't.

"Are you hurt?" I ask, bending down to pick up his pages.

"I don't think so." He shakes water from his coat like a dog just out of the sea and stoops to join me, scrabbling at the edges of the papers stuck to the pavement. "Feel like a damned fool, though. Are *you* hurt? That was quite a collision!" He speaks like the man from the Pathé newsreels at the picture palace, all lah-de-dah and lovely.

I check myself over. "I've a ladder in my stocking, but nothing that a needle and thread won't fix. At least I managed to stay on my feet. Should've been looking where I was going."

"Me too. It was completely unavoidable." He looks at me, the hint of a smile dancing at the edge of his lips, his eyes deep puddles of gray that match the weather perfectly. "Or perhaps it was necessary."

We grin at each other like the greatest fools, as if we are stuck and neither of us is capable of pulling away, or doesn't want to. London fades into the background as the rain becomes a gentle hush and the cries of the street vendors blend into a waltz in three-four time. For a perfect rain-soaked moment there is nothing to do, nowhere to be, nobody to worry about. Just the melody of a rainy London afternoon, and this stranger. I catch my reflection in his eyes. It is like looking into my future.

A ribbon of rainwater slips off the edge of the peppermint-striped awning of the florist's shop beside us, pooling in the crown of his hat. Grabbing the last of the papers, he ducks beneath the awning and the moment drifts away from us like a child's lost balloon and all I can do is watch it disappear over the rooftops. I join him beneath the awning as he pats at his elbows with a white handkerchief and inspects a small tear in the knee of his trousers.

"Damned new shoes," he mutters. "Treacherous in weather like this."

His shoes are smart two-tone navy-and-tan wingtips. I glance at my black lace-ups, hand-me-downs from Clover, as battered and worn as old Mrs. Spencer at the fish shop. I place one foot over the other, self-consciously. "That's why I don't bother with them," I say. "Old shoes are more reliable. Same with men."

My Lancashire accent sounds common beside him and I regret giving up the elocution lessons

I'd started last year. Couldn't stand the stuck-up woman who taught me. In the end I told her to get knotted with her how-nows and brown cows. Now I can't help feeling I might have been a bit hasty.

I watch as he fusses and fidgets to set himself right, adjusting his coat and replacing his trilby: nut-brown felt with a chocolate-ribbon trim. Ever so smart. Dark shadows beneath his eyes suggest a late night. He smells of whiskey and cigarettes, brilliantine and rain. I can't take my eyes off him.

"If you don't mind me saying, you look knackered."

He raises an eyebrow. "Are you always this complimentary to strangers?" That smile again, tugging at the edge of his mouth as if pulled by an invisible string. "It was a late night, if you must know."

"Hope she was worth it."

He laughs. "Well, aren't you the little comedienne! I needed some amusement today. Thank you."

As I hand him the sodden pages that I've rescued from the pavement, I notice the lines of musical notes. "Do you play?"

"Yes." He takes a page from me. "I write it actually."

"A composer? Blimey! Blues or jazz?"

"Blues, mainly."

"Oh."

"You sound disappointed."

"Prefer jazz."

"Doesn't everybody?"

I hand him another page. "Is it any good then, your music?"

He looks a little embarrassed. "I'm afraid not. Not at the moment, anyway."

"That's a shame. I love music. The good type, that is. Especially jazz."

He smiles again. "Then perhaps I should write some."

"Perhaps you should."

And here we are again, grinning at each other. There is something about this fox-haired stranger that makes me smile all the way from my sodden toes to the top of my cloche. Nobody has made me feel like this since I was eight years old and first met Teddy Cooper. I didn't think anybody would ever make me feel that way again. Part of me has always hoped nobody ever would.

"And what is it you do?" he asks. "Other than knock unsuspecting gentlemen down in the street?"

I hate telling people my job. My best friend, Clover, pretends she's a shopgirl or a clerk if anybody asks. "Nobody wants to marry a domestic," she says. "Best to tell a white lie if you're ever going to find a husband." I want to tell him I'm a chorus girl, or an actress in revue at the Pavilion. I want to tell him I'm *somebody,* but those gray eyes demand the truth.

"I'm just a maid," I say, as Big Ben strikes the hour.

"*Just* a maid?"

"Yes. For now. I start a new position today. At The Savoy." The chimes are a reminder. "Now, actually."

"A maid with ambition. A rare and wonderful thing." A grin spreads across his face as he chuckles to himself. I'm not sure whether he is teasing me. "Well, I mustn't keep you." He rolls the damp papers up and bundles them under his arm like a bathing towel. "Perry," he says, offering his hand. "Perry Clements. Delighted to meet you."

His hand is warm against the fabric of my glove. The sensation makes the skin prickle on my palm. "Perry? That's an unusual name."

"Short for Peregrine. Frightful, isn't it?"

"I think it's rather lovely." I think *you* are rather lovely. "Dorothy Lane," I say. "Dolly, for short. Pleasure to meet you, Mr. Clements." I gesture to the paper bathing towel under his arm. "I hope it's not completely ruined."

"You've done me a favor, to be honest, Miss Lane. Possibly the most dismal piece I've ever written."

And then he does something extraordinary and shoves the papers into a litter bin beside me, as casually as if they were the empty wrappings of a fish supper.

I gasp. "You can't do that!"

"Why not?"

"Well. Because. You just can't!"

"But apparently I just did. That's the fascinating thing about life, Miss Lane. All its wonderful unpredictability." He slides his hands into his coat pockets and turns to walk away. "It was terribly nice to meet you." He is shouting above the din of traffic and rain. "You're really quite charming. Good luck with the new position. I'm sure you'll be marvelous!"

I watch as he runs tentatively down the street, slipping and skidding as he goes. I notice that he carries a limp and hope it is an old war wound and not the result of our collision. He tips his hat as he jumps onto the back of an omnibus and I wave back. It feels more like an enthusiastic hello to an old friend than a polite good-bye to a stranger.

When he is completely out of sight I grab the bundle of papers from the litter bin. I'm not sure why, but it feels like the right thing to do. Something about these sodden pages speaks to me of adventure and, as Teddy said when we watched the first group of men head off to France, you should never ignore adventure when it comes knocking. Little did any of us know that the experience of war would be far from the great adventure they imagined as they waved their farewells.

Pushing the papers into my coat pocket, I run on

down Carting Lane, being careful not to slip on the cobbles that slope steadily down toward the Embankment and the river. It is pleasantly quiet after the chaos of the Strand, even with the steady stream of delivery vans and carts that rumble past. I head for the service entrance, sheltered by an archway, and turn to walk down a flight of steep steps that lead down to a black door. A maid is stooped over, rubbing a great lump of hearth-stone against the middle step. It seems to me a fool's errand with the rain spilling down and dirty boots and shoes everywhere, but as I well know, it is not a maid's place to question the sense of the chores she is given.

She looks up and wipes her hands on her sacking-cloth apron. "Beg pardon, miss."

I smile at her. "Don't let me stop you."

Her cheeks are flushed from her efforts. She is young. Probably in her first position. I was that girl not so long ago, scrubbing steps, polishing awkward brass door handles, hefting heavy buckets of coal, constantly terrified to put a foot wrong in case the housekeeper or the mistress gave me my marching orders. The girl looks blankly at me and drags her pail noisily to one side so that I can pass. I go on tiptoe so as not to spoil her work.

Above the door, a sign says FOR DELIVERIES KNOCK TWICE. Since I'm not delivering anything I pull on the doorbell. In my head my mother chastises me. *"Late on your first day, Dorothy Mary Lane. And look at the state of you. Honestly. It beggars belief."*

I hear footsteps approaching behind the door before a bolt is drawn back and it swings open. A harried-looking maid glares at me.

"You the new girl?"

"Yes."

Grabbing the handle of my traveling bag, she drags me inside. "You're late. She's spitting cobs."

"Who is?"

"O'Hara. Head of housekeeping. Put her in a right narky mood you have, and we'll all suffer for it."

Before I have chance to defend myself or reply, she shoves me into a little side room, tells me to wait there, and rushes off, muttering under her breath.

I place my bag down on the flagstone floor and look around. A clock ticks on the mantelpiece. A picture of the King hangs on the wall. A small table stands beneath a narrow window. Other than that, the room is quiet and cold and unattractive, not at all what I'd expected of The Savoy. Feeling horribly damp and alone, I take the photograph from my coat pocket, brushing my fingers lightly across his image. The face that stirs such painful memories. The face I turn to after every house-keeper's reprimand and failed audition. The face I

30

look at every time someone tells me I'm not good enough. The face that makes me more determined to show them that I am.

Hearing brisk footsteps approaching along the corridor, I put the crumpled photograph back into my pocket and pray that the head of housekeeping is a forgiving and understanding woman.

As she enters the room, it is painfully apparent that she is neither.

2
DOLLY

Wonderful adventures await for those
who dare to find them.

O'Hara, the head of housekeeping, is a furious Irishwoman with a frown to freeze hell and an attitude to match. She is tall and strangely angular, her hair frozen in tight black waves around her face. Her arms are folded across her chest, her elbows straining against the fabric of her black silk dress, like fire irons waiting to prod anyone who gets in her way.

"Dorothy, I presume?" Her voice is clipped and authoritative.

I nod. "Yes, miss. Dorothy Lane. Dolly, for short."

She looks pointedly at a watch fob attached to the chest panel of her dress. "You are five minutes late. Whilst I might expect poor timekeeping of flighty girls who work in factories and wear too much makeup and colored stockings and invariably come to a bad end, I do not expect it of girls employed at The Savoy. I presume this is the first and last time you will be late?"

Her words snap at me like the live crabs at Billingsgate Market. I nod again and take a step back. When she speaks the veins in her neck pop out, as if they are trying to get away from her. If I were a vein in O'Hara's neck, I'd be trying to get away from her too.

"Mr. Cutler is not impressed by tardiness," she continues. "Not at all. Not to mention the governor."

I have no idea who Mr. Cutler or the governor are, but decide that now is not the best time to ask. "I'm very sorry. I bumped into someone you see, miss, and the rain—"

A brusque wave of the hand stops me midsentence. "Your excuses do not interest me and I most certainly do not have time for them." She consults the watch fob again, as if it somehow operates her. "Hurry now. Get your bag. Come along."

She turns and sweeps from the room. I pick up my bag and scuttle along behind, following the familiar scent of Sunlight soap that she leaves in her wake. She moves with brisk neat steps, the *swish swish* of her skirt reminding me of Mam rubbing her hands together to warm them by the fire. We go up a short stone staircase that leads to a series of narrow sloping passageways, the plain walls lit by occasional lampless lights. We pass a large room where maids are stooped over wicker baskets sorting great piles of laundry, and another room where a printing press clicks and whirs and men with ink-stained aprons peer through spectacles at blocks of lettering. The air is laced with a thick smell of oil and tar. It is stark and industrial. Far from the sparkling chandeliers and sumptuous carpets I'd imagined.

"Your reference from Lady Archer was complimentary," O'Hara remarks, looking over her shoulder and down her nose with a manner that suggests I don't match up at all with the girl she was expecting. "And the housekeeper spoke highly of you."

"Really? That was very kind of them." I'm surprised. I can't believe Lady Archer would be complimentary about anything, let alone me. I worked for her in my last position at a house in Grosvenor Square. She can't have said more than a dozen words to me in the four years I spent there and most of them were only to remark on my appearance and suggest how it might be improved.

"It wasn't kind, Dorothy. It was honest. Kindness and honesty are very different things. You'd be advised not to confuse one with the other."

We walk on a little farther until she takes a sharp left and stops. "We'll take the service lift," she says, checking her watch fob again and tutting to herself as she bustles me into a narrow lift and instructs the attendant to take us to second. He mutters a good afternoon before pulling the iron grille across the front and pressing a button on a panel in the wall.

34

"I presume you haven't been in an electric lift before," O'Hara says as the contraption jolts to life and we start our ascent.

"No. I haven't." I push my palms against the wall to steady myself as the passage slips away beneath us. I'm not sure I like the feeling.

"The Savoy is the first hotel to be fully equipped with electricity," she continues. "Electric lifts, electric lighting—and centrally heated, of course. No doubt there'll be plenty of new experiences for you here." She pushes her shoulders back and stands proud. "You'll soon get used to it."

"Yes. I suppose I will." The sensation of the lift makes me queasy. My mouth feels dry. I could murder a brew.

Stepping out of the lift, I follow O'Hara along another corridor and into a large room, similar to the servants' room at Mawdesley Hall. She tells me this is the Staff Hall Maids' Room, where I will take all my meals. At least a dozen maids sit around a long wooden table, their faces lit by electric globe lights suspended on a pulley from the ceiling. The walls are distempered a sickly mustard yellow.

O'Hara waves an arm toward the table. "I'm sure you're capable of introducing yourselves. Afternoon break is ten minutes. Breakfast, lunch, and supper are all served in here. The tea urn can be temperamental. Wait there."

She departs in a rustle of silk. I put my bag down

and shove my hands into my coat pockets. "Seems like the tea urn isn't the only thing that's temperamental." I mutter the words to myself but one of the girls sitting closest to me hears. She spits tea with laughing.

"That's the funniest thing I've heard all year. Where'd they find you then, the music halls?"

I have that uncomfortable feeling of being the new girl at school, unsure whether I should sit down and join the others or wait for the irate Irishwoman to return. The girls at the table chatter away like a flock of starlings. They pretend to pay no notice to me, but I can tell they are all trying to sneak a glance without obviously staring. A couple of them smile at me. One glares at me so intently that I wonder if I've worked with her before and offended her in some way, although I can't place her.

The youngest-looking girl pours tea from a pot and hands me a cup. "You been for a swim in the Thames?" she says. "You're soaked. And you're leaving puddles on the floor."

I look down. A small pool of water has gathered on the floor as the water drips from the hem of my coat. I take it off and bundle it under my arm, telling the girl that it's cats and dogs outside.

The girl who spat her tea asks if I've ever heard of a thing called an umbrella. "Sissy, by the way," she says. "Sissy Roberts."

"Dorothy Lane," I reply. "Dolly, for short. I

36

never bother with umbrellas. Too much bumping into people and apologizing. Anyway, a bit of rain never hurt anyone."

Sissy laughs. "It'll hurt the governor's Turkish carpets if you drip all over *them*."

As I take my first sip of tea, O'Hara sweeps back into the room. "Come along now, Dorothy. I'll show you to the maids' quarters." She stops and stares as if noticing me for the first time. "Goodness, girl! You're soaked. Did you swim here?"

Her comment sets the others sniggering again. Sissy mouths a "good luck" as I reluctantly leave my tea and rush along after O'Hara like a gosling following a mother goose.

We walk down another long passage that leads to a narrow staircase where two porters are struggling with a heavy-looking crate of champagne. One of them winks at me as they shuffle past. Cheeky sod. We pass a maid whose cap is just visible above a towering pile of linen balanced in her arms, and then a young page in a powder-blue uniform who stands obediently to one side to let us pass. He reminds me of a toy soldier with his smart white gloves and epaulets. He wishes O'Hara good morning and gawps at me like he's never seen a girl before. I flash him my best smile, setting him blushing like a ripe peach. O'Hara tells him it is rude to stare and to straighten his cap and to hurry along with whatever message he is delivering. His cheeks flare scarlet under her castigation.

"You'll share your room with three other maids," O'Hara explains as she bustles on ahead. "I suggest you get out of those damp clothes straight-away or you'll have pneumonia before you've even changed so much as a pillow slip. Your uniform is laid out on your bed: two blue print morning dresses, two black moiré silk dresses for afternoons and evenings, three white aprons, two frill caps, black stockings, and black shoes. Laundry is sent out on Mondays. The hotel has its own laundry out Kennington way." The mention of Kennington sets my heart tumbling, but I have no time to dwell on the memories stirred as O'Hara rabbits on. "Sissy Roberts will show you around the areas of the hotel you are permitted in. Pay attention. Nobody likes to see a maid where she isn't supposed to be. I'll stop by later with the house list."

I haven't the foggiest what the house list is. I would ask, but my mouth is dry and my tongue feels as fat as a frog.

"Second floor is live-in staff quarters," she explains. "Heads of department are accommodated on eighth. The governor—Reeves-Smith—keeps an apartment here, although he usually stays at our sister hotel, the Berkeley. Each guest floor has an assigned waiter, valet, and maid for floor service. You'll take instruction from them, as necessary."

The corridor is brighter than the passages below.

Electric lights shine from sconces along the walls. My sodden shoes squeak against the nut-brown linoleum as I walk, the sound setting my teeth on edge. I follow O'Hara to a paneled door, where she stops and takes a key from the impressive collection hanging from her waist. She opens the door and we both step inside.

The room is neat, functional, and comfortably furnished. Far nicer than the sparse little room I'd shared with Clover at the top of the house in Grosvenor Square. It smells of furniture polish and lavender. A Turkey rug sits in the middle of the room, worn in patches from the footsteps of countless maids. Each of the four iron bedsteads is neatly made up with a white candlewick counterpane pulled tight across the sheets and mattress. O'Hara strides toward a narrow sash window and pulls it shut.

"The maids' bathroom is across the corridor," she says. "The necessary is to the right. You'll be attending to guest rooms on floors four and six. All rooms are turned out daily, starting with unoccupied rooms for incoming guests, and then on to occupied rooms as soon as the guest departs for the day. Knock three times before announcing yourself by saying, 'Housekeeping.' You'll hang a MAID AT WORK sign on the door and always close the door behind you. Nobody wishes to see the work in progress, as it were." She tugs at the edge of a counterpane and plumps a pillow. "Should a guest return unexpectedly, you must vacate the room and finish it when instructed to do so. Things happen at peculiar and unpredictable times of the day in a hotel, Dorothy. You cannot expect the rigidity and routine of a regular household."

"No. Yes. Of course." My mind dances with thoughts of the hotel's impressive guest list. Hollywood stars. Privileged American heiresses. The darlings of London society. Far more impressive than the stuffy old ladies who visited Lady Archer for boring bridge evenings and dreary at-homes.

"You'll attend to various other duties throughout the day—sorting the linen cupboards, occasional sewing for guests, that sort of thing. You'll pull the blinds and curtains and turn down the beds in the evening. You must greet guests with a polite good morning, good afternoon, or good evening, and use their full title."

I try to take everything in as O'Hara reels off her endless lists of instructions, but I'm preoccupied with thoughts of who the other three beds belong to, whether my roommates are pleasant, whether we will become good friends.

O'Hara chatters on. "I'm sure I needn't remind you that the utmost discretion is required at all times." She raises an eyebrow. "Maids may occasionally see or hear things that are, shall we say, out of the ordinary. My advice to you is to turn a blind eye."

"Yes. Of course."

"You have a ten-minute morning tea break. Lunch is at twelve or one, depending on which relay you are on from week to week. Tea is at five, and supper—if all your chores are complete—is cocoa and bread and butter at nine. You have Wednesday afternoons and alternate Sundays off. I presume you'll be powdered and painted and heading off to the picture palaces or the dance halls like the others." She tuts as she straightens the hearth rug. Her words fall off me like raindrops. All I can remember is cocoa and bread and butter at nine and my stomach rumbles at the thought. "Curfew is ten o'clock. Sissy Roberts will accompany you on your rounds today and tomorrow. Then you are on your own. Watch and learn, Dorothy. Watch and learn."

I set my bag down beside the bed where my uniform is laid out. "It's Dolly," I mutter. "Dolly, for short." She doesn't hear me, or if she does, she chooses to ignore me as she stoops to pick up a piece of lint from the rug.

"Any questions?"

I have dozens. "No. Everything seems straightforward. I'm sure I'll soon pick it up."

"Very well. Then welcome to The Savoy, Dorothy. She is quite wonderful when you get to know her. I hope you will get along very well."

She closes the door behind her, leaving me alone with the sound of the rain pattering against

41

the window and a nagging voice in my head wondering how I'll ever remember everything.

Hanging my sopping hat and coat on the stand beside the door, I take a better look at the room. Beside the beds, occasional items on the nightstands suggest a hint of the other girls who sleep here: a framed photograph of a soldier in uniform, a copy of Jane Austen's *Persuasion*, a scallop-edged gilt powder compact that I can't take my eyes off, a well-thumbed copy of *The Sheik*, and a pile of *Peg's Paper* magazines. Clover's favorite.

Dear Clover. I wish she were here with me. She'd tell me to stop worrying. She'd say something to make me laugh. While I wonder about things, Clover just gets on with them, accepts her lot, and makes do. She teases me about my dream of a life on the stage, but she also believes in me. "There's something about you, Dolly," she says. "Something in your eyes. I saw it the very first time I met you. And you're as stubborn as an old Lancashire goat. If anyone can get onto that stage, you can. I'd bet my best knickers on it."

Her belief in me has only ever been matched by Teddy. He always said I would become someone special, that the little girl who twirled and danced her way through childhood when she should have been sitting still or feeding the chickens would find greater things. It was Teddy who found

The Adventure Book for Girls in the laneway behind the house all those years ago when we were just children. "It's yours now, Dolly," he said, brushing the mud off the cover with his elbow and pressing the book into my hands. "Finders keepers." And then he ran off to chase a butterfly. Teddy was always chasing butterflies. He never kept them though. Said he just liked to admire them close up before he let them go.

The Adventure Book for Girls was heavy, filled with 236 pages of stories, but it was the inscription inside that intrigued me the most: *Wonderful adventures await for those who dare to find them. With much love, Auntie Gert.* Those words crept into my heart and since nobody knew who the book belonged to, or who Auntie Gert was, I kept it. My sisters squabbled about it, saying it wasn't fair. My taunting response of "Finders keepers, losers weepers" only made things worse. Mam eventually put the book out of reach on top of the grandfather clock and told us it would stay there until we could learn to be nice to one another.

It was a week before that book came down.

My sisters soon lost interest, but I read every page, a dozen times at least. As time passed, the book was discarded by all of us in favor of other things—bicycles and boys mostly. The last time I saw it, it was being used to balance out a wobbly leg at the kitchen table, but I've never forgotten those adventure stories, nor Auntie Gert's words.

They whisper to me still, blowing my dreams onward despite everything that has happened, and everyone I have loved and lost in the years between.

Shivering against the cloying damp of my clothes, which now feel horrible against my skin, I step out of my shoes and strip down to my underwear, draping my brown serge dress, slip, and stockings over a wooden clotheshorse that stands in front of the fire. They hang there like a wilted version of myself in shades of tea and stout as I place my shoes on the hearth, despairing at the dull practicality of them. More than any cap or apron, I've always felt it is a maid's shoes that really distinguishes "Them" from "Us." I stand in front of the fire, first to the front, then to the back, just like I did as a young girl standing beside my two sisters, our reedy bodies convulsing as we tried to get warm after the weekly bath. I smile at the memory. What would they say if they could see me now, standing half naked in The Savoy hotel in London? I squeeze my eyes shut and say a silent prayer to them.

When I'm a little warmer I take the photograph from my coat pocket and set it on the hearth to dry. "We made it," I whisper, resting my fingers lightly on the image of his face, my heart contracting and expanding in great waves at the thought of him. Beside the photograph and my shoes, I lay out the pages of music, wishing I could understand the black dots and squiggles dancing across the lines. The heat from the fire lifts the faintest scent of him from the paper: whiskey and cigarettes.

Perry Clements. Peregrine Clements. Mr. Clements.

The name skips through my mind as I picture him staggering to his feet; fox-fur hair, gray puddles for eyes. The thought of our brief encounter sends goose bumps running over my skin and makes me smile, and yet at the same time I am saddened to know that it is someone other than Teddy who occupies my thoughts and sets my heart racing.

I always knew the day would come.

I always knew it would be too soon.

I have to leave, Teddy. For reasons I can't explain, I have to go away. I will never stop loving you, and if only things were different there is nowhere I would rather be than by your side.

My thoughts are disturbed as the bedroom door flies open and three maids come tumbling in. I shriek and run to my bed, pulling off the counterpane and wrapping it around my shoulders to cover myself. I recognize Sissy from the maids' room. She takes one look at me and bursts out laughing.

"I'd get dressed if I were you," she says, throwing herself down onto the bed beside mine and putting on a snooty accent. "This isn't one of *those* hotels. *This,* darling, is The Savoy!"

3

LORETTA

"Hope is a dangerous thing, darling.
It is usually followed by
disappointment and too much gin."

The soothing lilt of the piano drifts around the Winter Garden at Claridge's. With a pleasing jazz medley the pianist captivates us all, the music mingling with polite chatter and the jangle of silver teaspoons against fine china cups. The sounds of afternoon tea. The sounds of luxury.

I sit alone at my usual table for two, my brother being habitually late. One would think I would be used to his tardiness by now, but I find it irksome and unnecessary. Seated behind a huge date palm, I at least have a little privacy while I wait. A little, but not too much. The spaces between the foliage afford the guests an occasional glimpse, sending whispered speculations racing across the crisp white tablecloths. "Is it her?" "I thought she was in Paris." "Yes, I'm certain it's her."

I smile. Let them whisper and wonder. It is, after all, part of the performance.

I sip my cup of Earl Grey as I watch the raindrops slip down the windowpanes. Mother always insists that tea tastes better when it rains, something to do with precipitation and dampness bringing out the flavor in the leaves. She is full of such tedious nonsense. It is one of the reasons I visit her as infrequently as possible. The fact that she can barely stand to be in the same room as me being another. In any event, despite the inclement weather, my tea tastes peculiar, and there is nothing more unsettling than peculiar-tasting tea, particularly at Claridge's.

I sniff the milk jug as discreetly as it is possible for one to sniff a milk jug in public. It has definitely turned. Mother would be appalled by the very fact that I take milk in Earl Grey at all. I look around for a waiter but think better of it. I don't like to make a fuss. Not at Claridge's. I'm awfully fond of Claridge's, and besides I can't summon the enthusiasm to make a proper fuss about anything recently. I decide to forgive this small oversight, assign the bad taste to too many gin cocktails last night, and reserve my annoyance for my wretched brother.

I'm quite aware that Peregrine tolerates our ritual of afternoon tea simply to humor me. He has complained about it since we first started meeting here when he was a jaded young lawyer and I was a bored society debutante. He thinks it unfair that I only invite him to tea and not our older brother, Aubrey, but as I remind him frequently Aubrey is too busy and too married and too full of his own self-importance to contemplate tea with his little sister and brother. We are better off without him.

"But must we take afternoon tea *every* Wednesday, Etta?"

"Yes, Perry. We must."

"Might I ask why?"

"Because afternoon tea is predictable and charming—qualities that should be preserved wherever possible. Because it is one of the few things in my life that I can do without a chaperone, and because if we stop meeting for afternoon tea, who knows what we will stop doing next. Eventually we'll stop seeing each other altogether. We'll become distant strangers, like Aubrey, communicating only through a few thoughtless lines scribbled on tasteless Christmas cards. One day we'll realize that we miss afternoon tea on a Wednesday terribly, but it will be too late, because one—or both of us—will be dead."

Perry laughed and called me melodramatic, but he kept showing up nevertheless. In the end it wasn't his lack of enthusiasm that brought an end to our little arrangement, it was war.

Overnight, the carefree privileged life we knew came crashing to a halt as a new and terrifying existence settled upon us all like a suffocating fog. My brothers went to France to serve as officers on the Western Front. I enrolled as a

Voluntary Aid Detachment nurse. Simple pleasures such as afternoon tea became a distant memory until the war ended and my brothers returned. We were all changed irrevocably by the long years between. Now I cling to Perry and afternoon tea at Claridge's like a life raft, holding on with grim determination, even if his habitual tardiness irritates me immensely and gives me a daylong headache.

"Would you care for another pot of Earl Grey while you wait, Miss May?"

I glance up at the waiter. A handsome young chap. All taut-skinned and vibrant-eyed. The treasures of youth. "I suppose another can't do any harm."

"No, miss. Not on such a dreadful day. And another slice of Battenberg, perhaps?"

I nod. Even the waiters at Claridge's know my preferences and tastes. It makes life extraordinarily dull at times. "And a fresh jug of milk," I add.

"Very well, Miss May."

He moves with the precision of a principal ballet dancer, pirouetting behind the great ferns and Oriental screens that segment the room into private nooks and crannies. I almost call after him, tell him I've changed my mind and to bring Darjeeling and Madeira cake instead, but I don't. Sometimes it is simpler to keep things as they are.

The pianist plays ragtime as the rain thrums in time against the window. All is a colorless gray smudge outside, weather for reading a racy novel, or for playing backgammon by the fire if one isn't easily enthralled by the notion of illicit love affairs. Bored and restless, I drape my arm casually over the back of the chair beside me the creamy white of my skin visible where my sleeve rides up over my wrist. A gentleman at the table to my right can't take his eyes off me. I stretch out a little farther, languishing like a cat. I am still beautiful on the outside, despite the cracks that are appearing beneath the surface.

The waiter returns and pours the tea as I shuffle in my chair, fussing with the pleats and folds in my skirt, checking my reflection in the silver teapot: perfect golden waves, crimson lips, penciled eyebrows over hooded eyes, green paste earrings that swing pleasingly as I tilt my head from side to side to catch the best of the light from the chandeliers. Claridge's has always had flattering light. It is one of the reasons I insist on coming here.

I check my watch. Where the devil can Peregrine have got to?

I fiddle with the menu card, tapping it against the edge of the rose-patterned saucer. Lines of script whirl through my mind like circus acrobats as carefully choreographed steps play out on my feet beneath the linen tablecloth. I cannot sit still. My nerves rattle like the bracelets that knock together on my arm.

It is always the same. Always at three o'clock on the afternoon before opening night when the butterflies start dancing and the jitters set in. Tomorrow is opening night of a new musical comedy at the Shaftesbury, a full-length piece, the female lead written especially for me. The Fleet Street hacks and society-magazine gossip columnists are waiting for me to fail, desperate to type their sniping first-night notices: *Miss May's acting talents are obviously limited to revue and the lighter productions that made her a star. She would be well advised to leave the more challenging roles to accomplished actresses, such as the wonderful Diana Manners and the incomparable Alice Delysia.* I feel nauseous at the thought.

The new production, *HOLD TIGHT!*, is a huge personal and professional risk. I don't know how I ever let Charles Cochran talk me into it. Presumably it had a lot to do with the wonderful Parisian dresses he promised, and the large volume of champagne we drank on the night the contracts were signed—not to mention the fact that I cannot deny darling Cockie anything. But it isn't just opening night that has my nerves on edge. There are other matters troubling me, matters far more important than forgotten lines and missed cues. Matters that I do not wish to dwell on.

My only small comfort is in knowing that I'm not the only one feeling anxious today. It is early in the autumn season. New productions open nightly across the city and everyone in the business is skittish. Final dress rehearsals are grueling fourteen-hour-long marathons. Tempers and nerves are as frayed as the hems on unfinished costumes. The precariously balanced reputations of writers, composers, producers, actors, and actresses are all at stake. Everybody wants *their* show, *their* leading lady, to be the big sensation. For established stars such as myself, there is the added threat of the new girls—ambitious beautiful young things who will inevitably emerge from the chorus to become the darling of the season. That dreadful Tallulah Bankhead has already gone some way to shaking things up with Cockie engaging her in the lead role of *The Dancers*. The gallery girls find everything about her so exotic: her name, her beauty, her quick wit and overt sexuality. Under the glare of such bright young things, is it any wonder I feel dull and worn? It wasn't so long ago when ambition and beauty were synonymous with the name Loretta May, when I wore my carefree attitude as easily as my Vionnet dresses. I was the darling of the set, wild and free, outdazzling the diamonds at my neck. But things move quickly in this business. What shines today glares horribly tomorrow. We all lose our luster in the end.

As the pianist plays "Parisian Pierrot," a popular number from André Charlot's new revue *London Calling!*, I spot Perry crossing the road. I urge the pianist to play faster and finish the piece. Perry is fragile enough without hearing the most popular number of the season so far, written by one of his friends. While Perry struggles to write anything at all, Noël Coward could write an address on an envelope and it would be a hit. Thankfully the final chords fade as he is shown to our table, limping toward me like a shot hare, apologizing all the way. He is as sodden as a bath sponge and has a tear in the knee of his trousers. Disapproving stares follow him.

"Sorry, sorry, sorry." He leans forward to kiss me, his stubble scratching my skin. He smells of Scotch and cigarettes. I tell him to sit down. Quickly.

"You're an absolute fright, Perry Clements. You look like a stray dog that has been out all night. Where on earth have you been to get into such a state?"

"In the rain mostly. I bumped into someone near The Savoy. Quite literally. She sent me skittering across the pavement like a newborn foal."

"Anyone interesting?" I ask.

"No. Just some girl." He takes a tin of Gold

Flake from his breast pocket, lights a cigarette, and takes a couple of long, satisfying drags. "Damned nuisance really. And then the omnibus got a flat, so I decided to walk the rest of the way. Anyway, I'm here now, and while I know you're desperate to lecture me on appearance and send me straight off to Jermyn Street for some smart new clothes, I'd rather like it if we didn't squabble. Not today. I have an outrageous headache."

"Scotch?"

"And absinthe. Rotten stuff. Don't know why anybody drinks it."

"Because the Green Fairy is wicked, and everybody else does. I have no sympathy for you, darling. None whatsoever."

Much as I'd like to, I can't be cross with him. I don't have the energy. I take a Turkish cigarette from my case and lean forward for a light, studying Perry through the circles of smoke I blow so expertly. He isn't unpleasant to look at. A little shoddy around the edges perhaps, but nothing that couldn't be improved with a little more care. I'm sure he could find a perfectly decent wife if he tried a little harder. There are plenty of young girls in need of a husband, after all. The divine Bea Balfour, for one. But that is a romance I fear I will never see flourish, despite my best efforts to get the two of them to realize they are perfectly matched and to get on with it.

"So who was this girl anyway?" I ask.

"Hmm? Which girl?" Perry inspects the delicate finger sandwiches and miniature cakes on the stand, lifting each one up as though it were a specimen in the British Museum. He takes a bite from a strawberry tart, curls his lip, and replaces it. I smack the back of his hand.

"The girl you bumped into. Who was she? Anyone we know?"

"Why do you ask?"

"Because you paused after you mentioned her. I know you too well, darling. Whoever it was left a mark on you as clear as that unsightly tear in your trouser knee."

He smiles. "You've been reading Agatha Christie novels again, haven't you? We'll make a detective of you yet!" I glare at him. I am in no mood for jokes. "Oh, all right. She's a maid. Not the daughter of an earl, or a beautiful American heiress. I know what you're thinking and she was most definitely not marriage material. Pretty young thing, though. Eyes to make you wonder. She made me laugh, that's all."

"Goodness! Well, I hope you invited her to dinner. Perhaps she could make you laugh more often and we could all be cheered up."

He pours milk into his tea. "I'm not that bad. Am I?"

"Yes, you are. Honestly, darling, sometimes it's like spending time with a dead trout. And you used to be such tremendous fun." I stop myself from saying *before the war,* and take a sip of my tea. The milk is fresher, and the tea tastes better. Perhaps Mother is right about the rain.

Perry relents a little. "Well, perhaps I have been more serious of late. But the way the others carry on is ridiculous. Fancy-dress parties and all-night treasure hunts. Did you see the photographs of them dancing in the fountains in Trafalgar Square? Were you there?"

I laugh. "Sadly not. It looked like terrific fun, though. The society columnists can't get enough of them. Bright Young People, they're calling them. You shouldn't be so serious, darling. They're just shaking off the past. Living. You do remember what *that* feels like?"

"Running around like bored children, more like. Did you hear they had one of the clues baked into a loaf of bread in the Hovis factory?"

"I did. And they had to take one of Miss Bankhead's shoes from her dressing room in a scavenger hunt last month. Of course, she adores the attention. I suppose I'd be part of it if I were ten years younger. When a woman reaches her thirties it seems that she can't be referred to as a 'young' anything, bright or otherwise."

"Well, I think it's all a lot of foolish nonsense."

I can feel my irritation with him growing. "I wish you *were* plastered all over the front page of the *Times* or hanging around in opium dens or literary salons. Anything would be better than hiding away in that dreadful little apartment of yours eternally stewing on things." I grab hold of his hand and squeeze all my frustration into it. "You can't change what happened, darling. You can't bring them back. None of us can."

We've skirted around the same conversation so many times. I cannot understand Perry's enduring guilt about what happened under his command in France and he cannot understand the apparent ease with which I have put the war behind me. If only he knew the truth.

I take a long drag from my cigarette and change the subject. "So, you say this maid amused you?"

A smile tugs at the edge of his lips. "A little. She was different. Honest. She told me I looked tired. 'Knackered,' actually."

"Eugh. Vulgar word, but she's right. You do." I lean back in my chair. "Was that it? She insulted you and now you can't stop talking about her?"

He stares out of the window, watching the rain. "It's you who keeps talking about her! She just seemed different, that's all. There was something about her. Some infectious indescribable thing that made me want to know her better. For someone in her position she seemed so full of hope."

"Hope!" I laugh. "Hope is a dangerous thing, darling. It is usually followed by disappointment and too much gin."

He casts a wry smile from behind his teacup.

"Anyway, that was that. She went her way and I went mine. The shortest love story ever told. Now, enough about me. Tell me about tomorrow night. Who'll be there?"

"Bea Balfour."

"Anyone else?"

"The usual. But especially Bea."

He crushes his spent cigarette in the cut-glass ashtray. "You'll never give up, will you?"

"Not until I see the two of you married. No."

"Then I'm afraid you'll be waiting a very long time. I missed my opportunity with Bea. And anyway," he continues, glumly pushing crumbs around his plate, "she deserves better. What prospects does a struggling musical composer have to offer a woman like her?"

"You could always go back to the bar. A successful barrister would be hard to decline."

"What, and give Father the opportunity to gloat and prove that he was right all along; that I would never be a good enough composer? I'd rather end my days a lonely old bachelor and see Bea happily married to someone else."

I sigh and take a sandwich from the tray. I am simply too tired to argue with him.

We spend a tolerable hour together chatting about this and that, but like the withered autumn leaves tugged from their branches outside, my thoughts drift and swirl continually elsewhere. I think about the houselights going down and the curtain going up. I think about the third scene in Act Two. I think about a rapturous standing ovation and the cries from the gallery, "You're marvelous! You're marvelous!" I think about the letter in my purse that I have written to Perry but cannot bear to give him.

After kissing him good-bye and imploring him to smarten himself up for tomorrow's opening night, I take a taxi to the theater for a final dress rehearsal. A fog has rolled up the Thames and the streets are lit by the orange lamp standards, giving everything a sense of winter. The fog makes my eyes smart and sticks to my face. I feel choked by it and long for the warmth of spring and the flowers that brighten the Embankment Gardens.

As we approach the Shaftesbury Theatre, I see a line of fans already gathered outside the ticket office. The gallery girls: factory girls and shopgirls, clerks and seamstresses, ordinary girls and women who would give anything to live my life. Their adoration and enthusiasm can make or break a star quicker than any society-magazine columnist. I know they adore me and desire my beautiful dresses. If only they knew the truth my costumes conceal.

The front of house sign blazes through the dim light: LORETTA MAY IN HOLD TIGHT! My name in lights, just as I'd imagined when I was a starry-eyed novice in the chorus. Except it isn't my name. It is the stage name I chose in my desire to leave the real me, Virginia Clements, behind. She was the respectable daughter of an earl, the daughter who had failed to secure a suitable marriage, the daughter who was suffocated by expectation. Loretta May set me free from the starchy limitations imposed on titled young ladies such as myself. She allowed me to be somebody daring and new.

Virginia Clements. Loretta May. Just names, and yet I wonder. Who am I? Who am I really?

That's the curious thing about discovering one is dying: it makes one question absolutely everything.

4
DOLLY

"If only the mess we make of our lives
could be tidied as easily."

While I wriggle into my maid's dress I learn that
my roommates are Sissy, Gladys, and Mildred.
Sissy does the introductions. She reminds me of
Clover, all round-cheeked and generous-bosomed
with bouncy blond hair. I feel comfortable around
her and know we'll get along. Gladys is much
quieter. She offers a distracted "hello" as she
studies her reflection in the scallop-edged powder
compact I'd admired earlier. She's very pretty
with a peaches-and-cream complexion and her
hair perfectly styled in chestnut waves, just like
Princess Mary of York. The third girl, Mildred,
barely acknowledges me as she perches on
the edge of the bed beside the nightstand with
the Austen novel. She is prim and rigid, like the
governess in Grosvenor Square who Clover used
to say was so brittle she would snap in two if she
bent over. Mildred is the girl who had stared at
me downstairs. Something about her is familiar,
and although she busies herself, I know she has
one ear firmly tuned to the conversation.

Sissy props herself up on her elbows and flicks through a well-thumbed copy of a *Woman's Weekly* magazine. "So, where'd you come from, then?" she asks, turning down the corner of a page with an advert for a new Max Factor mascara.

"Grosvenor Square." My words are muffled as I pull the black dress over my head.

"No, you great goose. I mean, where are you *from?* Not where did you get the omnibus from this morning, 'cause that's not a London accent, or I'm the Queen of Sheba."

I shimmy the dress down over my stomach and hips. It fits perfectly. The moiré silk fabric feels so much nicer against my skin than the starchy cotton dresses I'm used to. "Oh. I see. I'm from Lancashire. A small village called Mawdesley, near Ormskirk. You wouldn't know it."

"So what brought you to London, then? Or should I say, who? Bet it was a soldier you met in the war. Told you he loved you and you followed him here only to find out he was already married with five children?" She laughs at her joke. Gladys tells her to stop being a nosy cow and to mind her own. Mildred sits like a stone statue on the edge of her bed.

"It wasn't a soldier," I say, tying my apron in a neat bow at my back. "It was work. That's all."

Sissy puts down her magazine. "None left in Lancashire?"

"Only the usual. Domestic service. Tea shops.

Textile factories. London offered . . . more." My explanation is as limp as my damp clothes hanging beside the fire. How can I explain what really brought me here? "I had an aunt who worked in a private home in Grosvenor Square. I started as a maid-of-all-work and worked my way up. Gave my notice a month ago."

"Let me guess. It was stuffy and boring and Madam was a miserable old cow?"

I smile. "How did you guess?"

"Always the same. Anyone who ends up here wants more than picture rails to dust and fires to lay and chamber pots to empty. We all fancy ourselves a cut above the ordinary housemaid. And then of course there's some like our Gladys here who spends far too much time at the picture palaces and doesn't think being a maid at The Savoy is good enough." Sissy winks at me. "Has her eye on Hollywood, this one does. Fancies herself as the new Lillian Gish. I keep telling her it'll never happen. Silly dreams. That's all."

Gladys is plucking her eyebrows. "It's not silly dreams, Sissy Roberts. It's called ambition."

Sissy chuckles to herself from behind her magazine, but I'm interested.

"Did you ever audition, Gladys?" I ask.

"Dozens of times. Most of them turned out to be with seedy old men full of empty promises, but some Hollywood bigwig arrived last week. We think he'll be staying for the season, and I'm

63

going to make myself known to him. You see if I don't."

I'd love to talk more to Gladys but Sissy's disregard for her "silly dreams" makes me reluctant to share my own, so I say nothing and sit down on the edge of my bed, pulling a stocking over my toes before working it carefully up my leg. I don't notice Mildred walking over to the fireplace.

"What are these?" she asks.

I look up. She has my photograph in her hands, and one of the pages of music. In my hurry to dress I'd forgotten all about them. I jump up from the bed and rush over to her.

"Nothing. Just some papers that got damp on my way here." I snatch the page from her, gather up the rest from the hearth, and push them under my pillow.

"That's piano music," Mildred remarks. "Do you play?"

"No. I'm just minding them for someone."

She seems more interested in the photograph anyway. "And who's this?"

My heart leaps. For a moment, I am back with him. I see his face, my hands trembling as I open up the lens on the little VPK camera. "It's my brother," I say, grasping for an explanation and holding out my hand to take the photograph from her.

She looks at the image a moment longer and

hands it to me. I place the photograph under my pillow along with the pages of music and sit protectively beside them as I pull on the other stocking. Mildred walks back to her bed. She glances at me over her book, her silent interest in me unsettling.

"What's the house list?" I ask, desperate to change the subject. "O'Hara mentioned it."

"Ah, the famous house list." Sissy rolls onto her back, sticking her legs straight up in the air like fire irons. She doesn't seem to care that her dress falls around her hips and shows her knickers. "That's the most important thing. It's the list of guests. We're given a copy each day and expected to remember who's staying in which apartment and suite. We need to know the names of their valets and lady's maids, their secretaries—even their silly little dogs."

This is bad news. I'm awful at remembering names. "Doesn't it get confusing?"

"You get used to it. The regulars always ask for the same rooms. Some of the apartments have the same residents for months at a time." She stands up and walks over to the window. The rain is still coming down in torrents. "The *Mauretania* docks in Southampton tonight, so we're expecting a load of Americans to arrive on the boat train tomorrow. We'll be rushed off our feet." She turns around and leans her back against the window, amused by the look of panic on my face. "Don't

65

worry. The Savoy is a tightly run ship. It's like clockwork, all the parts clicking and whirring together to move us all around to the right place each day. I don't think about it anymore. I just go from here to there, and there to here. I grab a cuppa and a bite to eat when I can, and fall into bed at night exhausted. Don't even have the energy to take off my undies sometimes. But it's all worth it when you see Fred and Adele Astaire dancing on the rooftop."

"Did you see them?" I ask. "Really?" I have a picture of them both in my scrapbook. I would give anything to dance as wonderfully.

"Yes! Really! I was polishing windows one minute and the next, there they were, dancing a quickstep and a photographer taking pictures of them. You never know what'll happen at The Savoy. Better get used to it."

This is what I had imagined when I thought about working here: stars dancing on rooftops, Hollywood bigwigs. This is the magic I heard in the words "The Savoy."

"So, what are the Americans really like?" I ask as I pull on my frill cap. "Are they as glamorous as everyone says?"

"Dresses and shoes to make your head spin. More importantly, they tip well. You'll do fine as long as there's Americans upstairs. Save those half crowns and you'll soon have enough for a pound note. Before Christmas, you'll have a fiver in your purse." She nods toward Gladys. "Or a fancy powder compact, if that's your thing."

I gaze at the compact on the bed beside Gladys. "Oh, it *is* my thing."

"Selfridges," Gladys brags. "Had my eye on it for months. Isn't it the bee's knees?"

"Think *you're* the bee's knees," Mildred mutters.

I'd almost forgotten she was in the room. Gladys and Sissy roll their eyes at me.

I stand up and slip my feet into the shoes that have been provided for me, black as night but at least they have a strap and button. I spin around to face my roommates.

"Well. Will I do?"

Gladys smiles. Mildred's left eye twitches. Sissy nods. "Yes, Dorothy," she says, mimicking O'Hara's Irish accent perfectly. "You'll do very nicely. We'll make a Savoy maid of you yet."

I wish I knew her well enough to throw my arms around her. I wish I could kiss her dumpling cheeks and thank her for the vote of confidence. Instead, I tug at the counterpane on my bed, straightening the creases I've made by sitting on it. A habit of mine. If I can't untangle the knots in my heart, it seems that my life must be spent untangling everything else, setting things straight, making neat all that has been messed up.

Wonderful adventures await for those who dare to find them.

67

I think of Auntie Gert's words and feel the flutter of restless wings on the edge of my heart. If adventures are waiting for me here, then I'm ready to find them.

"Right, then," I say. "Where do I start?"

While Gladys and Mildred head out for their afternoon off, Sissy takes me down to the hotel storerooms and back-of-house operations, a bewildering maze of corridors and rooms housing all manner of weird and wonderful things. She shows me the audit room where male clerks hunch over desks, the stationery and fancy goods stores, stores for glassware and china, and even a silversmith's repair and replating room. In the linen stores we collect bedsheets, pillow slips, and chamber towels and load them onto a trolley. Then we fill a wicker basket with cleaning products and supplies: feather dusters, scourer, polish, chamois cloths, soap tablets, tissue paper, drawer liners, and pomanders. When we have everything we need we push the trolley down another long passageway that leads toward a service lift. A cool draft blows through an open door. I shiver in the thin fabric of my dress and hope I haven't caught a chill from standing around chatting to strange fox-haired men in the rain.

As we make our ascent to sixth, Sissy consults several pages of foolscap paper clipped together. The house list. "We'll do suite 601 first," she says. "Occupied by a Miss Howard, traveling from Pennsylvania. Arrived yesterday evening. Daughter of an American shipping magnate. Plenty of expensive shoes to try on."

I gasp. "You do not."

" 'Course I do. We all do." She leans casually on the pile of towels. "Perk of the job. We'll never live their lives, but what's the harm in a dab of perfume or a quick try-on of a silk shoe?"

I'm shocked. "But what if you get caught?"

"You don't—or . . ." She makes a dramatic slicing gesture across her throat. "Gone. Marching orders. On the spot. Never get a reference or work in service again and then it's a life of prostitution and vice for you, my girl."

She sees the look of horror on my face and bursts out laughing as the lift jolts to a stop. She slides back the grille, pulls the trolley out behind her, and strides off along the corridor.

Stepping out of the lift, I'm struck by the decor. It is rich and sumptuous, a noticeable contrast to the stark functionality of the rooms below. Elegant ferns and great palms drape like chiffon over willow-pattern pots. Impressive gilt-framed paintings of seascapes and ballerinas pattern the walls. Tiffany lampshades cast a soft creamy light and huge chandeliers dazzle like icicles above our heads.

Sissy calls over her shoulder. "Stop gawping. Wait till you see the river suites, and the Grand

Ballroom. Makes these corridors look like the staff passage."

I hurry after her, my feet sinking into the plush pile of the carpet. We pass two gentlemen discussing a painting of a ship being tossed around on a stormy sea. It makes me feel queasy just looking at it. One of the men wears small round spectacles. He is portly and dressed for dinner. The other man is dressed casually in cream slacks and a blue shirt with a mint-green knitted vest. He wears a lemon-colored cravat at his neck and his black hair is slicked neatly to one side. He leans against the wall, his crossed ankles revealing plaid socks. The man with the spectacles looks up as we pass.

Sissy acknowledges them both. "Good afternoon, sir. Good afternoon, Mr. Snyder."

They bid us both good afternoon in reply as the elder of the two gentlemen stares at me. "I don't believe I've seen you before," he says. "Are you new?" His tone is authoritative, but not unkind.

I mumble a reply. "Yes, sir. I just started today."

"Ah. A new recruit! Splendid. Welcome to The Savoy—the largest and finest luxury hotel in the world."

His colleague laughs. "In *your* opinion, old man. The manager of the Waldorf Astoria may not be inclined to agree!" His accent is American. Brash and confident. As he speaks, his eyes travel from my shoes to my cap and everywhere in between.

I feel uncomfortable under his gaze. "But your standards are most definitely going up," he continues. "Much prettier staff than last year. A carefully planned business strategy of yours, I presume? Anything to drag the punters in!"

My cheeks redden as they both laugh at the joke.

"Don't let us hold you up," the older gentleman says. "Plenty of work to do. *Tempus fugit.*"

I follow Sissy along the corridor. As we turn a corner, I glance over my shoulder. He is still staring.

"Who was that?" I whisper.

"The governor. Reeves-Smith."

"No. Not him. The younger man with him."

"That's Lawrence Snyder. Larry to his friends. Big Hollywood somebody or other. Comes over every season to spot the new talent. Entices them to America with the promise of starring roles in the movies. He's the one Gladys has her sights on. Can't blame her. He's so handsome. And that accent!"

"I thought he was vile. Did you see the way he looked us up and down?"

"Looked *you* up and down, you mean. Serves you right for having those great big eyes and shapely ankles. Anyway, all the gentlemen look at the maids that way. The prettier ones, at least. You'd better get used to it, Miss Dorothy Lane."

My stomach lurches at her words. I instinctively place a hand to my cheek. Sometimes I can still feel the pain; the sickening thud of his fist.

Reaching a white paneled door, Sissy knocks firmly and calls, "Housekeeping." Hearing nothing in reply, she turns the key and steps inside. I hang the MAID AT WORK sign on the handle and close the door behind us.

The suite is breathtaking, a dazzling display of crystal chandeliers and polished walnut. An ornate chaise sits by a low window and Hepplewhite chairs are arranged beside a mahogany coffee table. The famous Savoy bed is big enough for half a dozen people to sleep in. Even with its crumpled linen and creased pillow slips, it is quite something. Following Sissy's lead, I check the blinds, switch the electric lights on and off to make sure they are all working, and turn the bathroom taps to make sure they're not dripping.

"It's funny to be among the things of someone I've never met, and probably never will," I remark as we strip the bed. "I'm used to doing out the rooms of young ladies I'd see every day."

"I like the anonymity," Sissy says, bundling the dirty sheets into a neat pile. "It suits me to come in and set things right while they're out having lunch and cocktails. Never cared for all that gossip and familiarity in a private household. Part of the fun of working here is imagining whose room you're in. Look at those black opera gloves over that chair. What do you reckon? A tall redhead with a dirty laugh?"

"Or maybe a short brunette with thick ankles?" I add.

We giggle as we conjure up increasingly awful images of who Miss Howard from Pennsylvania might be and as I lift beautiful necklaces from the dressing table, I imagine the pale neck they will decorate with their emeralds and jade. I replace the cap on a lipstick and see perfect crimson lips and the mark they will leave on a champagne glass. I breathe in the scent of sandalwood and rose as I dust beneath perfume bottles and face creams. I admire a small traveling pillow, running my fingers over the outline of a butterfly expertly captured by silk thread. I feel the rich fabric of each elegant dress, the soft satin of each shoe, the smooth gloss of every Ciro pearl, and for a delicious moment I am not Dorothy Lane, daughter of a Lancashire farmer, I am the daughter of an American shipping magnate with exquisite things to make my life perfect.

We work methodically following a careful routine, making neat hospital corners, plumping downy pillows, folding thick towels, replacing the scented lining paper in drawers, and placing freshly baked Marie biscuits into the silver boxes on the nightstands. The work is intense and time passes quickly.

As we finish the last room on our round, I pull at a final pucker on the counterpane. The room, once again, set straight. I step back to admire our work and think of something Teddy once said as he watched me iron the laundry until everything was as smooth as glass. *Life can't always be starched sheets and perfect hemlines, Dolly. Sometimes creases and puckers will sneak in, no matter how much you tug and smooth.* He had such wise and lovely words. It makes his silence all the more unbearable.

Sissy is watching me. "Penny for your thoughts."

I let out a long sigh. "If only the mess we make of our lives could be tidied as easily. That'd be something, wouldn't it?"

She studies me for a moment. "What's his name, your mess? Mine's Charlie. Ran off with my best friend."

I hesitate. I don't often talk about him, but something about Sissy makes me want to open up. "Teddy. He's called Teddy."

"And what did Teddy do to make a mess of things?"

I look at her and then I look down at my feet. "Nothing. Teddy did nothing at all."

5
TEDDY

Maghull Military War Hospital, Lancashire
March 1919

> "I wonder if I might see your face among the
> clouds, because sometimes I forget you."

My bed is the last in a long row of twenty on the ward. It means that I'm the last to be fed and the last to be seen by the doctors on their rounds, but it also means that I am beside the window, and for that I would come last at everything.

With a simple turn of the head I can look out at the sky and the distant hills. I can watch the clouds and the weather rolling in across the Irish Sea. I can turn my back on the rest of the ward and forget that I am here at all.

Today the sky is a wonderful shade of blue. Bluebell blue. A welcome sight after yesterday's relentless sheets of gray rain. My nurse tells me she hopes to take a walk in the park later.

"It's lovely out," she says, her voice cheery and bright. "Looks like spring has arrived at last."

I don't speak. I barely acknowledge her as I

stare at the window and watch a butterfly dancing around the frame. Unusual to see them at this time of year. A Peacock. Or maybe it's a Painted Lady. I forget. I used to know my butterflies so well. Whatever it is, the nurses have let it out several times but it always comes back in.

"I've brought some more of the letters to read," the nurse continues. "Shall I start?"

I turn my head toward her. She sits in a small chair beside the bed. Smoothes her skirt across her knees. Tucks a loose hair behind her ear. I nod. What else can I do? She's here now. She says the letters will help me remember.

She unfolds the page, and starts to read.

October 5th, 1916

My dearest Teddy,

I looked at the sky this morning. Not just a quick glance because a bird flew overhead, but really looked, like you always told me to. I stood perfectly still and did nothing but look up. It was all peaches and raspberries. Yesterday it was soft velvet gray, like moleskin. I wonder if the sky looks the same in France. I imagine it is different somehow. Darker.

Do you remember when we used to meet at the stone bridge and sit with our legs dangling over the edge, swaying like the bulrushes in the breeze? "Listen to the river," you would say. "What can you hear?" I laughed at you. All I could hear was the water. But when I really listened I heard other things: the rush of wind through the grass, the hum of dragonfly wings, the splash as a fish took a fly from the surface. When I looked at the water all I could see was our reflections and the shadows of the clouds. But you told me to look beyond the surface and slowly my eyes would adjust and I'd see a fish. And like magic, an entire shoal would be there. They'd been there all along, but I couldn't see them. I wasn't looking properly. And then all sorts would appear from the murk: the glint of a coin, a child's rattle, the flash of pink and gold as a trout flickered beneath the surface.

I remember.

It comforts me to know that we are looking at the same sky. If we look hard enough, what might we see, Teddy? I wonder if I might see your face among the clouds, because sometimes I forget you. I struggle to catch the image of you, like I struggled to see those fish. But I keep looking, keep searching, and suddenly there you are, as clear as if you were standing in front of me. As if you'd been there all the time.

I just need to keep looking and there you'll be.

Don't forget me, Teddy. Look for me.

Your Little Thing,

Dolly

X

P.S. I've been catching the leaves and making a wish like you showed me. I don't need to tell you what I wished for.

The words of the letters upset her. Sometimes she dabs a little cotton handkerchief to her cheek to wipe away the tears. Perhaps she wrote letters like this to someone too. Perhaps they stir memories of her own.

"Would you like me to read another?" she asks. I look back to the window; stare at the trees with their buds promising new life. I shrug. "I know it's difficult," she says, "but it's good for you to hear them." She places a comforting hand on my shoulder. "They'll help you remember. In time."

I turn my head slowly to look at her. My eyes feel dull and tired. She looks distant; far away. Picking up another envelope from her lap, she removes the pages and continues.

November 12th, 1916

My dearest Teddy,

It is eight months since you left, and everything has changed so much.

Conscription is so cruel. Everyone who is able to fight has gone now, even the married men. Those who are left—too young, or too old or infirm—drift around the village like dandelion seeds. They feel guilty and useless and wish they were out there fighting with you all. I tell them they should be grateful they're not and that I'd give anything to make you a year or two younger so you'd still be here with me.

We are all doing our bit. I seem to be knitting, mostly. Socks, gloves, and other comforts. It turns out I'm almost as bad at knitting as I am at sewing, but if I keep trying I might improve. Others are making Christmas puddings to send to you all and everyone's helping out on the farms. The Land Army, it's called.

I finished up at the big house and work in the munitions factory since I turned eighteen. It's hard work, but anything's better than domestic work and it pays better. We wear trousers! We clock in and out and fill the shells with TNT powder. They call us "canary girls" because the powder stains our skin yellow. The work is dangerous—there was a big explosion at a factory in Faversham down south—but at least I feel like I'm doing something to help, and sometimes, when we sit out on the grass on tea break, we feel quite happy. I know we shouldn't because there's a war on, but Ivy Markham says you can't be maudlin all the time. We all feel terrible when one of the girls gets the King's Telegram. Oh, that's so awful, Teddy. We don't know what to say and I know everyone else feels the same as I do deep down—relieved that it wasn't news about our own, and that's an awful thing to think when someone's just lost somebody dear to them.

I'll try to write with happier news next time. Mam says I shouldn't be telling you sad things. She says the job of the women back home is to cheer you all up.

Your Little Thing,

Dolly

X

P.S. The camera arrived safely. I think you are right to send it back, considering the ban from the War Office. It would be silly to get into trouble if your officers found that you still had one, and worse still if it fell into enemy hands. I'll keep it safe until you come home.

The room is silent apart from the occasional cough from another patient. I look out at the distant chimney pots of the factories, reaching up toward the clouds like grubby fingers. The nurse tells me they made bombs in that factory during the war. They make ladies' gloves there now. Sometimes it all seems so pointless.

"Another letter?" she asks.

I shake my head. What's the point? She must have read these letters to me a dozen times and still I cannot remember this girl called Dolly who says such nice things. I hold out my hand and take the pages from her. They are watermarked and stained with the filth of war. She told me they were found in the breast pocket of my greatcoat. A great bundle of them, carried against my heart. I fold the pages as neatly as I can, following the worn creases. The tremble in my hands makes hard work of what would once have been such a simple task.

She takes the pages from me and pats my hand. "Tea?"

I nod.

"Two lumps?"

I nod again. I can remember that much, two lumps of sugar in my tea. I can remember the name of my cat, the date of my mother's birthday, how to make a corn dolly. Trivial things. Everything else is a distant fog, my once apparently happy life slowly erased by years of war until I am left only with the nightmares that haunt me.

The doctors are troubled by my condition. They prod me and poke me and write things down.

Words I don't understand for a condition they don't understand: delusions, hallucinations, hysterical mutism. I've seen their notes. But despite their many treatments—hypnosis, electric shock, basket making, warm baths—they can't make me better and they won't send me home. They have labeled me "Not Yet Diagnosed, Nervous." A fancy name for what the men called shell shock. We all knew someone who was sent back from the front, suffering with their nerves. Lacking Moral Fiber, was another label the officers stuck on it. The young lad in the bed beside me says I need to pull myself together, that if I keep screaming at night and talking about the things I've seen they'll send me off to the county asylum. And this girl in the letters, this Dolly, she tells me of so many wonderful things I have seen and done. It seems such a shame that I can't do them anymore.

The guns are silent, but I am still fighting my war.

It is all I have now. War, the nurse, and the butterfly at the window.

6
DOLLY

"You look at things. Imagine things.
I bet you see shapes in the clouds."

The hotel room is dark and unfamiliar when I wake. I lie still, listening to the rise and fall of the girls' breaths, the pop of a mattress spring as they move, the rustle of bedsheets as they fidget in their sleep. It is all so strange and new. I didn't think I would ever miss Clover's snoring, but I do. I hear other noises as the hotel wakes up: the rush of water through distant pipes, the yawn of a straining floorboard overhead, the whistle of a porter, the jangle of milk bottles in the courtyard below the window. I think of the sounds I woke to in Mawdesley: the cockerel, the wind in the eaves, the *knock knock knock* of the wonky leg at the kitchen table as Mam scrubbed it with sugar and soap until her fingers bled. She scrubbed that table for weeks, as though she might somehow scrub away the words on the telegram that told her my father had fallen in the line of duty. That relentless knocking became the sound of our grief until I couldn't bear it any longer and propped up the wonky table leg with *The Adventure Book for Girls*.

The knocking stopped. Mam's tears continued. I had nothing to prop her up with.

Instinctively, I reach beneath my pillow for the photograph but my fingertips find the pages of music. The touch of them reminds me: gray eyes, russet hair, a moment of something unspoken. I think about the music on the pages; unplayed, unloved. It nags at me like an itch I can't scratch. I feel again for the photograph and take it from its hiding place, pressing it against my chest as I pull back the bedcovers, wrap a blanket around my shoulders, and creep across the cold floor to the window. The gas lamps cast an eerie glow over the courtyard at the back of the kitchens, lending just enough light to the room for me to see his face. My heart collapses at the sight of him. So many questions I can't answer. So much pain. So much hurt and anger—and yet still so much love; an instinctive yearning to hold him in my arms. I clutch him tight to my chest, just as I did the day the photograph was taken. If only I could feel the warmth of him once more. That would be enough.

Beneath the window, porters and deliverymen are lifting supplies off wagons and carts after their trip to the markets. They work quickly, the men on the carts tossing pallets of fruit and vegetables to the next man, and on down the line. A rotten tomato lands on someone's head and I smile as the unlucky recipient throws one back in reply. Soon everyone is pelting each other with whatever they can grab: oranges, lemons, walnuts. "Silly buggers," I whisper.

A mattress spring pops behind me. I look around to see Sissy sitting up in bed watching me. I startle at the sight of her, making us both giggle.

"What are you doing?" she whispers.

"Looking."

"At what?"

I shrug. "Nothing much."

She wraps her blanket around her shoulders and joins me at the window. We stand for a moment, our foreheads pressed against the cold glass as we watch the porters larking about.

"You're a dreamer, aren't you, Dolly."

"What do you mean?"

"You look at things. Imagine things. I bet you see shapes in the clouds."

She is right. I do.

We watch as the lamplighter makes his way along the street with his long pole and ladder, extinguishing the lamps as a dove-gray dawn settles across the sky.

"Did you lose someone?" she asks.

I falter. What is the definition of loss? I place my fingertip on the glass, drawing patterns into the condensation formed from our breaths. "Yes."

"Me too. The Somme. He'd only been there a couple of months. My brother, Davey." She turns and points to the photograph on her nightstand. "That's him. Handsome bugger."

I place my hand on hers. "I'm sorry." It never sounds enough.

"Left a wife and two babies, a mother, and a sister. We're all sorry. His missus says she could bear it a little more if he'd written a good-bye. But there was no last letter in his pocket. Not our Davey. He wasn't one for words or soppy sentiments." She draws a heart onto the glass and we watch as it fades away. "What about yours? How did he die?"

Our conversation is interrupted as something lands with a clatter against the glass, making us both scream and jump backward. We peer down to see one of the porters grinning up at us. He has a handful of walnuts and sends another rattling against the window.

Sissy pushes up the sash. A blast of cold air nips at my skin as she sticks her head outside. "Oi!" she shouts. "Watch it!"

The porter blows her a kiss and carries on with his work.

"Cheeky sod," she says, closing the window and pulling the blanket closer around her shoulders.

"Do you know him?"

"Billy Morris. He's taken a fancy to me."

"And?"

"And what?"

"Have *you* taken a fancy to him?"

Her cheeks redden as a smile crosses her lips. "Might have."

"What's all the noise?"

We both turn around to see that Mildred is awake.

"It's Dolly," Sissy says. "She's flirting with the porters."

I cuff her on the shoulder. "I am not!"

Mildred looks at me with that same knowing look. "Well, Dolly should be careful or she'll get herself a reputation before she gets her first pay packet."

Sissy and I look at each other and burst out laughing.

Mildred throws her covers back and steps out of bed. "Honestly. It's like being back at school." She leaves the room, slamming the door behind her.

"What's got into her?" I ask, clambering back into bed and hugging my knees tight to my chest for warmth.

"Nothing," Sissy says. "That's the problem. Needs a good roll in the hay, that one does. She's as stiff as a fire iron."

The maids' bathroom is like Piccadilly Circus on a Friday evening. A couple of the manicurists from the hairdressing salon are washing their stockings in the sinks. I catch snippets of their conversation, something about a Hollywood movie producer being sweet on one of them. I'd love to hear more, but they leave as the bathroom fills up with a dozen chattering maids.

"The manicurists think they're above us," Sissy

says. "They don't live in, but they'll happily use our bathroom when it suits. Don't know why they can't wash their smalls at home."

The narrow counter below the mirror is a jumble of caps and hairpins as we all fuss and fidget to make sure we look just right. Skinny arms and sharp elbows in matching blue print dresses jostle for position. I stand on my tiptoes, peering above the heads in front of me. It isn't the first time I wish I were taller. *"Not tall enough. Next, please."* I've heard those words so many times, sometimes before I'd even danced one step.

Sissy gives me a shove in the back, pushing me forward. "Come on, girls. Give someone else a turn."

With a ripple of annoyance, the sea of bodies in front of me slowly parts and finally I get in front of the mirror. I look pale and tired from my restless night and pinch my cheeks to draw some color to them.

"Here. Have some of this." Gladys hands me a pot of rouge. "Never know who you might bump into." She winks and rubs a little onto her cheeks. "Got to look your best."

"I thought we weren't allowed to wear makeup."

"We're not. You just wear enough to look a bit less dead, but not enough for O'Hara to notice."

I pass up the offer and concentrate on pinning my unruly curls into some sort of order, before fixing my frill cap in place.

Sissy passes me a lipstick. "Got it in Woolworth's last week. It's called Vermillion." She's already applied a little to accentuate her Cupid's bow, just like the actresses in the silent pictures. She puckers her lips and pouts at herself in the mirror. "Well. What d'you think?"

I turn to look at her. "Very Mary Pickford!"

She laughs and wipes it off with a tissue. "Here. Try it."

I can't resist. I twist the bottom of the golden case. The beveled edge slides easily over my lips. I press them together and rub them from side to side as I lean closer to the mirror to take a closer look. "It's lovely."

A girl beside me tells me it suits me. "You new?" she asks.

"Yes. I'm Dolly."

"Pleased to meet you, Dolly. I'm Tallulah."

She mimics Tallulah Bankhead's southern drawl perfectly. I laugh. "Did you see her in *The Dancers*? She was so beautiful."

"Went every night for a week," she replies. "Lost a shoe in the rush to get to the gallery the first night. Walked home in my stockings. Earned myself a clip round the ear from my mam."

Sissy claps her hands together, drawing everyone's attention. "Now, girls," she says, in her best Irish accent. "Everything must be neat and tidy and just so. The white frill cap and apron worn in a particular way, the shoes polished like glass, the hair curled and pinned perfectly." She stops and looks at me. "For the love of all that's holy, Dorothy Lane. Look at your cap. That won't do at all!"

I giggle as she helps me fasten my cap properly, but our good mood is interrupted by a sharp knock at the door.

"I hope this jolly attitude will remain with you through your day's work, girls."

"Who's that?" I whisper to Gladys.

"Head porter. Cutler."

The voice continues beyond the door. "Far too many surly expressions in the corridors recently. It's not good for the hotel's *ambience*. Now, hurry downstairs. It is nearly half past. Mrs. O'Hara will be along for her inspection soon."

Gladys explains that Cutler is a moody old sod. "Nice as pie one minute but he'd fire you on the spot for anything inappropriate. Keep your nose out and your hands clean and you've no need to worry."

But as we file out of the cramped bathroom, I do worry. There's so much to remember, so many new faces to know. I've already met several floor-housekeepers, dozens of maids, floor-waiters and valets and lift attendants, not to mention the various members of the management team. As we rush down the staff stairs, the swish of our dresses mingles with the rumble of heels against the linoleum. I try to suppress the memories that lurk in every squeak of my shoes against the floor. In the Maids' Hall I take a seat at the long table and pour a cup of tea. It is good and strong. Not like the pale sweepings I used to get at Mawdesley Hall. Triangles of toast sit in steel racks with pats of bright yellow butter in ramekins dotted about the table. The kitchen maids have been busy. I see the young girl who was scrubbing the steps yesterday and smile at her. She's so engrossed in her chores she hardly notices me. I tuck into porridge and bread that's still warm, fresh from the ovens of the hotel bakery. I let a piece melt slowly on my tongue and remember how me and my little sister, Sarah, used to stand outside the bakers with a pillowcase, ready to fill it with whatever we could get for the sixpence Mam had given us. Mostly it was those awful flat brown loaves—cowpats we used to call them. If we were lucky, we'd get a roll to scoff on the way home. I'd tell Sarah to brush the crumbs from her lips and her pinafore so Mam wouldn't notice.

All too soon, we hear brisk footsteps and O'Hara appears, the great bundle of keys jangling at her hip like a restless child. We all stand as she enters the room, chair legs scraping against the stone floor, spoons clattering against bowls and cups. The kitchen maids start to clear the breakfast things as O'Hara calls us to line up in the corridor. I follow the others, copying them as they fall into a long line: shoulders back, feet together, chin up, hands behind the back. I cross my fingers and say a silent prayer as O'Hara walks briskly along the line like a drill sergeant major, handing each girl a neatly typed house list. She stops occasionally to tug at a twisted apron strap or to inspect hands and nails. She stops in front of me. My heart pounds beneath my dress as I look straight ahead, trying not to focus on anything and avoiding O'Hara's cold stare. She considers me for a second before leaning forward and brushing a fingertip along my upper lip.

"Lipstick, Dorothy?"

Bugger. I forgot to wipe it off. The girl to my right takes a sharp intake of breath. My heart thumps.

"We are not at some backstreet picture house now," O'Hara snaps. "Lipstick has no place on a maid's lips until she clocks off." She passes me a handkerchief. "And even then it is quite unnecessary. Get rid of it. Immediately."

"Yes, miss." I rub the handkerchief frantically at my lips, turning to the girl beside me, who nods to confirm it is gone. As O'Hara continues down the line Sissy leans forward and mouths an apology. I shush the voice in my head that wonders if she might have done it on purpose to land me in trouble.

Finally, O'Hara is satisfied. "Everything seems to be in order. Let's have a good day's work and remember . . ."

The girls all join in a chorus of rehearsed instruction. "The smallest things can make the biggest difference. Attention to detail in everything. Our guests are our priority."

O'Hara nods approvingly. "Quite so. Now, off you go—and, Dorothy . . ."

What now? "Yes, miss?"

"Sissy Roberts will assist you with your rooms again today. Tomorrow, you're on your own."

"Yes, miss."

"Any questions?"

"No, miss."

"I presume we won't be seeing any crimson lips tomorrow?"

In my head I tell her it's Vermillion. "No, miss. We won't."

My inquisitor nods firmly and swishes away with her sticky-out veins and pointy elbows. I lean back against the wall and breathe a sigh of relief. "Yes, miss. No, miss. Three bags full, miss."

Sissy digs me in the ribs. "Cheeking the head of housekeeping already? I'd keep those thoughts to yourself if I were you. You'll land yourself in trouble muttering under your breath like that. The hotel has eyes and ears. The less said the better."

"Well, she looks at me funny. Like I'm something she scraped off her shoe."

"She *will* scrape you off her shoe if she hears you bad-mouthing her. Keep your mouth shut and your corners neat." She grabs me by the elbow.

"Sorry about the lipstick. Next time, wipe it off before you come downstairs, you silly sod. She'd have marched you straight to Cutler if it wasn't your first morning. I'm certain of it."

"Let's call it beginner's luck, then, and forget all about it."

Sissy checks the new house list as we make our way to the storerooms. "Well, look at this. Beginner's luck indeed. First room on your list, Miss Dorothy Lane, is occupied by a Mr. Lawrence Snyder. Friend of the governor. Manager to the stars."

"Snyder? That vile man we saw yesterday?" I think about the way he looked at me. I think about the way I've been looked at like that before.

"The very same. Gladys will be as sick as a dog when she hears. She's convinced he'll have her on the next boat to America." She nudges me in the ribs. "Well, come on. We won't get much done standing around daydreaming. The rooms won't clean themselves."

I follow her as she strides off toward the linen stores, but my thoughts are elsewhere and my heart has rushed back to my room and wrapped itself around the photograph beneath my pillow.

The service floor is even more confusing than it was yesterday. A steady stream of porters, maids, chefs, and waiters fills the narrow corridors. When anyone in livery or formal dress passes, we step aside to make way for them. Sissy points out the head chef, a formidable Frenchman who forbids anyone, other than kitchen staff, to enter his storerooms. I catch a glimpse of some of the recent deliveries: gallons of cream in great vats, mountains of fresh pineapples, tanks full of live lobsters, vast saddles of venison, haunches of ham, and great slabs of beef. The hotel bakery alone is the size of a small house. My mouth waters at the aroma of freshly baked loaves being lifted from the ovens on huge paddles by red-cheeked young boys and burly men. Sissy swipes two milk rolls from the nearest tray, earning herself a friendly flick at her backside with the end of a paddle.

"Do you ever see the guests when you're in their rooms?" I ask when we've loaded our trollies. "Gladys was telling me that the ladies sometimes keep maids talking for hours, to pass the time."

"They ask for more soap to be sent up, or hand towels, but really it's just an excuse to have a bit of company. Bored, you see. I suppose there's only so many times you can admire yourself in the mirror. It's mainly the hairdressers and manicurists who are personally requested in the guests' rooms. They spend hours up there, drinking coffee and eating delicate little cakes. Get sent bouquets and earrings and perfume and all sorts by their regulars. And they always get a good tip. Half a crown if they're lucky."

"Really?"

"Mind you, I've heard some guests show their gratitude in ways that might not be appreciated as much as a bouquet of roses, if you know what I mean."

She winks as we step into the lift and ask the attendant to take us to fourth.

"I didn't think things like that would go on here," I whisper.

Sissy scoffs at my naïveté. "Same old divide. There's us downstairs, and there's them upstairs. A maid is as easily taken advantage of at The Savoy as she is anywhere else. You'd be a fool to think otherwise."

The lift jolts to a stop and we step out as a gentleman emerges from a room to the left. He tips his hat as he passes. Larry Snyder. We stand to one side and wish him a good morning.

"And to you both." He looks at me. "The new girl. Am I right?"

"Yes, sir." I touch my fingers self-consciously to my lips, hoping the last traces of Sissy's Vermillion have been rubbed away.

"So my suite is your dress rehearsal!"

"I'm not sure what you mean, sir."

"Movie stars. Actresses. Chambermaids. I suppose we all need somewhere to practice. My suite is all yours. Feel free to fluff your lines—or should I say pillows!"

He smiles warmly and I mutter a thank you.

"Would you like your room attended to now, sir?" Sissy asks.

"Indeed. I shall be gone for the day." He walks on a few paces, stops, and turns around. "There might be a few papers scattered around the place. Leave them where they are, would you. Work in progress on a new script."

"Of course, sir."

At the guest lift we hear him greet a friend. "John McArthur! What the devil has you at The Savoy?"

"The wife, Snyder. The wife has me at The Savoy, and both my bank balance and I are suffering dreadfully as a consequence."

Sissy and I burst out laughing and enter Snyder's room.

As I sip my cocoa over supper that evening, my feet throb and my arms ache. I glance at the clock on the wall. The productions across London will be reaching their final act by now, the girls in the gallery hoarse from shouting their appreciation, the restaurants and nightclubs ready to welcome the after-show crowds for supper and dancing. I'm so tired even the thought of dancing makes me feel weary, and when I climb into bed I'm too exhausted to even read one page of Sissy's magazine.

I shuffle under the blankets, listening to the scratch of Mildred's pen on the page as she writes in her diary. I can't think what she can possibly have to write so much about. Her life seems to consist of nothing more than the hotel. No hobbies. No interests. No dreams. By the time she turns out the light, Gladys is fast asleep and Sissy is already snoring. The room is plunged into darkness, but I know the lights from the hotel suites and the restaurant and ballroom still shine all around me. For a while, I listen to the distant sounds of music and laughter that float along the corridors, enticing me to follow, until I grow sleepy and close my eyes and I set my dreams free to drift and dance among those who have already made theirs a reality.

7
LORETTA

*Sometimes I would happily swap
the lonely peaks of stardom for
the jolly camaraderie of the chorus.*

The Shaftesbury is sold out for opening night of *HOLD TIGHT!* Dear Cockie is delighted. Yet again he has shown his critics that while those who take risks in this business sometimes fall on hard times, they can also bask in the glory of success when it comes. From the ladies and gentlemen and distinguished guests dressed in their finery in the stalls and dress circle and boxes, all the way back to the raucous throng squashed together high up in the gallery, there isn't a spare seat in the house, nor any space to stand. If ticket sales are a measure of success, we already have a hit on our hands, but experience has taught me that there's a long way to go and many pages of script and musical score to be convincingly delivered before the final curtain falls.

As the audience roar their approval for the first act, the heavy velvet curtain drops in a dramatic swoop in front of me and the spotlight goes out, plunging the stage into a dead blackout. I savor the moment; the cocoon of pitch black. In that dark silence, I can pretend that nothing matters, other than the fading applause. I stand as still as stone and breathe. In and out. In and out. I wonder what my last breath will feel like.

A fine dust drifts down from the gantry high above, disturbed by the stagehands as they hoist and lower scenery. I stifle a cough as it settles on my arms and sticks to my clammy skin. My moment of silence interrupted, I walk offstage, feeling my way with the toe of my satin shoe down the five steps that lead from the wings.

Backstage is already a hive of activity. Stage-hands, assistants, the pianist, and my leading man all congratulate me as I pass.

"You're terrific, Miss May."

"A wonderful first act!"

"Fabulous, darling! Fabulous!"

"Word perfect. Simply divine!"

I smile graciously, letting the compliments and platitudes wash over me. They are expected now, arranged by my people, regardless of how good or bad my performance. I don't care for insincerity. Only dear Jimmy Jones, the stage-door manager and my unlikeliest of friends, remains silent. We have known each other through some of the hardest years we will ever know. He understands when words are not needed. He simply smiles, gives me a reassuring pat on the arm, and presses a bundle of carefully audited cards and messages into my hand. Only the kindest words, the most sincere letters of adoration from fans and amusing offers of marriage from respectable gentlemen ever make it past Jimmy's careful scrutiny.

As I make my way to my dressing room a young girl from the chorus runs past. She stops as she recognizes me. She is a beauty, all wide-eyed and wondering, no doubt envying my leading role and my name in electric lights front of house. Little does she know that it is I who envy her and the other chorus girls with youth and vitality on their side: training from noon till four, twenty-five half-dressed girls crammed into one dressing room, stepping on each other's corns, sharing makeup and jokes and a cup of pickled onions for a snack before curtain up, and all the while waiting for Friday when "the Ghost Walks" so they can run straight to the shops to spend their hard-earned pay. Sometimes I would happily swap the lonely peaks of stardom for the jolly camaraderie of the chorus.

It wasn't so very long ago that I was a defiant society girl with an unforgettable face and an unrelenting mother; the girl who found her place on the stage despite the disdain her parents expressed toward such an unseemly profession. That girl had fought and rebelled. That girl had shunned her chaperones to drink and dance to the exotic music of the Negro bands and mix with the chorus girls and actresses she admired. That girl was starry-eyed and carefree. She had passion and belief, just like the young girl in front of me now.

"You are wonderful, Miss May," she gasps, all breathless and starstruck. "Just wonderful."

I step forward and take her face in my hands. "And so will you be. Keep practicing, keep believing, and you can have whatever you dream of." She gazes at me, adoringly. "Now run along and get changed before the wardrobe mistress has a fit."

"Yes, Miss May. Of course."

I watch her as she runs off into the shadows and wish I could run with her, disappear into obscurity, and never have to tell anyone the awful truth of it all.

Stepping around tins of paint, precariously balanced props, ladders, and endless rails of costumes, I hurry along the cramped passageways, relieved to reach my dressing room and close the door on the noise and chaos behind me. Jimmy has been busy, arranging the boxes of chocolates and bouquets from gentlemen callers and well-wishers. I take a cursory look at some of the cards as Hettie, my seamstress and dresser, pushes several larger displays to one side so that I can see my reflection in the mirror. I slump down in the chair at the dressing table and look at the flowers surrounding me. A beautiful arrangement of pink peonies catches my eye. The rest are ghastly.

"Why can't people send roses, Hettie? Nobody sends roses anymore. They're forever trying to outdo one another with gaudy-colored orchids." I lift up some vile yellow blooms. "I don't even know what these are."

"Shall I remove them?" she asks.

I take off my dance shoes and slip my aching feet into silk slippers. "No. Leave them. Ask Jimmy to arrange a car to send them to the hospitals after the show."

"Of course."

"Tell him to leave the peonies. I'll take them home." I run my fingers over the blooms, remembering my wedding posy. Pink peonies. Roger stole one for his buttonhole. It was all such a rush that buttonholes hadn't been considered. He placed a single bloom in my hair and told me I looked more beautiful than the stars. *My very own slice of heaven.*

Hettie places a silk housecoat around my shoulders and pours me a glass of water. I'd far rather she pour me something stronger but she fusses about my drinking, especially during a performance, so I say nothing and take a couple of dutiful sips as she fetches my dress for the next act.

"The audience love you tonight, Miss May."

"Hmm? What?" I'm distracted by my thoughts and the many pots of pastes and creams on the dressing table. Gifts from Harry Selfridge. He really is a darling man, if a little too American at times.

"The audience," Hettie repeats. "They love you. The gallery girls especially."

"The audience always love me, Hettie. And as for the gallery-ites, I can do no wrong as far as they are concerned. It's the press I need to worry about."

"Well, I'm sure they'll love you too. You could hear the shrieks of laughter back here."

She sets to work, fiddling with last-minute adjustments to hems and seams. I stand up and turn around as instructed, the electric bulbs around the mirror illuminating my skin. I look tired and drawn, the delicate skin around my lips pinched from too many cigarettes. My thirty-two years look more like fifty-two.

"Do I look old, Hettie?"

She is used to my insecurities. She knows me better than my own mother at this stage. "Not at all," she mumbles through a mouth full of pins. "You're as beautiful now as the first day I saw you."

I catch her eye. "You are very kind, Hettie Bennett. You are also a terrible liar."

She smiles, finishes her adjustments, and leaves me alone for a blissful five minutes before curtain up. Those few minutes of peace are like a religion to me. Like afternoon tea with Perry, they are mine. Everything else about tonight—what I wear, what I say, what I sing, where I stand, where I will dine after the show and who I will be seen dining with—is all decided for me, all part of the performance. I sit down and stare at my reflection without blinking until my image blurs and I can almost see the young girl I once was.

Ironically, it was Mother who introduced me to the theater. She shunned the teaching of regular subjects, instructing my governesses to focus on poetry, singing, and the arts. As a young girl, I was often taken on trips to the London theater, where I was enthralled by the provocative dancing of Isadora Duncan and Maud Allan's *Vision of Salomé* and the exotic *Dance of the Seven Veils*. As I approached my debut year, I embarked on a strict exercise regime to improve my fitness. I enrolled in dance classes, determined to learn how to move as gracefully as those incredible women I had watched on the stage. I worked hard, and while Mother considered my dancing "a pleasant little hobby," my heart was soon set on it becoming far more than that.

Shortly after my debut season, I developed a talent for escaping my chaperones. While other debutantes diligently danced gavottes in the austere rooms of elegant homes across London, I discovered the heady delights of the city's nightclubs. I met theater producers and actors, writers, artists, and dancers. I was captivated by them as much as the gossip columnists were captivated by me. My exceptional beauty and extraordinary behavior became a regular feature of the society pages. As the years passed, my parents increasingly despaired of my unladylike behavior and my failure to secure a suitable husband. I, however, reveled in the exciting new circles I mingled in.

But it was the arrival of war that gave me my first real taste of freedom. We were told the fighting would be over by Christmas, but it soon became clear it was going to last much longer than that. Losses were heavy. Help was needed. I couldn't bear to stand idly by as Aubrey and Perry and dear friends of mine fought for their lives at the front. Going against my mother's express wishes not to, I enrolled as a Voluntary Aid Detachment nurse at the Royal Herbert Hospital. The work was difficult and exhausting, but I took comfort in knowing that I was helping. Photographed in my uniform, I became something of a poster girl for the VAD. Other society girls soon followed my example.

The sleeping quarters of the shared hospital dorm were cramped and inelegant, but the freedom of dorm life was thrilling to a girl who had been educated at home. On my evenings off I relished the opportunity to dance and drink and forget the awfulness of war for a while. It was during those evenings away from the hospital that

I first met Charles Cochran. It was Cockie who saw my charm and my talent and encouraged me to dance in his little revue at the Ambassador's. It started as a bit of fun, a distraction from the shocking realities of nursing. I took to the stage with audacious poise and a new name, Loretta May. While Lady Virginia Clements put in long shifts at the hospital, Loretta May became a shining star of the stage. Night after night, Virginia was dismantled as easily as a piece of scenery, replaced with the dazzling smile and beautiful costumes of my new persona. That I danced in secret whilst under the glare of the brightest spotlight was nothing short of thrilling.

Small speaking parts soon saw my reputation soar. Sassy, beautiful, beguiling—the hacks lavished praise in their emphatic press notices and it didn't take them long to discover the truth behind this intriguing new star. The papers couldn't print their headlines quickly enough.

PEER'S DAUGHTER TAKES THEATER BY
STORM! LADY VIRGINIA CLEMENTS
EXPOSED AS DARLING OF
THE WEST END, LORETTA MAY.

By day, I attended to the sick and wounded. At night, I entertained those whose lives were falling apart. While the revelation about my true identity saw Mother take to her bed for a week, it only made the gallery girls and society pages love me even more.

And then the first letter arrived, and everything changed.

> My dear Miss May,
> You must forgive me, but I have fallen hopelessly in love with you and I'm afraid I must tell you that you are now inextricably linked to my survival in this dreadful war.

"One minute to curtain. One minute to curtain."

The cry of the stagehand cuts through my thoughts. I check myself again in the mirror, touch up my rouge, and apply more kohl to my eyes. The mask of theater. Who cares that my head is pounding and my bones ache dreadfully. The show must go interminably on.

I open the dressing room door and call out into the dimly lit corridor: "Does anyone have an aspirin?" but my words evaporate in a cloud of powder and perfume and glitter as the chorus girls scurry past, their heels clicking and clacking along the floor as last-minute adjustments are made to zips and straps, buckles and laces.

Only Hettie hears me. "Should I go and find one?"

"One what?"

"An aspirin."

"Yes. Please." I wave her away with a distracted hand. I have no idea why the poor thing puts up with me. I treat her dreadfully at times. I don't mean to. I just don't seem to know how to treat her any differently.

I listen at the door until I'm certain the last of the girls have gone. Only then do I reach beneath the dressing table and open the bag I keep hidden there. I pull out the bottle of gin. A quick slug. Purely medicinal. What I wouldn't give for a shot of sweet morphine, to slip into that delightful abyss of nothingness where nobody can hurt me and nothing dreadful has ever happened and Roger is coming home and I am perfectly well. There was a time when I took morphine for fun, to numb the emotional pain of war. Now the doctors tell me I must take it for the physical pain that will eventually bring about my demise. I take two long gulps of gin, coughing as the liquid burns the back of my throat, before returning the bottle to the bag and rushing from the dressing room, the sharp tang of liquor flooding through me, suppressing my pain and my fear and my doubts.

"Miss May! Your aspirin!"

I ignore Hettie and carry on along the passageway, climbing the steps into the wings. I hear the chatter and rustle of the audience as they settle back into their seats. As the houselights go down I take a deep breath, close my eyes, and allow everything to dissolve into a muzzy warmth as I step onto the stage.

The curtain goes up. The spotlight illuminates me. There is an audible gasp from the ladies in the stalls as they admire the beauty of my red velvet cape. I know the reporters for *The Lady* and *The Sketch* and the other society pages will be scribbling down every detail. The gallery girls burst into rapturous applause, screaming my name and standing on their chairs. "Miss May! Miss May! You're marvelous!" I open my eyes, the audience a blur of black against the dazzle of the footlights. My leading man, Jack Buchanan, gives me the cue.

I step forward and deliver the line. "Honestly, darling, *must* we invite the Huxleys for dinner. I think I would rather curl up in a ball and die."

The audience roar with laughter, unaware of the cruel truth contained in my words.

8
LORETTA

"It isn't my place to tell you when you're dreadful, especially not on opening night."

A heavy fog smothers London by the time the show is over. Outside the door to Murray's, the soot-tainted air catches in my chest, making me cough. It is sharp and painful. Far worse than anything I have experienced before.

Perry looks worried. "You really should go to the doctor about that cough, Etta. It's definitely getting worse."

When I've recovered and caught my breath I take a long drag of my cigarette and tell him to stop fussing. "Was I all right tonight, darling? Really?"

He shivers, pulls his scarf around his neck, and claps his hands together for warmth. "You were fabulous, sister dear. Everybody said you were splendid."

I wrap my arms across my chest and sink the fingertips of my gloves into the deep pile of my squirrel-fur coat. "Of course they did. They always do. Anyway, you wouldn't tell me even if I was beastly. Would you?"

111

He says nothing. I pinch his arm.

"Ow! That hurt."

"Good."

"Etta, I'm your favorite brother, and one of only a handful of people you deem worthy of calling your friend. It isn't my place to tell you when you're dreadful, especially not on opening night. There are plenty of people being paid perfectly good money to do that."

I pinch him again. "You're a dreadful tease, Peregrine Clements. First-night notices are ghastly things. I'm nervous. What if the critics hate it? I really can't bear to think about it."

He crushes his cigarette beneath his shoe. "Come on. Let's get disgracefully drunk. By the time the notices are in, you'll be too blotto to care."

But despite the cold and the lure of champagne cocktails, I'm reluctant to go inside. "Walk with me around the square?"

"What? It's freezing. You need a gin fizz, dear girl, not an evening constitutional."

"Please, Perry. Just once around. It was so dreadfully stuffy in the theater tonight, and the club can be so suffocating at times."

He sighs and offers his arm. "Very well. I've lost most of the sensation in one leg. I might as well have a matching pair."

Looping my arm through his, I rest my head wearily on his shoulder as we stroll. I enjoy the sensation of his cashmere scarf against my cheek;

the sensation of someone beside me. For a woman constantly surrounded by people, I so often feel desperately alone.

We walk in comfortable silence. For a few rare moments we are nothing more remarkable than a brother and sister enjoying an evening stroll. Much as he frustrates me, I love Perry dearly, although I can never bring myself to tell him so. Even when he came back from the front I couldn't say what I'd planned, couldn't say the words I'd rehearsed in my head and written in dozens of unsent letters. Old habits die hard. Our privileged upbringing might have left us with proper manners and a love of Shakespeare, but it also left the scars of unspoken fondnesses and absent affection. We are as crippled by our emotions as Perry is by the shrapnel wound to his knee.

"How did the meeting go with Charlot today? Did he like your piece?" I hardly dare ask. Perry's meetings with theatrical producers have been less than successful recently.

He yawns. A habit of his when he isn't telling the truth. "Not bad. He didn't hate it. Didn't love it either."

I stop walking. "You didn't go, did you?"

"Damn it, Etta. Are you having me trailed? How do you know everything about me?"

"Because you are about as cryptic as a brick, darling. Anyway, it doesn't matter how I know. But I *would* like to know *why* you didn't go."

We continue walking as he explains. "The sheet music was ruined by the rain when I bumped into that girl yesterday. And it was a lot of miserable old rot anyway. Charlot wants uplifting pieces. The phrase he used last time I saw him was 'whimsical.' He told me people want to be amused, that Londoners have an appetite for frivolity. I haven't a whimsical bone in my body, Etta. Why put myself through the embarrassment of rejection again?"

For months it has been the same. Unfinished melodies. Missed appointments. All the promise and talent he had shown before the war left behind in the mud and the trenches.

"You need to get out more, Perry. You need to meet interesting people and find inspiration. It can't help to spend so much time in that apartment of yours. It's the least whimsical place I've ever had the misfortune to drink a cup of tea in."

"I'm here now, aren't I? Escorting you on an impromptu evening promenade, about to mingle with the set."

"I do appreciate that you're trying, Perry. Really, I do. All the same, I think you spend too much time alone."

"I'm not alone. Mrs. Ambrose comes and goes."

"Mrs. Ambrose is a middle-aged charwoman. You need vibrancy and excitement in your life, not floor wax and sagging bosoms and woolen stockings."

He laughs. "I can't argue with that."

"I've been giving it some thought, as it happens. I know what you need."

"And what might that be?"

"A muse."

"A *muse?*"

"Yes. A muse."

"And why would I want a muse?"

"To spark your creativity. You need to find someone whose every word, every movement, leaves you so enraptured that you can do nothing but settle at the piano and write words of whimsy about them. Look at Noël Coward. I doubt he would have written anything notable if it weren't for Gertie Lawrence. And Lucile Duff Gordon. How do you think she produced such incredible costumes for Lily Elsie—and for me? They adore those women so much they simply cannot wait to dress them or write songs or books about them." I feel rather pleased with myself as we walk on. "Yes. That's absolutely what you need. A muse."

Perry clearly isn't convinced. "And where might one find a muse these days? Does Selfridge sell them? I hear he has all manner of whimsical things in his shop."

"Don't be factitious. You need to look around. Take more notice of people." I cough and pull my collar up to my chin as we turn the final corner and walk back toward the entrance to the club. "Either that or put an advert in *The Stage*." I laugh at my joke as the doorman holds the door for us and we step inside.

The tantalizing beat from the jazz band drifts up the narrow stairs. The cloakroom attendant takes my coat. I turn to check my reflection in the mirrored wall tiles, twisting my hip and turning my neck to admire the draped silk that falls seductively at the small of my back. I'm glad Hettie chose the pewter dress, the fabric shimmers fabulously beneath the lights. I shake my head lightly, setting my paste earrings dancing. I shiver as a breeze runs along my skin. Murray's is one of my favorite clubs in London. I feel safe here. I can let loose for a while and forget about things among the music and dancing and cocktails.

Turning on the charm, I glide down the stairs. My evening's performance isn't over yet.

Perry orders us both a gin and it from the bar. We sit at the high stools and sip the sweet cocktail, perfectly positioned for people to see us. I watch the band with their glorious café au lait skin. The pulse from the double bass and the shrill cry of the trumpet seep through my skin so that I can feel the music pulse within me. The bandleader acknowledges me, as he always does, and leads the band in my favorite waltz of the moment, "What'll I Do." I smile sweetly and applaud when the song ends.

When we are quite sure we've been noticed,

Perry leads me to our table. The others are already there, the usual set of writers, poets, artists, and anyone who is vaguely interesting in London. Noël Coward, Elizabeth Ponsonby, Nancy Mitford, Cecil Beaton, and, of course, darling Bea, who—I am delighted to see—makes a special fuss of Perry. I kiss them all and settle into the seat between Noël and Cecil.

"You were brilliant, darling!"

"Simply divine. Your best yet, without a doubt."

I wave their words aside. "You are all wicked and mean to tease me. You've been sitting here drinking cocktails all night. You didn't even see so much as the HOUSE FULL boards outside."

"But she was splendid, of course," Perry adds as he pours us both a glass of champagne. "Regardless of what the notices might say in tomorrow's papers."

I ignore his teasing and take a long satisfying sip. The bubbles pop and fizz deliciously on my tongue. *Do* I care what the critics say? It's been so long since I've taken any real notice of the reviews. I haven't needed to. It has simply become habit to read flattery and praise. My housekeeper-cum-secretary, Elsie, cuts out the notices from all the papers and sticks them into a scrapbook with an almost obsessive diligence. The slightest mention of me falls victim to her scissors—photographs, passing references to supper at The Savoy, charitable events, after-the-show reports, costume reviews—nothing escapes her scissors. I tell her I really don't give two figs what they say, but she persists. She says it is important to keep a record; that people will be interested in my career in years to come. She's too polite to say "when you're dead," but I know that's what she means, and it occurs to me that perhaps she is right. The more I think about tonight's performance, the more I realize that the notices *do* matter. There's an astonishing honesty required of oneself when faced with one's own mortality. The notices and observations in Elsie's silly little scrapbook will soon become the record of what I am—who I was. It is how I will be remembered. It matters immensely.

I tip my neck back to savor the last drop of champagne and hold my glass toward Perry for a refill, hoping that nobody notices the tremble in my hand.

The night passes in a heady oblivion of dancing, laughter, and playful flirtation with handsome men who invite me to dance. I allow myself to be guided around the dance floor to quicksteps and tangos, spinning and twirling among elegant young couples who twist and turn as deftly around each other as the champagne bubbles that dance in my glass.

As the night moves on, the band picks up the pace, holding us all spellbound on the dance floor, our feet incapable of rest. I say all the right things to all the right prompts, but despite the gaiety of it all and the adoring gazes I attract whenever I so much as stand up, part of me grows weary too soon and my smile becomes forced as I stifle a succession of yawns. As I watch the midnight cabaret show the room becomes too hot and the music too loud. I long to slip quietly away and walk along the Embankment to look for shooting stars. I was just six years old when my father told me that they are dying stars. "What you are looking at is the end of something that has existed for millions of years," he said. It was the saddest thing I'd ever heard, and in a champagne-fueled fog of adulthood, the thought of it makes me want to cry.

"Miss May. Would you care to dance?"

I turn to see who is addressing me. "Mr. Berlin. What a joy! It would be my pleasure."

What I really wish is that he would hold me in his arms while I rest my head on his shoulder and weep, but that is what an ordinary girl would do, and I am not an ordinary girl. I am Loretta May. So I stand tall and look beautiful and allow myself to be led to the dance floor, where the music thumps and the bodies of a hundred beautiful people twirl and sway in a wonderful rhythm of jazz-fueled recklessness. The gin flows, beaded fabrics ripple against slim silhouettes, ostrich-feather fans sway in time to the music, the soles of satin shoes spin and hop, and legs in silk stockings kick and flick flirtatiously as the band plays on and on.

I play my part perfectly well.

Shooting stars, and the wishes and tears of an ordinary girl, will have to wait.

9

DOLLY

"Sometimes life gives you cotton stockings.
Sometimes it gives you a Chanel gown."

After an exhausting week getting lost in the hotel,
finding my way around my chores, and trying to
keep in O'Hara's good books and out of trouble,
my first afternoon off can't come soon enough.
Mildred slopes off somewhere before anyone
notices. Sissy and Gladys are disappointed I
won't join them at the Strand Palace, but I
explain that I've promised to meet Clover for the
weekly *thé dansant* at the Palais de Danse in
Hammersmith and only a fool would break a
promise made to Clover Parker.

Clover and I have been to the Palais every
Wednesday since my first week in service at the
house in Grosvenor Square. I was looking for a
distraction. Clover was looking for a husband.
Along with hundreds of others who swarm to the
dance halls once a week to shake off the memories
of war and the strict routines of work, Clover and
I pay our two and six and forget about the troubles
that weigh heavy on our shoulders as we foxtrot
and waltz our way around the vast dance floor.

After years of rolling back the carpet in our shared bedroom and practicing the latest dance steps over and over, we are both reasonably good on our feet. More than anything, I love to dance, to lose myself in the music until it wraps itself around me as tightly as the arms of my dance partner. More often than not, this is Clover. Such is the way of things now. There aren't enough men to go around and we can't always afford the extra sixpence to hire one of the male dance instructors, so us single girls make do, taking it in turns to be the man. Clover is a decent substitute, but even when I close my eyes and really imagine, it isn't the same as having a man's arms to guide me. It isn't the same as having Teddy's arms around me. He was a wonderful dancer. It was Teddy who first taught me to dance. It was Teddy who encouraged me to chase my dreams. It was always Teddy.

Changing out of my uniform as quickly as I can, I clock out at the back of the hotel and step outside for the first time in a week. It is still raining but I don't mind. The cool breeze and damp air feel lovely against my cheeks as I turn up the collar on my shabby old coat and walk through the Embankment Gardens toward the river. I think about my collision with Mr. Clements a week ago and the pages of music still hidden beneath my pillow. Although I've tried to push him from my mind, I can't stop thinking about those gray eyes and that rich russet hair, and I can't help wondering about the music I rescued from the litter bin. I feel a strange sense of duty to hear the notes played.

After the hushed order and sophistication of the hotel, London seems particularly grubby and alive. I notice things I've never really noticed before: the soot-blackened buildings, the pigeon droppings on the pavements and railings, the noise from the tugs and wherries on the Thames that toot to one another like gossiping girls, the smell of roast beef from the kitchens at Simpson's. I dodge around smartly dressed ladies in rain-flattened furs who try to avoid the puddles that will leave watermarks on their expensive satin shoes. To them, this is just another dull October afternoon, but to me it is an exciting medley of noise and chaos; a place without restrictions and rules. To me, the pavements dance beneath the raindrops. To me, the roads sing to the tune of motorcars and puddles. To me, everyone quicksteps and waltzes around each other.

In the Embankment Gardens, I feel the vibrations of the underground trains through the pathway beneath my feet and smile as I watch two pigeons squabble over a piece of bread. Beyond the Gardens, I follow the bend of the river along the Embankment where the over-night work of the screevers—the pavement artists—has been spoiled by the rain. Only one drawing of a young girl is just visible. Beside it is written the word "hope" in a pretty looping script. I'd like to take a closer look but I'm already late, so I hurry on. Clover gets cross with me when I'm late, and she's already cross with me for leaving my position in Grosvenor Square.

She hadn't taken well to the news of my position at The Savoy. Her reaction was twenty-two minutes of snotty weeping. I'd watched the clock over her shoulder as I consoled her in the A.B.C. teashop.

"Things won't be the same, Doll. They'll lock you up in that fancy hotel and you'll get all sorts of notions in that pretty head of yours and I'll never see you again. I know it."

"I'm only going to The Savoy, not the moon!"

"Might as well be going to the moon. You'll make new friends and forget all about me. I can feel it in my waters."

Clover feels everything in her waters. "Don't be daft. How could I forget *you?*"

"Then promise we'll still go dancing on our afternoons off."

"Of course we will."

"Promise."

"I *promise*. I'll meet you at the Palais every Wednesday. Same as usual. Cross my heart."

I didn't say "and hope to die." Nobody says that anymore. And I have every intention of keeping my promise. Clover Parker gave me friendship, a shoulder to cry on, and a Max Factor mascara when I had absolutely nothing. I've grown to love her like a sister and can't imagine sharing my makeup, my ciggies, or my worries with anyone else. But things had to change because I'd made another promise. A promise that I would make something of my life. I had to. Otherwise, how could I ever make peace with what I had done?

"Why does everything always have to change, Dolly? Why can't things stay as they are?"

"I want more, Clover. Look at me. I'm as dull as a muddy puddle. When I watch those girls on the stage, I want to be there with them. I want silk stockings on my legs and silver Rayne's dance shoes on my feet. I want Chanel dresses against my skin. I want to cut my hair and rouge my cheeks, not flinch every time I hear footsteps following me down the back stairs. I want to be appreciated, not discarded like a filthy rag. I feel like a stuck gramophone record, going round and round, playing the same notes of the same song over and over. I want to dance to a different tune. Don't you want that too?"

She doesn't. Clover is happy with her lot. A reliable job as a kitchen maid and a quick fumble with Tommy Mullins at the back of the dance hall is enough for her.

"I don't think about it, Dolly. I just am what I am. All I know for certain is that Archie Rawlins ain't coming home and he was the only bugger ever likely to marry me. I'll more than likely end up an old spinster with ten cats to keep me company. But there's no use complaining. Sometimes life gives you cotton stockings. Sometimes it gives you a Chanel gown. That's the way of it. You just have to make the most of whatever you're given."

Part of me wishes I could be more like Clover, settle for a life as a housemaid, marry a decent enough man, make do. But I have restless feet and an impatient heart and a dream of a better life that I can't wake up from.

I'd been told that The Savoy prefers personal recommendations of employees from its current staff, and a discreet word by a friend of Clover's cousin led to my engagement. Clover's opinion is that a maid is still a maid, however fancily you package it up, but I disagree. The Savoy attracts movie stars and musicians, poets and politicians, dancers and writers; the Bright Young People who fill London's newspaper columns and society pages with their extravagant lifestyles. The people who excite me. The people who fill my scrapbooks and my dreams.

At Trafalgar Square, I jump onto the back of the omnibus and take a seat downstairs, paying my tuppence to the conductor as I pick up a copy of *The Stage* left behind on the seat opposite me. I flick through the pages of adverts for dancing shoes and stage props, fat-reducing soap and seamstresses, and turn to the theater notices, hoping to find something for my scrapbook.

In his latest production, *HOLD TIGHT!*, Cochran has taken something of a gamble with his leading lady, Loretta May. It is a gamble that has more than paid off. Miss May—one of the hardest-working actresses on the London stage—dazzled, captivating the audience with her acting and singing talents, and her comic timing. Miss May brings the stage to life in a way that many others simply cannot. The costumes were equally remarkable, Mr. Cochran exceeding his previous best in this department. The gasps of admiration from the ladies in the audience could be heard all over town.

In her first full-length musical comedy, Miss May was triumphant in *HOLD TIGHT!* at the Shaftesbury. Her departure from revue was launched amid scenes of tumultuous applause. Kitty Walsh, the chorus girl selected at the very last minute to play the role of Miss May's daughter, was captivating. She is most definitely a young actress to watch. The audience yelled themselves hoarse and refused to let the curtain go down.

I close my eyes, imagining what it would be like to be that young chorus girl, to sing and dance on the West End stage. The notices go on: Gertrude Lawrence "splendid" in Charlot's revue *London Calling!* Noël Coward's musical score "triumphant." Bea Lillie "radiant" in Lelong. The descriptions of the costumes take up as many column inches as the commentary on the performances.

Miss Bankhead's costumes in *The Dancers* were admired repeatedly. Her first outfit was à la Egyptienne—composed entirely of silver sequins. Another outfit was lilac chiffon and green satin, adorned with lilac trails. Her final costume—a slim "magpie" dress, a back of black charmeuse and a front of white, ending in white lace encrusted with black and crystal beads—was undoubtedly the finest we have seen on the London stage since Lucile Duff Gordon's creations for Miss Elsie in *The Merry Widow*.

Turning the pages, I read the calls for auditions. Chorus girls are wanted all over town, the bad fogs wreaking havoc with the health of many dancers and leading ladies so that understudies are needed for the understudies. I imagine the long lines outside the theaters, another batch of disappointed girls and crushed dreams traveling home on the omnibuses and trams later that day. I've been that girl so many times, watching with envy as the final name is announced for the callbacks. *"The rest of you may leave. Thank you for your time."* The words we all dread.

As I read down the column of audition calls, something catches my eye. The print is small and I lift the page closer to read it.

WANTED: MUSE
Struggling musical composer seeks muse
to inspire. Applicants must possess a
sense of humor and the patience of a saint.
One hour a week—arranged to suit.
Payment in cherry cake and tea. Replies,
outlining suitability, for the attention of:
Mrs. Ambrose, c/o Apartment Three,
Strand Theatre, Aldwych

I read the notice several times and tear the page from the paper. I'm not really sure why, other than that the words set my heart racing.

"You need to stop asking why, Dolly. The question to ask is, why not?"

I hear Teddy's voice so clearly, his gentle words, his belief in me. I see his face, the empty stare, the uncontrollable tremble in his arms, the damp stain at his groin. No dignity for men like him. No future for would-be wives like me.

I read the notice once more, fold it into neat quarters, and place it in my purse as Auntie Gert's words whisper to me. *Wonderful adventures await for those who dare to find them.* Why not?

Clover is already standing outside the Palais when I arrive. She runs to greet me as I step off the bus, nearly knocking me over as she throws her arms around me as if we'd been apart for months, not days.

I hug her tight. "I've missed you, Clover Parker."

"Liar. Bet you've hardly thought about me." She loops her arm through mine as we walk up the Palais steps. "Go on, then. Tell me. What's it like, this posh hotel of yours? I know you're bursting to tell me."

I can't help smiling. "I wish you could see it, Clo. Your eyes would pop out at the ladies' dresses and shoes, and the gentlemen are so handsome and the hotel band plays the hottest sounds. I can still hear it sometimes when I go to bed. Ragtime and the latest jazz numbers."

Clover lights a cigarette for us both. "Told you. Head full of nonsense already! So, what are your roommates like? Please tell me they're awful and you wish you'd never left Grosvenor Square."

"They're nice, actually. One of them, Sissy, reminds me of you. Gladys is quiet, but nice enough. Very pretty. She wants to be a Hollywood

130

movie star and I wouldn't be surprised if she makes it. The other one, Mildred, is a bit miserable. Never has a word to say, and she looks at me funny. We didn't work with anyone called Mildred, did we?"

Clover thinks for a moment. "Doesn't ring any bells. Why?"

"I've a funny feeling I've met her before, but I don't know where. Anyway, I don't want to talk about her. Let's get inside and dance!"

The Original Dixieland Jazz Band is playing a waltz when we enter the dance hall, a sea of bodies already moving, as one, around the dance floor. I love it here. The Oriental decoration, the music, the dancing, the sense of freedom and letting go. We sit at a table and order tea and a plate of sandwiches. Clover is wearing a lovely new dress, which I admire. Lavender rayon with a lace trim.

"Made it myself," she says, twirling around and sending the hem kicking out as she spins. "Three yards of fabric from Petticoat Lane for two pounds. Hardly need any fabric to make a respectable dress these days. If Madame Chanel raises her hemlines a bit higher, I'll be able to make a whole dress for sixpence."

"It's lovely," I say, conscious of my faded old dress, which looks like a sack of potatoes beside Clover's. I keep my coat on and complain of being cold. It isn't a complete fib. I've had an irritating cough since arriving at The Savoy and it seems to be getting worse. Sissy says it serves me right for wandering around in the rain without an umbrella.

"So, how are things at Grosvenor Square?" I ask. "Is Madam as bad-tempered as ever?"

"Everything's exactly the same. A new girl started as a kitchen maid to replace you. It's strange to wake up and see her in your bed. She doesn't say much. Her fella was killed in the war. When her work's done, she knits endless pairs of socks. Seems to think they're still needed at the front. Completely batty."

I'm dying to show Clover the notice from *The Stage* and take the folded square of paper from my purse.

"Before you say anything, I know it's a bit strange, but I couldn't resist."

But she isn't listening. She's distracted by Tommy Mullins, who has just arrived and is standing across the other side of the dance floor. Clover makes a big show of taking her lipstick from her purse and applies it as seductively as she can as he starts to make his way over. Tommy is a weasel of a man. I don't care for him at all.

"I wish you wouldn't encourage him, Clover," I whisper, placing my hand protectively on hers. "Don't dance with him. Not today. Wait for somebody else. Somebody better."

She laughs. "You and your *better*. Somebody better. Somewhere better. There might not *be* anything better. This might be as good as it gets. Beggars can't be choosers, Miss Dolly Daydream with your head in the clouds. I'm not being left on the shelf like a forgotten bloody Christmas decoration." She stands up as Tommy reaches our table. "One dance," she whispers, "then I'm all yours. Promise."

As I watch them walk to the dance floor, giggling like teenagers, I fold the piece of paper and put it back into my purse. Clover would only tell me to forget about it anyway. And she'd be right. I probably should.

I pick up a limp ham-and-paste sandwich as Clover waves over to me. I wave back and pour the tea. It is as weak as my smile.

When the afternoon session ends, we head back up west, to Woolworth's, where Clover insists on trying on the makeup. We rouge our cheeks and pat pancake and powder over our noses and squirt Yardley perfume onto our wrists until we feel sick with the smell of them all and go to admire the button counter. After Woolworth's, we go to the picture palace, buy two singles and a packet of humbugs, and huddle together in our seats as the picture starts. There are the usual public-service announcements followed by the Pathé newsreel.

"I met a man last week who spoke like that," I whisper. "Ever so handsome."

"And?"

"And nothing."

"Then why did you mention him?"

"I don't really know!"

We burst out laughing, earning a sharp *shush* from a sour-faced woman behind us. We slide down into our seats as the silent movie starts. We are shushed three more times as we comment on the picture and unwrap our humbugs, but this only makes us giggle even more.

When the picture ends and the houselights go up, we make our way outside, where London has become a blaze of lights and color. The restaurants are buzzing. Strains of jazz and ragtime drift through open doors as lines of motor cabs wait outside the theaters to take the excited audiences home or on to supper parties. Smartly dressed page boys shout and whistle to hail passing motor cabs outside the hotels. A flower seller walks by, hawking her posies. Clover and I link arms and stroll together, arm in arm, as far as the corner of Wellington Street, where Clover hops onto her omnibus.

"See you next week, then," I say, kissing her on the cheek.

"Wouldn't miss it for the world."

I feel guilty for the spring in my step as I walk back toward the Strand. Truth is, I want to run. I want to race along the pavement as fast as an express train, away from the soldiers who beg outside the theaters and remind me of war, away from my memories of Mawdesley and everything I left behind there. I think about the notice from *The Stage* neatly folded in my purse, and I curl my fingers instinctively around the photograph in my coat pocket. I feel a desperate urge to keep moving forward, toward a future where I might see him again. I feel it, deep down in the pit of my stomach, like a tightly twisted knot of possibility. If only I could find a way to untangle it all.

Reaching the Strand, I linger for a moment on the opposite side of the road to look at the hotel; this place I now call home. The lights shine from the windows of the private apartments and suites, decorating the front of the hotel like a Tiffany necklace: THE SAVOY. Even the name oozes charm. I repeat it over and over, savoring the feel of it against my lips. "Savoy. Savoy. Savoy." I feel the flutter of hope swell and rise within me until I could burst.

Crossing the road, I stand just inside the hotel courtyard beside the hairdressing salon with its dazzling glass bottles of Parisian scent displayed in the window. I watch the beautiful creatures as they pirouette in and out of the swing doors. One after the other they come and go, dazzling visions in emerald silk, peacock-blue chiffon, ivory tulle, and ink-blue crepe, each dressed more exquisitely than the last. Damson and chestnut velvet cloches complement the matching fur-trimmed coats, sitting flawlessly over fashionable crops and glossy waves. Shoes are silver damask, mint-green silk, and gold brocade. These are not just women who walk, they are creatures who glide. Creatures whose silk stockings and satin evening gloves I pick up and fold, creatures whose private hotel-apartment doors—and the private worlds they conceal—have been opened up to me. I am enchanted by them.

A page boy jumps to attention as a silver Daimler glides to a halt in front of the hotel doors and a liveried doorman moves forward to open the car door. The vision that steps out takes my breath away: perfectly waved hair, sable fur, gold Louis heels, crimson lips, and smudged black kohl around those famous hooded eyes. Tallulah Bankhead. I would know her anywhere. I can't take my eyes off her as she steps through the swing doors of the hotel and disappears into a world I can only imagine.

"Front entrances are of no concern to a maid, other than when she is scrubbing the steps or polishing the handle."

I hear Piggy Griffin's caustic words and feel the cheap cotton of my stockings more than ever. I pull my shoulders back, hold my head high, and make tight, determined balls of my fists. Piggy Griffin can get well and truly knotted with her steps to scrub and her bootlaces to be ironed and petticoats to be mended. I'll show her. I'll show them all.

"One day, Dorothy Mary Lane, you'll walk through that swing door. And when you do, you'll be dressed so beautifully and be so famous that *everybody* will notice you."

I say this to nobody in particular, and to Miss Bankhead, and to anyone who has ever stood in my way, or trampled on my dreams, or told me I wasn't good enough. Taking a deep breath, I blow my words into the night sky, wishing them all the luck in the world as they rise above the rooftops and drift across St. James's Park and up, to mingle with the stars.

Reluctantly, I leave the gliding creatures to their evening of cocktails and jazz, and run around to the back of the hotel, where a line of vehicles blocks the way to the service-entrance steps. I stand in the shadows for a moment and watch as instruments are off-loaded from trucks. The new hotel band must have arrived. Sissy told me they were due to arrive this week, the current resident band having left for a tour of Australia. A smartly dressed gentleman picks up a trumpet and starts to play, right there in the laneway. He is very handsome with slicked-back hair and a slim mustache.

As he finishes the tune, he notices me watching and tips his hat. "Good evening, miss."

I'm embarrassed at being caught and mutter a good evening in reply.

He smiles. "Getting a free performance? You're

lucky. The guests inside pay good money to hear me play."

I'm glad of the darkness that conceals my blushes. "I'm sorry. I didn't mean to . . ."

"I won't tell anyone if you don't tell Wilfred I was messing with his trumpet."

"It's not yours?"

"Gosh, no. I'm the pianist. And the bandleader. Debroy Somers. You work here, I presume?"

"Yes. I'm a maid."

"A maid who likes jazz?"

"Yes."

"Then you must try and catch a rehearsal sometime. We're in the Ballroom most afternoons. My trumpet isn't bad, but I'm a far better pianist. Ragtime, jazz, foxtrot, Charleston. Whatever the guests demand."

"Maids aren't permitted in the Ballroom, sir."

"And pianists aren't permitted to mess around with expensive trumpets, but we all bend the rules every now and again, don't we?"

Big Ben chimes the first stroke of ten. A reminder that I should be elsewhere and not loitering outside, talking to the hotel bandleader, regardless of how charming he might be.

"I'm sorry to seem rude, Mr. Somers, but I have to go."

"Don't forget. Afternoons in the Ballroom."

He steps aside so I can pass as I run down the steps and inside, along the dark passageways, praying that I don't bump into O'Hara or Cutler or any of the management team. I clock back in just before the last chime of the hour rings out and don't stop running until I'm back in my room. Even then, thoughts of unplayed music beneath my pillow and of a muse wanted by a struggling composer swirl and dance through my mind, and all the while Auntie Gert whispers to me of adventures. And I am listening.

Applicants must possess a sense of humor and the patience of a saint. One hour a week— arranged to suit. Payment in cherry cake and tea.

I will write my reply first thing in the morning.

10
DOLLY

"But I do exist, Mr. Cutler," I whisper.
"And I will be seen."

The thick fog that has blanketed London for a fortnight finally lifts and is replaced with a wonderful autumn sun. My cough eases and my heart soars as long shafts of sunlight stream through the windows of the river suites, brightening the rooms with light and warmth. The chandeliers send shimmering reflections against the floor and I pretend I'm walking on fragments of crystal as I go about my work.

The hotel is at full capacity and my days are busy. Boat trains arrive daily into the capital, bringing new fashions, new music, and new stars of the screen and stage on the Atlantic steamers. The theaters open to packed houses every night. The maître d' of the Grill sets extra tables and chairs to accommodate the post-theater supper crowd. The Grand Ballroom heaves to the thumping sound of Mr. Somers's band, the thrilling beat of jazz rocking the chandeliers until the early hours of the morning. Everyone, from the potato peelers to the head porter, is rushed off their feet, but we are all in high spirits. Even Mildred almost smiles when she passes me in the corridor. There's so much to remember that I barely know my own name as I climb into bed at night, exhausted, my feet and back aching with the satisfaction of a job well done. I don't even have the energy to loosen the bedcovers, letting them cocoon me like a swaddled infant, and while the shadows of my past still linger, they don't cling to me as tightly as they once did.

The last room on my morning round is always Larry Snyder's. Thankfully, I haven't encountered him again since my first morning. Gladys, on the other hand, doesn't seem to be able to stop bumping into him. She insists he's a perfect gentleman and is convinced he'll offer her an audition before the season is over. I don't trust him an inch, but I, of all people, can't deny Gladys her desire to dream.

Finishing my morning rounds, I take a moment to rest my cheek against the window, enjoying the warmth of the sun. London looks so lovely from up here. The Thames twists like a silver ribbon across the city as a steady stream of black motorcars snakes along the road beside it. The flagman guides the trams in and out of the tunnel from the Embankment to Kingsway as ladies stroll arm in arm with their gentlemen up Savoy Hill toward the Strand. Simpson's for lunch, no doubt. I strain my eyes to read the poster bills on the passing omnibuses, promoting the new season's shows and stars. I imagine my own name in large black type: DOROTHY LANE. Perhaps they would give me a stage name. Perhaps I would become somebody entirely new. Twisting the lock, I push up the sash window, lean my head out, and close my eyes. Lost in a daydream, I find my thoughts traveling across the London skyline, through the English countryside and home, to Lancashire.

I imagine Mam looking out of our small cottage window, remembering happier times before war took her husband and influenza took two of her daughters. I haven't written to her yet to tell her about my new position. She always thought my love of dancing and endless talk of actresses was a phase that would pass; the product of a young girl's imagination. Mam is old-fashioned. She has funny notions about actresses and chorus girls. If I tell her I'm working at The Savoy, she'll make a fuss about hotels attracting unsavory types. Worse still, she'll find an excuse to travel to London and try to convince me to go back home. I'm not ready for that. Just as the people we love the most can sometimes cause us the deepest pain, so it is with places. Mawdesley holds too many painful memories.

I open my eyes as a cloud passes in front of the sun and close the window, leaving my secrets and my dreams to drift over London's rooftops.

• • •

After morning break, I'm about to leave the Maids' Hall when one of the porters rushes in.

"You. You'll do." He shoves a mop and a bucket into my hands. "Front Hall. Someone's dog knocked over a vase. There's water everywhere."

Before I can say anything he rushes off, leaving me standing there with the mop and bucket in my hands.

"Well, go on, then."

I turn around. Bessie, the potato peeler, is watching me. "But . . . we're not supposed to . . ."

"Nobody ignores the Front Hall," she says. "I'd get yourself up there if I were you. Quick sharp."

Against my better judgment, I make my way down the stairs and rush along the back-of-house corridors until I reach the Front Hall. I hesitate behind the curtain that separates "Them" from "Us" and drink in the scene. It is busy and yet strangely calm, everyone going easily about their business: porters carrying packages and suitcases, ladies in beautiful dresses and furs chatting in small groups, gentlemen in dapper suits resting against the concierge desk, small dogs minded by immaculate children who look like the porcelain dolls in the windows of the department stores. Polite chatter mingles with the elegant lilt of piano. The air is laced with the scent of cigars and the perfume of freshly cut Oriental lilies that stand in tall vases on bone-china pedestals. Huge

143

palms and ferns reach toward the ornate marble ceiling. It really is breathtaking.

I step hesitantly onto the black and white floor tiles, trying desperately hard not to stare at anyone as I keep my eyes to the floor and walk toward the pool of water beside the door. I'm nearly there when someone grabs my elbow and steers me sharply to one side until I'm concealed behind a particularly large fern.

A tall man with bulging eyes and an immense mustache confronts me. He isn't liveried like the lift attendants or porters, but dressed in black tie, like the governor.

"What on earth are you doing?" he hisses. "Maids do *not* enter the Front Hall!"

"A porter told me to come," I explain. "He said a vase had been knocked over."

I feel my cheeks redden as I'm bustled back behind the curtain and down a short flight of steps toward a glass-paneled door. The tall man leans into a small office and hands a ledger to a young girl who is patting powder onto her nose.

"Report from the night porter," he says. "I need it for the three o'clock meeting."

"Anything special happen?" she asks, snapping the powder compact shut and barely glancing over the tops of her tortoiseshell-rimmed spectacles.

"Nothing much. A delivery of champagne to one of the suites. A doctor called out. The usual."

She opens the ledger and starts typing. The

clack clack of the keys ends the conversation abruptly.

He turns back to me. "You. Follow me."

I do as I'm told and follow him into another small office. A plaque on the door says MR. P. CUTLER—HEAD PORTER. I remember Gladys's words. *Moody sod. Nice as pie one minute but he'd fire you on the spot for anything inappropriate.* He settles himself at a seat behind a cluttered desk and picks up a pencil.

"Name."

"Dorothy. Dorothy Lane. I'm new." My voice is thin and apologetic. He looks at me, raises an eyebrow, and scribbles something onto a piece of paper. "Am I in trouble, sir?"

He leans forward, rests his elbows on the desk, and steeples his fingers. "What do *you* think? Do you consider yourself to be in trouble?"

"It was a mistake." I refuse to let myself cry. "The porter told me to come." The mop and bucket feel like lead irons in my hands.

"Hotels have rules and regulations. Order and routine. And for good reason."

"It's just . . ."

"Just what?" He thumps the table with his hand, making me jump and setting my heart racing. "You thought you could waltz in here and act like a big house maid-of-all-work and that nobody would mind where you decided to hang about?"

"No, sir. I just . . ."

"Might I remind you that The Savoy is one of the most highly regarded establishments in London. In the world. Our guest list comprises some of the most famous names of our time and I can assure you that they do *not* wish to encounter a maid with mops and buckets as they arrive."

"Of course not, sir." I curl my toes inside my sensible black shoes and fidget with my fingers.

"Back-of-house staff must *not* be seen. As far as our guests are concerned, the staff are invisible. *You,* Dorothy Lane, do not exist." His words sting like a slap to my cheek. "Do you understand?"

I hang my head. "Yes, sir."

"I've a good mind to pay you for the week and get rid of you. Plenty of girls waiting to fill those shoes, let me tell you."

I can't bear the thought of being given my notice after only a month in the job. I look up at him, blinking back the tears in my eyes. "It won't happen again, sir. You have my word."

He finishes writing on the piece of paper and stamps it with an officious thump. "Off you go. I do not want to have reason to speak with you again. This was your second chance. There are no more."

"Yes, sir. Of course."

He waves me away and I leave the office, making my way to the staff stairway. His words pound in my ears. *"Back-of-house staff must not be seen . . . they are invisible. . . . You, Dorothy Lane, do not exist."*

146

"But I do exist, Mr. Cutler," I whisper. "And I *will* be seen."

A dark cloud follows me around the hotel for the rest of the day. I'm anxious about the consequences of my mistake and dread the repercussions when O'Hara finds out, but more than that, I'm angry. I'm angry with the porter. I'm angry with Bessie for encouraging me to go. I'm angry with Cutler for his cruel words, but mostly, I'm angry with myself. As I dust and sweep and wrestle with my temper and great piles of bed linen, I think about the notice from *The Stage* and the reply I have written but not yet found the courage to send. *One hour a week, arranged to suit.* One hour a week is perfect. I think about it over lunch and all afternoon and I am still thinking about it over supper as I sip my hot chocolate.

Sissy sits down beside me. "Heard you got into a spot of bother earlier."

"How do you know?"

"The hotel has ears, Dolly. Told you. Nothing goes unnoticed around here."

The chocolate tastes bitter. The bread is dry in my mouth. "It was a misunderstanding. That's all."

Sissy takes my chin in her hand and turns my face toward her. She scrutinizes me as if I were a polished candlestick being inspected for missed thumbprints. "Don't mind old Cutler. His bark's worse than his bite." She smiles sympathetically. "We all mess up from time to time. You're not the first girl to be marched into his office. The Savoy does funny things to people, Dolly. Makes you feel like a movie star one minute, and a heap of muck the next."

There's a kindness in her eyes and I'm grateful for her words. "Thanks, Sissy. You're a good friend."

"And don't forget it when you're a famous actress drinking cocktails in the American Bar!"

I haven't told Sissy about my dreams of a life on the stage. I've wanted to, but something has always stopped me. "How did you know?" I ask.

"Saw it the first day you arrived. You've got that distant dreamy look about you. Same as Gladys. Stars in your eyes. It's like there's a part of you somewhere else. And you talk about the theater all the time. Miss Bankhead this. Loretta May that." She chuckles to herself. "I think you're soft in the head, but good luck to you anyway. There's something about you, Dorothy Lane. People watch you. They notice you."

I laugh. "Nobody ever notices me!"

She stands up and walks to the door. "Oh, but they do. You're just not paying attention."

As I settle into bed and pull the blankets tight around my chin, I think about Sissy's kindness. I miss having someone to tell me it will all be fine, to take me in their arms and protect me, just as Teddy used to. I miss the blush to my cheek brought on by his wink, the feel of his hand in mine, the racing of my heart as I savor the words of his latest letter. I miss the sensation of being loved, of being someone who matters so much to someone that they want to share their world with you.

Teddy was always showing me things, spotting things that I would have missed: kingfisher, hawk, rabbit, pike. "Look," he would whisper, gently taking hold of my arm and pointing to where he was looking. "Do you see?" Most of the time I didn't. I was always looking in the wrong direction, or at the wrong thing.

It was Teddy who saw *The Adventure Book for Girls* as we walked back from the stone bridge. We'd been fishing for sticklebacks that day. Teddy had a whole jam jar full of them. I hadn't caught one. He knew I was disappointed. Even at the age of ten he was a sensitive soul. When he found the book, I said that we ought to find who it belonged to.

"We already have," he said. "It belongs to you. They're your adventures now."

They're your adventures now.

Dear Teddy. Like a silent-movie reel, images of him flash through my mind, fleeting glimpses gone before I can hold on to them. Teddy, silhouetted against the setting sun at the end of the street. Teddy, running through the field with his butterfly net. Teddy, waving his white handkerchief from the window of the train. Private Teddy Cooper, ashen-faced and gaunt. He looks at me, and yet he doesn't. I take hold of his hand but he pulls it away as if I am a candle flame that burns.

It is too painful to remember. I close my eyes and sweep the splintered fragments of my life into a corner, like embers to be taken out later.

11
TEDDY

She is like spring sitting beside me,
my very own daffodil.

I sit in my favorite chair at the window, my trembling hands folded neatly on my lap. I look out at the rooftops, the soaring chimney stacks of the textile mills, the distant slag heaps of the collieries. Black smoke billows skyward, smothering the sun, blotting out the shadows. I like to watch the clouds with all their changing colors; sometimes dark and moody, sometimes delicate fragile feathers. They are racing each other today, scudding by, blown on invisible winds.

Through the distant chatter of the other patients, I hear the nurse approaching. Soft black rubber soles. Each sticky step peeling away from the floor, like the rip of shells through the air. I still hear it. I press my palms against my legs to control the shaking.

"Tea, Teddy. Thought you might fancy one."

She sets the cup and saucer down on the small table to my right and places a hand on my shoulder. I don't look at her. I stare at the scene beyond the window. Life always happens beyond the window these days. I don't go outside.

"How are you today?" she asks, sitting in the empty chair beside the bed.

Her voice is a blackbird, all singsong and breezy. She is like spring sitting beside me, my very own daffodil. I can't remember her name and I'm too embarrassed to ask.

She follows my gaze to the window. "I see your butterfly is still there. Can't say I blame it. I wouldn't want to go outside today if I was a butterfly. It'd be blown to Ireland in that wind!"

I almost smile.

"Are you ready for another letter?"

I shrug. Take a sip of tea. Extra sugar. She's very kind, this nurse. I close my eyes as she clears her throat and starts to read.

April 15th, 1917

My dearest Teddy,

The cat had eight kittens! I've never seen anything so helpless and tiny. I wish you could see them. The smallest is a tortoiseshell. She's so beautiful. Her eyes are bluer than yours. Mam doesn't know what to be doing with them all but she's promised she won't drown them in the river. I think Smudge will be a great mother until we find a home for them. Bunty Brown says she'll take two, and the vicar's wife wants a good mouser for the vicarage. I'm keeping the smallest. I've called her Poppy.

Jack Elvidge came home with a shrapnel injury. They thought he might lose his leg but he's made a miraculous recovery and is being well fed by his mam. He won't be going back to the front, what with him being injured. He says he wishes he could go back to carry on fighting alongside you all. I tell him that's silly talk and that he's done his bit and should be grateful that his life—and his leg—were spared. I gave him one of the kittens to cheer him up. He called it Private.

So, you see, some good news.

I'm now part of the factory football team. We call ourselves Mawdesley United. We play against the other munitionettes in the neighboring factories. Turns out some of us have a bit of a knack for football. I've been told I have quick feet. I reckon that's from all the dancing you taught me.

Write to me soon. The weeks between your letters feel like months. I long to hear from you, Teddy. I worry so much and hope you will be home on leave soon.

I will close now.

With fondest love,

Your Little Thing,

Dolly.

X

Seeing no response from me, she carries on. I watch her take another piece of paper from another stained envelope. I close my eyes again, and listen.

October 20th, 1917

My dearest Teddy,

I hope that you are reading this on the train—that you couldn't wait a moment longer to see what words I'd written to you. How happy I was to have you back home. I have never known two weeks pass so quickly. I'm so pleased you found your mam and dad well.

I enjoyed our long walks to the stone bridge. It was so lovely to feel the warmth of you beside me, to just sit with you. I found the silence between us a little strange at first, but I understand that sometimes words are not needed, and I know your thoughts were with your brothers, back in France. I know you were anxious to get back to them.

It is selfish of me to wish you had refused to go back. You are a brave man, and I have to try to understand that you had to return to France to fight and to give someone else the chance to go home to their mam and the girl who loves them.

I pray that this will all be over and that you'll be home for good soon. Until then, know that I am thinking of you always.

Your Little Thing,

Dolly

X

She folds the letter and slips it back into the envelope. She sits beside me for a while, not reading, not talking. I watch the butterfly open and close its wings, basking in the sunlight at the window, and I cannot stop the tears that prick my eyes at the thought of this girl in the letters who writes all these wonderful words to me.

I wish I could remember.

With all my heart, I wish I could remember her.

12
DOLLY

"Get a job in a shop. Marry a nice young chap.
Leave the dancing to someone else."

Remembrance Sunday arrives with scudding
gray clouds and a decision to deliver my reply to
the musical composer. Teddy always said that
when you're not sure about something, you
should let the weather decide. Today is wild and
willful. There's a reckless urgency to everything
that I can't resist.

As I leave the hotel I feel every blast of the
eager east wind swirling around my ankles and
gusting at my back. Before I go to the Strand
Theatre, I step into the dark interior of the small
chapel beside The Savoy. I remove my hat and
hurry to the altar to light a candle, my cheeks
burning from the wind. I settle at a pew and say
my prayers. I think of the photograph in my
pocket, and pray for him; for his well-being and
his happiness. I pray for strength and forgiveness
for myself.

My prayers said, I head back outside, the wind
pushing me down the sloping path toward the
Embankment. I pass a bootblack and a coffee

156

seller and the regular pavement artists. There are several gathered today, including a young woman who kneels on a piece of cloth and chalks her drawings onto the flagstones. I drop a penny into her hat. She thanks me and tells me she's collecting for the British Legion. A little farther along, a man is drawing a field of poppies. He has already completed an image of a young woman and a view of the Houses of Parliament. His likenesses are very good. Lines of poetry and verse are scrawled among his images. I drop a penny into his hat too and walk on.

Back on the Strand, the roads that usually teem with trams and motorcars are empty, the pavements free of the crowds of shoppers and street sellers, the awnings of the shops pulled in until trading starts again on Monday. The significance of the date lends a sense of somber reflection to the city, and at the corner of Lancaster Place I buy a poppy, pinning it to my coat with a sense of pride and sadness. The guns will be fired at eleven as the wreaths are placed at the Cenotaph at Whitehall. We will all stop and reflect for two minutes, and then we will carry on, as we have always done, as we always will. What else can we do?

I walk on, passing wine merchants and tobacconists. I catch my reflection in a furrier's window. Despite the sweep of Gladys's rouge and Sissy's lipstick (applied as soon as I'd escaped the beady eyes of O'Hara and her notions of flighty girls), I look as drab as a dray horse. The envelope in my pocket tugs at my thoughts as a gust of wind tugs at my hat. I hold it tight against my head and hurry on, pulling my collar around my neck. I'm glad I've resisted the lure of the shingle bob. As it is, I feel every cheap fiber of Clover's old coat as I scurry along Lancaster Place toward the Aldwych. It is a walk of only five minutes with the wind at my back. I wish it were longer.

Too soon, I arrive at the Strand Theatre. I must have walked past it a hundred times but have never really paid it any attention. Now I scrutinize it like O'Hara at her morning inspection. It is an elegant gray building, wrapped around the corner of Wellington Street and the Aldwych. My eyes travel toward the windows on the upper floors. They remind me of castle turrets. I wonder which window belongs to apartment three. I wonder if he is up there, looking out. If he might be watching me.

Crossing the road, I push open the swing doors and step onto a beautiful mosaic floor. The lobby is empty. I almost turn around and walk straight back out, but the wind rattles the glass in the panes and whistles through the gaps at the door hinges and I'm glad to be inside for a while. The dusky pink marble walls send back an echo of my footsteps. Above me, the ceiling reaches up into an ornate glass dome.

Look up, Dolly. Look at the stars.

For a moment, I stand perfectly still, looking up at the glass. I wrap the fingers of my left hand around the envelope in my pocket. The fingers of my right hand settle around the photograph.

"Can I help you, miss?"

I turn around to see an elderly woman watching me from behind the window of the ticket office. I walk toward her with small hesitant steps and am reminded of the post office in Mawdesley, of hesitant steps walking toward Mrs. Joyce, her wrinkled old hand ready to snatch my words from me and send them off to France. I was never quite ready to let my words go, afraid they would be unheard; unanswered.

I stop in front of the narrow window. The woman smiles. Her face is as plump as a sponge pudding, her eyes dark little currants. Several chins fold like melted candle wax toward what would be her décolletage, if it were visible. But there is a kindness in those currant eyes; a warmth to her smile.

"Can I help you?" she asks again.

"Where can I leave a letter for apartment three? Care of a Mrs. Ambrose."

"You can leave it with me, duck."

"Thank you. I'm . . . well, thank you."

I push the envelope beneath the window. The woman's fingers touch mine as I hesitate to let go, but she pulls it from my grasp.

"Come along now. Don't be making a fuss. It'll be much easier if you just let go." The awful tugging of my fingertips. The hollow ache in my arms; the weight of his absence. A woman in a yellow coat, the color of daffodils.

She places my envelope in a pigeonhole on the wall behind her. "Did you want to buy any tickets, miss?"

"I'm sorry?"

"Tickets? For the show. A Noël Coward farce. Did you want any?"

I'm too distracted to think properly. "No. Thank you. Not today. I just wanted to hand in the letter."

The woman nods, folds her arms across her chest, and closes her eyes.

I watch her for a moment. "Excuse me."

She opens one eye. "Yes?"

"Do you know the occupant of flat three?"

Her currant eyes sparkle. "And what if I do?"

"I just wondered what he's like. Whether he's decent enough. You know. Pleasant."

The woman chuckles, sending her chins wobbling like a jelly pudding. She leans forward. "I'll tell you this much, love. If I had a daughter looking for a nice husband, I'd send her right on up to flat three and I'd lock the door behind them until he offered her a ring. Couldn't meet a nicer gentleman, in my opinion. Could do with being a bit tidier about the place, mind, but what man couldn't?"

I breathe a sigh of relief. "You will make sure he . . ."

"Gets the letter. I will."

Taking one last look at the envelope, I silently wish it good luck, push open the swing door, and step out into the street. Like a needle settling in a groove on a gramophone record, all I can do now is wait for a reply; wait for the music to play.

Despite the cold, I walk through Covent Garden, past the bookshops on Charing Cross Road and on toward Trafalgar Square, where Nelson's column reaches proudly toward the salt-and-pepper sky and the lions languish on their plinths. I walk along Haymarket and through Piccadilly Circus, where a long line of girls snakes around the Pavilion Theatre, all the way from the stage door around the front of the building and along Coventry Street.

An audition call.

Their excited chatter and shrieks of laughter are infectious. I detect the scent of shoe polish, hair pomade, and perfume in the air as I pass. They are all immaculately turned out, aware that being hired will depend as much on how they look as how they perform: fashionably bobbed hair, the best stockings and shoes they can afford, smart cloches, vermillion lips, dark kohl around the eyes. Every inch the jazzing flapper they talk about in the newspapers. I'm horribly conscious of my plain clothes and oversized coat and yet a familiar shiver of excitement runs along my spine as I remember the thrill of anticipation as the doors open and the names are taken and the lines called forward, "Next, please," a dozen girls at a time. So often, I've been that hopeful girl waiting in line, teeth chattering, toes numb in too-tight borrowed Mary Janes.

I pull my coat closer around me as the wind gusts, blowing the girls' skirts dangerously high up their glossy legs. They won't feel the cold. They'll be warmed by excitement and adrenaline, not to mention a tot or two of gin, and yet, in a few hours' time, most of these pretty young things will have had their hearts broken and their makeup ruined by their tears. Kicks too low. Toes not pointed. Loose arms. Too much flesh around the waist. Not pretty enough. Not tall enough. Too pretty. Too tall. Too talkative. Too serious. There are any number of reasons why a girl won't cut it. From this long line, only two dozen will make it into the chorus, and only half of them will ever make it to the front line. One or two will become lead chorus with the stage to themselves for a few precious moments, and perhaps only one of these hopeful faces will ever land the starring role they've dreamed of.

My last audition was for a part in the second chorus in *The Water Babies* at the Palace. Baxter was his name. Cecil Baxter. One of the biggest musical-theater producers in town. I'll never forget his words to me when I muddled my steps and asked him for a second chance. "There's no such thing as second chances. Not anymore. There was a time when we couldn't fill the chorus— had to stretch the line and dress the girls in yards of material to fill the gaps. But since the war everyone wants to dance, and those who don't want to dance want to be actresses and film stars. I'd give up now, miss, if I were you. Go back to polishing the silverware, or whatever it is you do for a living. Get a job in a shop. Marry a nice young chap. Leave the dancing to someone else."

He couldn't have said anything to make me more determined to succeed.

"Dorothy Lane?" I stop at the sound of my name and turn around as a girl steps out of the line and stares at me. "It *is* you, isn't it?"

"Yes. I'm Dorothy Lane." The girl looks familiar, but I can't place her.

"I knew it. I'd recognize that face anywhere." She throws her arms around me. "You don't remember me, do you?"

I shake my head. "I'm sorry. No."

She laughs. "Edie. Edie Bishop. We was in the hospital together. Remember?" Edie Bishop. The name smothers me. "You was in the bed next to me," she continues. "I had twins. Two of the little buggers. No wonder I was the size of a house!"

I can barely speak. Distant memories creep

forward. Names and places I had pushed from my mind raise their voices and shout to be heard.

She laughs at my dumbstruck silence. "You don't remember me at all, do you?"

"Yes. Yes, I do. The Mothers' Hospital." I grasp the photograph in my pocket and try to control the tremble in my legs. "How are you keeping?"

"Oh, you know. Making do. Still turning up to the auditions. I'm working for a dressmaker in Hackney. It was her told me about this audition. We've never been so busy with costumes for the shows. How about you?"

"I'm a maid. At The Savoy."

"Sounds fancy."

"It's a job."

She leans forward and whispers in my ear. "Did you ever hear anything?"

I shake my head. "No. Nothing."

"Me neither. For the best. Put it behind you and carry on. Isn't that what they told us?"

She grabs my hand and squeezes it tight. I want to hold on to her. After so many years of agonizing silence, I want to talk. I want to ask questions and remember, but my thoughts are interrupted by the somber chimes of Big Ben.

The eleventh hour. The first boom of cannon fire ricochets off the buildings around us.

We all bow our heads. Ten more times the guns are fired, each one a blow to the heart, a memory. For two minutes, London falls silent. The pages and porters stop rushing and calling for cars. The omnibuses, motorcars, and trams pull up to a halt. Gentlemen remove their hats. Ex-servicemen stand to attention. Mothers and wives blink back their tears. England stands still and remembers. Even the wind drops to a respectful hush. Two minutes for all that was lost. It hardly seems long enough. As I stand with my head bowed, I try to shush the memories stirred by Edie Bishop and try to focus on Teddy, but his sweet face is a blur. Like a reflection in rippled water, I cannot quite grasp the image of him.

I envied him and the boys from the village when they left for France; envied the adventures awaiting them. I read his early letters with naïve eager eyes, devouring the sights he described as he passed through pretty French villages. I could almost smell the bread from the *boulangeries* he wrote of. Even the French words were exciting. I liked to roll them around my tongue like a humbug, teaching them to my sisters: *boulangerie, château, église, campagne.* We giggled at our awful pronunciations. But Teddy's letters changed. His descriptions of poppy fields became descriptions of mud and death. His words became those of a frightened boy, not of the brave soldier who had kissed me good-bye and taken my breathaway and promised he'd be back for Christmas.

Nobody came back for Christmas.

As the boys marched on, so did the years, until I began to lose all hope of ever seeing him again. The comfortable life I'd once imagined for us with a family of our own was trampled into the French countryside as life became a muddle of strange new normalities: death, grieving, extraordinary exchanges of love in letters written to and from the front. My job at the munitions factory was a welcome distraction. My sisters found work in the textile factories, sewing secret messages of hope into the pockets of greatcoats. What was once so strange became familiar. A new normal. And then the war ended, the boys returned, and we were unsettled all over again.

Relationships didn't slot back into place as we'd imagined they would. Some homecomings were as natural as the sunrise, but many more were as awkward and faltering as the soldiers on their crutches. It was painful to watch. I couldn't understand why the girls were so hesitant to touch the men they had longed to see, disturbed by the masks their loved ones wore to conceal the disfigurement of their once flawless faces. I knew I would love Teddy as soon as I saw him, whatever wounds and scars he carried. I would love him just the same.

But he didn't come back with the others. In many ways, Teddy didn't come back at all.

• • •

When the two minutes has passed, London begins to move again, albeit with a heavier heart. The theater doors open, sending the line of girls flapping and squawking like a bunch of starlings.

Edie grabs my arm. "Looks like we're going in. It was nice to see you again, Dolly."

"And you, Edie."

She rushes back into the line and checks her face with a compact. "Wish me luck," she calls.

"Good luck! See you in Hollywood."

She winks at me and laughs.

I walk on, pushing my hands deep into my pockets, feeling for his photograph. *The hollow ache in my arms; the weight of his absence.*

By the time the war was over, my heart was broken, my dreams were shattered, my hopes were bruised. Without ever stepping onto a battlefield, I too was wounded.

13
LORETTA

". . . it seems to me that children
are like marriages. They are often better
imagined than experienced."

There is something mesmerizing about a sunny
autumn day in London. While part of me wishes I
was still languishing in bed with a breakfast tray
and the newspapers and the blinds only partially
open, I have to admit that I find myself charmed
by my surroundings.

Green Park is aflame with autumnal beauty, the
trees adorned with shades of rust and copper, ruby
and ochre. I lean back on the bench, allowing
the warmth of the sun to radiate through me. It
reminds me of a wonderful lost afternoon with
Roger: reddened ivy climbing the walls of the
hotel, long shadows reaching across the pier as he
stole a lingering kiss, the glow of the setting sun
against his face. Our time together was callously
brief, but it could not have been more perfect. No
arguments. No jealousy. No weary compromise.
No tedious resignation. Only love. Three perfect
days of love and a bundle of letters—that is all I
have to remember him. I don't even have a

photograph. I don't need one. I often see him, right there in front of me, smiling in that lopsided nonchalant way of his. I place a hand to my chest, instinctively holding the ache in my heart.

My thoughts are disturbed as a leaf flutters down from the beech tree above me and lands in my lap. I pick it up. It is a rich crimson, perfectly symmetrical and unblemished. Just a leaf, and yet the irony of it landing plumb in my lap is not lost on me as I watch Bea prance among the dappled shade, shrieking as she tries again and again to catch a leaf as they fall around her. I chuckle at her foolish capering. She is like an excitable puppy, all bounce and energy until she collapses in an exhausted heap. I can hardly believe we are the same age. Watching her, I feel as ancient as the Tower of London.

It was Bea's idea to come to the park. She is one of those exhausting outdoorsy types, always keen to be out among the elements, wind in her hair, rain on her cheeks, the sun at her back. I blame Miss Austen. Her novels are full of excitable young ladies forever wishing to be outdoors, and look what happened to poor Marianne Dashwood, nearly dying from the chill she caught from her walk in the rain. Why people must always go for a stroll on a chilly autumn day is one of life's peculiarities, but Bea insisted. She is my best friend—the sister I never had—and I cannot deny her anything. She, in turn, plays me like a fiddle.

"Got one, darling!" I wave the leaf above my head like a hunting trophy.

Bea stops her capering and whirls around. "You have not!"

"Fell straight into my lap. Almost like it wanted me to have it."

"You rotter!" She squeals with injustice and rushes over to inspect the captured specimen. "That's absolutely not fair. You haven't even moved since we got here."

"That's because chasing leaves is a silly game for children. Anyway, darling, I haven't the energy. I'm exhausted just looking at you charging around like a panicked squirrel trying to find his winter nuts. I didn't get home until three this morning and I'm getting one of my heads."

Bea smiles and plonks herself down onto the bench beside me. "You can be such a stick-in-the-mud sometimes, Etta. It's fun. And it's such a beautiful day." She takes off her hat and runs her fingers through her hair, honeyed by the sun. She's recently had it shingled. It's as sleek and polished as glass and falls perfectly back into place. Bea makes everything seem so effortless and jolly. "Did you make a wish?"

I laugh and toss the leaf to the ground. "No, I did not. Wishes are for fools." I check my watch. It is past two o'clock. "Can I tempt you to a cocktail? It's a perfectly respectable time of day."

Bea scowls at me and picks up the leaf. "No,

you cannot. It would be a sin to be indoors on such a wonderful afternoon. We can do cocktails when it's pouring. I promise."

"Very well. But you're no fun."

Bea places the leaf back on my lap and folds my fingers around it. "You have to make a wish. I absolutely insist."

She has that look in her eye that tells me there is little point in arguing. The only daughter of friends of my parents, Bea Balfour and I have known each other since we were young girls making daisy chains on the lawns at Nine Elms, my family home in East Sussex. The Balfour family annual pilgrimage from the north of England to the south coast was an event much anticipated by Aubrey, Perry, and me. Aubrey, for the chance to talk to Bea's father, Bertie, about politics. Me, for the infectious enthusiasm and wonderful dresses Bea always brought with her, and Perry, for the joy of simply watching her and being the occasional recipient of a smile that could light up a room on the dreariest of winter days.

"Oh, all right, then. But it's all a lot of silly nonsense." I close my eyes and make a wish.

When I open my eyes Bea is perched on the edge of the bench, staring at me. "Well?"

"Well what?"

"What did you wish for?"

"I can't tell you, or it won't come true."

"Thought it was a lot of silly nonsense."

"It is. Still, there's no point in breaking the magic, is there?"

"I hope you wished for something delicious and fun."

I place the leaf in my coat pocket. "Such as what?"

"Oh, I don't know. A romantic love affair. Or a starring role on Broadway. Or a kissing scene with Valentino. Imagine it, Etta. I'd simply die. Those lips!"

As we watch more leaves spiral to the ground, I think about Valentino's lips, imagining myself as Lady Diana to his Sheik Ahmed. It would, indeed, be pleasant. My wishes, however, are required for more somber matters.

I pick up my script and start to read, but the pages are illuminated by the sun so that the words on both sides blur into a confusing mass. Bea chatters on like a train beside me, twitching every now and again as she is tempted to run after another leaf. Finding it impossible to concentrate, I give up and put the script down. We sit for a moment and watch a child pushing a sailing boat around the edge of the pond with a stick while his nanny looks anxiously on.

"Adorable little thing, isn't he? Do you wish you'd had children, Etta?"

I falter for a moment as I watch the boy screw up his face with grim determination. "Certainly not. Beastly little things. I don't mind other people's but I wouldn't care for any of my own. From what little experience I've had of them, it seems to me that children are like marriages. They are often better imagined than experienced."

Bea cuffs me on the shoulder. "You're wicked to say such things." But she laughs, despite herself. "I always wanted six children. Three boys and three girls, all with different shades of hair."

She falls silent. I know what she is thinking; that it is too late for her now.

We watch the boy until his stick falls into the boating lake and he starts wailing when the nanny won't allow him to jump in after it.

I turn to Bea. "See. They always have to spoil things with their silly little tantrums."

She scowls at me. "Much like actresses."

I bat her playfully on the hand.

She smiles and turns her head to one side so that the sun catches her cheek. She really is exquisite. I can't blame Perry for being so infatuated with her. It would bring me such joy to see the two of them married, but the shadows of war stretch between them and Perry's stubborn pride and eternal guilt prevent him from asking her.

She stands up, pulling me reluctantly to my feet and tugging me away from thoughts of match-making. "Walk with me. I'm bored."

"You're always bored. You've been bored since the day you were born. Unless there's a handsome man pouring you a cocktail or telling you how

173

beautiful you are, you will always be bored. Why didn't you bring a book to read?"

"I don't just mean now. I mean with life. With me. With everything." She picks at a button on the cuff of her coat. "Marriage is all anybody talks about. *'Who will she marry now that her fiancé is dead? Such a shame. They were the perfect match.'* It's all so tiresome, Etta. Sometimes I wish we were still at war and that I was still nursing. I felt useful then. I felt that my life had a purpose." She looks at me with her big blue eyes. "Is that a dreadful thing to say?"

"Yes, darling. It is. But I'm sure you're not the only woman to think it. We all felt useful when the men were away, more useful than we'd ever felt, or possibly will again. But they're back now. They had to return to the lives they'd left behind and we must return to the roles we once had— even if it is nothing more exhilarating than awaiting a proposal of marriage."

She lets out a long sigh. "You make it sound so exciting."

Sometimes I forget how young and inexperienced we were when war broke out. Like me, Bea had bravely stepped forward as a VAD nurse. Like me, she was a naïve twenty-three-year-old who'd never had to do so much as draw her own bath. She was eager to do her bit as soon as she could, and surprised everyone with her stamina and her aptitude for nursing.

I pull her closer. "You mustn't forget how dreadful it was in the hospitals, Bea. Yes, we helped some men to recover, but we helped many more to die. Do you forget the screams of pain and the stench of infected wounds?"

She shakes her head. "How could I ever forget?"

"We were a hand to hold," I continue. "A kind face to see them on their way as they wept for their mothers. We were no Florence Nightingale. You shouldn't romanticize the war, nor wish yourself back there. Those days were far darker than you might recall under the benefit of a stroll in the park on a sunny autumn afternoon."

They were far darker than any of us could ever have imagined.

Mother laughed when I told her I'd enrolled as a Voluntary Aid Detachment nurse at the Royal Herbert Hospital.

"What nonsense, Virginia. You know absolutely nothing about nursing. You've never even been in a hospital! Besides, a hospital in Woolwich is no place for the daughter of an earl. What on earth will people think? You must write and tell them you have reconsidered. I absolutely forbid it."

Her ignorance and misplaced notions of class and status left me speechless. And furious. Her cheek was reddening from my slap before I realized what I was doing.

I wasn't sorry, even though she has never

forgiven me. I don't wish her to. I want her to feel the sting of that slap every time she meets someone whose injured son recovered in hospital because someone like me, the daughter of an earl, had volunteered to help.

She was, however, right about one thing. I was desperately unprepared for hospital life.

War had been a distant thing in the early months, something happening to other people far away. But as more of the dashing young men I'd flirted and danced with at lavish garden parties and summer balls headed to the front, I knew I couldn't simply stand by and watch. I had to do something. I gladly stepped out of my chiffon dresses and into the starched cotton of the nursing uniform. I can still smell the bitter stench of camphor and iodine; still see the nauseating wounds that I bathed and dressed. It was a frightening, bewildering experience, but it was *my* experience and there was something undeniably exhilarating about that.

Bea and I stroll along the path beside the lake, both of us lost in thoughts of the past.

"You seem distracted today, Etta. Is something wrong?"

I stop walking. "I'm sorry. I know I'm not much fun. It's an anniversary."

Her hands fly to her mouth. "I'm so sorry. I'm such a fool. It's Roger, isn't it? Was it today?"

I nod.

I still feel nauseous when I think about the letter. I can still see the look of helplessness on Jimmy's face as I crumpled to the floor like a discarded dress. I can hear the roar of the audience as I stepped onto the stage for the final act, and yet I don't remember delivering a single line or singing any of the songs, my performance a dream I wasn't quite part of.

"Is there anything I can do?" Bea asks. "Anything to make you feel better?"

I shake my head. "What can any of us do, darling? There are wives and mothers, sisters and brothers, sons and daughters all over the country who wake up once a year and remember. It happens every day, and yet none of us know. We go about our business and pass a woman strolling through Green Park and we haven't the slightest indication that she can barely find a reason to keep placing one foot in front of the other. We step onto the stage and we turn on our smiles and we carry on, because what else *can* we do?"

The strengthening breeze sends a flurry of leaves tumbling from the branches above us, spiraling to the ground. Bea pulls her arm free of mine and runs beneath a great oak, darting after one leaf and then another.

"Let's not be sad," she shouts. "Come on! There's heaps of them coming down!"

Eventually she catches one and rushes back

177

to me, her cheeks attractively flushed by her exertions. She is the very picture of health and vitality. Everything that I am not.

She closes her eyes and makes a wish.

"What did you wish for?" I ask. "I hope it was a good one after so much effort."

"I wished for a Poiret gown, a summerhouse in Monaco, a motorcar, and six children."

"Perhaps you should have wished for a husband first?"

She laughs and grabs my hands. "Now I've told you, so you have to tell me."

How can I possibly tell her? How can I tell anyone? I feel for the leaf in my pocket. "If you must know, I wished for courage."

"Courage? For what?"

"For everything."

She scrunches up her nose. "You should have wished for Valentino."

"Perhaps." I smile and kiss her on both cheeks. "I'm afraid I have to go, darling."

"Rehearsal?"

"Yes. Cockie isn't happy with the third act. Honestly, he can be such a stubborn brute sometimes. And I promised I would pick up a new suit for Perry."

"You do mother him! How is he?"

"Same as ever. Melancholy and alone. I've told him to find himself a muse to inspire him. I think it's a marvelous idea."

"I just wish he could find someone to make him happy."

I look at her knowingly. "He already has, darling." She smiles awkwardly. "To be perfectly honest I think he's happiest when he's miserable."

She laughs as she wraps her arms around me in a wonderful embrace. "Don't let me keep you. And send him my love."

"I'll do no such thing. He's in a bad enough mood as it is without letting him know I was dashing around Green Park with you. You know he's never forgiven you for breaking his heart that summer at Nine Elms."

"I was eight years old and he was eleven! Even Romeo and Juliet were a little older than that when they were married!"

"And what if he asked you now? Would you still tell him he's a silly boy and run off to your mother?"

She sighs. "He will never ask, Etta. That is all in the past now."

I think back over the years to the annual spring ball at Nine Elms, the color draining from Perry's face when it was announced that Bea—the young woman he had quietly loved since he was a boy—was engaged to Oscar Howard, his childhood friend. I, alone, knew that Perry had planned to ask her that very evening. His hesitation was Oscar's gain, albeit briefly. Before the year was out, Oscar was shot for desertion, the horrors of war too much to bear any longer. Under orders from his superior, Perry was among the firing squad.

As I leave Bea and Green Park, I think about all that we have loved and lost and the new battle I must now face alone. My fingers curl instinctively around the crimson leaf. Childish game or not, the wish in my pocket gives me hope.

14

LORETTA

"A muse has to be discovered,
darling, not appointed."

Autumn season marches on and *HOLD TIGHT!* is
settling into its twelve-week run. The forgotten
lines and missed cues of early performances are a
distant memory, the HOUSE FULL sign placed
outside for every performance. The critics and
gallery girls have already decided on their hits
and flops of the season, sealing the fate of us all,
such is their influence on the theatergoing public
and the city financiers. Thankfully—they adore
us. Others are not so fortunate.

The shows with the lowest ticket sales and
most scathing reviews have already closed, the
producers and theater owners left to count the
extent of their financial losses while the cast
return to auditions and urgent meetings with
agents and directors. Several leading ladies have
withdrawn with exhaustion or nerves, unable to
cope with the stresses and strains of life at the
top. I'm not surprised. The schedule and the
demands of my own performance are exhausting.
I'm onstage for nearly three hours every night.

Some days I can barely tolerate the thought of getting out of bed, but a dangerous cocktail of adrenaline and gin, Veronal for insomnia and morphine when the pain becomes too much, somehow keeps me going.

From the outside, I look no different. Makeup and lighting can mask even the harshest of illnesses. Yet inside I feel myself falling apart faster than a house of cards. The doctors urge me to tell close family members, they say it will help to prepare them—and me. But I cannot. I cannot bring myself to say the words; cannot bear the thought of the pity and sympathy. If this is going to be my final performance, I'm determined to go out with a bang. If I really must die, I will do it with my name on everyone's lips and my face in all the papers. I will die as I have lived: spectacularly.

It is Wednesday afternoon and that means Claridge's.

As the driver pulls up outside the hotel entrance, a liveried doorman steps forward and opens the car door. I swing my legs to one side and step elegantly onto the pavement, pulling my hat down over my ears and my lynx collar up around my neck. The press photographers know I come here on Wednesdays and a small crowd is already waiting. A great noise starts up as soon as they recognize me. "Miss May! Miss May! Over here!" All of them clamoring for my attention.

I turn and flash them a well-rehearsed smile and a graceful wave, giving them the perfect picture for their front pages. The magnesium bulbs pop and fizz around me. I blink away the dazzle of the flash as the doorman holds open the door and I step inside the hotel.

The concierge immediately leaps to attention, taking my coat to the cloakroom attendant as a floor waiter shows me to my usual table in the Winter Garden. Sometimes I have an overwhelming urge to brush all these endless assistants aside and tell them I am perfectly capable of opening a door myself, but that would not be the proper order of things, and people would start to talk. There will be time for talking soon enough.

I walk slowly through the room, a well-rehearsed sway of the hips, just enough to make sure that the guests catch a glimpse of me. I stand tall, lift my chin, throw the end of my fox-fur stole around my neck, and walk with poise and grace, just as I was taught to do by my ballet teacher when I was a little girl with an imaginary pile of books balanced on my head. I glance occasionally toward the tables, smiling warmly, moving like an angel through the whispers and gasps that gather around me like an autumn mist. I'm glad of the extra waves in my hair; pleased with the work of the gentlemen in the salon. That I don't feel so much as a wing beat in my stomach is of no surprise. I have long ago stopped feeling the excitement of fame and adoration. It is my job to be seen and admired and talked about, and like anything one is required to do for one's profession, there is, quite often, a sulky reluctance within me to do any of it at all.

"Mr. Clements arrived early, Miss May. I hope you don't mind, but he insisted that I show him to your usual table."

I stop walking and turn to the waiter. "Did you say Mr. Clements arrived early?"

"Yes, miss."

"Well, I never. How extraordinary."

Perry stands to greet me as I reach the table, the most idiotic grin on his face.

"I am astonished," I say, removing my gloves. "For the first time in ten years of taking afternoon tea, you are actually on time."

"Early, in fact. What is seldom is wonderful, sister dear."

"It most certainly is."

He kisses me lightly on both cheeks. I detect Scotch, as usual, but am pleased to note that he has at least shaved. His skin is smooth and his hair neatly combed. I settle into the chair and wait while the maître d' fusses with my napkin and pours a cup of Earl Grey from the pot Perry has ordered in advance.

"And to what do we owe this rare pleasure of punctuality?" I ask as I place a cigarette in my holder and lean forward for a light.

He slaps an envelope down onto the table, sending the sugar tongs toppling off the edge of the bowl. "This!"

"What is it?"

"A reply."

"To what?" Clearly he is in the mood for a guessing game. I feign interest as I take a sip of my tea.

"To my advertisement for a muse."

"An *advertisement*?"

"Yes. In *The Stage*. Your idea, I believe."

I swallow my tea the wrong way and start coughing dramatically. In seconds, several waiters are around me, passing me water and flapping at my face with napkins. The commotion sends a ripple of concern across the room, so that everyone stops what they are doing and turns to look. Even the pianist stops playing. Perry jumps up and sharply pats my back until I recover. I take a sip of iced water and dab at the makeup streaming from my eyes.

"Thank you, gentlemen. I am quite well." I turn to the gawping audience. "You can carry on."

I am dreadfully embarrassed at causing such a scene and relieved to hear the pianist resume his playing and the hum of conversation start up again. The attention soon moves away from Perry and me and back to the gossip and declarations of love that were being exchanged at the neat little tables dotted around the room.

Taking a long drag of my cigarette, I study my brother intently. "You were saying?"

"I took your advice. To find a muse. I put a small notice in *The Stage*. Didn't really expect anything to come of it—but it did. This arrived a few days ago." He pushes the envelope across the linen tablecloth. "Read it."

I take the page from him and read it aloud. "'Dear Struggling Musical Composer.'" I raise an eyebrow at that. "'I read your recent notice in *The Stage* and am interested in the position of Muse. I have a keen sense of humor and know most of the numbers from *The Shop Girl*, *The Cabaret Girl*, and *Sally* ("Look for the Silver Lining" is one of my favorites). I love jazz and I like cherry cake. I get Wednesday afternoons off and alternate Sundays. Please send word to the attention of Clover Parker, Poste Restante, Cambridge Circus.'"

I fold the letter and carefully place it back into the envelope. I sip my tea and cut a small corner from a slice of Madeira cake.

"Well?" Perry leans back casually in his chair, his good leg crossed over his bad. There is a hint of curiosity in his eyes that I haven't seen for a long time. "What do you think?"

"Cherry cake? Really?"

"That was just a detail to make it sound friendly. What do you think in general?"

"I think it was a preposterous thing to do."

He laughs and snatches the envelope from the table, slipping it into the inside pocket of his jacket. "This is what you wanted, isn't it? For me to take risks and chances and find something—someone—to inspire me."

"Yes. I did. But I didn't actually think you would place a notice in *The Stage*. Finding a muse isn't the same as finding a knitting pattern for winter gloves or a new position for a picture-house pianist. A muse has to be discovered, darling, not appointed. A muse is a rare bewitching sort of person whom one meets unexpectedly and feels strangely drawn to, like salt on ink, absorbing their very essence. I'm sorry, darling, but you don't know anything about this Clover Parker, or anyone else who might reply." I sit back in my chair. "My guess is that she's seen an opportunity to get a ring on her finger. That's all any young single girl wants these days. Replying to a notice in *The Stage* might be the only chance she has of finding a husband."

Perry listens and looks at me through narrowed eyes. "Perhaps. And yet, perhaps not. She might be looking for something to add a little color to her day. Perhaps she's already married and can't stand the sight of her husband, or the sound of her children bawling all day long, and longs to listen to music and escape from it all for a while. She might very well be bewitching. We can't know, can we? Not until I meet her."

I sigh and take my compact from my purse. I dab at my nose with the powder puff, angling my face toward the better light. My skin is dull and tired-looking, lacking the dewy luster I was once renowned for as the face of Pears soap. Age is such a dreadful thing.

"So, what are you going to do?" I ask. Perry looks at me, and smiles. "You've already replied, haven't you?"

"I've invited her to meet me. What's the worst that can happen?"

I laugh. "The worst that can happen is that you realize she's an ordinary dowdy girl who couldn't inspire a flea. You'll send her back to wherever she came from and she'll feel that her life is even worse than it was before. You'll break the poor girl's heart. That's the worst than can happen."

He shuffles in his seat. "It would make a change from mine being the broken heart, wouldn't it?"

I feel myself soften a little. Perry really has been desperately unlucky in love. "Yes. I suppose it would." I rub a little rouge onto my cheeks. "So, when are you meeting her?"

"In two weeks, hopefully. At the Lyons' Corner House on Coventry Street. She gets Wednesday afternoons off. I thought I should give her a little advance notice."

"Wednesday afternoons?"

"Yes."

"But you meet *me* on Wednesday afternoons." I

snap my compact shut. "You can't go. You'll have to reschedule."

"I can't reschedule. I've already sent my reply." He drains his coffee. "I'm sorry, Etta. It will only be this once, and if we agree to continue the arrangement I'll make sure we meet later in the day, or on a Sunday."

So this is how it starts. This is how my life begins to unravel and fall apart. This simple little ritual I have grasped hold of for so long is finally slipping away from me. I should be angry with him, but when I look at Perry his eyes sparkle and I see my own reflection in them. He hasn't looked this alive for months.

"Very well. Go. Meet her. But don't say I didn't warn you if she turns out to be your undoing."

He laughs. "Let her do her worst. There isn't much left of me to undo." He takes a long drag on his cigarette. "And what if she turns out to be the perfect muse. What then?"

"Then you can thank me for giving you the idea in the first place."

We talk for a while about mutual friends and who might be going to the Mitfords' New Year's Eve party. We share snippets of news, pleasantries, niceties, and all the time the letter in my purse and the doctors' voices nag at me. *Tell him, Etta. Tell him.* But it gives me such joy that we can spend time together like this and I can't bear to spoil it. If I can just get through the autumn and winter months, I'm sure I'll feel better. So I say nothing. I keep my secret locked away like the flowers beneath the frozen ground, and enjoy whatever time I have left with the brother I hadn't really known for much of my life, but who I can now call my friend.

We were never especially close as children, Perry and I, and I was even more distant from Aubrey, whose purpose in life, even from when he was in short trousers, was to prepare himself to become heir to the Clementses' title and estate. Our childhood was a strict routine that didn't provide for emotion or affection. At best, we were brought down from the nursery to the drawing room at four o'clock, paraded like dolls to be dandled on our parents' knees until the warmth of fat little legs set unsightly creases in skirts and flattened carefully pressed creases in trousers. We were like little shadows in that great house, unsure of the loud vivacious people we called Mother and Father. Watching my brothers go to war stirred new emotions within me. I knew Aubrey would be all right, he always was, always will be. But Perry, I worried about.

He had never quite fit within our family. Like a shoe half a size too small, one always sensed a kind of niggling discomfort around him, and I didn't pay him much attention. He was just Perry, the shy young boy who preferred music to trains and dancing to cricket, the second brother sent off to boarding school and brought home for the holidays, the gawky adolescent who shied away from my giggling friends and sought the company of the ivories on the piano above the company of others. As had always been expected, he studied law at Oxford and entered the legal profession, just like his father and Aubrey before him. Yet where they had excelled, Perry hated every minute of it.

He couldn't wait to get to the front, away from the pressures Father exerted on him and the stifling constraints of a profession he despised. Yet even in war, Perry was unconventional. Father scoffed at the letters he sent from France, proudly telling us how he had become involved in the divisional concert parties and was a firm favorite, composing songs and comedy skits for the privates and other officers. "Not even a real soldier," he sneered. "Can't even go to war properly. Always has to be a damned disappointment."

My brothers survived. Aubrey was decorated a hero. Perry was acknowledged as a loyal officer. It was, perhaps, the best any of us could have expected of him. Their return to Nine Elms was a joyous occasion, although we all knew that it was Aubrey whom Mother and Father were the most grateful to have safely home. I was grateful too. If we had lost Aubrey, Perry would have crumbled beneath the pressure of becoming Father's heir. He had crumbled enough as it was.

"Etta? Etta, are you listening to me?"

The room becomes unpleasantly hot. I fan myself furiously and sip my water as a wave of pain washes over me. The lilting strains of the pianist fade in and out; soft then loud. A baby takes up a great bawling from somewhere nearby. The sounds prick at my ears as a shooting pain grips my chest, numbing my skin. I hold the edge of the table.

"Etta? Are you quite all right? You're ever so pale."

Perry's words take on a strange muted quality. He moves in circles in front of me. I need the child to stop crying; the pain to go away. I try to place my hands over my ears but feel myself drifting away, slipping underwater until I cannot hear anything other than my name.

"Etta? Etta!"

"Air, Perry. I need air."

My words sound as though they belong to someone else. I try to stand up and knock a teaspoon to the floor. Perry grabs me and helps me to my feet, placing his arm around me for support as he escorts me briskly from the Winter Garden, furtive whispers like rushing water following in our wake. I cling to Perry, gasping for air as we step outside.

"Loretta! Loretta! Miss May!"

The magnesium bulbs from the photographers

pop pop pop until I am blinded by the fizzing white light. The maître d' is already there with our coats. The page flags a motor cab. My hand waves in front of my face to shield my eyes from the glare of the camera lights and then a deep darkness surrounds me and I allow myself to drift away to a safer place, where Roger is with me and his hand feels so perfect in mine.

I wake in my bedroom the next morning. The sun streams through the window. Outside I can see the rooftops blanketed with a white dusting of frost, sparkling like diamonds beneath the sunlight. Perry is asleep on the chaise, his jacket draped over him as a blanket. He may be silly and irritating at times, but he cared enough to stay with me, and that gives me great comfort.

Elsie has brought a tray. Not wishing to disturb me, she has left it beside the bed. In a small white vase, a single pink peony. I slowly sit upright and pour myself a cup of tea. It is good and strong. I nibble at a triangle of toast, my appetite soon stimulated. The fire crackles in the grate. Such simple things, and yet I am so grateful for them all.

I will have to tell them soon.

The carriage clock on the mantelpiece chimes the hour of nine. I have three hours before I must be at the theater. Ample time to pull myself together. The spotlight may be fading, but the curtain hasn't fallen for me yet.

15
DOLLY

My dreams are what anchor me.
Without them, without hope of
making a better life, I am nothing.

My first six weeks at The Savoy pass quickly.
With time comes a new assurance in my abilities,
so that I can almost find some enjoyment and
satisfaction in my work, and yet beneath the
smooth linen sheets and carefully ordered routines,
my heart remains a crumpled, complicated mess. I
can't stop thinking about Edie Bishop. Forgotten
names. Suppressed memories. *"Put it behind you
and carry on. Isn't that what they told us?"* When
I wake in the dark of the morning, I instinctively
reach beneath my pillow, my fingers feeling for
the rough edge of the photograph. My heart beats
a little easier to know that he is there, but it isn't
enough. I feel it like a hunger pain deep within
me; a longing to know that he is loved and cared
for. And all the while the pages of Perry
Clements's music lie idle, the notes and melody
remain unheard.

Since my encounter with Debroy Somers, I've
often thought about the resident hotel band. I've

stepped aside in the corridors so that they can pass by with their high waistbands and slicked brilliantine hair. Sissy says they act like they own the place. "They've their own dressing room and valets and God only knows what other privileges. Stuck-up, the lot of them. Wouldn't give the likes of us the time of day." But I remember my conversation with Debroy Somers, and while I haven't yet gathered the courage to find him in the Ballroom and ask him to play my pages of music, I know that I will. When the time is right.

The daily delivery of the house list is always a cause for excitement. Sissy, Gladys, and I read through it together, looking for names of American movie stars against our room allocations. I secretly hope to see a new occupant in suite 401, Larry Snyder's room, but while other guests come and go, he seems intent on staying for the season. I always leave his room until last, work quickly when I'm in there, and breathe a little easier when I'm done.

It is where I am now, folding the last few chamber towels, when the door flies open and Snyder strides into the room. We both jump at the sight of each other. My heart thumps beneath my dress.

He looks at me and then at his pocket watch. "I thought you would be finished by now."

"I'm almost done, sir. I can leave these and come back later." I place the towels on the foot of the bed and make for the door, but he steps in front of it, blocking my way.

"No need to leave on my account. Stay and finish. I just popped back for some papers."

His hair is as black as the coalhole downstairs, slicked perfectly to one side. His face is sharp and angular, free of any creases or lines, like a freshly ironed bedsheet. He has an olive hue to his skin, the California tan that all the American guests from the West Coast have.

I stand awkwardly beside the bed, my hands fumbling with the edges of the towels as he busies himself, rifling through the piles of paper spread over the writing desk. I was careful not to disturb them as I cleaned around them a short while ago, although I couldn't help noticing that they are pages of script for a new Broadway play.

"Ah, found them. The show *will* go on!"

He stands upright and grins at me. I stare at the towels and wait for him to leave, but he doesn't.

When I look up, his head is tilted to one side, studying me as if I was one of the paintings displayed in the corridor. He rubs his fingers along his slim mustache.

"A smile wouldn't go amiss. A surly maid can ruin a hotel's reputation, you know."

Somehow I force a weak smile. "Yes. Of course."

"And look how pretty you are when you manage it." He tilts his head the other way. "Quite intriguing. Did anyone ever photograph you? Professionally."

I shuffle my feet and pull at a loose thread on my apron. "No. Never."

He makes a square with his fingers, holding his hands out in front of him and squinting at me with one eye closed, as if looking through a camera lens. "I'd say you'd be a natural in front of the camera. Good bone structure. Symmetrical features."

There is nothing sensible I can think of to say in reply. I continue to fold the towels as he walks toward me. He smells of expensive cologne and shoe polish. He takes a towel from my hand, his fingertips sweeping over mine as he does. My stomach tumbles.

"I'm sure I can manage to fold these myself. Go. Grab an extra few minutes' break or something."

I don't like to leave the towels unfolded, but I'm not especially keen to stay in the room with him either. I mumble a thank you and walk toward the door, fumbling with the handle as I try to pull my trolley behind me at the same time.

"One moment." I turn around. Snyder is standing right behind me. A small white feather is pressed between his thumb and forefinger. "It was on the back of your dress," he says. "I thought the White Feather Brigade had stopped with the war."

He laughs, but his words bite through me. I stare at the feather in his tar-stained fingers and see my mother standing up in church, passing the feathers to the men who had refused to fight. I see myself tug at her coat sleeve, the shame and embarrassment staining my cheeks red as I beg her not to.

My breath catches in my throat as he hands it to me. "It must have fallen from a pillow," I say.

"I suppose it must." He looks deep into my eyes, a cold emotionless gaze. He leans forward so that I can feel his warm breath against my cheek. "Lucky feather."

He laughs too loudly and walks back toward the window, whistling a show tune.

I step out into the corridor, my heart racing as I close the door behind me. I stand for a moment with my back against the door and let out a long breath before I gather myself together and push my trolley toward the service lift. My legs tremble. The carpets feel stiff beneath my feet. The paintings look gaudy in their ornate gilt frames. A bulb on a wall light flickers and goes out.

The hotel is unsettled and so am I.

I try to forget about Snyder as I stand in the post office at Cambridge Circus later that day, waiting for the postmistress to check if there is anything for me. I hope Mam will have replied to the letter I'd eventually plucked up the courage to send, although I'm not looking forward to hearing what she has to say about my new position. And, of course, I'm hoping to hear back from the musical composer. I presume he will reply, even if to say I'm not the sort of person he had in mind.

I pick at the quick on my fingernail as the woman peers into various pigeonholes and removes bundles of envelopes, adjusting the spectacles on the end of her nose so that she can read the addressee. I wish she would hurry up. As she searches I think about the years I spent writing letters to Teddy and waiting for his reply, everything an agonizing interval in the weeks and months between. His letters, his words, became everything to me.

I'd never written a letter before the war. There was no need. Anybody I wanted to say something to was in the next room, or the next house or the next street. I wasn't one for writing anyway, reading was what I loved the most, despite the meager collection of books at home. My written school-work was described as "rushed and untidy," the schoolmistress saying that if I could apply myself to the task of writing as much as I did to the task of reading, I would be "a much improved girl." But I didn't have the patience to practice my writing and I remained unimproved.

When war came, letters were our lifeline, the only way to communicate with our loved ones. The writing of letters became the most important thing to me in the world. I asked the school-mistress to help me put into words all the emotions I felt, and when I was done I walked to the post office, my letter in my coat pocket. I dreaded it. There was something so final about handing my letter to Mrs. Joyce, so I would delay and linger, let people go ahead of me until I was the only one left and she was closing for lunch. "Come along then, Dolly," she'd say. "Hand it over. I'm parched." Everyone knew how much Mrs. Joyce enjoyed her lunchtime cuppa and a roll-up. No matter who was waiting, or what was happening, she would close the hatch and lock the door. Reluctantly, I would hand over my envelope and walk home, blinking back the tears. So many emotions were contained within that neat little envelope. So much hope. So much fear. What if he didn't reply? What if it was the last letter I would ever write to him?

More than once I ran back to the post office, hammering on the door until poor Mrs. Joyce thought the world was at an end and abandoned her cup of tea to open it. I would beg her to give me the letter back and then I would run home, throw it in the fire, take up a fresh sheet of paper, and try to find some better words; words that would tell him how much I loved him without admitting that it broke my heart to think that I might never see him again. We had to be brave so as not to make the soldiers worry. Positive news.

Happy thoughts. Wonderfully proud. That sort of thing. And when the postmaster cycled past with the sack of mail on the start of its long journey to France, I would run to the end of the lane and wish my words a final farewell and pray that I would hear back soon.

By some miracle, a reply always came. He wrote of the birdsong he heard in the early morning, and the pleasure the boys got from the gifts we sent from home. Sometimes, his reply was a standard-issue form with the boxes ticked in all the right places. Sometimes, his words were censored, blacked out. But always, always he told me to never give up hope, to always love life and to chase adventures.

Hope. Love. Adventure.

That was all that mattered, he said. That was all.

And then the war ended. The guns fell silent. And so did Teddy.

"Ah, yes. Here it is. For a Clover Parker, you say?"

The postmistress hands me a slim envelope. "Yes, that's right." I take it from her. "Nothing for Dorothy Lane?"

"No. Nothing today, dear."

I thank her, and rush from the post office, ducking down a narrow side alley to read the composer's reply. I tear the envelope open, my hands shaking.

Dear Miss Parker,

Thank you for your reply, which I was delighted to receive. Might I suggest that we meet at the Coventry Street Corner House at 4 P.M. on Wednesday, November 28th.

My method of finding inspiration must seem rather unusual, but I can assure you my intentions are entirely honorable. A public meeting in the tearooms will hopefully allay any concerns you might have.

I look forward to meeting you.

Sincerely,

S.M.C. (Struggling Musical Composer)

A grin spreads across my lips. A flutter stirs in my heart. I read the letter twice more before putting it back into the envelope and slipping it into my purse.

There is a bounce to my step as I stroll back along the Charing Cross Road and through Trafalgar Square. Even the pigeons amuse me.

At the Palais, Clover and I dance until our legs feel like they're going to drop off. The band plays foxtrots and tangos, swinging jazz numbers and the new dance called the Charleston. The dance instructors demonstrate the steps. Clover says they look like they're having a fit the way their limbs jerk about, but I rush to the dance floor to give it a try. I spend most of the afternoon perfecting the steps until I can do it quite well.

After dragging Clover away from an amorous embrace with awful Tommy Mullins, we head to the teashop for a simple supper of poached eggs and coffee. She has a new hat, plum velvet, which I admire and envy at the same time. She tells me one of the ladies at Grosvenor Square passed it onto her. Last season's color. She sees the flash of jealousy in my eyes and promises to give me the next hand-me-down.

As we settle at a table by the window, I take the advertisement from *The Stage* from my purse and pass it to Clover. "What do you think of this?"

She leans forward onto her elbows, peering at the small print. "What is it?"

"Found it in a copy of *The Stage* left on the omnibus a few weeks back. Read it."

She picks it up, reads it, puts it down, and peers at me over the top of her coffee cup.

"So?" I prompt. "What do you think?"

"I think you've already replied and want to know what to do next." She raises an eyebrow. "Am I right?"

I nod sheepishly.

"You're daft in the head. The only reason anyone would place a notice like that is to get a gullible young girl like you trotting round, and Lord knows what trouble you'll end up in."

I wince. We both stir sugar into our coffee, willing her words away.

"Sorry," Clover says. "I didn't mean it to come out like that. But men can't be trusted." She lights a cigarette. "I take it you're planning to meet this 'struggling musician' or whatever they call themselves?"

"He sent a reply. He wants to meet me at the Corner House on Coventry Street next week." Clover studies me through narrowed eyes. "It's not like I'll be on my own or anything, and there's no harm in meeting him, is there?"

"Well, don't say I didn't warn you."

I pick the page up off the table and read it again. "Don't you think it's strange that I noticed it in the first place? Do you think it could be a sign?"

She takes a long drag of her cigarette. "You and your bloody *signs*. Tea leaves this and full moon that. Yes. It is a sign. A sign of a murdering lunatic who wants to lure girls to his apartment." She shakes her head, but smiles at me in that knowing way only a true friend can. "You don't need to reply to adverts in the papers, Dolly. You'll make it, you know. One day. You just have to keep practicing and turning up to auditions."

I fold the piece of paper and slip it back into my purse. I try to concentrate as Clover chatters on, telling me how she's been laid up sick most of the week and how the housekeeper caught the new girl dancing to a song on the wireless when she was supposed to be polishing the silver, but my thoughts drift constantly away. All I can think about is the reply in my pocket. *My method of finding inspiration must seem rather unusual, but I can assure you my intentions are entirely honorable.* I think about the endless line of girls outside the Pavilion Theatre. Everyone who makes it needs a bit of luck along the way. Maybe this little piece of paper is mine. I don't blame Clover for imagining all sorts of awful things, but I'm not just a girl who walks around with her head in the clouds. My dreams are what anchor me. Without them, without hope of making a better life, I am nothing. Without them, he will remain forever absent from my arms. And that is a thought far more frightening than any of Clover's grim predictions.

As the chimes of Big Ben strike eight we leave the teashop. Clover says she has a headache and needs to go back to Grosvenor Square. I see her onto the omnibus and make my way back to the Strand. I wonder if I might tell Sissy about the musical composer. Or Gladys. She might understand. Then again, she might try to talk me out of it also.

It is a cold clear night. I tip my head back to look up at the stars, just like Teddy and I used to do. They shone so brightly in Mawdesley; so brilliantly. Here, the lights and fogs obscure them and I have to look closely to see any at all.

205

I walk on, passing the night screevers who are busy etching their drawings onto the paving stones with such patience and care. A small crowd has gathered to watch one of the artists. He's copying a cover of *Life* magazine, a flapper girl with butterfly wings, the original propped up against the railings for him to use as a guide. He copies it very well. The word "love" is written in place of the title of the magazine. It prompts a memory of Teddy chasing butterflies with his net. He never kept them. He said he just liked to admire them for a while, that some things are so beautiful they're worth chasing, even if you can't keep them.

I think about his words, wrap my fingers around the photograph in my pocket, and head back to the hotel.

16
TEDDY

Maghull Military War Hospital, Lancashire
May 1919

> ". . . lavender-, violet-, and rose-colored
> clouds, and wispy white clouds
> of goose feather."

Someone has brought a gramophone player onto the ward. The music has everyone as giddy as goats. The nurse tells me the names of all the songs and how she loves to dance. She says everything is better with music and talks for an age about Nellie Melba and Gertie Lawrence. She comes alive when she talks about these women. It is quite infectious.

A group of other nurses pair up and waltz around the room, earning a round of applause when the music ends. Someone calls for another and they dance a tango. As it ends, Matron enters the ward. She chastises the nurses for getting the patients overexcited and tells them that is quite enough tomfoolery for the day. They fall around laughing when she leaves, but the fun is over and we quickly get back to the business of being melancholy.

My young nurse settles into the chair beside me. Her cheeks are flushed from her exertions, her eyes bright. She takes the paper from the envelope. "It'll have to be more letters, then, if she won't let us dance."

I close my eyes and listen to her voice. It is far nicer than any gramophone record.

July 12th, 1918

My dearest Teddy,

Here is a picture for you to keep in your head. Today I walked in the hills. I climbed to the top of the highest hill, spread out a blanket, and had a picnic for us both. I had two of everything. Two plates, two cups, two forks, two knives. I set everything out, just as we used to do, and imagined you were there with me.

What a day we had, Teddy, even though rationing made for slim pickings. I'd collected blackberries and gooseberries from the garden and we stuffed them into our mouths in great handfuls until our chins were purple with juice. And then we ran over the hills with the breeze whipping around us and the sun blazing down until our skin went pink and the fork handles were too hot to hold.

And then we lay on the blanket, side by side, heads together as we watched the clouds: lavender-, violet-, and rose-colored clouds, and wispy white clouds of goose feather. It was so perfect, Teddy. We snoozed away the afternoon until the sun sank low on the horizon.

Is it silly of me to imagine such things? Am I wrong to think that this will all be set right when you come home, that we can put things back the way they were? Mam says we can't expect things to be the same; that it isn't like an upset tea tray that we can set to rights. She says I should prepare myself for things to be cracked and spoiled.

Some mornings, when I see the postmaster's bicycle coming along the lane, I prepare myself for the worst. Some mornings I think about how we will be married in the spring with the daffodils dancing in the breeze to cheer us along.

Some mornings I can't think of anything at all.

I will close now. Mam needs me to help with some chores.

Your Little Thing,
Dolly
X

August 23rd, 1918

My dearest Teddy,

I haven't heard from you for so long and I worry terribly. I know you are well because Alfie Barrow speaks of you in his letters to his mam, but he says you're finding it hard out there, and I wish you would write.

I have wrapped the parcel especially well to make sure everything reaches you safely. I've sent more OXO cubes since you complained about the soup. I've also sent a pencil, a candle, and some paper—you know what I wish you to do with them—and a photograph from the newspaper. This is the munitions factory football team. I'm the goalkeeper. I've saved more goals than anyone else in the league.

Remember to look at the sky and the stars, Teddy. That's where I am. That's where you'll find me.

Your Little Thing,
Dolly
X

When she has finished reading, she tugs at the bedsheets and plumps the pillows behind my head. Swift, sure movements. Clear and precise. I envy her the assurance of hands that move as she wishes. I can barely manage the buttons on my trousers; can't even go for a pee without needing somebody's help. Like a child, I am helpless and unsure. I let her do her work and distract myself by watching the butterfly at the window. It is something of a companion now. The first thing I see when I wake in the morning. The last thing I see before I go to sleep.

She places a bunch of grapes in a bowl and tells me she has some woodbine for me.

"This place gets quieter every day," she says. "I'm sure they'll let you go home soon."

Half the beds on the ward are empty now, their occupants recovered and sent home to their loved ones to carry on with whatever life they have left. Many of the voluntary nurses have also finished up. Their services no longer needed. I hope my nurse has a little while longer yet.

I turn my face to look at her. She's a pretty thing. So young to be dealing with all this horror. There's a brightness to her face, a gentleness in her eyes. I try to smile at her but my muscles can't remember how and the smile becomes a grimace. I turn away so that she can't see, and settle my gaze on the butterfly instead.

"That silly butterfly," she says, opening the window. "I don't know why it doesn't fly away."

She stands and looks at me for what feels like an age before moving toward the bed and sitting on the chair beside me.

"You're making good progress, you know. By the end of the summer you'll be running through those fields outside." She squeezes my hand as reassurance but I pull away and slip my hand beneath the bedcovers. "On a warm summer's day, you'll be able to sit out in the gardens and listen to the birds singing and watch all the butterflies." She dabs at her cheeks with a cotton handkerchief. "Won't that be wonderful?"

I'm tired. I want to doze. I close my eyes but leave them open the smallest fraction so that I can still see her. She stays beside me for the rest of the afternoon, sometimes talking, sometimes dozing in the warmth of the sun. It is pleasant, just the two of us. When you feel at ease with a person, you don't need grand gestures or loud music or wild dancing. There is an undeniable truth in those companionable silences. Just to know that she is there beside me is enough.

17

DOLLY

"The Savoy is much more than a hotel, Dorothy. It has a personality all of its own."

After the now familiar routine of breakfast and O'Hara's inspection, Sissy, Gladys, and I scan the house list as usual. I'm not expecting any changes to my room occupancy and hardly pay attention to the names on the list when Gladys squeals and grabs my arm.

"You are the luckiest cow ever, Dolly Lane!" She snatches my copy of the list from my hands and presses it to her chest. "You'll *never* guess who's coming?"

Her excitement is infectious. "I don't know. Nellie Melba?"

"Nope. Better than that."

"Tallulah?"

"No."

"Valentino?"

"God, you're hopeless." She shoves the list into my hands. "Alice Delysia!" Her eyes shine with excitement. "And she's staying in one of *your* rooms!"

Sissy is unimpressed. "Who's Alice Delysia?"

I stare at her in disbelief. "You *must* know her. Star of Broadway and the West End. One of Cochran's discoveries. Famed beauty. She's wonderful. She's really coming here?" I grab the list off Gladys to see for myself.

"Yes. She's really coming here," Gladys says. "You're the luckiest maid in London. Not here two months and you've two of the biggest names in town. Snyder and Delysia. He's her manager."

I can't believe it. There it is in black ink against suite 602. "Alice Delysia! I'll die if I see her. I wonder if she's as beautiful up close. I saw her in revue last year. I was hoarse for a week from cheering. Who do you both have?"

Sissy scans her list. "I've got an American actress I've never heard of. An unbearable diva according to one of the other maids. Mildred has an Indian prince of some sort and Gladys has a Russian business tycoon. The manicurists love it when he stays. He gives them the most extravagant gifts, but they can't understand a word he's saying!"

I'm not listening. I'm already lost in thoughts of Alice Delysia and Parisian dance shoes and Poiret dresses and what I will say if I see her.

The "French Actress," as she becomes known, arrives on a frosty November morning. The hotel is fidgety at the prospect of this important guest.

214

Tea trays have been dropped, bedsheets scorched by forgotten irons, fingers pricked by errant needles, and silverware has clattered to the ground. Everyone senses it. Even the doorman and the pages at the entrance are jittery.

I've persuaded one of the manicurists to let me watch Mademoiselle Delysia's arrival from their little cubbyhole beside the Grill. I press my nose to the glass, watching every car that sweeps into the narrow courtyard as the doorman stamps his feet and claps his hands together to warm them in the crisp air. Across the courtyard I can see the florist at her window, peering around her displays to get a better view.

Eventually, the sleek lines of a black Rolls slide to a stop. The doorman steps forward and opens the back door. A white-gloved hand emerges, followed by the woman herself. She's dressed in a fashionable wool day dress in rose pink and a cranberry velvet coat with sable trim. Her hair is a vision of perfect marcel waves. I almost forget to breathe, I am so mesmerized by her.

The porters lift her many trunks and cases onto a trolley as she adjusts her gloves, making sure she looks perfect before she makes her entrance. She takes a moment to say something to the doorman before she disappears through the famous swing doors. What happens on the other side is not for the likes of me to know.

I'm counting linen in the storeroom when O'Hara finds me later that morning. I'm so engrossed in my work I don't hear her enter.

"Might I have a word, Dorothy?"

"Crikey, miss! You shouldn't go sneaking up on people like that. Nearly gave me a heart attack."

O'Hara doesn't blink. "I might be about to give you another. We have a minor crisis with one of the guests which I hope you can help with."

"What is it, miss?"

"One of the guests is missing her lady's maid. Caught a fever in Calais or something. The end result being that she finds herself without her maid and would like to borrow someone while her people arrange a replacement. I checked your file and see that you have some experience as a lady's maid, albeit fleeting. I'm hopeful it will suffice for a day or two."

My experience as a lady's maid was over Christmas several years ago. A guest was left without her maid who'd been delayed by a snowstorm. I was the only one with sufficient experience to step in. Apart from my being hopeless with the curling irons and almost ruining the woman's hair, it had gone surprisingly well.

"It was only for a short while, but I'd be happy to help if I can," I say.

"Very good. I'll inform Mademoiselle Delysia straightaway."

My heart thumps. "Alice Delysia?"

"*Mademoiselle* Delysia. Yes. Is there a problem?"

"No. No problem at all. I'm a huge fan of hers. Have you seen her? She's very beautiful. I saw her in *Mayfair and Montmartre* last year and . . ."

O'Hara folds her arms across her chest and gives me that look of hers. I stop talking.

"Can you do the job or not? I'm quite certain Mademoiselle Delysia won't want a giddy gallery first-nighter fussing over her. Perhaps I should find somebody else."

"I can do the job, miss. What does she need me to do?"

"I have to discuss matters with her. I don't expect it will be much. Laying out her clothes, dressing her. That sort of thing. She'll use the hotel hairdresser." That's a relief. "And of course this doesn't mean you are relieved of your normal duties. I'll expect you to sign in at six thirty each morning as usual. Mademoiselle Delysia's demands must be worked around your usual routine. I'm sure she'll find a replacement before the week is out."

"Of course." I have no idea how I'll get everything done, but I'm determined to find a way.

O'Hara looks at me. "You're coming along quite nicely, Dorothy. I'll admit that I didn't have the greatest of hopes for you after your first day and

Mr. Cutler's report of a minor transgression in the Front Hall, but you have redeemed yourself amply, and you work hard."

I stare at her, speechless.

"Carry on, then. I'm sure you've plenty to do."

I place my hands to my cheeks. They are flushed with excitement. Alice Delysia! Maid to Alice Delysia!

Giddy with excitement, I hitch up my skirt and dance around the storeroom, a broom as my partner. I knew some good fortune would come to me if I was patient. This is the start. I can feel it. This is where my adventure begins.

Within the hour, it is all confirmed. Over lunch, O'Hara tells me I've been summoned to the governor's office.

"Mr. Reeves-Smith wishes to speak to you, Dorothy."

"To me?"

"Yes. No doubt he wishes to impress upon you the importance of the extra duties you have been assigned."

I leave my lunch and make my way from the Maids' Hall.

"And remember your manners," she calls after me. "Don't say more than is necessary. I know how you girls like to let your tongues run away with you."

She rushes off in a rustle of silk as I head in the

opposite direction toward the service lift and ask the attendant to take me to eighth.

"Eighth?"

"Yes, Thomas. Eighth."

I frown at him. The lift attendants really do think themselves something special.

The governor's office is a river suite, commanding impressive views over London. The dome of St. Paul's and the towers of Westminster Cathedral dominate the skyline, while oil paintings of similar scenes decorate the walls around his desk. My eyes are drawn to a collection of butterflies in a glass case, their wings pinned against a white card. They remind me of the library at Mawdesley Hall. One of the sons was an avid collector. He kept dozens of butterflies and moths beneath glass cases. I hated dusting them. The sight of them gave me a chill down my spine.

I perch, childlike, on the edge of the chair across the desk from the governor and worry at a loose thread on the edge of my apron.

"I understand from Mrs. O'Hara that you are assisting with one of our most esteemed guests?"

I nod. "Yes, sir. Mademoiselle Delysia. The actress."

"I am aware of her profession." I blush and lower my eyes. "And Mrs. O'Hara assures me that you have adequate experience and suitable references." I nod again. "It is a sudden and unexpected promotion of duties, which, I trust, you will handle appropriately?"

"I will. Yes, sir."

"The fact is, Dorothy, that guests like Mademoiselle Delysia are of immense importance to a hotel such as The Savoy. Her stay provides the sort of publicity that the other London hotels would long for. This is far more than turning out a room and ensuring the taps are working." He stands up and walks to the window, turning his back to me as he continues to talk. "I am quite aware that working at The Savoy gives an ordinary girl such as yourself access to the lives of some of the best-known and greatest stars of our time. Undoubtedly thrilling as this is, you are—I presume—aware of the need to turn a blind eye as you turn down the bedcovers?" He looks over his shoulder at me and raises an eyebrow.

"Yes, sir."

"Things *occur* within the privacy of a hotel suite which may not occur elsewhere. I don't need to remind you that what happens in the private suites at The Savoy is nobody's business but the person paying the bill, and is most definitely of no concern whatsoever to a maid."

"No, sir."

"The Savoy is much more than a hotel, Dorothy. It has a personality all of its own. It casts a sort of spell on people the moment they walk through the door and step into the Front Hall. Even our most frequent guests tell me that they still sense something quite extraordinary about her."

I shuffle in the chair and wonder why he is telling me all this. I've a lot to be getting on with.

"To you, the hotel may seem to be nothing more than surfaces to clean and polish, picture frames to dust, pincushions to place on the dressing tables. But soon it will become like a familiar friend to you. You will sense the hotel's moods. You will know when she feels frivolous and gay. You will sense when she is petulant and irksome. She moves to the rhythm of the pistons in the engine rooms and the great pendulums that swing in the clocks, but she also moves to the rhythm of our guests and their unpredictable whims. They may be difficult and demanding. They may be pleasant and charming, and we all feel it, every single one of us. From the potato peelers in the kitchens all the way up here, we react to the shift and change, to the comings and goings, even though we might not realize it."

He pauses, thankfully, and removes a cigar box from a drawer in his desk. He takes a moment to make his selection, lifting several cigars to his nose and inhaling deeply. Satisfied with his choice, he commences a lengthy ritual of cutting and tapping and sniffing before finally lighting the blessed thing. He takes a series of short puffs before relaxing into his wingback chair and placing his feet up onto the edge of the desk.

I stifle a cough. "Might I go now, sir?"

He studies me through the smoke that drifts in the space between us. "Tell me something, Dorothy. What is it you wish for?"

"I'm not sure what you mean, sir?"

"In life. What is it you wish to do, because much as I would love you to tell me differently, I suspect that your ambition is not to turn out rooms at The Savoy for the rest of your life?"

I'm not sure how to respond. I presume he is testing me, trying to trick me, to prove that I don't care and am not worthy of a position here.

"I'm very happy with my position here, sir."

"I'm sure you are. But do you dream of marrying, perhaps?" he continues. "Of children? Of a life as mistress of a grand home in the country with servants and a pond full of carp?"

He chuckles to himself. I wonder if he has been at the sherry.

"I think you may be teasing me, sir."

He drops his feet to the floor and leans forward. "Not at all. I see something in you. I saw it the very first time I met you. You won't remember. I was discussing the merits of a Monet seascape with Snyder. You had recently started your employment with us."

I nod. "I do remember." I remember how uncomfortable I had felt under Larry Snyder's unwelcome gaze.

"I've seen it once or twice before in the girls

here. A longing for more. Of course, most of them never achieve whatever that 'more' is. But very occasionally, they do. I have a feeling you might be one such girl."

I take a deep breath and sit upright. "I wish for nothing more."

He taps the ash from the end of his cigar into the cut-crystal ashtray beside him. "Very well. Then look about you. Pay attention. Let the hotel become your friend and you never know what she might give you in return." He stands and walks back toward the window. "Now off you go. I believe you have work to do. That is, after all, what we pay you for, is it not?"

"Yes, sir. Of course."

I leave the room, closing the door quietly behind me. "I wish for so much more, Mr. Reeves-Smith," I whisper, as I make my way back to the service lift. "I wish for more than you could ever imagine."

As instructed by O'Hara, I arrive at suite 602 later that afternoon and knock tentatively on the door. My knees rattle like milk bottles in a crate. I can hear voices inside, low and distant.

After a moment, a young man opens the door. I recognize him as Mr. Snyder's valet. He stares at me. "Yes?" He looks at me as though I'm a piece of dirt on his shoe. Valets always think themselves above their station.

"I'm Dorothy," I say. "The temporary lady's maid for Mademoiselle Delysia. The head of housekeeping told me to come."

He turns and walks back into the room. "Yes, yes. You'd better come in."

I step into the apartment. I'd only cleaned it earlier that morning. Already it is in disarray.

The valet walks into an adjoining room. I hear voices before he returns. "Well, close the door, then."

I close the door behind me. After what feels like an age, Alice Delysia enters from a door to the left of the fireplace. She is exquisite, dressed in a white satin housecoat with an ostrich-feather trim, her feet in lavender silk mules. It takes all my self-control not to gasp at the sight of her.

She walks toward me. "Your name is . . . ?" Her voice is like spun sugar, soft and oozing in her seductive French accent.

"Dorothy Lane, ma'am." I curtsy instinctively.

The valet smirks and leans against the ornate mantelpiece. A small dog lies on a rug beside the fire.

Mademoiselle Delysia nods. "I dine at seven thirty, followed by dancing. I will need a dinner dress, gloves, shoes, headdress, and jewels. You will help me dress and arrange my night attire."

I nod, thoughts of dazzling evening dresses spinning through my mind. "That is all for now. I must leave the hotel shortly, but I will return for afternoon tea. After that, I will dress for dinner. You may go."

I mumble a thank you as she glides back into the adjoining room.

The valet smirks at me. "That'll give you plenty to gossip about over your tea break." He affects a female voice. 'She wore this. She said that. She was so beautiful.' He laughs at himself. "You're all the same. So easily starstruck."

He calls the little dog after him and disappears into another room.

Opening the door to leave, I jump at the sight of Larry Snyder, his hand raised, ready to knock. He startles, dropping a bundle of papers.

"I'm so sorry," I say, dropping to my knees and scooping up the papers: sheet music, and lines of script. It is all horribly muddled. I think of Mr. Clements and rain-soaked music; a silent moment shared between us. But unlike Mr. Clements, Larry Snyder merely laughs and stands over me as I fumble about and try to pick everything up.

"We really must stop meeting like this . . . goodness, I don't even know your name."

"Dorothy," I mutter. "Dorothy Lane."

"Well, Dorothy Lane, we really must stop meeting like this or people will start to talk."

I glance up. "I don't know what you mean, sir."

He smiles and winks. "Oh, I think you do."

I scoop the pages up as quickly as I can, stand

up, and hand them to him, adjusting my cap and straightening my apron.

He looks at the mixed-up papers. "Well, if Mademoiselle can make any sense of the scenes now, she really does deserve the part." I look blankly at him. "I'm her manager," he explains. "We work very closely together. Are you the maid for her room too?"

I nod. "I've been asked to stand in for her lady's maid. She's been struck down with a fever in Calais."

"Then I expect we will see even more of each other, Dorothy Lane." He looks at me through narrowed eyes, placing the papers under his arm and making a square of his fingers again, framing my face between them, just as he did in his own room. "Really quite alluring. No doubt you've dreamed of being on the stage, or the screen?"

I shrug my shoulders. What business is it of his?

He smirks. "Very well. Be coy and demure. But if you ever want a professional photograph, or if you'd like to audition . . ." He pulls a business card from his inside pocket and hands it to me.

I hesitate.

"Take it. Throw it in the garbage if you wish. Or keep it. It's entirely up to you." He folds his arms across his chest. "But remember this, Dorothy Lane, nobody ever made it in this business by being coy and demure. Fortune favors the brave. Isn't that what they say?"

He holds the card closer to me. I take it from him, shove it into my pocket, and hurry off down the corridor.

As I leave the dazzle and glitz of the upstairs and travel back down to the darker corridors of the staff floor, I think about the butterflies trapped in their case on the governor's office wall. I take Snyder's business card from my pocket and think of the face in the photograph beneath my pillow. The person I long to be will always be pinned down by the person I once was.

After attending to my extra duties, I am late for supper and arrive in the Maids' Hall to great excitement.

Sissy grabs my arm. "Where've you been? It's snowing. Look!"

She drags me toward the window. The snow is coming down thick and fast. Some of the porters are having a snowball fight in the laneways below. We stand and watch for a while before Sissy pushes open the window and leans out, turning her head up to catch snowflakes on her tongue.

Soon we all join in, taking turns to lean out into the cold air, and for a wonderful moment I am neither trapped in my past nor reaching for my future. I am exactly where I belong. Not looking forward. Not looking back. Just laughing, and catching snowflakes as they tumble from the sky.

18
LORETTA

I look for him on every street corner,
in every passing car, in every silent flake.

There is a curious stillness about London when it snows. Like everyone else, I feel compelled to gaze skyward and marvel at the spectacle. As I look up, I give space to my private thoughts, to matters more important than hats to buy and rehearsals to attend and what one should wear to unwelcome invitations to tedious dinner parties. Something about the crisp white of the snow gives me the courage to face my darkest fears.

The first light feathers soon become thick fat flakes that form a white blanket over the roof-tops and gas lamps and shop awnings of Regent Street. I find it extraordinarily pretty, delighting in the scene despite the fact that I know the snow will be the ruination of my good silk shoes. A young boy—a scruffy urchin from the East End by the look of him—hurries past with his mother, sticking his tongue out to catch the flakes. I smile as I watch him from the warmth of the car, envying his childish ways. I wasn't permitted such vulgar habits as a child. In many ways, I wasn't permitted a childhood at all.

My driver comes to a stop outside the stage door where the gallery-ites are already waiting for me, undeterred by the weather. I stop to sign a few autographs, my gracious gesture sending the girls into a hysterical frenzy until Jimmy Jones tells them politely that that will be all and ushers me inside.

I'm looking forward to the performance. We are at that wonderful point in the show's run where the cast all have great confidence in each other and know their way around the stage and the script as well as they know their way around their own homes. We have perfected our timing and costume changes so that we can relax and truly enjoy what we are doing. In another fortnight we will be stale and lazy. A week after that we will be longing for the run to end. For now, we are in that wonderful sweet spot and I feel myself falling in love with the profession all over again.

Like a lover's return after a long absence, I revel in the sensation of familiarity and give a tremendous performance. The crowd show their appreciation with a long standing ovation and the cast reciprocate with several curtain calls. I make a short speech of gratitude. As I'd feared, the photographs of my sudden departure from Claridge's made the front pages, accompanied by spurious claims of a nervous breakdown.

I'm determined to put an end to the rumors.

"You have all been marvelous in your recent concern and well wishes, and I am most grateful for it. However, as you can see, I am perfectly well. Better, in fact, than ever! I, ladies and gentlemen, am a reminder that one shouldn't always believe what one reads in the newspapers. Nervous breakdowns are for anxious lady drivers, not for Loretta May!"

I sweep from the stage to thunderous applause and I hope that is the end of it.

It is still snowing as I step out of the taxicab in The Savoy courtyard for the after-show supper party. I tip my head back to look at the falling flakes.

"Beautiful, ain't she?" I turn to see the doorman looking skyward beside me. His cheeks flare red against the cold air.

"I'm sorry?"

"London. She's beautiful when it snows."

"She most certainly is. It makes one feel quite childlike." I stick my tongue out, mimicking the urchin I'd seen earlier.

He laughs. "Have a good evening, Miss May."

"You too, Bert."

Pushing a manicured hand against the swing door, I'm pirouetted into the warm interior of the hotel. The lights of the chandeliers dazzle against the frosted glass paneling of the ceiling. The scent of cigar smoke and expensive perfume wraps itself around me, the lilt of the piano mingling gloriously with the clink of silverware and crystal and the merry chatter of post-theater diners in the Grill. Cocktail pages dressed in white and gold flit about like butterflies. A waiter waltzes past with a silver tray covered in gemstone-colored cocktails, cloakroom attendants busy themselves with coats and umbrellas, and the headwaiters stand to attention, ready to receive late diners for the restaurant. Everything blends into a beautiful symphony of charm and elegance. I can't blame Reeves-Smith for his gloating. This really is London's finest hotel.

I walk slowly toward the concierge desk, leaving whispers and glances in my wake. I may not be the beauty I once was, but I can still stop people in their tracks.

"Good evening, Miss May."

I turn to greet Reeves-Smith, offering him my hand and a dazzling smile. "George! How wonderful to see you." George Reeves-Smith takes great pleasure in fawning around his more esteemed guests. He has a rare talent for making one feel like the only important guest in the hotel.

"What a pleasure to see you," he gushes, leaning forward to kiss the air to the side of my cheek as he clicks his fingers behind my back and motions discreetly for a cloakroom attendant to take my cape.

I feel as light as air as the silk lining slips from my shoulders and the great weight of velvet and mink is lifted from my narrow frame. "And it is always a pleasure to see you, my good man, and your wonderful hotel." I know how he likes to be flattered.

He flushes with pride and tugs at the dickey bow around his neck. I run my fingers flirtatiously along my string of emerald beads.

"And to what do we owe the honor of your presence with us this evening, Miss May?"

"I have an overwhelming yearning for one of Ada's cocktails, George, and band music that only your esteemed establishment is capable of supplying. Where else could one possibly wish to be?"

He escorts me personally to the ballroom, following the sweeping stairs and wide corridors. I am dressed in gold lamé and lace. Eyes turn to admire me as I glide along the marble floor, shoulders back, chin high. Seeing the others already seated at our table at the very front of the stage, Reeves-Smith bids me a good evening.

We drink and gossip and smoke cigarettes as Mr. Somers's Orpheans band plays wonderfully, but it is only when I am halfway through my third martini cocktail that I begin to fully relax. I'm delighted to see that Perry and Bea are getting along rather well. She and the others are all talk of a midwinter's eve party they are planning with

Elizabeth Ponsonby. Of course, it isn't any usual sort of party. There is talk of a strict dress code of white clothing only and Cecil Beaton is planning to set up a studio to photograph the guests posing with paper moons and stars. It all sounds rather glorious.

I accept an invitation to dance with André Charlot, another great theater producer and rival of Cochran's. The two of them are in constant competition with one another to put on the biggest hit of the season. Charlot has wanted to engage me for his revue for years. He has come very close to charming me with his seductive French ways on more than one occasion, but my loyalties lie firmly with dear Cockie, the man who first discovered me and has never let me down. Nevertheless, I admire Charlot's work and I wonder if I might put in a good word for Perry.

"Is that brother of yours writing anything decent at the moment?" he asks as he leads me expertly around the dance floor. "I'm looking for something different for next season. The audiences are becoming bored of the same numbers and the same format of revue. I want something different. Something exciting."

I tell him Perry is working on new material. "He's even found himself a muse, André. Imagine that. I can hardly wait to see what wonders he starts to produce!"

"I would love to discover a new young star," he

says. "It has been an age since we discovered anyone really special. Someone such as yourself when you first started out, or Tallulah."

"Surely there are any number of girls *you* could turn into a star."

He brushes aside my flattery. "I find that everyone is too polished these days, or too similar to everyone else. There's no spark. Nothing original. I want someone imperfect. Someone I can mold. You might let me know if you notice anyone promising in the chorus."

I laugh as he leans me gently back for the end of the number. "I will do no such thing, Mr. Charlot! Promising stars you will have to find on your own. But I will certainly mention the music to Perry whenever I can drag him away from Bea Balfour."

Tiring of the conversation around the table, I stay on the dance floor. For once, I enjoy the fuss and attention of the endless line of gentlemen who wish to dance with me. The flurry of snow has everyone childish and gay. I drink and dance too much and the night passes in a heady blur.

As the band strikes up the exhilarating new Charleston number that everyone is so mad about, I excuse myself to powder my nose, walking more than a little unsteadily as I cross the room. And that is when I see him, and my world comes crashing in around me.

It is unmistakably him, standing at the bar,

cigarette in hand, hat on his head, a silk scarf draped elegantly around his neck. And yet, it can't be.

He leans with one elbow on the bar, his hand under his chin. His ankles are crossed so that I can see his socks. Plaid. His favorite. His jacket falls aside to the left and I see blue braces, the very same blue braces I had so admired in Harrods and insisted on buying for him, despite his protestations.

"Roger?" His name is a whisper on my lips. "Roger. Is it you?"

Everything slows down, my steps labored as I move toward him. He takes a sip from his glass. Hennessy XO. I am certain of it. The thump of the band, the laughter of the guests, the sumptuous surroundings of the Grand Ballroom all fade into the background as I slip underwater. There is nothing but him. I reach out my hand, but he is too far away. "Roger!" He cannot hear me and everyone is rushing to the dance floor and I cannot see him. I strain my neck, rise up onto my tiptoes, and wave my hand in a strange sort of greeting. "Roger! Roger!" I am shouting now, and I am being jostled backward. I am moving away from him. I stumble and push against the tide of eager young things rushing to the dance floor, until they pass and I am at the bar.

But he is gone.

I look around, to the left and the right, frantic

to find him. An empty tumbler sits on the bar. I lift it to my lips. Hennessy XO. I can smell him.

"Miss May? Is everything quite all right?"

The bartender has hold of my hand. I am shaking. "He was here. Right here. Did you see him?"

He looks puzzled. "Mr. Snyder? Is that who you mean? Yes, he was here."

"No. Not Snyder. Roger. Officer Dawes. He was right here." I am panicking, my breaths coming fast and shallow.

He gives me a sympathetic look. "I'm sorry, miss. I only saw Snyder. He always drinks XO."

The pain shoots through my head like daggers. I falter for a moment and grip the edge of the bar.

"Would you ask for a driver? I need to leave immediately. Tell my brother I have a headache. And not to cause a fuss."

The snow is still falling in fat dizzying flakes as I am driven back to Mayfair. I look for him on every street corner, in every passing car, in every silent flake, but he isn't there. He will never be there, his absence a dull ache within me that no amount of morphine can ever suppress.

I've heard them talk about women who see their dead husbands and sons. Delayed grief, they call it, another of the neat little labels the War Office attached to things we had no words to explain. And yet I was so certain he was there.

I stumble into the apartment, and make for the writing table where Elsie keeps her scrapbooks. I throw everything aside, my reckless noise waking her in the process. She emerges from her bedroom to see what all the commotion is.

"Leave me," I tell her. "I need to be alone."

Except I don't. I need to be loved. I need to be held.

I find the small package I'm looking for at the back of a drawer, tied with silk ribbon. My letters to him, my photograph captured in a newspaper cutting, the image of the beautiful actress he had fallen in love with before he even knew my name. SOCIETY DARLING AND BRAVE NURSE VIRGINIA CLEMENTS REVEALED AS WEST END STAR LORETTA MAY! All of it now melded together into a strange singular bulk.

They told Roger's mother he must have kept the letters in the breast pocket of his greatcoat, where they were found when they discovered his body beneath the earth and twisted metal. They told her it was the heat from the explosion that had caused them to melt into this strange mass. Reading my name and the address of the theater on one of the letters, his mother had sent them on to me, along with the terrible news of his death. She didn't know of the love affair we had engaged in through years of writing to one another. She didn't know of the passionate three nights we'd spent together. She didn't know he left a widow to grieve for him.

Only Jimmy Jones, the stage-door manager, ever knew that we had corresponded. Only he knew about the whirlwind wedding we arranged when Roger came home on leave. But even Jimmy didn't know about the child I carried for three months and lost one beautiful summer's day. That was my secret; a secret I carry alone, deep within my heart.

I hold the letters in my hand as I allow Elsie to help me dress for bed, too weak and exhausted to protest any longer. She makes tea that I refuse to drink and I sulk like a child until she brings brandy. She waits with me, like a patient mother, until the tears stop. I want to thank her, but I can't. I want to talk about him, but I don't, because if I do, if I open up this secret part of me, I don't know how I will ever stop.

19
DOLLY

"Everything might be the start of
something wonderful, but it usually
turns out that it isn't."

After a week of juggling my regular chores and
fitting in the requirements of Mademoiselle
Delysia, I'm relieved when my afternoon off
comes around again. Since it was Clover's
birthday at the weekend, we both pay for a sixpenny dance with a male instructor at the Palais.
I'd forgotten how lovely it feels to be whisked
around the dance floor with confidence and
poise and strong arms. I let the dizzying sound of
trumpets, banjo, and piano envelop me as the
instructor's arm circles my waist and he guides
me around the dance floor.

Clover has new paste beads. A gift from
Madam for helping with a large luncheon. Life at
Grosvenor Square has certainly improved since I
left. I don't remember staff ever being given a gift
apart from the traditional one on Boxing Day.
Still, I can't begrudge Clover nice things, not on
her birthday. Sitting down for a short break, we
talk about our week, but I can't concentrate. I can

only think about my meeting with the musical composer in the tearooms.

Clover tires of repeating herself as my thoughts continually wander. "What's got into you, then?" she asks. "'Cause something's on your mind." And then she remembers. "It's today, isn't it? Your meeting with the composer."

I stare into my tea. "Yes. Four o'clock at the Lyons' Corner House on Coventry Street."

She leans back in her chair and blows out a long trail of smoke. "You're still going then?"

I nod.

"Who is he anyway?"

"I've no idea. That's why I'm meeting him. To find out." She says nothing. Her silence is unsettling. "I don't have to meet him again if he's dreadful," I continue. "And it's a public place, so there's no danger of him kidnapping me or anything else you're imagining. He might be a perfect gentleman, Clover. This could be the start of something wonderful!"

She sighs and takes hold of my hand. "I wish I could have some of that optimism of yours, Dolly. Everything might be the start of something wonderful, but it usually turns out that it isn't." She looks deep into my eyes. "But I know you well enough by now. There's no point me saying anything. I can tell you're set on meeting him."

"I am."

"Then go. Have a cup of tea and a slice of cake.

See what he wants his *muse* to do, but don't say I didn't warn you if it isn't as straightforward as he makes out in that little notice of his." She sees a flash of doubt in my eyes. "I'll come with you if you like. I'll hide around the corner. Keep an eye on you. Make sure he doesn't follow you back to the hotel or get up to any funny business."

I like the idea. I *am* apprehensive, although I won't admit it to Clover. "Would you do that? Really?"

"What are friends for, eh? You can give me a signal if you think he's genuine."

"What sort of signal?"

"I don't know. Drop something and pick it up. Jump up and down. You can sing the bloody national anthem for all I care. As long as you're happy, Dolly, that's all that matters. And I know you're never happier than when you're chasing those dreams of yours."

For the first time that day I notice how tired she looks. "Is everything all right, Clover?"

She pushes a loose hair behind her ear and stands up. " 'Course it is. Come on, then. I've been practicing the new Charleston step. Let me show you how to do it properly, and then we'll go and meet this mystery man of yours."

We laugh and rush to the dance floor and let the music transport us to a place where dreams always come true and everyone is the perfect gentleman.

• • •

We arrive at the Corner House twelve minutes early. I'm bursting for the lav and jiggle around, my nerves not helping matters. I glance at my watch again and again, but the minutes drag along. Now I know why I'm never early for anything—waiting around is awful.

With Clover lurking a little distance behind, I distract myself by admiring the window display of biscuits and cakes and handmade chocolates that all look too good to eat. I linger in front of a florist's shop beside the tearooms, watching a lady dressed in black who fusses and tweaks at blooms in tall vases although they seem perfectly arranged to me. The flowers are a lovely splash of color among the gray murk. They remind me of a rainbow and a summer rainstorm when me and Teddy had watched the rain pelting against the kitchen window while I grumbled about not being able to get out for our picnic. He'd kissed the frown lines from my forehead and lifted my finger to chase the raindrops down the glass. Then we blew warm breaths onto the windowpanes and drew shapes with our fingers. "Some days try to suck the color and joy from everything and everyone, Dolly," he'd said. "Same with people. Don't let them. Don't let them spoil things for you." We had our picnic in the end, rain and all. Soggy sandwiches. Damp cake. Cold tea. Clothes that clung to us like weary children and a perfect rainbow arching above us as the rain stopped and the sun peered through sulky clouds.

It was the loveliest picnic we ever had. It was also the last.

"Excuse me. I don't suppose you would be Clover Parker?"

I turn around at the sound of the voice behind me. I recognize him immediately.

Gray eyes stare back at me. A sandy mustache curves into a broad smile. "My goodness! It's you!"

He remembers me. After all this time, he remembers me. "Mr. Clements!"

"Miss Lane, isn't it?" he asks, holding out his hand.

My relief at seeing his familiar face is so immense that I grasp it as if I am drowning and might never let go. "Yes. Dorothy Lane. Dolly, for short."

He holds on to my hand longer than necessary. Perhaps he is drowning too. "Dorothy Lane. The girl who knocked me to the ground."

"The girl who helped you to your feet."

He laughs. "And that, Miss Lane, is the fundamental difference between people—the manner in which they experience things." He looks at me, as if trying to work something out while I feel myself falling into those gray puddles. "I must apologize, Miss Lane. You'll think me awfully rude, but I'm actually here to meet someone."

I glance down at my feet. "I know. Clover Parker."

He releases my hand. I put it deep into my coat pocket and wrap my fingers around the photograph.

"Yes. Clover Parker. How on earth . . ."

"It's me, Mr. Clements. *I* replied to your notice. I had no idea it was you, and I'm ever so glad that it is." We stand and grin at each other. For a moment we are back in the rain on the Strand. "I used a friend's name," I explain. "I'm not really sure why."

He takes off his hat and runs his hands through his hair. I still want to touch it. My heart hammers. My mouth is as dry as paper. I think about the pages of unplayed music beneath my pillow and I want to hear the melody more than ever.

He whistles through his teeth. "Well, I'll be dashed."

"Me too."

My words are making no sense. I catch a glimpse of Clover over his shoulder. She is pointing at him and waving frantically but I'm too distracted to acknowledge her.

"So, shall we have that cup of tea? Of course, I quite understand if you would rather not. Now that you know who wrote the notice. I'm sure you think it most irregular. I'm really not in the habit of advertising for such things. It was all my sister's idea. She's an actress. They have

ridiculous notions like that rather too frequently."
I can think of nothing sensible to say as he opens
the door and stands to one side. "Perhaps I can
explain a little better inside."

I walk ahead of him. He smells of musk and
lemons and Scotch. With all thoughts of sinister
men forgotten, I hold my head up high and walk
into the tearooms. I forget to give Clover the
signal. Like the most dreadful friend, I forget
about Clover entirely.

The Corner House is lovely. Far nicer than the
places Clover and I usually go. There's a gentle
background noise of polite chatter, and a soft fog
of cigarette smoke adds an intimate atmosphere.
I feel horribly underdressed as the waiter takes
my coat; my plain navy cotton shift has seen
better days. I'm grateful for the sweep of Sissy's
Vermillion on my lips.

We sit at a jolly little table beside the window.
Mr. Clements moves a vase of red carnations to
one side so we can see each other without having
to peer over them. We both order coffee and he
orders two slices of cherry cake. He drinks his
coffee steaming hot, while I stir sugar into mine
and send half of it sloshing into the saucer. I fidget
in my chair, crossing and uncrossing my ankles
beneath the linen tablecloth as if I am knitting
with them. I knock over the pepper pot as I reach
for the milk.

He lights a Gold Flake. "Do you?" he asks, offering them to me.

"I shouldn't really, but I do."

"Doesn't everyone?"

"They say cigarettes help to keep us ladies slim."

I take one and lean forward as he strikes a match and lights it for me. My fingers are trembling so much that the cigarette bounces up and down on my lips. I take a long drag. It is much stronger than the cheap cigarettes I'm used to and the rush of nicotine goes straight to my head. I admire the imprint of red lipstick on the tip.

"I suppose your friends thought you were meeting some sort of lunatic?"

I laugh. "Yes! They're expecting to find me floating in the Thames tomorrow morning. You can tell me now if that's your plan and I'll finish my coffee and be off."

He leans back in his chair. "I can assure you I have no intention of going anywhere near the Thames. Never did care for the water. I'm not a great swimmer."

"Me neither."

"Then let's stay on terra firma, shall we? I get the feeling we would be quite hopeless at rescuing one another."

That familiar feeling I had the first time I saw him comes flooding back. There is something about the way he talks. So assured and precise. I want to tell him about the music that I fished out of the litter bin. I want to tell him it has been beneath my pillow and in my thoughts—that *he* has been in my thoughts—ever since. But I don't.

We talk easily as we work our way through the slices of cherry cake. He tells me about the music he has written and the theaters he has played in. I listen, wide-eyed, hooked on every word. I tell him about life at The Savoy and how I love to dance at the Palais on a Wednesday. The conversation is easy and comfortable. We laugh, we smile, we blush in awkward pauses and show the very best of ourselves. He is awkward and bumbling at times. Cracked and flawed. Not the perfectly polished gentleman I'd imagined him to be. He is far more interesting than that. I haven't felt this relaxed in a man's company since Teddy.

Teddy.

After all these years, there is still a sense of betrayal within me when I think of him; a voice that wants to be heard. I gently close that door in my mind. For now, I want to focus only on the man sitting opposite me.

Time passes quickly in Mr. Clements's company. I drink far too much coffee and have to excuse myself to visit the conveniences. When I return, he isn't at our table. Presuming he has taken a trip to the gentlemen's room, I settle back into my chair. But he doesn't appear, and after sipping on the dregs of cold coffee and feeling rather silly, I catch the waiter's attention.

"You didn't see the gentleman I was with, did you?"

He nods. "He asked me to give you this, miss."

He hands me a folded sheet of paper. I wait for him to busy himself at another table before I open it up.

Dear Miss Lane,

It was very kind of you to meet me and I appreciate your time. How strange that we should meet again! However, I'm sorry to say that you are not quite what I am looking for. I need someone with more experience in the theater. I am terribly sorry for wasting your time. I thought it might be easier to explain in this short note and save you the embarrassment of a protracted farewell.

I do hope you can forgive me and I wish you well in your position at The Savoy.

Peregrine Clements

The color drains from my cheeks and sinks through my body all the way to my feet. I don't understand.

The waiter appears at my side. "Is everything all right, miss? Can I help you with anything?"

I stare at him. "No. No, thank you."

"The gentleman paid the bill before he left. Should I fetch your coat?"

"Yes. Please."

He can't bring my coat soon enough. I rush outside, desperate to get away from the whispers and curious looks. I stand on the pavement, hoping to catch a glimpse of him, but he has vanished. Clover is nowhere to be seen either and only now do I remember that I was supposed to give her a sign.

I read the note again . . . *you are not quite what I am looking for* . . . We were getting along so well. What did I do wrong? What did I say?

Scrunching the paper into a ball, I throw it to the ground and stamp on it in a temper. Peregrine Clements may consider himself to be a gentleman, but he has made me feel as cheap as a backstreet prostitute.

I walk away from the tearooms, my feet thudding against the wet pavement, tears pricking at my eyes. I was a fool for believing in fairy tales. Piggy Griffin was right. I am a girl who will never get on in life. Never become anything. Never be good enough.

As I walk, an omnibus passes me, splashing filthy rainwater all over my stockings and shoes. I stop walking. All the bravado of grand adventures and new beginnings seeps out of me like spilled milk as tears of frustration fall down my cheeks. Nearly two months have passed since I started at

The Savoy and here I am, back where I started, alone in the street with sagging stockings and wet feet. I am no closer to finding him. No closer to making a better life for myself. No closer to my dreams.

Placing my hands into my coat pockets, my fingers find Larry Snyder's business card. He may be as oily as a rag in the printing room, but if Alice Delysia trusts him, why shouldn't I?

". . . remember this, Dorothy Lane, nobody ever made it in this business by being coy and demure. Fortune favors the brave. Isn't that what they say?"

I walk on, stomping through puddles, letting myself get drenched. I will swallow my pride and ask Larry Snyder for an audition. Sod Mr. Peregrine Clements and his silly little notices. Sod him altogether.

20
DOLLY

"You are like a cat with nine lives, Miss Lane.
The Savoy seems determined for you to stay."

On my return to the hotel, I am met by stern
expressions and anxious glances in the Maids'
Hall, where everyone is assembled. I don't even
have time to remove my coat or hat before I'm
instructed to stand beside the table with the
others. I look for Sissy and Gladys, but they won't
meet my gaze.

O'Hara stands in front of us all, her face scarlet
with rage. "Something has occurred which causes
me great concern." We all look at each other,
fearing the worst. "A hair comb is missing from
one of the guest suites. We have reason to believe
that it has been stolen."

A gasp ripples through us like a breeze.
Everyone averts their eyes, the guilt implicit on
each of our faces, even though we know it wasn't
us. We shuffle uncomfortably in our shoes.

"I am quite sure that I need not spell out the
severity of the punishment for anyone found
guilty of tampering with guests' possessions, or
stealing from guest apartments. This particular

251

item is missing from a suite on sixth. Sixth-floor maids, remain here. Everyone else may return to their rooms."

I smile awkwardly at Sissy and Gladys as they disappear. I know I have nothing to worry about, but there's something formidable about O'Hara's outrage. There are four of us left. I stifle a cough, the irritation in my chest bothering me again.

O'Hara stands in front of us. Arms folded. Veins protruding. "If anyone would like to own up, now would be a very good time to do so. Otherwise, I will be forced to inspect your rooms. It is an indignity that I am sure none of us wishes to endure unnecessarily." There is a terrible pause. The clock ticks loudly on the wall behind me. "Very well. I can only wonder how such a thing as a hair comb could really be worth it."

Leaving the Maids' Hall, O'Hara commands us to follow her. There is a stony silence as we walk along the corridor. Outside my room, I'm surprised to see Snyder.

O'Hara approaches him. "I have spoken to the maids, Mr. Snyder, and I'm afraid that nobody has come forward. I am left with no choice but to carry out a search."

"Would you mind if I wait?" he asks. "Mademoiselle Delysia would very much like the comb returned as soon as possible." My breath catches in my throat. Mademoiselle Delysia? I feel guilty merely by association. "It belonged to her mother," Snyder continues, "and carries a great deal of sentimentality. Such matters would usually be handled by her lady's maid but, as we know, she is indisposed."

O'Hara is flustered. "Yes, of course you may wait. It won't take long."

My heart thumps beneath my dress. My legs feel like lead. Snyder leans casually against the wall, ankles crossed. I smell Virginia tobacco as I walk past him into my room. I can feel his eyes settle on me, but I refuse to look at him.

Sissy, Gladys, and Mildred are already waiting in the room.

"Did you do it?" Sissy whispers as I walk in.

"No!" I reply. " 'Course not!"

Sissy shrugs her shoulders. Gladys keeps her eyes fixed firmly on the floor. Mildred stares straight ahead.

The four of us stand near the window as O'Hara opens drawers and cupboards and lifts books on nightstands. Her inspection revealing nothing, she tells us to get ready for bed, and makes to leave. As she does, Mildred asks if she might have a word in private. They step to one side and lower their voices so that I can't hear what is being said. Nodding as she listens to whatever Mildred has to say, O'Hara turns back to us.

"Remove your bedcovers and lift up your pillows."

I can't wait for this to all be over. I've had a bad

enough day as it is what with Mr. Clements running off like that, and it's unsettling to know that Snyder is lurking outside the room, especially when I've decided to approach him about an audition and have absolutely no idea how to mention it without making myself sound desperate and needy. He strikes me as the sort of man who would be quick to take advantage of a desperate, needy girl.

I lift my pillow and hug it to my chest, the crumpled pages of sheet music exposed for all to see. I think of my embarrassment at being left in the tearooms and want to throw them into the fire. At least my photograph is safe in my coat pocket, away from prying eyes. I bend to pick up the papers but O'Hara snatches them from me, holding them by a corner as if they were infected with the Spanish flu.

"And these might be?"

"Just some papers," I say. "I'm minding them for a friend."

"Under your pillow?" I nod. "Do you keep many things under your pillow?"

I shake my head. "No, miss."

She takes the pillow from my hands, giving it a slight flick of her wrist to loosen the cover. An ornate silver hair comb tumbles from the fabric and settles on the bed sheet.

I take a step back. I feel choked, my breaths thin and shallow. "But . . . how did that get there?

I swear I didn't do it. I didn't take it. I've never seen it before!"

Sissy and Gladys look horrified. Mildred remains stony-faced. O'Hara snatches up the comb and grabs me by the wrist. Tears spring from my eyes as she marches me from the room, where Snyder is still lurking in the corridor.

O'Hara stands in front of me and hands him the comb. "The good news, Mr. Snyder, is that we have found the missing hair comb."

"That's a relief. Mademoiselle will be very pleased."

"The unfortunate news is that we have a thief in our midst. I shall take her straight to Mr. Cutler and have her collect her things."

I plead for O'Hara to believe me, protesting my innocence as she drags me along the corridor. Tears stream down my face. I see Mildred close the door to our room, shutting me out.

Snyder follows us. "Perhaps the girl should at least be heard."

O'Hara stops. "There is nothing to be heard, sir. The hair comb did all the talking for her."

"Perhaps. But I wonder if I might propose something."

He looks at me. I can't bear to meet his gaze and stare at the floor, everything blurring as I wipe hot tears from my cheeks with the palms of my hands.

He lowers his voice as he takes O'Hara to one

side of the corridor. I can just make out what he says. "Mademoiselle is an extremely generous person. She would not wish to see someone turned out at her expense. Perhaps some other punishment might be considered. Reduced wages. Or extra duties? I am sure we can reach a more satisfactory conclusion than seeing this young girl cast out onto the street. It is approaching the season of goodwill, after all. I presume that extends to maids as well?"

O'Hara looks flustered. "Well, I really should . . ."

Their conversation is interrupted by the appearance of a porter at the top of the stairs. He runs up to O'Hara. "Sorry to bother you, Miss. Spot of bother in a suite on seven. A young lady thinks she's going into labor. They've asked for more towels and a doctor."

O'Hara looks at the porter and at me and at Snyder.

"I'm very happy to handle this," Snyder says, nodding in my direction. "I'll take her straight to the head porter. Cutler, isn't it?"

O'Hara nods. "Very well. Take her straight to his office. I'll join you there as soon as I can."

She rushes off to attend to the emergency, leaving Snyder and me alone in the corridor.

"Somebody must have put it there. You've got to believe me," I plead. "I've never seen it before. I promise."

He says nothing as he guides me down the staff

stairway. On the ground floor, we walk to Cutler's office, where he raps on the doorframe.

Cutler looks up from a great pile of paperwork on his desk. "Ah. Snyder." He stares at me as I wipe the tears from my eyes. "Nothing wrong, I hope?"

Snyder lowers his voice. "Would you mind if we stepped inside, dear fellow? Spot of bother with one of the maids. I told your head housekeeper I would handle it. She was called to attend to another matter."

"Of course. Come in. Come in." Cutler flaps about and pushes the papers to the side of his desk. He tugs at his bow tie to straighten it.

"I didn't take it. I promise." I start sobbing again as Snyder offers me a handkerchief. I can smell his cologne as I dab at my cheeks.

Cutler is confused. "Take what? Whatever has happened?"

Snyder relates the events in a low tone and I notice him slip something into Cutler's hand before he leaves us.

I sniff and sob. I am utterly wretched and confused. "I don't know what's worse, sir. Being accused of something I didn't do, or knowing that someone dislikes me so much that they intended for this to happen."

Cutler pours himself a sherry and turns his back on me to drink it quickly. "Yes. Well. Snyder, being a capital fellow, has asked, on behalf of

Mademoiselle Delysia, to have the matter overlooked. He believes that you didn't take the hair comb, and are the unfortunate recipient of a malicious prank. He wishes no more to be said about the matter. He assures me that would be Mademoiselle's wish."

I wipe my nose. "Really?"

"Yes. Although if it were up to me . . ."

"So, can I go?"

"*May* I go? *Sir.*"

"May I go, sir?"

He sits back in his chair, blows onto his spectacles, and rubs the lenses with his handkerchief. "Yes, you may go, but for the life of me I'm not sure why you should. You are like a cat with nine lives, Dorothy. The Savoy seems determined for you to stay." He glowers at me and replaces his spectacles. "I am, nevertheless, quite sure that Mrs. O'Hara will have more to say on the matter when she is relieved of the other crisis she is dealing with. Consider this a reprieve. Nothing more. Your name is appearing too often in my ledger."

"Yes, sir."

I skulk from the office and make my way back to second, my mind whirling with thoughts of who would have done this, and why. The only person I can possibly think would do such a thing is Mildred, but I don't know how she would have got hold of the hair comb in the first place, or why she should dislike me so much.

Exhausted after everything that has happened, I'm relieved to get back to the room and find that it is empty, the others using the bathroom. Alone for a few moments, I dress for bed and climb wearily beneath the covers.

Mildred is the first to come in. "Still here, then."

I glare at her. "Snyder intervened. I've been given a reprieve."

"You're lucky. Most girls would have been out on their ear."

"I didn't take it anyway. But I think I know who did."

She sits on her bed and fusses with her hair. "I know you think I did it, but you're wrong. I have no wish to cause trouble for anyone."

"Then who did?" I ask.

"None of my business."

She picks up a sheet of writing paper. I watch her for a moment as I pull on my nightcap. "Why are you so quiet, Mildred? So secretive?"

She puts her pen down and looks at me. There's a lost look in her eyes that I haven't noticed before. "It's perfectly acceptable to be quiet, isn't it? We don't all have to bounce around like an omnibus or be constantly powdering our nose, do we?"

I shrug my shoulders. "Suppose not."

She keeps looking at me as the fire crackles in the grate. "You don't remember me, do you?"

I shake my head. "I thought I recognized you,

but I'm not sure where from. And I've never known a Mildred."

"But you've known a Vera Green."

In an instant I know her. Edie Bishop and Vera Green. From the Mothers' Hospital.

"Come along, now. Don't be making a fuss. It'll be much easier if you just let go." The awful tugging of my fingertips. The hollow ache in my arms; the weight of his absence. A woman in a yellow coat, the color of daffodils.

"Vera Green." My words are a whisper in the dim light of the room. "Vera Green. From the Mothers' Hospital?"

She nods and puts her pen and paper on her nightstand. "We all have secrets, Dolly. We all have a past."

She settles beneath her bedcovers as Sissy and Gladys barge back into the room. Gladys doesn't say much to me, but Sissy is all talk about the incident with the hair comb.

"I can't believe you weren't given your notice. You lucky cow!"

I explain how Snyder intervened and arranged for the whole matter to be overlooked. Sissy wants to go over it all again and again but I ask her if we can leave it for tonight. I tell her I'm worn out from all the drama.

The truth is, I'm too distracted by thoughts of Mildred and the Mothers' Hospital and too angry with Mr. Clements and too ashamed at having to accept the help of awful Larry Snyder. I pull the bedcovers tight up to my chin and wait for Sissy to turn out the light.

As I lie in the dark, the ghosts of my past creep closer. I think about him. I see his sleeping face as I lean over his cot. So innocent, unaware that he is about to be taken from me, unaware that another woman will soon press her cheek to his and feel the unfathomable lightness of him as she rocks him in her arms. I remember how Teddy's little camera shook in my hand as I fumbled to expand the lens and press the shutter. I can still hear the click and whir of the mechanism as his image
was captured within the tiny machine. Just one exposure left on the film. The only chance I would have to remember him. A face in a photograph.

My little Edward.

My child.

My reason for everything.

ACT II

Love

LONDON
1923–24

There is a gallery first-nighter—a girl or woman with a shrill treble—who most disconcertingly persists in screaming to actors and actresses, good, bad, and indifferent, “You’re marvelous! You’re marvelous!”

—Newspaper review,
V&A Museum Theatre Archive

21
LORETTA

There is an art to dying convincingly.
Apparently, I do it rather well.

I suppose one shouldn't need a reason to visit
one's brother, but I have such an aversion to his
dismal little flat above the theater that I must find
compelling motives to go there at all. Discovering
what happened with his muse is one. Telling him
about my illness is another. Whilst I've thus far
managed to admirably cover up my episodes with
excuses about exhaustion and headaches and too
many cocktails, I don't know how much longer I
can keep up the pretense. And yet I struggle to
find the words to tell them: Perry, Bea, Cockie,
Elsie, Hettie, Aubrey, Mother and Father. How
exactly does one bring such a grim and depressing
matter into the conversation?

"Ice and a slice?"

"Yes, please, darling. Oh, and by the way, I'm
dying. They tell me I have a cancer. Dreadful
nuisance, isn't it. Anyone for croquet?"

If only somebody could write the script. If only
I could rehearse the lines and deliver them as if it
were all another performance. I have died at least

a dozen times onstage. There is an art to dying convincingly. Apparently, I do it rather well. But this is not a performance. This is frighteningly real.

My hesitation not only comes from my staunch denial that I am ill at all, but from the knowledge that as soon as I tell people, everything will change. I won't be me anymore. I'll be someone who is dying. People will look at me in that awful sympathetic way and nobody will know what to say. They'll tell me how dreadfully sorry they are and we'll all feel crushingly awkward until it is me consoling them. I cannot bear it, and so my illness remains as silent as an unplayed gramophone record.

Perry's apartment at the top of the Strand Theatre is small and overfurnished with distasteful pieces collected from here, there, and goodness knows where. It is horribly suffocating in the summer and depressingly damp in the winter.

"How on earth Mrs. Ambrose can even begin with the dusting is beyond me," I say, sweeping my glove across a wonky shelf cluttered with ghastly china dogs and blown-glass figurines of deer and swans. The trail my finger leaves behind in the dust suggests that dusting it is beyond Mrs. Ambrose too.

Perry ignores me and stares at his reflection in a small hand mirror perched on a shelf above the washbasin. The crack in the mirror has been there for as long as I can remember. He says it is a reminder of his imperfections.

I watch as he rubs at the lines on his forehead as if to erase the memories etched into them. He looks older than his twenty-nine years. Dark shadows beneath his eyes suggest another restless night. He has seen countless doctors, but they tell him there's nothing they can do for him, apart from the drafts they prescribe to help him sleep. They say the memories that haunt him will fade, that he'll forget, in time.

I light a cigarette and sit down on a couch that has seen better days in some far-distant past. "Can't you speak to the management about fixing the lift? It really makes me cross to think of you climbing those stairs every day. You are wounded, Perry. You aren't as physically capable as you used to be."

He scoffs at my concerns. "Wounded! I have a limp, Etta. A bloody limp. Couldn't even get injured properly, could I?"

"*Perry!* That's a dreadful thing to say."

"Well, that's what Father thinks. Some poor buggers came home without their legs or arms. After everything they did for this country, they're reduced to begging outside the train stations. *That's* what makes *me* cross." He splashes water over his face and stares into the mirror. "In the grand scheme of things, I really don't think it is such an imposition to walk up a few stairs. Do you?"

He ignores my mutterings and disapproving tuts. "Anyway," I continue, "I don't understand why you choose to live here at all when there are so many nicer places you could have."

"I like the location. And this place has character. It talks to me."

"It's the damp you can hear talking to you, darling. It talks to me too." I take a bottle of perfume from my bag and spritz a little here and there to mask the musty smell.

The truth of the matter is that Perry doesn't want to live in luxury in Mayfair or Belgravia. He's had enough of grand houses and the stuffy rules they come with. I can't say I blame him. When I first started touring with productions, I relished the freedom of distant hotels and boardinghouses in much the same way that I had relished the freedom of the hospital dormitory. Cockie always made sure we stayed somewhere respectable and I came to enjoy the liberty those places provided. Even when I performed in London, I preferred to board at the Theatre Girls' Club in Soho rather than return home to Nine Elms. It was a shocking departure from the living standards I'd grown up in, but it was convenient and daring. More importantly, it was somewhere my mother wasn't.

Perry passes me a gin and tonic and pours himself a Scotch. I swirl the liquid around in my glass, silently lamenting the absent clink of ice. "So, are you ever going to tell me what happened with your *muse* or am I going to have to play a tedious game of charades?"

"You don't have to say *muse* like that. You can just say 'muse.' " I roll my eyes at him. "She was very pleasant."

"Oh dear."

"What do you mean, 'oh dear'?"

"Pleasant is a dreadful way to describe someone. It's like saying someone is nice. Pleasant and nice people are like flat champagne. They're no fun."

"Then she was delightful."

"Better."

"I already knew her, as it happens."

"Oh?"

"She was the girl I bumped into outside The Savoy a few months ago. Do you remember? I was on my way to meet you for afternoon tea."

"Yes. I remember. You had a hole in your trousers and you made a show of me in Claridge's. The very same girl? How extraordinary."

"Isn't it." He takes a long drag of his cigarette. That telltale pause of his.

"And?" I prompt.

"And I walked out on her."

"You did what?!"

"I walked out on her. I left her in the Corner House."

"Without saying good-bye?"

"I left her a note." He takes a big slug of Scotch. "And paid the bill."

"Oh, well, that's all right, then. I'm sure she was perfectly happy and hasn't given it a second thought." I stand up and walk to the fireplace to warm my hands. "What a beastly thing to do, Perry. One doesn't invite a person to tea and then simply disappear. You're not Harry Houdini, for goodness' sake. You're impossible. Really and truly."

I'm restless. On edge. With every pause in the conversation I try to summon the courage to tell him, but the words won't come. I move over to the window seat and take a long drink as I look out of the large curved window, focusing my frustration on the busy street below. I watch a mother bend down to comfort her child who has fallen and grazed her knee. It is such a simple gesture, the two of them lost in a private moment as the world goes on around them. Little things like this catch my attention now. Quiet moments. Connections.

"So, what was wrong with her?" I ask.

Perry sits in his favorite chair beside the fire. He picks at his fingernails. Fidgets with his mustache. "Nothing. Nothing at all."

I take a long drag on my cigarette holder. "Then I simply don't understand. You're so infuriating!"

Perry runs his hands through his hair, sending it sticking up this way and that. "I don't understand it myself. It just all felt too . . . sudden. The truth is that I haven't stopped thinking about that girl since I bumped into her. There was something about her that day; something different. And of all the people in London, *she* was the one to reply to my silly little notice. I know you don't believe in such things as love at first sight, Etta, and I know it sounds ridiculous and unconventional, but after spending half an hour in her company, I think I felt myself falling in love with her."

"You *think?*"

"Yes. I'm not sure. How can one be?" He drains his drink and slams the glass down onto the mantelpiece. "That's why I left her, and that's why I can't see her again, because the notion of falling in love terrifies me."

I know he is thinking about Bea, that he is weighed down with the regret and guilt he carries heavy in his heart over her. I have no words to comfort him.

The room falls silent other than the crackling of the fire and the rumble of underground trains that rattle the glass in the window frames. Now would be a good time to tell him, but the words stick in my throat.

"Did she really leave that much of an impression on you? After one meeting?"

"Yes. And it's been two meetings. And a letter." He pokes sulkily at the fire. "But she's just a maid.

How can I possibly fall in love with a maid? Mother would die of shame. And as for Father. It doesn't bear thinking about."

"Ah. I see. *Just* a maid. Not good enough for a Clements boy. That's what you're afraid of—other people. My goodness, Father was right. You really are a coward." My words are unexpectedly harsh, smothering the room with an atmosphere as thick and heavy as the acrid fog outside. "There. I've said it. And now you hate me and will probably never speak to me again. But I'm not sorry. Sometimes the truth needs to be spoken, Perry, regardless of how painful it is to hear or to say. In fact, there's something I've been meaning to—"

"I don't hate you, Etta. I'm not especially fond of you at this particular moment, but I don't hate you." He walks to the writing desk and sits at the chair, his shoulders slumped like an old man. "You're right. I *am* a coward. I didn't have the courage to stand up to my convictions. I shot men who were far braver than me. They stood by their principles, laid down their arms, refused to fight. I was just a puppet following orders, taking instruction, just like I always have." He kicks against the writing table in frustration. "I'm a coward and a failure. I can't even be pleasant to a bloody hotel maid."

His voice is choked. It is uncomfortable to hear. I wish I could throw my arms around him and tell him it will be all right, but I don't know how. I stand stiffly by the window, as inanimate and cold as one of his silly little figurines on the shelves.

"You know what people are like, Etta. They have standards. Expectations. I could never take someone like Miss Lane to the Mitfords' New Year party. I'd be the laughingstock. They all think I'm enough of a joke as it is."

"Miss Lane. So she has a name after all." I sigh and stretch my arm behind my head. "What was in it for her, anyway, this arrangement of yours? Why did she want to be your muse?"

"I don't think she did particularly. She wants to be a dancer. Wants to be on the stage. Lead a more exciting life. I expect she was attracted by the prospect of getting to know someone in the business."

"So she was using you to her own advantage?"

"I suppose she was."

"Good for her. I rather like the sound of this Miss Lane." I finish my cigarette, crushing it in the ashtray on the sideboard. "In fact, I wonder."

"What do you wonder?" Perry eyes me suspiciously. "You worry me when you wonder."

"I wonder if we might not be able to come to some sort of arrangement whereby she inspires you and we improve her."

He looks at me. "What do you mean, *improve* her?"

"What if you were to have your weekly tête-àtêtes, let her amuse you and distract you from your melancholy, let her inspire your compositions, and in the meantime we teach her how to behave more like the sort of person you *could* take to the Mitfords' party. It can't be that difficult. Rosie Boote was as sophisticated as a stick when she first started in the chorus. And now look at her, the Marchioness of Headfort! If Rosie Boote can become a lady, anyone can." The more I think about it, the more I like the idea, and I'm quietly confident that Perry's lifelong affections for Bea will never be replaced by those for a maid. If I can just encourage him to play along, to let this girl into his life, it might lift him out of the doldrums he's been languishing in for far too long. "I can help with the more feminine things. I can give her dance training if she's serious about it. Does she get time off?"

"Yes. Wednesday afternoons and alternate Sundays."

I am suddenly full of purpose and in a tremendous hurry. I grab my coat off the back of the battered old sofa. "Let me find her and apologize on your behalf. We can improve her together. It'll be fun."

He looks doubtful. "You make her sound like a toy."

"I'm serious, Perry. In fact, I'm most exhilarated at the prospect. Is she pretty?"

"Yes, but . . . this is madness, Etta. I'm the last

person she'll want to see after my appalling behavior. And how on earth will you find her?"

I sigh and place my hands on my hips. "How many hotels do you know in London called The Savoy? Honestly, darling, have a little sense. I'll talk to Reeves-Smith. I could find her this afternoon if I wanted to. And in the meantime, you can start working on a new piece. Charlot was asking about you. Says he's looking for something new. Something different."

"Like what?"

"I don't know. You're the composer. Write a piece about Miss Lane."

"But I hardly know anything about her."

"Precisely. You know enough to be afraid of falling in love with her, but not enough to have discovered her flaws and irritations and annoyances. There is no better time to write a song about her. Use your imagination. What does she look like?"

A small smile plays at his lips. "Deep brown eyes to get lost in. A face like a love heart. Perfect vermillion lips and a smile to brighten the dreariest day."

"My goodness. You really have fallen, haven't you?" He shrugs. "Imagine if you could see those lips every day, could kiss them, taste them. Send your heart on a rampage, dear boy, and the music will follow."

I pick up my hat and gloves and bend to kiss

him on both cheeks. As he looks up at me I see something of hope in his eyes.

"I'll see you next Wednesday," I say. "Don't be late."

Despite my enthusiasm for this little project, I walk slowly down the three flights of stairs, each step reprimanding me. You should have told him, Loretta. You should have told him. But when I see how lost and confused he is, I realize how much Perry needs me. Like so many others, he relies on me. Cockie, Jack Buchanan, the rest of the cast, the girls in the gallery who have saved everything to come and see me—they all rely on me in one way or another.

I can't burden them with my sadness.

I must entertain. That is all. I must stand in the spotlight and play my part because that is what I do, what I am good at, what made me who I am.

I may not know how to die, but I do know how to live and I do know how I can help my brother. Right now, that is all that matters.

22
DOLLY

I close my eyes, imagining that
I am dressed in lavender chiffon;
soft silver dance shoes on my feet.

An entire season has passed since I arrived at The
Savoy. The last golden touches of autumn have
made way for the bare branches of winter. A
biting wind blows off the Thames with a temper,
pushing people along the pavements, billowing
out coats and skirts and turning umbrellas inside
out. The fogs come thick and often, the days are
short, the gas lamps in the street and the lights in
the hotel suites burn ever longer. Another year
nearly over. Another year in which my child has
not known me.

Mildred and I haven't spoken again of our
shared past. She keeps her distance and remains as
frosty as the glass at the windowpanes. While
part of me wants to talk to her, wants to ask a
thousand questions, I'm afraid she won't have the
answers I long to hear. The matter isn't discussed
between us again.

The incidents that blighted my first weeks are
thankfully no longer spoken about, although I

know that a record of my misdemeanors is written in stark black ink inside Cutler's ledger. I'm learning that life in a hotel moves in peculiar ways. An incident with a stolen hair comb can be hushed up at the request of an influential guest; a crisp note slipped from one hand to another can see the end to a matter. The inevitable gossip about my own indiscretions has faded as new mistakes are discussed around the breakfast table: an undelivered urgent message, a too-hot iron left against a couture dress, a badly timed fumble with a delivery boy at the back of the storerooms, an overheard derisory remark about a guest. While O'Hara watches me like a hawk, I try to put the past behind me, and as the weeks come and go I begin to understand the governor's romantic sentiments about the hotel. I feel myself drawn to it as if it had a personality of its own. It lives and breathes, shocks and surprises me as much as the guests who occupy the suites.

The anticipation of Christmas fizzes through London's streets. The freezing December air licks at my ears and snaps at my cheeks. I sometimes feel exhilarated, sometimes exhausted; sometimes hopeful, sometimes despairing. When I tell Clover about the disastrous ending to my meeting with Mr. Clements, she takes me to see the window displays in Harrods and Selfridges, Hamleys and Liberty to cheer me up. The winter hats and gloves, coats and shoes are beautiful: thick felts

278

and velvets in all the latest colors, heavy furs in mink and sable. Like scruffy children from the East End peering through a sweetshop window, we stare in admiration. Londoners flock in their thousands especially to see Mr. Selfridge's spectacular displays. I listen to the gasps of rosy-cheeked children as they press their noses to the glass, squealing with excitement at the sight of nutcracker soldiers, pretty dollies, teddy bears, and wooden trains. I see small hands nestling in woolen mittens, held tight by fretful mothers and nannies. My own hands have never felt more idle.

Clover has another new coat for me to admire and envy—another hand-me-down. She treats herself to a new lipstick and a mascara in Woolworth's and insists on buying me a pair of real silk stockings, wishing me a happy Christmas as the shop assistant wraps them up for me. I don't know how she can afford all these things, but she tells me she's been saving her wages.

"What's the harm in treating yourself now and again?" she says. "There's no bugger else going to buy these for me, is there?"

She's right. There isn't.

The Christmas theater trip is a tradition of ours. We've saved for the tickets for weeks and queued for hours to secure our place in the gallery at the Shaftesbury.

We sit at the very top of the theater, a collection

of shopgirls and clerks, seamstresses and domestics, growing more hysterical by the moment. We've all come to watch our favorite stars; the beautiful women who occupy our thoughts as we stitch and type, scrub and sell. This is where we come to forget the dull monotony of our jobs. For a few magical hours we are not just ordinary girls, we are Tallulah Bankhead, Gertrude Lawrence, Bea Lillie, and Loretta May. From our perch high up in the Gods, we are as far away from the stage as it is possible to be, yet we will never feel closer to the people who fill our dreams.

Everyone is restless as we wait impatiently for the houselights to fall and the curtain to go up. Weeks of anticipation mingle with the swirling cigarette smoke that dances around the chandeliers suspended high above the gathering crowds. The excitement grows with each passing minute, fueled by the prickle of nerves that escapes from the dressing rooms and drifts along the corridors and staircases until the entire theater has a desperate urge to fidget.

Clover fusses at her hair, waved especially for the occasion. She folds her program, fanning cheeks that burn crimson with excitement and heat. We wave to friends along the row and turn to the girls crammed beside us to speculate about the performance and Miss May's costumes and the chorus numbers.

Pressed against the rail at the very front of the

gallery, I fan my face with my hat. Beside me, squashed so tight that I can feel every rise and fall of her breath, Clover stands with her feet splayed, her back arched, and her puce face tipped up toward the ornate ceiling. I burst out laughing.

"What's tickled you?" she asks.

"You look like an overripe tomato! If you go any redder you'll pop!"

"I'm glad you find it funny. You won't be laughing when you're telling everyone how I passed out from the heat and that you had to carry me outside and we both missed the whole bloody thing."

I pass her my hat. "Here. Have a go with this."

Clover's hat was lost in the stampede on the gallery stairs when the doors opened. "Leave it!" she'd cried over her shoulder, bracing herself against the handrails to make a gap for me after I'd stopped to pick it up. "It's a rotten color anyway. Come *on!*" Clover wasn't going to let a hat stand in the way of a place at the rail. Hers wasn't the only one to fall victim to the gallery crush either. A trail of discarded possessions littered the back stairs as we thundered up. I saw at least four pairs of gloves and three lost shoes.

I watch as the stalls begin to fill up, wishing I could afford the three-guinea ticket to be down there.

"I really need a pee, Clo."

"Me too. But we'll have to hold it. Far too late

to go to the lav now. Jiggle about a bit until the urge passes."

As the bells ring in the lobby, we link arms and hold tight on to the rail with our free hand, refusing to give in to the shuffling and shoving behind us as others try to wheedle their way to the front. Being so slight, I'm glad of Clover's ample girth. She forms a sort of barricade around us with her bottom so that nobody can dislodge us.

Gradually, the ladies and gentlemen, theater and film stars, dignitaries and socialites arrive to take their seats in the stalls. We all gawp at the elegance. Furs and satin, diamonds and silk, shingled hair, necklaces of big sham pearls and silver beads, velvet capes and brightly colored dresses. The collective trill of excitement from the gallery gathers into a shrill crescendo, filling the theater with a sound not unlike that of the Portobello Market. I see a lady in the dress circle place her hands over her ears, but we continue on. Gallery girls don't care for the delicate heads of fragile ladies.

And then the houselights go down. My heart pounds. There is never a moment when I feel more alive than just before curtain up. An outburst of screaming and applause erupts from the crowd behind me. Someone bumps into me and I lose my balance for a moment, grabbing on to Clover to steady myself as the orchestra strikes up the opening bars. The music sends a tingle through my entire body. The dazzling white spotlight pierces the gloom and the curtains fall to each side of the stage in great swooping arcs. I lean forward, my knuckles white as I grip the rail. The chorus girls glide onto the stage, the rhythmic kick and tap of their heels against the boards sending a thrilling reverberation throughout the auditorium. Such precision. Such beauty in their costumes of cream silk and black feathers. Their perfectly synchronized dancing grows into a marvelous, thundering finale, their heels snapping like a rainstorm against the boards.

And then the woman we have all been waiting for.

Loretta May.

The darling of the West End. The darling of London society. The rebellious society debutante dressed by Poiret and Lelong, photographed by Beaton, painted by artists, and written about by poets in their salons. It is Loretta May we have been waiting for. She is the reason we have saved every penny from our weekly wage to buy a ticket to tonight's performance, to stand for hours just to see her in the flesh. She is the reason middle-aged women had taken in the milk off their doorsteps that morning and left their bewildered husbands without their breakfasts as they'd hurried off to Wellington Street to join the queue for the gallery door.

She appears from the wings amid a great

stamping of feet and a frenzied cheering from the gallery. Tears prick my eyes as I tighten my grip on Clover's arm. Miss May's costume is beautiful: lavender chiffon with powder-puff posies at the waist and handkerchief draperies falling from either side of the skirt. Shimmering silver shoes with heels the color of cyclamen. Even several gentlemen in the stalls cannot resist the urge to stand up and shout their admiration.

Her very first line has the entire theater in peals of laughter. The Loretta May magic is in full force.

The show passes in a blur of dance, song, laughter, and wild applause. The final curtain prompts a great outpouring of affection from the gallery girls. "You're marvelous! You're marvelous!" we cry, our words echoing around the theater as we call for Miss May's return to the stage. But she is gone, and it is over.

As the houselights go up, Clover tugs at my sleeve. "Come on. We might see her leave."

"You go," I say. "I'll follow in a moment."

As the others rush back down the steep stairs, hoping to get an autograph or perhaps an invitation to the dressing room, or at least a glimpse of Miss May as she leaves for the after party, I stand and stare at the stage. I close my eyes, imagining that I am dressed in lavender chiffon; soft silver dance shoes on my feet. I deliver my lines with deliberate sass and perfect timing. The audience roar for more and call my name every time I emerge from the wings.

"Not got a home to go to?"

I open my eyes. An usher is sweeping the floor around me. "Yes, of course. Sorry."

"Fancy yourself down there, do you?"

"Pardon?"

"On the stage? All the gallery girls think they'll be on that stage one day."

"And what's the harm in that?"

The woman has a sour face and sucks in her bottom lip with a great slurp. "No harm. Ain't never gonna happen, though, is it? I dunno. You young girls with your heads all full of nonsense!"

She chuckles to herself and carries on with her sweeping as I pick up my handbag and make for the exit where Clover is waiting for me.

Outside, London is lit up like a circus. I stop to look at the front of the theater. LORETTA MAY blazes out in electric lights. I link my arm through Clover's.

"I think 'Dolly Lane' would look well in lights. Don't you?"

"I thought it was going to be Ninette Faye," she says, reminding me of the stage name we'd concocted years ago. I giggle and pull her closer to me.

We stroll together along Shaftesbury Avenue and across Cambridge Circus, my head a jumble of thoughts.

Clover notices that I'm quiet; distracted. "What's going on in that head of yours now?" she asks.

I rest my head on her shoulder. "Things."

She guesses what it is I'm thinking about. "Why don't you visit the hospital? See if you can find him."

"I tried that before. All I found was a dead end."

"But that was a few years ago. They might be more helpful now. There's lots of girls have found their babies, or at least had word that they're safe and well cared for. It might put your mind at rest if nothing else."

"I'm afraid, Clover. What if I *do* find him? What if I find him and can't bear to lose him again? What then? I'd be right back where I started."

She pulls her arms around my shoulder. "But you won't know until you find him, will you. And you can't spend the rest of your life wondering."

As we walk, we pass a brass band of ex-servicemen playing Christmas carols. Their sound is beautiful and haunting, the music drifting above the crowds of shoppers and theatergoers and revelers. As we stand for a moment to listen, I wonder what their stories are. Where they fought. Who they lost. How different their lives are now.

I wonder if Teddy hears music.

I wonder if he remembers how we used to love dancing.

I wonder if he thinks of me at all.

23
TEDDY

Maghull Military War Hospital, Lancashire
June 1919

It reminds me of a sunset I once saw
but I can't remember where, or who I was with.
I suppose it was Dolly.
It was always Dolly.

More beds lie empty. I am one of only half a dozen patients left on the ward now. I seem to have become something of a medical marvel to the doctors. I almost wonder if they don't want to let me go home so they can continue to write their reports about me. Not that I really mind. I will miss the nurse if I go home. She's become something of a special friend to me.

"I found another letter," she says. "It was written on Christmas Day. It seems a bit silly to read on such a lovely summer's day, but I suppose it doesn't really matter. Would you like me to read it?"

I nod.

She takes the letter from the envelope, pushes a curl from her eyes, and reads.

December 18th, 1917

Happy Christmas, Teddy!

How can it be the end of another year already? How can you have been gone so long? There's been seven babies born in the village while you've been away—and the eight kittens. Poppy is getting very big. She's the most gorgeous cat. I tell her all about you.

I hope the socks and muffler fit. I knitted them myself. I'm afraid I'm not very good with the needles. Some of the other women and girls knock them out in their dozens, but I'm still all fingers and thumbs and keep dropping stitches. Mam despairs of me. But I insist on trying and these are what I made. Mam says if they're no use to you as socks you could always use them as an extra pair of gloves. I knitted them in the colors of our factory football team: black and white. The stripes are a bit wonky, but I don't suppose that will matter much when they're shoved inside your boots.

What will you do to celebrate Christmas? I hope everyone will stop fighting, even if only for the day, and take time to remember their loved ones back home. It is so awful to think of men killing each other at Christmastime. I've put a small bottle of rum and some extra smokes into the parcel. The pudding is from Mam. She insisted on making dozens for the men from the village. It gives her something to pass the time and take her mind off things.

We had the first snow flurries last week. I'd forgotten how pretty the village looks when it snows. Everything felt so calm and quiet for a while it was hard to believe we are a country at war.

I hope you see a little snow this Christmas, Teddy. Your socks will keep you warm if it does. Even with their wonky stripes.

With all my heart,
Your Little Thing,
Dolly
X

Wonky stripes.

I remember the wonky stripes on the socks. Black and white.

When I close my eyes, I can see them in my hands. I can hear myself laughing, knowing how hard she must have worked on them.

I remember. For the first time since I came here, I remember.

I open my eyes. Beside me, she folds the letter and dabs at her cheeks with a spotted blue handkerchief. I feel sorry for her; sorry that she has to be here in this awful place on such a lovely day. It is a day for walking. I know she'd much rather be outside.

I reach for her hand, wrapping my fingers around hers. They are soft, like velvet. I close my eyes to a world of crimson and mandarin as the sunlight settles against my lids. It reminds me of a sunset I once saw, but I can't remember where, or who I was with. I suppose it was Dolly. It was always Dolly.

She sits with me awhile, dozing with me in the sunlight. Only when Matron comes round for her daily inspections does she gather her things and leave. I watch her until she disappears through the swing door.

At the window, the butterfly spreads its wings, basking in a beam of sunlight. I sense that it is restless; that it will soon fly, and when it does I will watch it go, happy for its freedom.

It isn't mine after all. It isn't mine to keep.

24
DOLLY

"I'm not like that, Mr. Snyder.
I'm not that kind of girl."

Distracted by Christmas and the exhausting schedule of parties and luncheons, Mademoiselle Delysia appears to have forgotten about finding a new lady's maid. I've settled into a comfortable arrangement where I know her routine and little nuances and she trusts me to do what is necessary. I know which dresses and shoes to lay out for her various engagements and appointments, and although I rarely see her in person, when I do she speaks softly and smiles sweetly and I bathe in the glow of her attention for hours afterward.

As for Snyder, I still mistrust him and his motivations for helping me out over the hair comb, but I eventually found the courage to approach him about an audition. It was an uncomfortable conversation, which left me far less excited than it should have, but as I'm beginning to understand, dreams don't always arrive wrapped up in pretty packages. Sometimes they are awkward and misshapen and difficult to hold on to. I have to grasp any opportunity that comes my way.

When I'm alone, doing out my allocation of suites and apartments, I often think about Sissy telling me how the maids try on the ladies' shoes or take a spritz of perfume. I remember how she'd draped an evening dress across her front and pretended to waltz around the room on our first morning's work together, the hanger flapping down the back of her neck. She'd laughed at me when I told her she shouldn't. I've known lady's maids who have messed around with their mistresses' belongings, but that was usually done in temper, a reaction to years of being put upon and talked down to. While there is less cause for bad feeling and resentment in the hotel, temptation is still everywhere.

I especially admire Mademoiselle Delysia's dresses. She has the most magnificent Lanvin and Vionnet evening dresses in chiffon and satin that shimmer beneath my fingertips, and day dresses by Lucien Lelong with perfect pleats and soft lace trims. And apart from the dresses, her shoes are the most exquisite things I've ever seen. She owns a particular pair of dance shoes that catch my attention every time I see them. The silver brocade fabric is woven with a delicate pattern of roses and elaborate cutwork in the leather. Beautiful silver buttons secure the T-straps. The leather inside is embossed with the manufacturer's mark: *Perugia, Faubourg Saint-Honoré, Paris.* So many times I've picked them up to wrap them in tissue paper before placing them into their velvet pouch and back into their box. So many times I have paused, and wondered.

I hesitate now as I put them away, running my fingertips over the soft fabric as I lift them to the window to admire the way the light shimmers and shifts across the material. I place one beside my foot. They are my size. Dare I?

Rushing to the door, I press my ear to the wood-work, listening for sounds of anyone approaching. All is quiet. I make the decision quickly.

Perching on the end of the bed, I kick off my dull black shoes and slip my feet inside the soft leather. They feel wonderful. A perfect fit. I stand up and walk across the carpet and back. I do a twirl, a little hop, a step, and a kick. I stand in front of the looking glass to admire my reflection. My feet in silver shoes. So beautiful.

As quickly as I put them on, I take them off and return them to the wardrobe, my heart pounding with the thrill of having taken something without permission. As I attend to the rest of my work, billowing out the fresh bed linen, plumping pillows, rubbing thumbprints from gilt cigarette cases, my feet still feel the sensation of soft leather and the silver shoes nag and nag at my thoughts.

My audition with Snyder is arranged for nine o'clock on my Sunday off. He tells me to go to the stage door of the Prince of Wales Theatre. I have a borrowed dress from Clover, my dance leotard, and my battered old dance shoes. Apart from that, I have only my dreams for support.

He is standing outside when I arrive and grins when he sees me, crushing his spent cigarette beneath his shoe. "Ah. Good. You're here. You'd be surprised how many don't show up."

I look around. "Where are the others?"

"The others?"

"The other girls auditioning."

He laughs. "But this is a private audition, Miss Lane. Arranged especially for you. I suppose there has to be some benefit to cleaning a Hollywood manager's hotel suite!" He senses my hesitation. "Half the girls in London would be here in a heartbeat, but if you'd rather wait in a long line and take your turn . . ."

"No. It's fine." I offer a nervous smile and step into the dark corridor. Snyder closes the door behind me with a thud.

"Do you need to change?" he asks.

"Yes. Please."

"Dressing room's on the left. Take as much time as you need, then make your way to the stage."

I wander along a narrow corridor until I find the dressing room and close the door behind me. I look for a lock, but there isn't one. I drag a chair toward the door to block the entrance. It is better than nothing.

I place my bag on a stool and drape my coat over the back of a chair. The room is small and cold. I shiver and rub my arms to keep them warm. A long dressing table sits along one wall, electric lights around the mirrors reflect off the glass. Every surface is covered with costumes and props. The dressing tables are cluttered with makeup and glitter and open pots of cold cream, the deep grooves of finger marks left in the cream. The air smells of Pears soap and hair spray. It's as if the performers have just stepped out. I try to not let myself be distracted by the thought of where I am and who might have been here last night, and change as quickly as I can into my dance leotard, keeping one eye on the door. I do a few quick stretches and high kicks and make my way back along the corridor toward the stage. It's such a long time since I last auditioned. I feel rusty and unsure and I hesitate at the steps that lead to the wings. Concentrate, Dolly. Concentrate. Taking a deep breath, I step out onto the stage, my heels clacking against the boards as I walk toward the spotlight in the center.

The auditorium is dark and silent.

"Hello?" My voice sounds impossibly small and lost.

Snyder steps forward from the wings on the opposite side of the stage. "Don't worry. I haven't abandoned you." He gives me a quick once-over but doesn't remark on my appearance. "Did you bring any music?"

I hand him the pages of music, the same pages I've trawled around half of London over the last few years. He studies them for a moment and laughs. "Shouldn't we try something a little more modern? I presume you know the Charleston?"

"Of course."

"Good. I'll play and you give me your best steps." He hops down into the orchestra pit. "By the way, don't you want to ask me?"

"Ask you what?"

"Why I helped you out with that business over the hair comb."

I squint through the dazzle of the spotlight, raising a hand to my eyes to shield them from the glare. "I presumed you were just following Mademoiselle Delysia's wishes."

"You presume an awful lot for a maid. I don't recall hearing a thank you."

His words are cutting. I swallow hard. "Thank you. It was very good of you to step in."

"You should remember your manners, Miss Lane. Poor manners can land a girl in trouble."

I look down at my feet, hoping he can't see the reddening of my cheeks. This isn't how it should be. This isn't what I'd imagined at all.

He laughs. "Why so serious? I'm only teasing you! Pulling your leg—isn't that what you Brits say? That's all forgotten about. Yesterday's news."

He coughs and settles himself at the piano. "I'll count you in. Ready?"

I nod. My heart thumps in my chest. My legs shake like jelly. My mouth is as dry as an autumn leaf.

"Three, four . . ."

The first bars of music burst into life. He plays well. I try to shake off my nerves and think about how often I've watched the girls dance on this very stage, and I smile my best smile and tap and twirl and kick as high as I can, stretching my arms out on either side, imagining that I am part of a line of girls all dancing together and that I am not alone in this vast place with a man I do not trust.

As he plays the final bar, the chord fades and all is silent. I stand in the center of the stage, my breathing heavy.

I hear Snyder chuckling from the darkness as he offers some measly applause. "Not bad. A little rusty, but I've seen worse. I don't know why, but something about you amuses me, Miss Lane. You're really quite charming. You remind me of Bea Lillie when she started out. Charlot's little clown." He laughs to himself. "Do you sing?"

"A little."

"What do you know?"

My mind goes blank. " 'Look for the Silver Lining,' from *Sally*."

I give a dreadful rendition, during which I hear him snigger again. I apologize at the end. "I'm

297

very nervous, Mr. Snyder. I'm sorry. Should I start again?"

He hops back up onto the stage. "Dear God, no. Don't start again. Not to worry. We all suffer from nerves. Wouldn't be human if we didn't."

He stands in front of me, hands on his hips, looking at me.

"So, how did I do?" I ask, longing for this to be over.

"That depends."

"On what?"

"On what you can do for me in return."

In an instant, I am back at Mawdesley Hall, pressed against the wall of the butler's pantry, the squeak of his shoes against the linoleum floor, the stench of Virginia tobacco covering my mouth. My first instinct is to run from the stage, but I don't. Anger rises from somewhere deep within me. I'm tired of men like Larry Snyder trampling all over me.

I stand as tall as I can and look him straight in the eye. "I'm not like that, Mr. Snyder. I'm not that kind of girl."

He bursts out laughing; a cruel mocking laugh. "What? Oh, you hotel girls and domestics. You're all the same. One thing on your mind. I suppose when you've spent your life surrounded by filth it's bound to creep into your mind as well as under your fingernails."

I flinch at the cruelty of his words and walk

from the stage, my legs trembling so much that I can hardly put one foot in front of the other.

He calls after me as I step down from the wings, but I ignore him and run to the dressing room. As quickly as I can, I throw my dress over my leotard, grab my coat and bag, and run back along the corridor to the stage door and out into the street. I turn to check if Snyder has followed. He hasn't. I close the door behind me and burst into tears.

I stand in the street, not sure where to go as I pull on my coat and hat. My hands tremble as I try to do up my buttons. I look at the ugly calluses on my hands, the immovable marks of who I am and who I have been, the scars of a life surrounded by filth.

"Miss Lane?"

I look up, wiping my eyes with my coat sleeve. "Mr. Clements? What are you doing here?"

His brow furrows with concern as our eyes meet. "Goodness, Miss Lane. Is everything all right? You're crying."

He reaches a hand out to me but I pull back. "I'm fine. Everything's fine."

"Are you quite sure? You really don't look as if everything's fine." He takes a handkerchief from his breast pocket and passes it to me. I take it and blow my nose as he glances at the stage door behind me. "I'm not sure they open for a few hours yet."

I look down at my feet. "I'm not going in. I was just leaving."

"I see. Well, perhaps I could walk you somewhere?"

"I'd rather be alone. I'm good at being alone. Especially in tearooms."

He winces at my sniping remark. "Ah, yes. About that. I should explain . . ."

But before he has the chance, the stage door opens and Snyder walks out. "Still here, Miss Lane?" I ignore him. Perry looks from me to Snyder and back again. "You'd be advised not to spend too much time hanging around stage doors," Snyder continues. "You'll get yourself a reputation."

Perry extends his hand. "I don't believe we've met. Peregrine Clements."

Reluctantly, Snyder responds. "Snyder. Larry Snyder. Visiting from Hollywood." He looks at me. "She's not bad, if you're looking to fill the back row of the chorus."

"Actually, Mr. Snyder, I was just about to escort Miss Lane home."

Snyder scoffs. "Home! Well, I suppose a hotel is home to some. I'll bid you both good morning." He's still laughing as he turns the corner.

Perry puts his hands in his pockets. "Well, he seemed perfectly dreadful. I presume he's the reason for your tears."

"He's not the only reason." My words are sharper

than I'd intended, but I'm glad of them all the same.

Perry shuffles his feet awkwardly. "Are you quite sure I can't walk you back?"

"I'm quite sure." I'm angry with him—with everything—but there's a hopelessness in his eyes that I can't fully resist. "But thank you. For stepping in."

"It was the very least I could do, Miss Lane. The very least."

I offer a limp smile and walk away from him, part of me wishing he was walking beside me, part of me wishing I'd never set eyes on him, and all of me wishing I could crawl into my bed and hide from the world.

I walk along the Embankment to be beside the river. A stiff breeze tugs at my hat. The tips of my ears burn with the cold. I pass the pavement artists, the men and women I see here most weeks. I stop to watch them work for a while, particularly the artist who separates himself a little from the rest of the group. I've watched him work before, attracted by his use of vibrant colors. Today he has drawn several images of the same young girl. In one, her face is set within the trumpet of a daffodil. In another, she has butterfly wings. He works carefully, shading and adding definition until the girl looks as if she could almost fly free of the paving stones and walk among us. I put two pennies in his cap and walk through the Embankment Gardens to the hotel.

Back in my room, I change out of my dance leotard and pull my travel bag from beneath my bed, taking out the scrapbook I've kept since I was a young girl. *Dolly's Dreams*, it says on the front. The pages crackle as I turn them. The paper is yellowed in places, but the images are no less stirring. I remember each one, each beautiful face, each glowing review. There are not many benefits to working in service to a wealthy family, but one is having access to discarded newspapers and magazines. Nobody knew that as I scrunched up pages to lay the fire or dry the insides of sodden riding boots, I tore out the parts I wanted to keep and put them in my pockets. In the privacy of my room I trimmed the edges, making them perfectly straight before sticking the cuttings into my scrapbook with a paste of flour and water. I remember the tingle of excitement as I looked at those images night after night, by candlelight or gaslight. What would it be like to dance on a West End stage? What would those dresses feel like against my skin? These were the images and words that kept my soul alive as I emptied chamber pots and drew water from the frozen pump on a frigid winter morning. These are the images and words that light a fire in my belly now as I turn the pages, dozens and dozens of them, filled with my dreams.

I should probably give up. I should have given up many times before, but I can't. I keep coming back to these pages; to *Dolly's Dreams*, the naïve hopes of a young girl. I no longer chase a life onstage for myself. I chase it for a man called Teddy and a little boy called Edward, the boy I named in my mind, if not on paper, for the man who I had always imagined would be the father of my children. They are the reason I will keep going, keep trying, despite men like Peregrine Clements and Larry Snyder who dent my confidence and make me feel like dirt. I keep going for Teddy and Edward because if I stop now what on earth did I lose them for?

I turn the pages in the scrapbook until the cuttings end. The remaining pages are empty, a reminder that my dreams, and the column inches dedicated to theatrical reviews, were temporarily replaced with the stark realities of war.

As I close the book, my thoughts turn to my lost father and sisters, to Mam—alone in our little house in Mawdesley—distant fragments of my life, scattered across England. If only I could keep everything I have loved in one special place. If only I had a scrapbook to hold them all together.

If only.

The words that dreams are made of.

25
DOLLY

"If nothing else, it will give you the opportunity to tell him what dreadful manners he has."

Over breakfast the next morning, O'Hara asks if she might have a quiet word.

My heart sinks. "What have I done now, miss?"

She looks at me with something like compassion. "You've done nothing wrong, Dorothy. For once, I have no reason to reprimand you."

She takes my arm and guides me into a narrow linen cupboard in the corridor. In a hushed voice, she gives me the most extraordinary message. I am to meet a friend of the governor's at the Weeping Muse monument in the Embankment Gardens at two o'clock. The friend, she informs me, is a very well-known actress. Her name is Loretta May.

I barely feel the cold as I rush along the cobbles toward the river and the Gardens as the church bells across the city chime the hour of two. I see her immediately, a tall slender woman standing in front of the Weeping Muse, the monument to the composer Arthur Sullivan.

I hang back for a moment and watch her. She leans forward slightly, resting a hand against the back of the statue known as the weeping muse of music. I try to compose myself, but it is impossible. I am about to speak to Loretta May. I've seen almost every play she's been in. I've applauded her until my hands are sore. I've waited for a glimpse of her as she rushes from the stage door.

I move forward until I am right behind her. "Excuse me."

She turns around. She is even more exquisite close up. Dark gold hair like syrup, perfectly styled. Heavy-lidded eyes, seductively penciled with dark kohl. Arched eyebrows. Crimson lips. She smells expensive and luxurious. She dabs her eyes with a lace handkerchief and places it in her pocket.

"Miss Lane?"

I nod. "Yes. They told me. At the hotel."

"Thank you for coming." She extends a willowy arm and holds out a gloved hand.

I shake it and hope I can bring myself to let go. "It's such an honor to meet you, Miss May. You're very huge. I'm a beautiful fan. I mean, you're very beautiful and I'm a huge fan." I'm talking nonsense. My teeth chatter with cold and nerves.

She chuckles. It is a mesmerizing, seductive sound. "You're very kind to say so. I think!" A stiff breeze whips around us, ballooning out our coats and threatening to dislodge our hats. "Gosh, that wind. It brings tears to one's eyes," she remarks, dabbing at her eyes again. "Let's walk. It's far too chilly to stand about."

My steps fall in time with hers as we follow the path through the Gardens. I am walking beside Loretta May. Clover would die if she could see me.

"You must think this all terribly unconventional, Miss Lane."

"Yes! I can't actually believe I'm here. With you!"

She smiles politely, but I sense she isn't interested in flattery today. I scold myself for being so giddy and excited.

"It's about my brother, you see."

"Your brother?"

"Yes. I'm afraid he acted rather appallingly toward you." She stops walking and looks at me. "My brother is Peregrine Clements. You might know him better as a 'struggling musical composer.'" I am speechless. Loretta May is Perry Clements's sister. She starts to walk again. "Frightful business, abandoning you like that in the tearooms."

"He told you?"

"He did. And I told *him* he was beastly to do such a thing. Someone with his upbringing should have better manners."

I'm not sure what to say. "It was a bit of a shock. I thought we were getting on very well."

"It was downright *rude*. But he's dreadfully sorry. Truly. He's really a very decent chap. I think he panicked."

"Panicked?"

She turns to face me. "Look, it's rather difficult to explain, but the reason I wanted to meet you, Miss Lane, is to ask if you might give him a second chance."

I'm not sure what I was expecting when O'Hara gave me the message about meeting Loretta May, but it certainly wasn't this. "But he left me a note. He said I wasn't what he was looking for."

"Oh, never mind all that," she says, waving a gloved hand dismissively as she walks on. "He's a damned nuisance. Doesn't know what's good for him. You have every right to be furious with him and I understand if you never want to see him again—I'd prefer not to see him myself sometimes, but sadly one cannot choose one's family."

I *am* furious with him, but I haven't been able to stop thinking about him. Nor have I been able to throw his silly music in the fire as I'd promised myself I would.

Miss May sinks her chin into the fur collar of her nut-brown velvet coat and indicates that we should sit on a bench. "I'm intrigued, Miss Lane, as to why you replied to his notice in the first place. I presume there is more to this than the appeal of cherry cake and tea?"

I push my hands deep into my coat pockets, my fingers curling around Edward's photograph. "You think it was silly of me, don't you. My friend Clover said the same."

"I don't think it was silly of you at all. Actually, I think it was rather brave."

I've never thought of myself as brave. I suppose I was, in a way.

I look at this woman, my idol, beside me and see a warmth in her piercing green eyes, a sense of someone other than the famous actress hidden within them. I have nothing to lose, so I tell her the truth. "I want more than a life as a maid, Miss May. I dream of dancing on the stage and when I saw the notice, I thought it might bring me a step closer to that dream. If only for an hour a week." It all sounds so silly and unlikely as I say the words aloud.

She nods and places her hand on my lap. "I understand." She looks at me, *really* looks at me as she takes my chin in her hand and angles my head gently toward the sky. "There's something about you, Miss Lane. I see it in your eyes. A sense of something more." She pauses for a moment and lights a cigarette, offering me one. I decline. I'm trembling so much I'm sure I would drop it. "So, I'd like to propose one more meeting," she says, "in my apartment to keep things on neutral territory. If Perry does anything to remotely offend or upset you, I promise we will never bother you again. I will be there to make you feel more comfortable. I'll skulk about behind the door and you can call for me at any moment and that will be the end of it." She studies me, watching for a reaction. "You have Wednesday afternoons off, I believe?"

"Yes. And alternate Sundays."

"Then come on Wednesday afternoon. I'm at Fifty-Four, Berkeley Square." I think about Clover and our arrangement to go dancing at the Palais. She'll understand. "If nothing else, it will give you the opportunity to tell him what dreadful manners he has. I've always found something rather pleasing about having the last word in a disagreement. I'm offering you the chance to have yours."

There is a wonderful sense of mischief in her eyes. Clearly, this is a woman who is used to getting what she wants. "How can I say no to Loretta May?"

"Oh, you'd be surprised, darling. Plenty of people do." She stands up and we walk on. "You won't regret it, Miss Lane. I will make it my personal business to see that you don't."

It is easy to see why so many men have thrown themselves at her. She really is the most beautiful, enchanting woman I've ever met.

As we approach the end of the path and the steps

down to Embankment underground station, a few flakes of snow begin to fall. Miss May holds out her hand, letting the snowflakes settle onto her black glove.

"Did you know that every snowflake is unique, Miss Lane? That every one of these tiny fragile flakes is as individual as you and I. I find that remarkable. Just because we cannot see their beautiful little structures doesn't mean they're not there. They are all around us, and they are no less beautiful for our blindness."

There is a lovely musicality to her voice. I could listen to her all day.

"Well, I mustn't keep you." She offers her hand. "Thank you, Miss Lane. It has been a pleasure to meet you." I stand mute before her, too starstruck to say anything in reply. "My brother will not let you down a second time. I promise. Oh, and I almost forgot." She hands me an envelope. "Two tickets to my latest show. Do come along. It's rather jolly."

I can't take my eyes off her as she disappears beneath the archway and walks toward the river, shoulders back, head held high, neat dainty steps. I glance at my black shoes. How can I ever emulate such elegance when I'm cursed with such ugly footwear?

As I walk back through the Gardens, I pass the monument of the Weeping Muse. I must have walked past it a dozen times but have never stopped to look at it properly. I read the inscription above the bust of Arthur Sullivan.

Is life a boon? If so, it must befall that Death, whene'er he call, must call too soon.

I wonder what the words meant to Miss May. Whatever it was, they stay with me as I walk back to the hotel, pondering what has just happened.

I will go and see Perry again because Loretta May asked me to, and while I may very well end up wishing he would rot in hell, I already know that Loretta May I would follow all the way to the stars.

26
DOLLY

"But we all wrinkle and fade in time,
Miss Lane. Even the most beautiful bloom
must eventually wither and die."

Wednesday cannot come quickly enough. I am restless and distracted, rushing my work and snapping at Sissy when she asks me what's wrong. I haven't told anyone about my disastrous meeting with Perry Clements, or my awful audition for Snyder. The shame of both lingers around me, affecting my mood so that I am irritable and short-tempered. And while Mildred acts as if we had never spoken about our shared experience at the Mothers' Hospital, she still watches me, judges me. The sight of her stirs uncomfortable memories that nag at my conscience, telling me I should have done more to find little Edward.

As soon as my morning rounds are finished, I change into the neatest dress I own and take the omnibus from the Strand along Haymarket and Piccadilly to Green Park, from where I walk up Bolton Street and along Curzon Street toward Berkeley Square. I know the area well, it being only a few streets away from the Archer residence on Grosvenor Square. I skirt around the square and run past the sweeping crescents of Mount Street and Carlos Place. I have a note in my pocket for Clover to explain why I can't meet her at the Palais today.

I'm relieved that it is a new maid who opens the door rather than anyone I know—too many explanations and too much conversation would be needed and I don't have time for either. The maid tells me Clover has already left for her afternoon off.

"Will you give her this when she gets back?" I hand her my letter. She takes it from me and puts it in her pocket. "You won't forget. It's important."

She assures me she won't forget and slams the door in my face as her name is shouted down the passageway.

Rushing back to Berkeley Square, I arrive at number 54. The houses in the square are tall, terraced town houses; suites and apartments occupied by the very wealthy. I make my way down a short flight of steps to the deliveries door, ring the bell, and wait. I fidget and glance at the steps behind me. Should I forget all about Miss May and her brother and go dancing with Clover instead? I am here, and yet I am hesitant and unsure. I can't bear to be made to look a fool again. As I wrestle with myself to stay or leave, the door opens and a pleasant-looking woman invites me inside.

There's no going back now.

The woman tells me her name is Elsie and that she is the charwoman-cum-housekeeper-cum-secretary for Miss May. I follow her along a narrow passageway and up a short flight of steps into a wide hallway where we climb a sweeping staircase. My eyes are drawn to the many framed photographs and opening-night programs hung on the walls. LORETTA MAY. Her name in heavy typeface, her beautiful face captured by the photographers' flashbulbs. At the top of the staircase, I hear conversation in a large room to my left. Elsie asks me to wait a moment. I stand at the edge of the doorway, and peer inside.

The room is large and softly lit by the winter sunlight that streams through large sash windows on one side. Large bolts of different-colored fabrics cover a long table in the center of the room. A tailor's dummy stands in front of the window, a woman kneeling in front of it tugs at pleats on an emerald-green skirt. She grips pins between her teeth, removing one to secure an adjustment before leaning back to inspect her work and adjusting some more. Miss May is bent over a large book of sketches on a side table. There is a pleasant feeling of industriousness to the room, but I can't see Mr. Clements anywhere. I presume he has had second thoughts. Again.

A maid arrives at the top of the stairs, brushing past me as I stand to one side. I watch as she hesitates, unable to see anywhere to place the silver tea tray she carries, every surface covered with fabric or books. How often I have been that hesitant girl, not wishing to vex Madam or her guests by setting a tray down in the wrong place. A maid can be given notice for such indiscretions.

Miss May waves a distracted hand toward the sideboard without looking up. "Over there will do, Beth. Push the things to one side."

The maid does as instructed and sets the tray down. "Will that be all, miss?"

"Yes. For now. You may go."

The girl walks from the room, staring at me as she passes. "Well, are you going in, then," she whispers, "or are you going to stand there all day gathering dust?"

As the maid disappears down the stairs, Elsie invites me to step into the room. She smiles, pats me on the arm, and wishes me good luck as she closes the door behind her.

I stand awkwardly, just inside the door, until Miss May looks up from the sketch pad, a broad smile on her lips.

"Ah, Miss Lane. You came!" She takes my hands and squeezes them as if we were old friends. "I am *very* pleased to see you." She motions toward a chaise. "Please. Take a seat."

I move a few scraps of material and sit down, placing my purse on my lap. I feel horribly out of place and desperately underdressed. I cross my ankles and push my feet beneath the chaise so that my shabby shoes are out of sight.

Miss May pours tea from a silver pot. "Sadly it's a little too early for champagne, although all this costume planning is shockingly thirsty work, isn't it, Hettie?"

The woman kneeling beside the tailor's dummy looks up. "It is *never* too early for champagne, Miss May. Isn't that your golden rule?"

Loretta laughs as she hands me the tea. That same seductive laugh I heard in the Embankment Gardens and have heard so often in the theater. The laugh that has become something of a trademark and attracted so many admirers over the years. The laugh that catches in her throat and triggers a nasty fit of coughing, rendering her momentarily speechless. She sinks down into a chair and bends over, sipping from a glass of water until the coughing subsides and she recovers her breath. It isn't pleasant to watch.

The woman at the tailor's dummy fusses around her. "You really should see a doctor about that cough. It's definitely getting worse."

Miss May brushes her concerns aside. "I must introduce you to my dressmaker, Miss Lane. Hettie Bennett. She worries terribly."

I smile at the dressmaker. She smiles back. "A pleasure to meet you, Miss Lane. And if *I* don't worry, I don't know who will."

"Have you tried J. Collis Browne's?" I ask. "Or a dose of charcoal? My mam swears by it."

Miss May stands up and stretches her long arms high toward the ceiling. She reminds me of a willow tree; strong and yet so fragile. "Ghastly stuff. All of it. It's just the fog irritating my chest. Winters bother me. I'll be perfectly fine by the spring."

Hettie shakes her head and resumes her work as Miss May walks over to me. "It is very good of you to come, Miss Lane. My brother should be here shortly, although he is notoriously late for everything, so I wouldn't hold my breath if I were you."

"Does he know I'm here?"

"Absolutely not! You shall gain the upper hand with the element of surprise."

I smile and take a sip of tea. Earl Grey. It is like drinking a bottle of perfume.

"You must excuse the chaos," she continues, standing with her hands on her narrow hips and surveying the room. "We are costume planning for next season and for costume planning one must have chaos, it seems. Here, take a look."

She passes me the sketchbook she was consulting a moment ago. I place my teacup on a side table and flick through the pages, admiring the dress designs. "These are wonderful. Whose designs are they?"

"Mostly Lucile. Some Chanel. A few Poiret."

She settles beside me to take a closer look. "This one is described as woven sunshine. It will be ever so light to wear, gold and silver embroidery over oyster-white satin. The material will shimmer beautifully under the stage lights. And look at this one. Lucile is known for her floral embellishments. Garlands of pink silk rosebuds. Aren't they darling?" She turns to another page. "And this one is so elegant. Mademoiselle Chanel. Look at the bias cut of the skirt. She has the fashion world quite in a frenzy trying to work out how she makes her lines so clean and fluid. So feminine. How anyone can say this makes a woman look like a boy has clearly taken too much absinthe."

"They're very beautiful," I say. "I can't imagine how lovely they must be to wear."

She stands up and walks toward the window. "They are extraordinary to wear. The transformative power of a couture dress cannot be understated. I remember the very first time I met Lucy Duff Gordon. Cockie arranged the appointment."

"Cockie?"

"Sorry. Charles. Cochran. I knew Lucile had dressed Lily Elsie and other actresses. I was so excited I couldn't eat a thing for breakfast and was positively light-headed by the time I arrived at the shop in Hanover Square. She studied me so carefully as she made her sketches. Said I had beautiful lines and a talent for standing still.

Cockie said I was better at standing still than I was at dancing! Awful old man! I was never the best dancer, but I had charisma. That's why Cockie encouraged me to the stage. 'What you lack in rhythm, you make up for in charm,' he said. Cockie firmly believes that you can teach any girl to dance, but you cannot teach charisma."

I can't take my eyes off her as she talks. She's like an angel standing in the sunlight. She certainly has charisma.

She turns and rests her hands on the windowsill behind her. "Everyone needs a little luck, Miss Lane, somebody to see that certain something within us. I was fortunate. I had access to the best of the best. Lucile taught me how to move across the stage, how to style my hair to show off my face, how to hold my neck at the correct angle so that the stage lights would catch the best of me. She said I had 'lilies and roses' skin. I was a real beauty, you know!" She picks absentmindedly at a spray of roses in a vase on a pedestal beside her.

"You still are a beauty."

She smiles. "You are very kind to say so. I suppose everyone is beautiful to someone. But we all wrinkle and fade in time, Miss Lane. Even the most beautiful bloom must eventually wither and die." She sighs and sits back down beside me. "Do you dance, Miss Lane?"

"Yes. I love to dance. I go to the Palais in Hammersmith."

"Have you ever had lessons?"

"No. I've learned from watching the likes of yourself and the instructors at the Palais."

"Hmm." I wonder what she's thinking behind those piercing green eyes, but a door closes somewhere beneath us and distracts her. "Aha. That will be Perry. Come along, Hettie. We must make ourselves scarce."

"You're going?" I'm suddenly flustered and not sure I want to see Perry at all.

"Of course we're going! Think of this as a dress rehearsal. Best done behind closed doors, without an audience, so to speak. Do your best, Miss Lane. We'll be cheering you on from the wings."

And with that, they leave the room and I am alone.

I hear voices downstairs, a door closing, footsteps coming up the stairs. What will I say to him?

He opens the door as I stand up. "I know, I know, I'm late again . . ." He falters as he sees me. "Miss Lane! But . . . how on earth?"

"Your sister. She came to see me."

And there we are. Standing in an apartment in Mayfair, looking at each other, neither of us knowing what to say. I want to be angry with him. I *am* angry with him, but I'm also pleased to see him. I think of the times my sisters and I would squabble, determined to hate each other and yet forgetting our fight as soon as the sun came out and someone suggested a game of hopscotch.

He stands in the doorway, clutching his trilby across his chest. "I don't quite know what to say."

He looks like a lost little boy and I feel confident beside his unease. "Have you ever considered a job as a magician?" I ask.

"A magician?"

"Yes. You do a very good disappearing act." I drop my teaspoon purposefully against my saucer, wishing the clattering of metal against china was the clattering of my toe against his shins. He walks to the sideboard and pours tea.

"Ah. Yes. I see. Very good." He runs his hands through his hair, pacing up and down the Oriental rug like a bobbin on a loom. "I owe you an apology, Miss Lane. A proper explanation. I didn't get a chance when we met outside the theater. Leaving you in the tearooms was a terrible thing to do and I'm dreadfully sorry." He pauses and walks toward the dying fire. He throws several lumps of coal onto it, smothering the weak embers. I resist the urge to tell him he's doing it all wrong. "It was rude and ungentlemanly. I regretted it the moment I left, although I suppose that doesn't help much now." He turns to me. "I am truly sorry. What else can I say?"

I try to look indifferent as I sip my tea. "I've known market porters show more respect." He blushes and puts his hands in his trouser pockets. His hair sticks up at such peculiar angles that I would laugh in any other circumstances. "I suppose you're wondering why I'm here at all."

He nods. "I know I certainly don't deserve you to be here. I really didn't think you would agree to come."

"Everyone deserves a second chance, Mr. Clements; a chance to put right their mistakes. And if I *am* meant to be your muse or whatever you call it, it seems a shame to send me away." I take a long sip of my tea. "Also, your sister is Loretta May, and *she* was very nice to me. She's the real reason I'm sitting here."

He sits in the chair beside the fire and looks at me. That smile. Those eyes. In an instant, I'm back in the pouring rain on the day we bumped into each other, suspended in a moment I can't understand.

I walk over to the fire, take the poker from the companion set, and prod the lumps of coal to give the flames some air. They start to flicker immediately.

"Why didn't it do that for me?" he asks.

"They need air to breathe, Mr. Clements. Same as people."

He leans back, crossing one leg over the other. I can feel him studying me intently. "Still, I can't help wondering why."

"Why what?"

"Why you're giving me a second chance? Why you're here at all. Even if Loretta May *is* my sister."

I turn my face to his. I feel the warmth of the fire against my cheek, a flutter in my heart. The hesitant beat of a fledgling's wing. "The question isn't always why, Mr. Clements. The question is sometimes why not?" I put the poker down and sit back down on the chaise hoping that he hasn't noticed the tremble in my hands. "So, what is it you want your *muse* to do exactly? We didn't get round to discussing the details in the tearooms."

He takes a moment to light a cigarette as he considers my question. "Quite simply I want to write music again. I want to entertain people, make them laugh. My sister thought it might be helpful for me to meet someone who inspires me."

"And you were hoping for more than a maid."

"Not just a maid. A maid with ambition, if I recall."

I blush. So he has thought about me.

"Mr. Clements, I . . ."

"Miss Lane, I wanted to ask if you . . ."

We speak over each other, both stopping to allow the other to continue. Neither of us does.

I smile. He apologizes.

"Please," he says. "Continue."

"I was going to say that you must know a dozen beautiful ladies who could inspire you. Why would someone like you go looking for a girl like me?"

"Because they *don't* inspire me. They bore me, and besides, everybody knows everybody else's business in our circles. A chap can't leave a restaurant without everyone whispering about the woman on his arm, or the woman who isn't on his arm. I wanted to find someone new. Someone real. Someone honest." He hesitates before adding, "Someone like you."

"Well, nobody ever notices me. I could walk into the Savoy Grill and tip all the tables on end and nobody would bat an eyelid. I'm invisible, Mr. Clements. Unimportant." I remember Cutler's words. *"Back-of-house staff must not be seen. As far as our guests are concerned, they are invisible. You, Dorothy Lane, do not exist."* I feel suddenly weary and lean back on the chaise like a discarded coat as I drain the last of my tea. "I'd give anything to be whispered about as I left a restaurant."

Mr. Clements sits up in his chair. "Then perhaps Loretta is right. Perhaps we *can* help each other after all."

"What do you mean?"

"She can teach you to become visible."

I almost trip over myself as I try not to fall into those gray puddles. *"Can* you teach someone to become visible?"

"Of course! What do you think finishing schools are all about? What do you think ladies spend their days doing? Thinking about what to wear. How to style their hair. It is all to attract attention, all to stand out from the crowd. It isn't difficult. You just need to know what you're doing."

"And that's the problem. I don't know what I'm doing. I own three dresses and two pairs of shoes and all of them wouldn't look out of place at a jumble sale."

"But there's something about you, Miss Lane. I see it, and I know my sister sees it too. You could be so much more than a maid doing out rooms at The Savoy. You could be someone special. Someone *everyone* notices."

I laugh. "I think you've seen too many romantic plays, Mr. Clements. This isn't Act Three of *The Shop Girl*. We can't start again in tomorrow's matinee if we get it wrong today."

He leaps up and grasps my hands, pulling me to my feet. "You see! That's it! That's exactly what I'm talking about." He rushes to the writing desk and grabs a pen from the ink pot. I hear the scratch of the nib across the page.

"What are you doing?"

"Writing your words. Your wonderful honesty. Listen. *'I think you've seen too many romantic plays, Mr. Clements. This isn't Act Three of* The Shop Girl. *We can't start again in tomorrow's matinee if we get it wrong today.'* And cue the music for a wonderful duet."

His eyes sparkle. His hair sticks up like the top of a pineapple.

I start to laugh.

"What?" he asks. "What's so amusing?"

"You, Mr. Clements. You look ridiculous!"

He picks up a teaspoon and peers into the back of it. "Yes. Yes, I do. Who cares?" He rushes over to me and for a moment I think he's going to kiss me, but he just stares at me as if he's hypnotized. "What do you say, Miss Lane? Am I forgiven? Shall we do this, together, or would you rather walk away and forget we ever met?"

I glance at the grandfather clock in the corner of the room, the second hand sweeping time away. I think about *The Adventure Book for Girls* perched on top of the clock at home. I think about Teddy and how far away I am from him. If I agree to this arrangement I'll step even farther from the path I used to imagine for me, for us. The thought of it fills me with sadness and yet my heart dances with hope. The life I know in one hand. The life I dream of in the other.

"Very well, Mr. Clements. I'll help you write your music and you'll help me to become someone other than a maid." He claps his hands together so loud that I jump. "But you're going to have to stop being so unpredictable or I'll die of heart failure before you've written a single note."

I pick up my purse and hat from the chaise.

"You're going already?"

"Yes. Before you change your mind again. It would be nice to be the first to leave this time."

He joins me at the door and we stand for a moment, neither of us sure what to say next. I hold out my hand.

"Same time next week?"

"Same time next week. At my apartment. And thank you, Miss Lane. Thank you very much."

"Don't thank me. Thank your sister. And you can call me Dolly," I say.

"And you can call me Perry."

I look into his eyes. "I *can,* but I won't. I always call my employers by their full name. This is strictly business, Mr. Clements. Nothing more. Please thank Miss May very much for her hospitality."

Elsie shows me out. I follow her down the elegant staircase, somehow resisting the urge to turn around to see if he is watching.

I walk from the building with my head held a little higher than usual. Fat rose-tinted snow clouds have settled above the city again, lending a sense of magic to the air. I tip my head back and gaze up, appreciating its beauty. My steps feel light against the streets, my heart feels secretive and hopeful.

I feel hope in my heart and love in the air and wonderful adventures beginning.

27

LORETTA

Nobody had ever made me feel more loved or alive and I adored the very bones of him.

There is a moment just before curtain up when I feel completely alone in the world. I close my eyes, embracing the hush that settles across the auditorium; the orchestra's tune-up dissipating into the very last hum of a violin string until that too fades and is gone. There is no going back now. The lines of script have been memorized, the delivery rehearsed, the dance moves meticulously choreographed, the notes and harmony of each musical number sung time and again until everyone is pitch-perfect. I am surrounded by prop hands and directors, chorus girls and rigging assistants. I am anticipated by the audience, all of whom have come to hear my famous husky voice, to stamp their feet at my innuendo-laden lines, to gasp at the beauty of my costumes. And yet I remain entirely alone, my thoughts and fears, my doubts and insecurities my only companions. In that dark silence my thoughts meander back across the years to the night when Jimmy passed me the letter in the interval and my entire world shifted.

• • •

It was March 1917. The start of my second full season, and my first principal role. I was a triumph, that opening night. It was pure joy. Cockie didn't even see my performance. He sat with his back to the stage so he could watch the reaction of the audience. "Why would I want to watch the stage?" he said. "I know the thing inside out and back to front. It's the audience that matters now. I can tell immediately if a show will be a hit from the reaction of the first-night audience."

They adored the principals and fell in love with the chorus. Every one of our girls was beautiful, fashionable, and talented, a far cry from the corseted burlesque girls of vaudeville and music hall.

Lucile, Cockie, and I were a powerful team. Her clothes were so perfect for me that everyone wanted to copy them. Lucile laughed. She said there were few women who could wear her clothes with even a fraction of my style and elegance. And of course there were the streams of gentlemen callers. Stage-door Johnnies, we called them. Silly fools with romantic notions in their heads and lavish gifts in their arms. I was young and easily impressed. I adored the fame and attention, but I wasn't interested in them. Despite my best efforts to be rude and discouraging, the marriage proposals kept coming, some of them screamingly funny, others deadly serious. The colder I acted toward my admirers, the more in love with me they became. Men are such infuriating creatures that way.

The brilliant performances continued night after night and my name became synonymous with beauty and success. Every producer in town wanted to engage me for their latest production. My star shone ever brighter amid the curfews and blackouts of war.

Even the after-show parties and suppers continued, although we often felt more than a shade of guilt while we danced and drank. We all had a story to tell about a loved one we were missing and worrying about, but what use was there in locking ourselves away to be miserable? We couldn't stop the war, couldn't bring our men home. Blocking it out with a bottle of champagne or something stronger, putting on a dazzling show to provide a distraction . . . it was the only way we could carry on.

And then the letter arrived.

It was written by a Roger Dawes, an officer on the Western Front. Jimmy handed it to me in the interval. I thought about it all the way through the second and third acts.

Somewhere in France.

March 1917

My dear Miss May,

    You must forgive me, but I have fallen hopelessly in love with you and I must tell you that you are now inextricably linked to my survival in this dreadful war.

I know nothing about you. I have never met you, nor seen you perform, and yet I have an image of you stuck to the wall of my dugout. It belonged to one of the privates but I won it from him in a game of poker. The stakes were high, the prize was your picture, and I was the victor.

So now you are mine.

Please know that to see your beautiful smiling face each morning makes me determined to survive this wretched war so that I might one day watch you perform and meet you in person. I would like to see for myself how true the likeness is. Is it possible for someone to be so beautiful?

Please write a reply. You will make a lonely soldier very happy indeed.

Officer Roger Dawes

I replied.

We exchanged letters for six months. At first they were brief and frivolous. Roger joked about the holes in his socks and the trench rats, choosing not to dwell on what life was really like at the front. I wrote to him of life in London, of brighter things: my latest show, society gossip. I sent him photographs and notices from the papers describing my dazzling performances. But as the months passed our exchanges became more serious. He shared his deepest thoughts and darkest fears. I told him I took morphine to escape from the dreadful reality of it all. I told Roger things I had never told anyone, not even my closest friends.

I soon found myself waiting desperately for news, for Jimmy to hand me another little blue envelope. As the number of losses and casualties increased, a call was put out for more volunteer nurses. I told Cockie I was stepping out of the limelight for a while to concentrate on nursing full-time.

I relocated to Guy's Hospital, once again photographed in my nurse's uniform. The newspapers thrived on good news stories like this.

BRAVE THEATER STAR TO CONCENTRATE ON ASSISTING THE WAR WOUNDED

I worked a full shift during the day, and often continued through the night. I rose early every morning to help with the rounds of temperature checks and dressings and cooking the men's meals, all the while knowing that another wave of injured men would come through the doors that day, and the next, and the next. None of us knew when it might end, when our lives might return to normality, and through it all, Roger and I opened our hearts to each other.

For eighteen months we exchanged letters. Toward the end of that time, I had returned to the theater for occasional special performances. And then Roger sent word that he was coming home on a period of special leave. *I will return to battle the happiest man in the world if you would do me the honor of meeting me, my dear Loretta.* I wrote back immediately, telling him to come to the Shaftesbury and to give Jimmy, the stage-door manager, his name.

I could not have imagined a moment more wonderful or perfect than when he stepped into my dressing room, all smiles and peonies, his cap in his hand, his searching emerald eyes meeting mine. He was here. Roger. My darling Roger. Without hesitation, I flew into his arms and there I stayed for the most glorious time. I felt safe. I felt loved. I felt real.

I feigned a dose of laryngitis and informed Matron I would be absent for the week.

We spent our first night together at The Savoy drinking Ada Coleman's decadent cocktails in the American Bar and dancing the foxtrot in the ballroom while everyone watched, spellbound by the inescapable chemistry between us. I didn't care about the whispers and glances as we took the lift together to a river suite on the top floor. We gazed at the stars from the balcony and drank the finest champagne. We danced cheek to cheek to a gramophone record before he lifted me into his arms and carried me to the bedroom. He was the perfect gentleman. So gentle and yet so passionate. He insisted we leave the blinds open so that we could see the stars as we made love. He was so delicious that night, so perfect. He took my breath away.

I awoke to morning sunshine that spilled across the crumpled bedsheets, luxuriating in the warmth of Roger's naked body beside me. We were married by special license later that day, traveling on to Brighton for our honeymoon, like forbidden lovers eloping to Gretna Green. Roger was everything to me, and I to him. I reveled in the knowledge of Mother's disappointment when she learned that I had married a man like him: untitled, unimportant, Roger Dawes. Exactly what I had always longed for in a lover and husband. Exactly the type of man my mother loathed.

We spent our third day together blissfully alone and in love.

They were the most perfect three days of my life. He could not have been kinder, warmer, funnier, or more thoughtful. For the first time in my life, I felt loved for who I really was, not just admired because of my fame and my beauty. Roger had started with fame and beauty and spent eighteen months getting to know the real person behind the dazzle. When I told him my real name he insisted on calling me Virginia. Ginny. "It suits you," he teased. "It's especially perfect for someone who drinks so much gin!" Nobody had ever made me feel more loved or alive and I adored the very bones of him.

My heart shattered when he returned to France. I stayed in bed for two days, convinced that nothing could ever console me. But my misery then was nothing compared to what was ahead. Roger's letters stopped. I couldn't understand why, although I feared the worst.

He was killed exactly a week after we were married. A shell explosion in a deadly offensive near the Belgian town of Ypres.

I didn't find out until three months later, by which time the war was over and I was back at the theater full-time. Jimmy passed me the letter during the interval. It was from Roger's mother. She'd enclosed a bundle of letters found in his greatcoat. *My* letters. "It was as if they were trying to protect him," she wrote. "A barrier of love, wrapped around his heart."

My life as Mrs. Roger Dawes was at an end. The life I had carried secretly within me for three months ended soon after, a crimson bedsheet all I had to show that either my husband, or our child, had ever existed. I was left with nothing. Just a bundle of scorched letters and a broken heart.

The houselights go down, plunging me into darkness. The conductor taps his baton on his music stand. The orchestra settles and the pianist strikes up the first bar. The curtain goes up, the passing glare of the spotlight offering a glimpse of the audience. Couples in love, out for an evening at the theater together. Press reporters and society-magazine columnists, eager to write their reviews and gain the admiration of their editor. And way up, in the farthest reaches of the cheap seats in the gallery, I see the hopeful, adoring faces of the ordinary girls who wish to be everything that I am.

Right on cue I step forward, spread my arms wide, and smile. The audience cheer wildly as I search for him in the dark, willing my imagination to find him. And there he is, resting casually against a pillar at the back of the stalls. He smiles and blows kisses and Virginia Clements's heart breaks into a thousand tiny fragments, dragging her to her knees, crushed beneath the immense weight of her grief, and yet all the while, Loretta May dazzles. Loretta May keeps dancing, keeps performing and everybody in the auditorium loves her, unaware that her world is crumbling around her.

28
DOLLY

"Music is nothing without an audience.
We must have people to hear it;
otherwise it is just markings on a page."

There is a wonderful silence to the hotel in the predawn dark. While the guests lounge in their apartments and sleep off the effects of too many highballs, I lie awake, a hand on my chest, feeling the rise and the fall of a hundred beating hearts. I think about the governor's words; the connection with the hotel that he spoke of. I'm beginning to understand what he meant. I imagine the locked doors are closed eyes; the shutters and curtains tired eyelids, too weary to pull apart. And then I hear hushed whispers, soft footsteps in corridors as the hotel yawns, stretches, flexes its fingers, and gently wakes up.

Everything seems so simple in these silent hours. I think about my first meeting with Perry in his apartment. He called me Miss Lane. I called him Mr. Clements. He was clumsy and untidy. I was (he said) entertaining and intriguing. We drank pots and pots of tea, ate cake, and talked beyond the intended hour. He made me smile with his fancy notions of life. I made him laugh with what he calls "my northern outlook." I sensed a pleasant understanding developing between us. I think about him often while everyone else sleeps.

But more than anything, in these quiet moments, I think about Teddy and little Edward, both of them out there somewhere, distant and fading. I try not to dwell on the past, to keep looking forward, but it isn't easy. Like a shadow, my past lingers beside me always. Strange things remind me of them, small insignificancies that send my memories tumbling forward like water on a mill wheel: the smell of a rose in the Embankment Gardens, the song of a blackbird, a butterfly, the distant stars, the shape of my mother's hand-writing.

Her latest letter arrives with a Christmas package. She wishes me well and writes about the safe, predictable events that communities like ours have always relied on: marriages, babies born, the little runt who had thrived with the other piglets that spring. She doesn't write of the difficult realities we sweep aside when we choose to.

With the letter is a separate note scribbled on a scrap of paper.

Dear Dorothy,
I found these when I was clearing out your room. I thought you might like to

have them. Or maybe not. I wasn't sure.
I will be thinking of you this Christmas-time. I hope you are happy.
Your loving Mother
X

The package contains a lavender bag that I had made as a young girl, a yard of fabric, a bundle of letters, and a khaki-colored button from Teddy's tunic. I remember him giving it to me before he returned to the front from leave. I treasured that button as if it were a diamond, as if every part of him was contained within it.

With unsteady hands, I untie the string around the letters. His handwriting is so familiar, so haunting. He took to reading and writing poetry when he went to war. His writing became almost musical.

As I take the letters from their envelopes, I think of all the times I had longed to see his neat script, to read his gentle words. Now they only torment me.

Somewhere in France.

February '17

My dear Little Thing,

Do you sleep well? Sleep is broken and fleeting here. There is little to distinguish between night and day during these long winter months, so that I can't be sure if the sky is tricking me. We sleep in the dugouts, our bodies too wearied from marching and shivering to care about the discomfort. And to think that I used to complain of a broken spring in the mattress back home. What any of us would give for a mattress full of broken springs.

We long for the dawn, the first gray light to signal the end of another night of shelling and invisible enemies lurking over the top. The darkness plays tricks on the mind. The scratching of a rat becomes a German sniper, his gun barrel pressed against your temple. But that first sliver of light—the relief at knowing I have lived another day and that I am one day closer to seeing you again, my dear little girl. And the dawn is so beautiful, such color above all that is dreary and murk in the fields below. I think of you when I watch the dawn sweep across the sky. I imagine you sleeping as the light blooms through the window of your little bedroom. I imagine myself creeping in to sit beside you and I watch you sleep, until you sense me near and open a sleepy eye.

What do you hear, Dolly? Tell me what you hear when you wake in the morning, for I hear only dreadful things. Even in the silence I hear death and fear.

Please write to me, my dear Little Thing, and remind me of the whispers of the reeds on the riverbank. Tell me about the birdsong and the cries of the swallow chicks in the eaves. Tell me about the rumble of thunder and the hiss of a summer rainstorm on the tin roof of the hay barn. Tell me about the clang of the milk churns, the crackle of the knife through the crust of the morning's bread, the spit and sizzle of bacon frying. Do you hear the ringing of the school bell, the rumble of the coal cart, the cry of a newborn baby?

What do you hear, Dolly? Please tell me. Fill my ears with life again.

Yours always, Teddy

X

Somewhere in France.

November 1917

My dear Little Thing,

We are on the march in these short dark winter days. Just as the earth tilts away from the sun in the wintertime, so I feel a shadow fall over me as I move farther away from you.

How awful it was to leave you again. Worse than the first time we parted. I didn't know what awaited me then. Now I know what terrors await and I'm not ashamed to admit that my legs tremble at the thought.

They shoot the deserters and cowards. They are court-martialed and shot at dawn by firing squad. An example to us all. A reminder of how cowardice ends. But I cannot blame those poor boys. War can turn a man's mind inside out, so that the thought of being shot by your officer is better than being taken prisoner or torn apart by enemy shells. Who would ever have thought such decisions would have to be made? Who would ever have believed this was possible, Dolly?

Before I came home on leave, I scratched the days until I would see you into a wooden post in the dugout. I couldn't wait for the others to return so I could move up the list and get closer to seeing you. We all prayed for our brothers to come back so we could take our turn. And then I got my papers and I was walking away from that place and walking toward you, Dolly. There you were, hands on your hips, the sun in your hair, and I could not have been happier if I had seen an angel from heaven.

And now I have to tell you that I am afraid. I have a dreadful feeling that I won't see England again, that I won't see the great chimneys of the cotton mills or the blackened faces of the miners coming home from the pits. I think this is it, dear girl. And if it is, I want you to be brave and strong and I want you to go on and marry a man who is worthy of you and who will care for you and tell you he loves you when he wakes each morning.

You mustn't be frightened by these words. I have thought about keeping this letter somewhere safe so that they will find it when I go, but then I worry that it won't be found and you will never know what it was I wanted to say to you. So I am sending it now, and if my fears are wrong, and I live on, then I will write again, and again and again, and I will keep on writing until the stump of my pencil runs out and the candle dies, and we will carry on, my darling girl, as best we can.

Think of me often.

Yours always,

Teddy

X

Somewhere in France.

April 1918

I don't know how much longer I can stand it here, Dolly. I feel like I am a small boy again and I cry out in the night for my mother. I want to be tucked up warm in my little bed. I want to feel your hand in mine. I want to lie down and sleep.

Pray for me, my dear little girl. Pray for us all.

Teddy

X

Despite my efforts to forget and move on, I can't. The memories and the pain come flooding back with every word until the tears fall fast down my cheeks. He called me Little Thing. How my heart ached to hear him speak those words to me once more.

I was twenty years old when Teddy was demobilized and returned to England, but it was not the return I had imagined. I was not the naïve girl who had waved him good-bye. I was not the same girl who had spent years waiting for him to return. Waiting for Teddy, thinking about Teddy, writing to Teddy—it was all I ever did. "When Teddy is back," "after the war," was all I ever said.

Teddy returned a broken man. His body wasn't damaged; he carried his wounds on the inside. Shell shock, they told us. The empty stare. The tremble in his arms. The damp stain at his groin. It was so painful to see. I tried my best to help him heal, but I too was damaged. I carried my own invisible scars and it is hard to mend someone else when you, yourself, are damaged beyond repair.

That was why I had to leave.

Teddy always knew I would. He said my feet were too restless to walk forever along the narrow laneways of Mawdesley. "When the war is over, you'll go," he'd written. "Mawdesley isn't where you belong. You'll find a bigger stage to dance on than the village hall. And when you do, I'll be watching in the audience, and I'll clap and cheer, and blow kisses and throw roses at your feet."

But life doesn't always work out the way we hope.

There is no stage.

There are no roses.

I rest my cheek against the bedroom window, blowing a warm breath onto the cold glass. It fades too quickly. Everything is slipping away from me.

What do you hear, Dolly? Please tell me. Fill my ears with life again.

"I hear hope, Teddy," I whisper. "I hear hope and love and adventure."

The pages of Perry's discarded music remain unplayed beneath my pillow. I still haven't told him that I took them from the litter bin and I still haven't heard Mr. Somers's band rehearse.

Today is the day.

Taking my courage in my hands and a bundle of table linen in my arms, I make my way along the staff passageways that lead to a curtain at the back of the ballroom stage. I make a small gap at the edge of the curtain and peer around.

Half a dozen musicians are in full swing. Trumpet, banjo, violin, drums, trombone, and piano all mingle into a perfect melody as they play a favorite number of mine, "Tiger Rag." My feet tap in time as I gawk at the Oriental carpet and the huge ferns and palms that tower toward the ceiling at each side of a curved staircase. It reminds me of an illustration of an exotic Egyptian palace in *The Adventure Book for Girls*. Adventure lives in places like this; in the marble columns and crystal chandeliers, even in the scuff marks left by dancing feet on the wooden dance floor.

I wait until the band finish their last number and begin to pack away their instruments and then I whisper from my hiding place.

"Mr. Somers? Psst. Mr. Somers." He glances up from the piano but doesn't see me. I step out from behind the curtain and walk toward him. "Excuse me, Mr. Somers. I'm very sorry to bother you, but you did say for me to come and listen to a rehearsal." He looks at me, bemused. "I heard you playing the trumpet outside the deliveries entrance."

A look of recognition flashes across his face. "Ah, yes. The maid who got herself a free concert al fresco. I wondered when you might appear. So, how did it sound?"

I step a little closer, the bundle of linen still in my arms. "It was lovely. That last one's my favorite."

"Mine too. Well, I'm jolly glad you heard us." He closes the lid on the piano and steps down from the stage. "Nothing like a little music to see one through the day in good spirits."

"Actually, I wondered if I might ask you a favor, sir." My heart thumps beneath my apron. I'll be in terrible trouble if anyone sees me here.

Mr. Somers narrows his eyes. He wears little round spectacles that look comical against his rosy cheeks. He reminds me of a pet hamster my cousin used to keep. "Well? Spit it out."

"It's just . . . well . . . I wondered if you might play something for me."

"For you?"

"Yes." I feel silly for even asking.

"Of course. Which one would you like?" He opens the piano and sits on the stool, his hands poised over the keys. "Well?"

"Oh, no! Not one of *your* pieces."

He looks a little offended. "Mine not quite to your taste?"

I blush. "No. I mean, yes." I balance the linen in one arm and fish the folded sheets of music from my pocket. "It's just that I found some music a while back and I've never heard it played."

"Found?"

"Yes."

"I see." He looks at me, and shakes his head. "Well, we can't have unplayed music. That won't do at all. Music is nothing without an audience. We must have people to hear it; otherwise it is just markings on a page. It is the audience that brings it to life."

I hand him the folded sheets. He looks at the shabby state of them and frowns.

"They got a little damp," I explain. "I rescued them from a litter bin."

"A litter bin?" I nod. He smooths the pages before placing them on the music stand above the keys. "Well then. Let's see if their rescue was worthwhile."

I take a deep breath. Standing in this beautiful room where I am not permitted to be, I feel heavy with anticipation. It is desperately important that the music is special; memorable. My instinct to rescue it has to have been worthwhile. I close my eyes and listen to the rise and fall of the notes, the gentle trill of the top keys, the melancholy of the sharps and flats. The melody is beautiful; haunting. I stand perfectly still and listen to every note until Mr. Somers's fingers come to a rest and the final chord echoes around the room.

He speaks first. "It is quite beautiful, don't you think?"

I nod, afraid that if I speak I will burst into tears.

I want to run to Perry's apartment and tell him how lovely it is and how beautifully Mr. Somers played it and how silly it was of him to throw it away like that.

Mr. Somers hands the pages back to me. "Do you know this P. Clements chap? He has quite a talent."

"I'm getting to know him."

"When you next see him, tell him I know a producer looking for a song just like this for a new production."

"Really? Oh, yes. I'll tell him. And thank you, Mr. Somers."

I take the pages from him and turn to leave.

"And, miss."

"Yes."

"You might also ask him who the piece was written for."

"Oh, I don't think it was written *for* anyone. He seemed very unattached to it."

He laughs and stands up, closing the lid of the piano gently over the keys. "But of course it was written for someone. Every piece of music is written for someone: a lover, a friend, a friend you wish was a lover. Ask him. Whoever he was writing this for, he needs to write for them again. There is life and loss in this music. Real life. Real loss."

I tell him I will ask and step back behind the curtain. I rush down the corridors and staff stairways to continue my rounds before anyone sees me.

The melody follows me around the hotel for the rest of the day, playing over and over in my mind, and all I can think about is how delighted Perry will be when I tell him.

Yet something nags at me. Who *did* he write it for?

29
DOLLY

"It's only by trying and failing,
by losing something we really love,
that we discover how much we want it."

The following Sunday, I rush to the Strand Theatre to give Perry the good news. Mrs. Ambrose beams at me from behind her little window at the ticket office.

"Back again, Miss Dorothy?"

"Yes. Back again."

She winks and chuckles to herself, setting her chins dancing. "Glad to see it. Go on up. He's in."

I bound up the three flights of stairs and stop outside flat three, where I press my ear to the door and listen to the now familiar sound of piano keys, the same chord over and over, the lid being slammed shut, the keys reverberating in protest. My hand is raised to knock, but I hesitate. I get the feeling I've come at a bad time.

I jump backward as the door opens. Perry's hand flies to his chest. "Goodness, Miss Lane! You gave me a fright. I'd begun to think you weren't coming today."

"Sorry. I got delayed." Our eyes meet. I'm a

351

giddy child beneath his gaze. "You're obviously heading out. I'll go."

He reaches out, touches the sleeve of my coat. "Don't go. Please. I was only leaving because you weren't here."

His words dance in the space between us, twisting and turning with the suggestion of so much more. Color rushes to my cheeks as I glance down at my shoes. I try to suppress a smile.

"Well, I'm here now."

"Yes. Yes, you are."

He stands to one side and holds the door open. I step into the small apartment and just as I did the first time I came here, I feel instantly at home.

Perry closes the door behind me and dashes about, picking up cushions, pushing teacups and tumblers to one end of a table, and throwing open the curtains. "You must excuse the mess. Mrs. Ambrose hasn't been in today. Take a seat." He pushes a pile of sheet music off the end of the battered velvet couch. I perch on the edge as he stands in front of the fireplace, hands on hips, as awkward as a schoolboy. "Tea?"

"If you're making some."

While he clatters about in the small kitchenette, I glance around the room. I'd expected something much grander after seeing his sister's apartment, but Perry's little flat above the theater isn't much bigger than my sleeping quarters at the hotel. It is chaotic and eccentric. Candle wax spills over the edge of empty bottles of whiskey and absinthe. Ashtrays overflow with spent cigarettes. Discarded shoes loiter beneath chair legs. Scrunched-up balls of paper form a drift around the wastepaper bin. A teetering pile of novels leans against the fireplace and a teetering pile of music books rests against the sofa. Rugs are scattered about the floor and draped over chairs. A bizarre collection of art hangs on the wall and small ornaments sit on any available space on the shelves and mantelpiece. The room smells of Scotch and cigarettes, just like his pages of music when I'd placed them on the hearth tiles to dry.

O'Hara's veins would pop out of her neck if she could see this place, but I find something quite lovely about the chaos. It is full of character. Full of a life. In some ways, it makes the suites at The Savoy seem rather bland.

Eventually, Perry emerges with a tea tray, setting it down on a nest of tables beside me. Two generous slices of cherry cake are piled on a plate decorated with roses. The teacup is cracked and the pot dribbles when he pours. It reminds me of Mam's teapot at home, how she'd fussed and apologized as it dribbled over Teddy's trousers the first time he visited. *"It's the flaws that give things character, Mrs. Lane. Everyone talks about the teapot that dribbles. Nobody talks about the teapot that pours perfectly. If I were a teapot, I know which I'd rather be."*

I take a bite of cherry cake. "It's very good," I mumble, dropping crumbs into my lap.

"Mrs. Ambrose makes it. Secret recipe. Says she'll take it to her grave just to annoy her sisters."

He sits down and stands up again, pacing about the room, unable to sit still. He's always the same. I found it distracting at first. Now I find it quite charming.

"I have a confession to make," I say. Even the words make me blush. I shuffle in my seat.

He sits in the seat at the large bay window. "Oh?"

"Do you remember the first time we met, when we bumped into each other in the rain?"

"Yes. You knocked me down."

I sigh. "I helped you up."

He smiles. "Of course. How could I forget?"

"Do you remember putting your pages of music into a litter bin?"

"Ah. Yes. Miserable piece of rot."

"Well, that's the thing. I took those pages out of the bin. I kept them."

"You did what? Why on earth would you do that?"

"I'm not sure. It just seemed such a shame to throw them away. Anyway, that doesn't matter now. What I wanted to tell you is that I asked somebody to play the music."

Now he's intrigued. He walks toward the fire

and sits in his favorite threadbare old chair. "Who?"

"Debroy Somers. He's the pianist and leader of the hotel band."

"Somers? Of the Savoy Orpheans?"

"Yes."

"I know him. Decent sort of chap."

"Well, the thing is, he played your music. In the Grand Ballroom."

"He did?"

"Yes. And he liked it. He liked it very much."

"Really?"

"Yes. And so did I! I thought it was lovely. Really lovely."

For a moment neither of us speaks. Perry pokes at the fire as I sip my tea. I hope he isn't cross with me.

He runs his fingers through his hair. "I can't believe you took them out of the litter bin! And that you kept them all this time."

"Well, I did. Here." I take the crumpled pages from my purse and pass them to him.

He unfolds them, smooths them out on his lap. "Well, I never. You really did."

"But that's not all. Mr. Somers said he knows a producer looking for a piece of music just like it. He thinks it could be perfect for a scene the producer has been struggling to find a number for." Perry stands up and walks to the piano as I speak, setting the crumpled pages onto the music

355

stand. "And he asked if you'd written any lyrics to accompany the melody. Oh, and he also said that whoever the song was written for, you should write for them again because they clearly bring out the best in you."

I'm babbling. I take another bite of cherry cake to make myself stop talking.

Perry says nothing. He seems distracted.

"Would you play it for me?" I ask.

He hesitates for a moment before settling himself at the stool. "It would be my pleasure, Miss Lane."

He plays beautifully. The song sounds even better in his tiny little apartment than it did in the splendor of The Savoy ballroom. As he plays, I walk to the window. I can see Waterloo Bridge and the OXO Tower. I watch people and clouds scurry past.

When he finishes I turn around and clap. "See! It's lovely."

"I suppose it's not bad. Not as bad as I seem to remember, anyhow."

He joins me at the window, standing so close that our shoulders almost touch. My heart quickens as we stare at the moody sky together. "What do you see when you look at the clouds, Mr. Clements?"

He thinks for a moment. He's getting used to my strange questions. "Honestly?"

"Honestly."

"You won't laugh?"

"I won't laugh."

"I see a piano."

I laugh. "A piano?"

"Yes. It's always music with me. I can't help it. I see sharps and flats. I see unwritten music, notes and melodies. Have you ever seen the starlings gathering on the telegraph wires on a summer's evening?"

"Can't say I've noticed them."

"Well, I don't see starlings. I see a stave of music, each bird a note for me to play." He blows warm breaths onto the windowpanes and draws musical notes with his fingertip. "Sharps. Flats. Crotchets. Minims. My head is full of music when I'm standing here looking at the sky. But when I settle at the stool and try to write, to play, I feel suffocated by expectation. The notes disappear. They drift away like clouds and I can never find them again." He rests his forehead against the glass. "The others make it seem so easy: Coward and Berlin and Novello. They produce hit after hit and all the while here I am, scratching away with nothing to show for my work. Why is it so hard, Miss Lane?" He turns to look at me. "Why?"

"Because that's when we really learn, isn't it? When things are difficult. When it's a struggle and we're not sure. That's when we find out whether we care at all." I blow a breath onto the window and draw a butterfly with my fingertip.

357

"It's only by trying and failing, by losing something we really love, that we discover how much we want it."

The bells across the city chime the half hour. We stand, side by side, watching our childish scribbles fade on the glass.

"Thank you, Miss Lane."

"For what."

"For reminding me." He sits down in the window seat. I sit beside him. "During the war I was always waiting for tomorrow or thinking about yesterday. I was always somewhere in my future or pining for my past. It's hard to shake that off. Loretta says I need to live for the moment. She says I shouldn't spend the rest of my life waiting for my life to start. Does that make any sense to you?"

He raises his head to look at me and for a moment, everything else fades away. For a few seconds, a minute, an hour—who knows how long we sit there?—there is no Teddy, no war, no Edward, no shattered dreams. Just the two of us and a moment we can either grasp hold of or allow to pass us by.

I see a flicker in his eyes. A hesitation.

The vibration of an underground train sets the glass rattling in the windowpanes.

He stands up and the moment is gone. Like a fairground balloon tugged easily from a distracted hand, it drifts away to some distant place.

We didn't hold tight.

We didn't hold on.

Perhaps we didn't want it badly enough.

Over supper that evening, I'm interrogated by Sissy.

"So, where did you take yourself off to today?" she asks. "You missed a great picture at the Alhambra. Louise Brooks was fabulous in it."

I stir my cocoa, take a sip, and put the cup down onto the saucer. "I was out."

Sissy sighs and leans back in her chair. "Well now, that's never going to do, is it? *Where* were you out exactly?"

"Can't a girl do some things in private?"

"No." Sissy folds her arms and stares at me, waiting for an answer. "No, she can't. Not if she sleeps in a bed beside mine and shares my makeup."

I'm too weary to keep my secrets any longer, and the look in Sissy's eyes tells me she won't give in until I tell her. "All right. I went to meet a composer, if you must know."

"A composer?"

"Yes. It's a long story. A very long story." I tell her everything. I tell her about the notice in *The Stage* and my abandonment in the tearooms and my meeting with Loretta May and Mr. Clements's apartment and the music that I'd kept beneath my pillow. She sits and listens quietly, completely engrossed in my life over the past few months.

"So, what does he want you to do?" she asks. "What exactly does a muse do?"

"He doesn't really want me to do anything. He just wants me to keep him company. Talk. Tell him about my day."

"That's it?"

"Yes. That's it."

"And what do you get in return?"

"That's the best part. Miss May is going to help me with dance lessons and etiquette. You know, how to hold myself properly, and walk like a lady, and how to dine in fancy restaurants and what not."

"Ooo, lah-di-dah." Sissy laughs and sips her tea. "And what good is that going to do? I mean, it all sounds very nice, but what's the point?"

"The point is to make something of myself. Don't you want that, Sissy?" I look around the Maids' Hall, at the rows and rows of tables and chairs, exhausted girls hunched over their supper. "Don't you want more than this? Even if I spend the rest of my life here, at least I'll know I tried to improve myself, that I didn't just sit back and accept it. That I tried to walk in different shoes."

She shrugs. She's so like Clover. I know she doesn't really understand.

"I like it here, Sissy, and I care for you and Gladys like my own sisters, but I want more. Working here, seeing how the other half live, it's like having a taste of the most delicious cake and wanting a whole slice and then the whole bloody thing. Maybe Mr. Clements can help me taste a slice of the good life. That's not such a bad thing to want, is it?"

Sissy looks at me and sighs. "No, Dolly. I suppose it isn't. But be careful. Sometimes our eyes are bigger than our bellies. Just don't get too greedy."

Once in bed, I can't settle. I'm restless with hope and confused by my feelings for Perry. One minute I think of him like a brother; the next I find my heart racing as he stands beside me. It is hard to imagine myself loving someone else when I had always assumed it would be Teddy my heart galloped for.

I toss and turn and clutch little Edward's photograph beneath the bedcovers as I listen to the distant strains of Mr. Somers's band. My feet twitch and dance beneath the covers until I can't bear it any longer. I jump out of bed and push the window up. Mildred and Gladys are fast asleep, but Sissy is still awake.

"What are you doing?" she hisses.

"Listen," I whisper. "Can you hear it?"

She clambers from her bed and sticks her head out into the black night. The thump of jazz dances through the air.

"It's all I think about, Sissy," I whisper. "Music

and dancing. If only we had a gramophone player in here." We lean out farther as the pace of the music hots up. "When was the last time you danced?" I ask.

"Last week. At the Palace."

"I don't mean a quick twirl around a crowded dance floor with some awkward young bugger who doesn't know his foxtrot from his quick-step. I mean *really* danced. When you were so lost in the music that you became a part of it?" She stares at me as if I've gone loopy. "Come on," I whisper. "I'll show you!"

Grabbing her hand, I take the male lead, guiding her in an impromptu dance around the room. We rise and fall, spin and turn along with the music until the number ends and we grab our sides and try to catch our breath through our muffled laughter. The next number is a quickstep, a faster, jazzier beat. I begin to move my feet in the fashionable new Charleston step, kicking out my heels and swinging the opposite arm, turning my knees in toward my feet. Sissy watches and copies. It is clumsy and faltering but it's enough just to hear the music; just to be dancing.

"How do you know the steps?" she whispers. "You look like one of the ducks in Hyde Park!"

"I copy what I see the girls doing on the stage and in the pictures. You know—Jessie Matthews, Adele Astaire, Gertie Lawrence. I'd love to roll up the carpet and have a proper dance."

Sissy follows my movements until we forget about trying to be quiet and our thudding and jumping attracts the attention of O'Hara, who is passing on her rounds. We squeal when she opens the door and flicks on the light.

Mildred and Gladys rub their eyes as the electric light blazes in the room.

"What's going on?" Gladys mumbles. "Is there a fire?"

O'Hara stands in the doorway. "You'll have the chandeliers swinging in the Front Hall with all this racket. I suggest you close that window before you both catch your death of cold, and get some sleep. The ladies and gentlemen may be enjoying the exotic new rhythms of Mr. Somers's band, but they'll be able to sleep off the effects of their exertions until noon. You, on the other hand, will not. Now, into bed!"

As she closes the door, I'm certain I catch the hint of a smile at the edge of her lips.

I settle back under my bedcovers but I still can't sleep. The hotel is restless tonight and so am I. I listen to the music that comes and goes like waves through the dark. I close my eyes and imagine the ladies and gentlemen on the dance floor. I think about Perry. Why did he hesitate? Perhaps he was right to. I'm a silly girl with foolish notions of love between the likes of him and the likes of me. I imagine his arms wrapped around me, spinning and twirling me around the room. I see fox-red hair and gray puddles for eyes, and that smile tugging at the corner of his mouth. And then his image fades and it is Teddy who is whirling me around the dance floor and pressing his cheek to mine.

Rolling onto my side, I listen to the breaths of the other girls, and as my eyes grow heavy, I let out a long sigh. I imagine it as a living thing, slipping beneath the door, rushing through the softly lit corridors, past the night porter and the opulence of the Front Hall and out into the lamp-lit streets. On it goes, a rush of warm air, searching through the dark until it reaches the dazzling lights of Shaftesbury Avenue and the laughter and applause of the packed theaters. And there it finds a place to settle and waits for me to find it.

30
TEDDY

Maghull Military War Hospital, Lancashire
July 1919

> . . . her eyelashes fluttering against my skin.
> My very own butterfly.

I am one of only three left on the ward now. They tell me I'll be going home soon. I want to believe them, but sometimes it is easier not to think of anywhere beyond these stark walls and rows of empty beds.

She is here, as usual. I watch as she goes about her business with her familiar efficiency, light and breezy like the leaves that dance on the willow trees beside the riverbank. But there is something different about her today. She is restless. I watch her closely, really look at her, imprinting her image onto my mind like a flower between the pages of a press, so that I will always have it there.

She tells me she's read all the letters now. "I suppose I could start from the beginning." She can hardly bear to look at me. "Would you like me to read them again?"

I think of all the beautiful words. I shake my head.

She sighs a lot and fusses with her clothes. It occurs to me that she must be very warm with her coat on indoors. Ready for one of her walks, no doubt.

I close my eyes, pretending to sleep so that she might relax a little and stop fussing. She talks to me while she thinks I'm sleeping. Tells me secret things.

The afternoon passes in companionable silence as the sun shifts in the sky, taking its warmth and its light to a different part of the ward and casting a shadow across my bed.

"I have to go," she whispers. "I have to go, Teddy." I hear her gathering her things, sobbing quietly as she places an envelope on the table beside my bed. "There's one more letter," she says. "One I haven't read to you. It's for you to read, when you're ready."

And then she leans forward and kisses me on the cheek, her eyelashes fluttering against my skin. My very own butterfly.

"I'm so sorry, Teddy," she whispers. "So very sorry. I wish things could have been different for us. I hope one day you'll understand. That you can forgive me."

My darling Dolly. My dear Little Thing.

She was right here beside me all this time. Visiting me on her afternoons off, reading her own letters to me, her very own words, in the hope that I would remember her.

And I do.

I want to open my eyes. I want to tell her that I know her. I want to whisper her name and tell her that I love her. I want to keep her here beside me, always, but I can't. I have to let her go.

She squeezes my hand, stands beside me a moment longer, and then I hear her walk away. Only when I know she is at the end of the ward do I open my eyes a fraction. She turns only once to look back at me. Tears stream down her cheeks. And then she is gone. My girl. My Dolly.

I know the words inside the envelope are her good-bye.

"Thank you, Dolly," I whisper. "Thank you for everything." And then I sleep for a while, my head full of dreams of her.

I wake in the early evening. The Matron comes by on her rounds. She takes my temperature and plumps my pillows, encouraging me to sit up so I can drink a glass of water. As she writes on her charts, I lie perfectly still, listening to the song of a blackbird that drifts through the open window. I breathe in the sweet scent of freshly cut grass and watch the butterfly. My butterfly. Slowly, it spreads its wings, hesitates for just a moment and flutters away, dancing on the breeze.

"Oh! It flew away." Matron turns to me. "Your butterfly, Mr. Cooper. After all this time it has finally flown."

I close my eyes, and smile. "Yes," I whisper. "Yes, she has. She has gone in search of adventures."

31
DOLLY

"I wanted to know what it would feel like to *dance* in such beautiful shoes.
Walking in them would be a waste."

Christmas passes in a blur and New Year's Eve approaches. Time for the wealthy to indulge in grand parties and celebrations. Time for a young maid to sweep away the failures and doubts of the past and welcome a new year full of possibility. Nineteen twenty-four. I like the sound of it when I say it. I like the shape of it when I write it down. The prospect of a new year, smooth and unruffled, makes my heart flutter.

I lay out Mademoiselle Delysia's dress for the ball she will attend tonight: midnight-blue crepe de chine. I select matching satin opera gloves and a string of emerald beads. I already know which shoes she will want to wear. The silver dance shoes. I lift them from the wardrobe and place them at the foot of the bed. I would never take them off if I owned anything as lovely. I would sleep in them. I would dangle my legs over the side of the tub so that I could bathe in them.

My work finished, I tie up the bundle of bed

linen and make for the door, but the shoes tug at my thoughts, and I hesitate. Opening the door a crack, I peer out into the corridor, craning my neck and listening keenly. Certain that nobody is about, I close the door, quickly take off my black shoes, and slip my left foot into the silver shoe. It is like butter melting around my feet. Forgetting any concerns I once had about impropriety, I lift the right shoe and slide my foot inside. Fastening the delicate silver buttons, I lift first one foot, then the other, twisting my ankle so that I can admire them from all sides.

I walk over to the looking glass and once around the Turkey rug. It's like walking on a cloud, the soft kid leather hugging the soles of my feet so delicately I can barely tell that I have shoes on at all. How I could dance with these on my feet. I do a foxtrot. Slow, slow, quick, quick, slow, gliding effortlessly across the plush carpet. I slow to a waltz, rising and falling, the balls of my feet delighting in this new luxury, my arms wrapped around two pillows, my imaginary partner guiding me effortlessly in the dance. When I close my eyes, it is Perry in front of me, his eyes so close to mine. When I rest my cheek against the pillows, it is Teddy's cheek I rest against.

Perry. Teddy. Teddy. Perry. They mingle and change and I can't stop dancing. I close my eyes, my arms extended in front of me, locked in an embrace. His left hand in mine, his right hand resting lightly against the small of my back. "Close your eyes and let the music show you the way," he whispers. I hear the music so clearly, feel the warmth of his body against mine. "Can you feel the music, Dolly?" I lean into him. "Yes. Yes, I can." And then he leans forward to kiss me and I am a cloud floating in a lazy summer sky.

The click of the lock cuts through my thoughts. The door opens.

I drop the pillows and sink to a crouch in the middle of the room, my back to the door, my skirt covering my feet. I pull and twist desperately at the tiny pearl buttons but they are too perfect and smooth, not intended for urgent guilty fingers. I cannot undo them. The color drains from my face, my guilt and my shame flooding the suite around me. I look over my shoulder and my bones become jelly.

Snyder.

I pretend to pick lint from the rug and pray that he won't linger.

For an eternity he says nothing. The air prickles with danger.

"This needs to be cleaned," he remarks, dropping a dress casually onto the bed. "Mademoiselle insists on wearing it tomorrow evening."

"I'll send it to the laundry this afternoon." My voice is strangled. I tug at the buttons but I can't get them loose.

"You won't *send* it anywhere. This is finest

Parisian silk. Vionnet couture. You'll take it personally to the laundry and you'll bring it back."

"Yes. Of course."

"Jolly good." He stands with his hands in his pockets and rests a shoulder against the window frame, his back turned to me.

In the awful silence I somehow stand up, resting one hand against the back of a chair for balance as I try desperately to release the silver button from its clasp. My fingers are useless fumbling thumbs. I wobble, and steady myself. Wobble again. All the while he stands silently at the window.

"Leave them," he says, turning around. "Leave them on."

"I was just . . ."

"Just what? Trying on Mademoiselle's shoes? Yes, I can see that. I suppose the question that has to be asked next is, why?"

I refuse to give in to the tears that burn in my eyes. There are so many answers I could give, but how would a man like Snyder ever understand. "Because I am a fool," I whisper, lowering my head.

He walks over to the dressing table and picks up the gold cigarette case I have just polished. His fingerprints leave marks all over it. "I expected to find the room clean and tidy. Instead, I find it sullied with the worst kind of dishonesty."

"Everything is done, sir. I was just leaving."

"In those shoes?"

"Of course not. I would never . . ."

"Never what? Steal them. Just trying them on for fun, were you?" There is an edge to his voice that I haven't heard before. Threatening. Dangerous. I keep my head down, my gaze to the floor. "Wanted to know what it would feel like to walk in such beautiful shoes, did we?"

"Dance."

"I beg your pardon." His eyes glare at me, dark and brooding.

From somewhere deep within, I feel defiance rise within me. I refuse to be intimidated by him. I've been intimidated by men like Larry Snyder too often. "I wanted to know what it would feel like to *dance* in such beautiful shoes. Walking in them would be a waste."

He laughs. That great mocking laugh of his that reaches out and wraps itself around my throat so that I gasp for air.

He walks over to me, leaning his face close to mine. "I have seen you *dance,* Miss Lane, if one could call it dancing, and I can tell you now that you'll need far more than expensive silver shoes to ever make it. Far more." I swallow hard. He smells of stale Virginia tobacco and brandy. He has clearly been drinking. The scent of him settles on my face like dust. "You girls are so predictable. You think a few turns around the dancefloor at the local dance hall on a Saturday night will be enough to get you into the chorus of a Broadway show. You attend auditions without being properly prepared and you leave without so much as a 'thank you, Mr. Snyder.' "

"I wasn't expecting to be alone that day. I thought—"

"You thought I wanted to seduce you. You, with your mind in the gutter, thought that the favor I was asking was of a sexual nature." His speech is slurred. He lights a cigar and breathes smoke into my eyes. "You're all the same. Cheap as the cotton stockings on your legs. If you'd stayed to hear me out, you'd have realized that the only favor I wanted was for you to tell your roommate, Gladys, that I would like her to audition for me."

There is nothing I can say. I slump down on the edge of the bed and try again to take off the shoes. They feel like lead weights on my feet.

"You realize I could get you fired for this? First Mademoiselle's hair comb and now her shoes. My, my. You really don't want to be employed here, do you?"

My stomach lurches. I see my future dissolve before me like sherbet on a child's tongue. I want to protest my innocence over the hair comb, but there is no point. The shoes on my feet are far more incriminating.

Snyder stands at the window. "Hmm. What to do. What to do." His cigar smoke drifts around me like a fog. "I've a mind to frog-march you down to Cutler in those shoes. See what he has to say about the matter." My shame burns crimson on my cheeks, but I refuse to beg. "Or do I ignore this misdemeanor entirely. Let it be our secret. Goodness, what a dilemma I find myself faced with."

"You will do what you wish, Mr. Snyder. There is nothing I can say in my defense."

"Indeed, there isn't. But what, I wonder, would I get in return for keeping quiet?"

"I don't know, sir."

He looks at me with a cold hard stare and walks toward me. "Lift up your foot."

I stay perfectly still, although every part of me is trembling.

"I said, lift up your foot."

I raise my right foot tentatively. My leg convulses as he takes hold of my ankle. I flinch at his touch.

"I will say this for you, you have very shapely ankles, Miss Lane."

My flesh recoils beneath my stocking as he slowly undoes the tiny button and slips his fingers inside the leather, letting them rest there a moment before lifting the shoe gently from my foot. Hot tears of humiliation prick at my eyes as bile burns at the back of my throat. I am back in the butler's pantry at Mawdesley Hall. I can hear the squeak of his rubber soles against the linoleum floor; the sickening thud as his fist hits my cheek. I can hear myself begging him to stop, until his hand smothered my mouth.

"Please stop." The words from my past jump into my present. "Please don't." My voice is nothing but a whimper.

Snyder ignores me. "And the other."

I lift my left leg. Close my eyes. Wait for it to be over. I feel his hand against my ankle, on my calf. He lets his hand linger there for too long, drawing circles on the back of my knee with his fingertips. He runs his hand across the top of my foot before sliding his fingers inside and easing the shoe free. He places it slowly back onto the floor and leans forward, taking my chin in his hand and tilting my face toward the light, purring like a satisfied cat.

"I think you should put those shoes back where they belong, don't you?"

I can hardly breathe. My hands shaking, I wrap the shoes in tissue paper, place them back into the wardrobe, and close the door. I wish I'd never seen them as I slip my feet back into my plain black shoes.

Snyder stands behind me, so close that I can hear his breathing. Short, quick breaths. "You like to flirt a little, Miss Lane, don't you?"

"No, sir."

He yanks my hair sharply, pulling my face in front of the dressing-table mirror. "Liar. Look. There's a remarkable blush to your cheeks and your lips are plump. Anyone would think you were feeling aroused." I shake my head. He smirks and presses himself against me. "But I am, Miss Lane. I am very aroused. Isn't this what you wanted? What you were thinking about in the theater?"

I struggle away from him but his grip is too tight.

My vision blurs. *This isn't happening. It isn't real.* He leans into me, his lips against my ear. "Take the dress and go," he snarls. "This isn't over, Dorothy Lane. I have a feeling that you and I may need to discuss this matter again. In private."

I grab the bundle of linen and stumble from the room, everything spinning, my legs threatening to buckle beneath me at any moment. I run along the corridor and take the service steps down to the second floor. I reach the maids' bathroom just in time and retch into the basin, again and again, my body in spasms, desperately trying to purge itself of his touch. When I recover a little, I run water into the bath, pull off my stockings, and step into the water, tucking my skirts into my knickers as I bend down and scrub and scrub at my feet with a nail brush.

"Stupid, stupid girl." I scrub until my skin is red raw and my tears spill down into the water. "You stupid, stupid girl."

But no matter how much I scrub, I can't erase the memory of his hand on my ankle, nor the menace in his words. My indiscretion may have been momentary, but I know that it will follow me far.

32
DOLLY

They let me hold him for a while;
a feather in my arms.

The hotel laundry is in Kennington, a reasonable distance across the river and south of the city. Mademoiselle Delysia's dress sits in a packet of tissue paper on my lap as I rest my head against the side of the laundry truck and watch the boats on the Thames, barely visible through the fog. We rumble across Waterloo Bridge and on, along Waterloo Road toward the Elephant and Castle. It is an uncomfortable ride, the truck throwing me around like a rag doll as we judder over potholes and cobbles. I blow warm breaths onto the glass at the window and draw a butterfly absentmindedly into the mist. I think of the butterfly at Teddy's hospital window and wonder if it ever did fly away.

The truck trundles on, the driver humming and whistling at the same time—a noise that sets my teeth on edge. My nerves are rattled as it is. I can't throw off thoughts of Snyder; his touch, his threats, the stench of Virginia tobacco. I'm glad to be away from the hotel for a while and breathe a little easier knowing that he isn't around the next corner or behind the next door.

As we approach Kennington I stare more intently through the window. The buildings and shop fronts begin to look familiar and when we turn down Walworth Road, I know exactly where we are. I sit up straight and rub my breath from the window. There it is, right in front of me. Lime House. The Salvation Army Mothers' Hospital. The place that has haunted me since I first walked inside it four years ago.

Months before the Armistice was announced, rumors were rife that the Germans would surrender. None of us dared to believe it, not for a second, but the day we thought would never come finally arrived on a wet November morning. An armistice was declared. The war was over.

Before the month was out, the munitions factory was closed and I was back in my maid's uniform. I hated going back to Mawdesley Hall and the restrictions of domestic service, which felt stricter than ever after the relative freedoms of factory work. Mam couldn't manage on the widow's pension from the War Office, so off I trudged with reluctant feet, back along the sweeping drive-way to ask the housekeeper if they were looking to hire staff. They were.

Madam was delighted. She couldn't wait to fill her home with domestics and reinstate the proper order of things. Women like her were unbalanced during the war, their staff numbers depleted, their grand homes invaded by nursing staff, their privileged daughters required to nurse the sick and injured. The foundations of their superior status had been thoroughly shaken. But the narrowing of the gap was only temporary. Too quickly I settled back into my old routines. Any sense of independence I might have felt as a munitionette disappeared into the slop bucket along with the contents of the ladies' chamber pots. I was back at the bottom. When it came to "Them" and "Us," war had changed nothing at all.

Demobilization was a complicated and lengthy process. Our men came back in drips rather than the great emotional flood we'd imagined. Teddy was one of the first to come back, just after Christmas. Sent from a clearing station in London, he was admitted directly to the military war hospital in Maghull, denying me the romantic reunion of my dreams. The doctors said that Teddy was "Not Yet Diagnosed, Nervous" (which my cousin told me was hospital speak for shell shock). We were warned that it would be a long recovery process. I didn't care how long it took. I would be by his side.

On my afternoons off I traveled the long round trip to visit him, taking the bus to Rufford and then the train to Maghull. The doctors encouraged me to read my letters to Teddy. They thought it would help him remember. We'd communicated through letters for so long it felt normal to continue. I tried to be as cheery as possible, sitting beside his bed, reading my letters to him, my own words. He'd kept them in a bundle in the pocket of his greatcoat, close to his heart, just as he'd promised he would. It was strange to hear the war-torn emotions I'd ripped from my heart, to hear the words I'd struggled to find in the privacy of my bedroom, now read aloud in the stark daylight of a sterile hospital ward.

Occasionally there was a glimmer of recognition, but mostly there was only silence as Teddy stared out of the window. His voice, his words, had been stolen from him. He was locked in a horror too stark to release himself from, even though the trenches were miles away.

As the weeks passed I began to dread my weekly trip to Maghull. The hospital was exhausting; the sight of so many injured men was disturbing. But I kept visiting, kept reading my letters to him, kept hoping when there seemed to be nothing left to hope for.

The innocent flirtation with Madam's nephew was a harmless distraction; something to take my mind off things. That was all.

It started as a bit of harmless fun. An occasional smile, a wink, a careless hand trailed along the back of my skirt. All the maids talked about how handsome he was, an officer recently demobbed from Belgium, visiting from Scotland for rest and recuperation. His accent alone had us all giggling in the staff kitchen. Men were like precious gemstones after the war. We were dazzled by their presence, by the musky smell of them, by the sound of their deep laughter booming off the library walls. We'd forgotten how easily our hearts could be turned by the hint of a smile or a knowing look. We heard him cry out in his sleep sometimes, screaming as if he were still in the middle of the fighting. It made him seem vulnerable. It made him seem like one of us.

I was folding dinner napkins when he found me. Napkins.

He was drunk and aroused. I told him I had to get on, things to do, that I'd be in trouble if anyone found us, and that he shouldn't be hanging around in the kitchens anyway. He laughed and something changed in his eyes. He was oddly gentle at first, taking me by the hand and pulling me into the butler's pantry. He smelled of brandy and Virginia tobacco. My feeble protestations were like fuel to a fire, and something snapped. He grabbed my hair roughly and put his fingers to my lips. He told me if I made a single sound he would kill me. "I've killed men. Watched them die in agony. What does a kitchen maid matter?" I begged him to stop as he pulled up my skirts. I begged and pleaded, my words so quiet and weak and useless. His hands were so cold against my skin.

He wept like a child as he pushed himself inside me, the leather of his shoes squeaking against the linoleum floor, his hand smothering my screams. It was over quickly. In the distraction of his relief, I took the chance to bite down hard on his palm, earning myself a punch in the face. I remember the crack of his knuckles against my cheek, the jarring of my head as I fell to the floor, slumped against the riding boots I'd carefully polished earlier that evening. *Don't get blood on them. Don't spoil your hard work, Dolly.* He zipped up his trousers, straightened his waistcoat and cravat, and left as if nothing out of the ordinary had happened at all.

I lay there for hours. Too terrified to move. When I eventually did, I drew water from the pump outside and washed myself in the dark, the freezing water like tiny daggers piercing my skin, turning every part of me numb. It was as if my body belonged to someone else. It did. It belonged to him.

I told no one what had happened.

He was back in Scotland by the time I missed my monthly. I knew I'd be ruined if Madam found out I was in the family way. Nancy, the parlor-maid, told me to drink quinine and take hot baths in Beecham's Powders, but it was no use. I lifted the heaviest baskets of laundry I could find. I even threw myself down the scullery steps. Nothing worked. The bleeding and cramps I longed for wouldn't come. My skirts tightened around my waist as my belly began to swell and the sickness came over me in great waves. He had taken my dignity, broken my soul, and left me alone with the secret shame of a fatherless child.

I continued with my weekly visits to the hospital. All the time I sat beside Teddy, reading my letters full of love and hope, another man's child was growing within me. I stayed in Mawdesley as long as I could, until I couldn't conceal it any longer. I knew I had to take my shame and my secret to a place where nobody would know me. London. The perfect place to become invisible. The perfect place to become nobody.

Without telling a soul, I wrote to an aunt of mine who worked in service at a house in Grosvenor Square. I told her everything. She said she knew of a place out Kennington way, a Salvation Army hospital for unmarried mothers and that I could stay with her until my confinement at the hospital started. She made it sound like a prison sentence.

Mam and my sisters were heartbroken when I told them I was leaving to take up a position in London. Mam couldn't understand why I had to go all the way to London when I had a perfectly good situation in Mawdesley. I used Teddy as an excuse. Told her it broke my heart to see him that way; to know that he couldn't remember me. I showed her my scrapbooks, my collection of dreams. I told her London offered great prospects for a girl like me. After everything we'd been through, she couldn't deny me the opportunity to chase a better, happier life.

My last day in Mawdesley was a warm summer day. I said my good-byes to Teddy in a letter. It seemed we were forever destined to share our hopes and fears in the written word. I left the letter on the table beside his bed in the hope that one day he would read it and remember and understand. I left roses in a vase on the kitchen table and held Mam and my sisters tight against my heart. I didn't know it would be the last time I would see my sisters alive; that by the end of the month the last gasp of the Spanish flu epidemic would take them from us, just as it had taken so many others in its awful rampage across Europe.

As I walked to the bus stop that afternoon, a blackbird sang in a hawthorn bush and I felt the fluttering of my child from somewhere deep within me.

For nine months I tried my best to ignore the baby, concealing its existence behind loose-fitting coats and tightly closed doors, but one cold November night my child bawled its way into the world and took my breath away. I hardly dared look at him, afraid that I would change my mind. I'd heard of women who faltered at the last moment and took their baby home with them, preferring to face the anger and shame of their family than the reality of abandonment. I closed my eyes and pushed my hands against my ears to block out the bawling reality of his presence. Sensing my disregard for him, he clammed up like an oyster shell. The silence was unbearable.

They let me hold him for a while; a feather in my arms. Only when the moment came to let him go did I feel the immense weight of him. Only then did I realize that I loved him. Despite the painful memories he provoked—despite every-thing—he was my child and I loved him.

"Don't take him. Please don't." The words slipped from my lips as the faintest of whispers while my mind was a raging thunderstorm, bellowing across the room, deafening in my defiance. "You can't take him. He's mine." My panicked insistence was nothing but a whimper; I was too weakened by the efforts of labor to make myself heard.

"You're talking nonsense. The laudanum has you delirious. It's for the best. Now come along, you must let go. It wouldn't do to make a scene." The matron refused to meet my gaze as she leaned farther across the sweat-soaked delivery bed to tug and pull at the precious bundle cocooned in my arms. I felt suffocated by her sickening stench of bleach and soap, by the sharp sting of her words, by the hot breaths that fell against my cheek as she pressed against me.

"You can't take him. Please. He's all I have."

My anguished words as soft as goose down from a shaken pillow, drifting around me before slipping out of the open door, unheard, unheeded. And then the awful tugging and pulling, the wrenching and prizing apart of my fingers. It only took a moment, but felt like an eternity. The tiny bundle was lifted and taken from my arms. Taken from the room. Taken from my life. The edge of a blue blanket the last thing I saw as the door clicked shut.

I heard hushed whispers in the corridor and then only a dark, dark silence. Even my cries were muted by the weight of my grief.

I lay for hours, not moving, barely breathing, my arms still wrapped around the invisible form of the child I hadn't wanted and now couldn't bear to be without. *"It's for the best. Now come along. You must let go. It wouldn't do to make a scene."* Like an unwanted bundle of rags I had given him away, just as all the other unmarried mothers here would, not because they wanted to, but because they had no other choice. The cruel bastards like Madam's nephew who had held his hand over my mouth to smother my screams had taken away all of our choices, our dignity, our reputation, our children.

Sleep came just before dawn, a troubled anxious sleep muddled with distant memories of wounded soldiers and rousing song, the hypnotic whir of factory machinery, and the urge to dance. A dull ache settled in the empty crook of my arms and in my swollen breasts where my child should be suckling. And then the fever took hold.

For three days I lurched in and out of consciousness. The nurses attended to me as I fought against it. In my delirious mind I left the hospital and ran far away to an imaginary river where I filled my pockets with stones and stepped into the water. But I heard something in the distance. A voice, drifting through the open window. *"Wake up, Dolly. It's time now, time to wake up. You have to wake up."*

I opened my eyes. "Is he here?"

The nurse smiled and pushed the hair from my forehead. Such a tender touch. It reminded me of Mam and made me want to cry. "Welcome back, Dorothy."

"Where is he? Where am I?"

"You're in the hospital. Remember?"

I did. And all I wanted to do was fall into Teddy's arms and forget.

"A cup of tea. That's what you need. Tea will set you right."

But it didn't. The milk had turned. Everything was soured.

I placed the cup and saucer on the small table beside my bed, slid under the covers, and wept until the morning. I tried to recall the sound of my baby's cry, but all I heard was my own breath and the distant voice of a man I had loved. I had abandoned him too. I had abandoned them both when they needed me the most.

The truck driver pulls up outside the laundry entrance and I make my way inside. It is a hot, noisy place. The flat-iron machines hiss and whir as great armies of laundry maids pull bedsheets through huge rollers to stiffen and smooth them. Clouds of steam fog the washroom, so that I can just make out a blur of white and hear the rattle and thrum of the electric machines. One of the maids points me in the direction of the laundry manageress. I explain that the dress is needed for tonight and that I'm to take it back with me when it is ready.

"There's a tearoom on the high street," she says. "You can wait there." But I am not interested in tearooms. I already know where I'm going. Teddy always said that when you lose something you should go back to the start, back to the place you saw it last.

Leaving the laundry, I make my way slowly toward the Mothers' Hospital. I walked these streets once before, as hesitant then as I am now. I walk up the stone steps at the front of the building and push open the door. The smell immediately takes me back: bleach and sterilizing fluid. The smell of babies. The smell of him.

My heart pounding, I approach the reception desk. A girl behind the counter passes me a piece of paper without even looking up. "Fill in the form and hand it back when you're done."

"I'm not registering," I say. She looks at me over the top of her spectacles. I show her the photograph. "I want to find my son."

She sighs with a sense of having heard this a hundred times a day. "There's paperwork."

"Then I'll fill it in."

Leaving her chair, she rummages around in drawers and filing cabinets. Someone behind me coughs. Someone is sobbing into a handkerchief.

The girl returns and pushes several official-looking forms across the counter. I take a pencil from a pot and sit on a chair, carefully filling in as many details as I can remember. His date of birth. The date he left. My date of birth. My name. It takes a while but I complete everything as accurately as I can and take the forms back to the desk.

"When will I hear?" I ask as the girl clips the pages together and writes something in a ledger.

"We'll be in touch if there's any news."

It is a cold emotionless process. Forms are stamped. Papers are filed. The next young woman is called forward to take my place at the window.

As I step outside I turn to look up at the front of the building. A young girl stands at a window on the top floor. Pale-faced, blank expression. She is like an echo of myself not so many years ago.

The earlier fog has lifted by the time the laundry truck collects me, and as we drive back across the river I can clearly see the dome of St. Paul's on the skyline. It is a reminder. A reminder that I must be patient; that the fog will lift. Until then, I must keep hoping. Keep searching. Keep breathing.

33
DOLLY

I closed my eyes and wished
that whoever took my child
would be like her. Like spring.

In our cozy little bedroom at the hotel, we ring
in the New Year with hot port, the chimes of Big
Ben, and a rendition of "Auld Lang Syne." I can't
imagine a time when I didn't know this hotel or
this room or these girls: Sissy, Gladys, even
Mildred. They have become my family along with
the other staff. O'Hara and Cutler are like the
strict parents, the maids my sisters, the hotel the
grand home we all share with strange aunts and
cousins from all over the world. Sissy still makes
me laugh, Gladys is still all talk of Hollywood,
and Mildred and I still move awkwardly around
each other like strangers at a ball.

We haven't spoken of the Mothers' Hospital
again. She avoids being alone with me and I am
hesitant around her. If she's in our room and I
walk in, she leaves. If it's just the two of us in the
Maids' Hall after tea break or supper, she gathers
her things and rushes away. On her afternoons
and Sundays off, she disappears. Nobody knows

where to. Nobody asks. She writes her letters and remains sullen and withdrawn. It is only through a chance encounter in the linen stores that I finally get the chance to talk to her.

I'm counting chamber towels when I hear a strange wailing that at first I think must be a cat, but as I look behind a stack of wicker baskets I find Mildred, curled up on the floor, a towel folded in her arms like a mother holding an infant.

"Mildred?" Her face is blotched with tears. I step over a basket and bend down to her. "What's the matter? Has something happened?" I think immediately of Snyder. I'd hoped I wouldn't see him again after Mademoiselle Delysia was forced to return to France to recover from a nasty dose of laryngitis, but he returned last week. I know my indiscretion with the silver dance shoes won't have been forgiven; nor his threats forgotten. Maybe he has other maids in his sights. "Has someone been bothering you?"

She shakes her head and sits up as I shuffle into the narrow space behind the baskets and sit down beside her, pressing my back into the wickerwork. I pass her a handkerchief and we sit in silence until her tears subside and her breathing steadies.

"I try to forget," she says, "but I can't." She folds the handkerchief into a neat square and places it in her pocket. "Dorothy Lane. Edie Bishop. Betty Evans. All those names, all those memories, flooding back as you stood there in the

Maids' Hall dripping rainwater all over the floor. I'd wondered what happened to you all, and there you were, standing in front of me like a ghost."

"And what about Vera Green?" I ask. "What happened to her?"

"I gave my name as Vera Green so nobody would know it was me. I cut my hair the day I left the hospital. That's why you didn't recognize me. I thought I'd be able to leave Vera Green behind, but it's not that simple, is it?"

I shake my head. "No, it isn't."

"I remember them taking you from the ward," she continues. "You were hysterical with a fever. I never knew if you'd walked out of that place alive or if they carried you out in a box."

I think about those days and nights, drifting in and out of consciousness. "The nurses told me I'd been very ill, but the fever broke suddenly one night. I didn't know where I was when I woke up. At first I wished I'd never woken up at all."

Leaving day was the worst—the days the babies left. I'd watched the other girls on these days; heard their choking sobs. Too soon, it was my turn.

I washed him and dressed him and held him tight—so tight—his tiny heart a butterfly's wings fluttering against my chest.

I was cleaning the windows when I first saw her: red hair beneath a brown velvet hat, a ribbon of cream tied in a bow to the side, a coat the color of daffodils. She looked like spring; like she could love every single baby in the hospital and still have love to spare. I closed my eyes and wished that whoever took my child would be someone like her. Like spring.

I watched her again as she walked back down the steps a while later, a tiny bundle in her arms, and as she turned to step into the car I saw it: the matinée jacket, powder blue with a white ribbon trim stitched so carefully into the collar. The matinée jacket I'd made myself, sobbing with every click and clack of the needles.

I'd wished for her and I watched him go, knowing that I would never see him again; never feel his butterfly-wing heartbeat. All the loveliness of that spring day belonged to the woman in the daffodil coat, while I was left with an ache in my heart so dark and so deep I didn't know how I would ever recover.

I wept until I thought my bones would break.

The camera was all I had to remember him by, his beautiful little face captured by the shutter somewhere inside that little machine of Teddy's. When I developed the film I would be able to see him every day, and as I sobbed into my pillow that night, I vowed that every day without him would be a reminder to me to want more, to make a better life, to find the adventures and dreams I'd captured in my scrapbooks. I would do it for him. For little Edward.

Mildred sits silently beside me. We both stare at a cobweb being blown about by a draft.

"I went back last week," I say. "It was the first time I'd stepped foot in the place since I left. It smelled exactly the same. It smelled of him."

She turns her face to me. She's pretty, close up. There's a softness about her I hadn't noticed before. "What would you have called him?"

I can barely say his name. "Edward. He would have been known as Teddy, after the man who should have been his father."

"Why did you go back?"

"I hadn't planned to. I was running an errand at the laundry and there it was. It was as if I had to go back. Had to try to find out what happened to him." I pull at a loose thread on my apron. "They said it's very unlikely I'll hear anything."

"What if you do?" she asks. "What if they do find him?"

It is the question I have asked myself over and over. The question I have searched and searched for an answer to. "I don't know, Mildred. He came from such a dark place. I'm afraid all those memories will come back if I find him. Until then, I don't know." I close my eyes and see it all so clearly. "She had red hair, Mildred. Red hair and a yellow coat, the color of daffodils. I wished for someone like her to take him. There isn't a day has passed without me thinking about him;

wondering what he looks like, where he is, whether he is loved."

Mildred takes the rolled-up towel from her arms and stands up, shaking it out and folding it. "We have to believe they are loved, Dolly. What else can we do but imagine the happiness our babies brought to someone else's life; happiness where there was only sadness before. Think of that when you don't hear anything. Think of that when you look at his photograph."

She is right. "Did you ever think of taking your baby home with you?" I ask.

She shakes her head. "What life could I give her? The father was a soldier I met in a dance hall. He was on leave. Said he loved me and that we'd be married when the war was over. He'd gone back to Gallipoli when I wrote to tell him I was in the family way and that he was the father."

"What happened?"

"Told me to sort it out. You know, get rid of it. Turns out he was already married with a wife and kids. I never heard from him again."

"I'm so sorry, Mildred. Did anyone know?"

She shakes her head. "Didn't tell a soul. I booked myself into a place in Hackney where they sorted out girls like me, but I couldn't go through with it."

"Is that when you went to the Mothers' Hospital?"

"When I couldn't hide it any longer I told my

mother. She arranged for me to go to the Mothers' Hospital." She lets out a long sigh. "She'd been there too. She used to be a dancer, a chorus girl, but she gave it up when she married my father. When she told him she was expecting his child, he left her for someone else. Another dancer, as it turns out. She gave birth to me in the same hospital I gave birth to my daughter. History repeating itself. Except she was brave and selfless. She took me home. She said she couldn't bear to let me go."

My guilt surges within me. Why didn't I show such courage? "Your mother must be a brave woman."

"She is." Mildred hesitates for a moment. "In fact, you know her."

"Do I?"

"Her name is Kathleen O'Hara. Head of housekeeping."

I look at Mildred, wide-eyed. "O'Hara's your mother?" I can't believe it. "Why didn't you tell us?"

"Why would I? It only complicates things for everyone." She stands up and brushes dust from her skirt. "After I was born she moved back to her parents' house and got a position here as a potato peeler in the kitchens. Over the years she worked her way up. When I was old enough, I started in the kitchens, and we've lived in ever since. The governor was very kind to us. I'm the daughter she refused to give away, despite all the nasty comments and people looking down their noses at her. I'll always admire her for that."

I think of the stiff starchy woman who inspects us so thoroughly every morning. I think of the odd flash of something else I have sometimes seen in her eyes. "I can't believe O'Hara's your mother. All this time and I never knew."

"We all have a past, Dolly. There's always more to a person than the part they choose to show to the world."

I stand up and wrap my arms around her. She stiffens at first, but gradually I feel her give in to the gesture. "Thank you, Mildred. Thank you for talking to me. And I'm sorry for judging you."

"We all judge, Dolly. We'd be made of stone if we didn't." She wipes the last of her tears from her eyes and straightens her apron. "We'd better get on."

We leave the linen closet and I close the door behind us, turning the lock on our past and our secrets. If only they would stay there, locked away, hidden in the dark.

If only.

34
TEDDY

Mawdesley, Lancashire
September 1919

> "We are not just Teddy and Dolly. We are a damaged soldier and a broken heart."

They told me I could go home, that there was nothing more they could do for me. No miracle cure. No medical intervention. They'd tried everything: shock treatment, cold water, isolation.

"Time and patience, Mr. Cooper. That's the only medicine for you now."

Time and patience.

I am much improved from the broken man who had lumbered into the hospital so many months ago. I've watched the bare winter branches produce their first fragile buds. I've watched the blossoms blown on the wind, the birds build their nests, and the foliage burst into life beneath the warmth of the sun. Now it is my turn to grow new buds, green shoots, and strong branches.

The nurses helped me with my speech, and while I still sound like I've drunk ten pints of ale, people can at least understand me, and my words become clearer every day. They also helped me to control the tremble in my hands, mostly by drawing. Turns out I have a talent for art. They said I should keep it up when I got home.

Home.

Such a different place from the one I left and yet so familiar: the smell of hops from the brewery, the sweep of the sails on the flour mill. They tell me many were lost, ripped from our community by war and the influenza epidemic. Those who remain are forever changed by what they have seen.

But the biggest difference is that Dolly is not here.

Her mam tells me she went to London; that she found better employment than anything Mawdesley could ever offer her. I smile as she tells me. Dolly Lane was always going to leave. I only wish I could have said a proper good-bye.

At least I have her letters to remember her by. From the very first—now faded and stained, read so many times—to the very last, still crisp and white and read only once.

A good-bye is a good-bye after all.

July 1919

My darling Teddy,

This is the last time I will write to you and the hardest letter I will ever send.

I have to leave, Teddy. For reasons I

can't explain, I have to go away. I will never stop loving you, and if only things were different there is nowhere I would rather be than by your side.

War changed us all, Teddy. I am not the girl who wept for you on the station platform all those years ago and you are not the carefree boy who wiped the tears so gently from my cheeks. Those two people were lost, somewhere between the battlefields of France and the barley fields of home. We are not just Teddy and Dolly. We are a damaged soldier and a broken heart.

You are a good, good man, Teddy Cooper, and I wish you nothing but happiness. My only hope is that one day these words will mean something to you, and that you will remember me and all that we once had. And when you remember, I hope that you will find it in your heart to forgive me. More than anything, I can't bear the thought of bringing you any more pain.

You always told me to look and listen, to take notice of what was around me. I promise I will. I promise that I will always be looking for you; listening for you. I will see you in the stars and hear you in those silent moments.

Live your life, Teddy. Live your life with hope and love and adventure.

Your Little Thing, always.

Dolly

X

After reading the letter, I fold it neatly in half and place it in a special box I keep beneath my bed. And there it will stay. Her good-bye. Her final act of love.

35
DOLLY

*"And after all, every leading lady
needs a great understudy."*

London shakes off winter like an unwanted coat and spring arrives with a week of sunshine and curtains dancing at the open windows of the river suites. Daffodils and crocuses decorate the parks and gardens in yellow and purple, while cherry blossoms sway on the trees in shades of pink and white. On my Sundays off, I go to look at the displays of Easter hats and gloves, handkerchiefs and ribbons in the windows on Regent Street and Oxford Street. Without the din of weekday traffic and market traders, it is perfectly peaceful, the sounds of distant church bells and the clap of pigeons' wings my only companions. I pass the theaters on Shaftesbury Avenue, admiring the posters promoting new shows and the new stars for us to idolize. I close my eyes and imagine.

I've worked hard over the winter, practicing my dance steps and deportment, much to the amusement of Sissy, who laughs at my newly rounded vowels. She says I sound like Lizzie of York and that she wouldn't be surprised if I was invited to tea at the Palace soon! I don't mind her teasing. It's a sign that I'm becoming the girl I long to be.

As the months pass, my heart continually trips me up, confusing me with my feelings for Perry. With the infectious bloom of spring and a growing ease in each other's company, our arrangement to spend an hour together has gradually lapsed into many more. We often leave his apartment and stroll along the Embankment or through St. James's Park. On cooler days, we visit the British Museum and the Tate at Millbank. I enjoy spending time with him, learning from him. Without going any farther than a mile in either direction, my world is expanding around me. I've come a long way from the rain-spattered girl who arrived at The Savoy on a rainy October afternoon, but improved posture and the arrival of spring cannot fix everything.

Like the winter soot that clings to the rooftops and windows, my past clings to me. There is no word from the Mothers' Hospital. No letter. My child remains a face in a faded photograph, a distant memory of a fluttering heartbeat against my chest. Until I know that he is safe and loved, part of me will always remain tethered to that night in the butler's pantry; my wings will remain broken and useless.

But there is hope. Under Loretta May's careful guidance, I can feel myself transform. I still pinch myself when I walk into her apartment, but there are moments when I concentrate so hard on her exercises and instruction that I forget how famous she is and where I am. She is a determined teacher and I am an eager student. She shows me how to stand to make myself appear three inches taller, how to walk onto a stage, how to turn my head for photographers, how to extend my arms to make a movement more fluid, how to smile to break the hearts of men and capture the hearts of women. She tells me people are beginning to talk; rumors threading through the gossip columnists about a girl she is developing; a protégée. The pressure of expectation worries me but she dismisses my concerns. "Let them speculate," she says. "It will all help when you make your debut. There is no greater entrée than intrigue."

Each time we meet, she has something new planned for me. Today, I am to be measured for a new dress. She wants me to experience the boredom of standing still for hours at a time while measurements are taken and adjustments made. She insists that I must learn how to move in a couture dress to show it off properly, telling me "a couture dress moves differently than those dreadful shapeless things people buy from shops."

I arrive at the Berkeley Square apartment and wait in the drawing room, twiddling my thumbs until she sweeps into the room in an ochre caftan, great swathes of material flowing behind her as she flounces over to me and kisses me on the cheek. She wears an olive-green turban, embellished with onyx and amber. A long line of bangles along her arm click and clack as she moves.

"Now, Miss Lane. Straight to work. Strip down to your underwear and stand in front of the window." She senses my hesitation and tuts. "Use the screen if you must. You'll have to get used to people peering at you and commenting on how thin you are or how plump you've become. Come along. Get on with it. We've no time for prudery."

I step behind the screen and wriggle out of my dress and stockings. I emerge reluctantly and stand awkwardly as Miss May lights a cigarette and walks around me, prodding and poking her elegant fingers into my skin.

"Darling, you're like a dumpling." I pull my stomach in, but she already has a lump of doughy flesh between her fingers. I shriek as she pinches me. "Exactly. That is what laziness feels like. You'll never get a shriek from a girl who fits into her skin perfectly. You need exercise, Miss Lane, and plenty of it. Wait there."

I perch on the window seat as she sweeps from the room and reappears with a beautiful ivory chiffon dress over her arm. She holds it up against me.

"Lucien Lelong," she says. "Last season, but never mind. Put it on and let's see if you can carry it off."

I shimmy the dress over my hips. It feels like air against my skin, even though it is too tight here and there. As I twist my hips from side to side, the elaborate beading rustles. I twist faster, relishing the sound. Miss May fastens the hook and eye and places her hands on my shoulders, turning me back around to face her. Her face is inscrutable.

I glance at my reflection in the looking glass, standing on my tiptoes to make myself taller. "It's so beautiful," I whisper.

"A dress this beautiful will look good on anybody, but it will look incredible when you've lost a few pounds. Ivory is terribly unforgiving, but so wonderful under the spotlights."

As I wriggle out of the dress, a door closes downstairs and I hear voices. Miss May claps her hands together. "Ah, good. Here's Hettie."

Hettie arrives, out of breath and flustered. "I'm so sorry I'm late, Miss May. My sister isn't well, so I had to bring Thomas. He's downstairs with Elsie. He won't be any bother. I promise."

"Not to worry. These things happen. I'm quite sure Elsie can find something to entertain the little chap. Now, introductions. Hettie, Miss Lane. Miss Lane, Hettie." We smile and say hello, both too polite to remind Loretta that we've met before. "She's all yours, Hettie," Miss May continues. "I've told her she needs to lose a few pounds, so bear that in mind when you take your measurements."

She drifts over to the gramophone player and sets the needle on a record. Lazy jazz fills the room as she flops down onto the chaise, placing a satin mask over her eyes.

I feel self-conscious in my undergarments as Hettie walks over to the window and puts a sewing case on the table beside me. The sight of all the pins and needles and reels of different colored cotton reminds me of Mam. I feel a sudden longing to see her.

Hettie takes a measuring tape and a box of pins from the case. "Stand as straight as you can. Shoulders back. Chest out." She takes hold of my limbs and positions me as if I were a mannequin. "That's perfect. Place your arms out to the side. I won't be long."

She is quick and efficient with her measurements, scribbling notes onto a small pad of paper and making a few preliminary sketches. I talk about The Savoy and the famous guests I've met. She tells me about the actresses she's dressed. From downstairs, I catch the occasional sound of a child's laughter.

"It sounds like they're having fun down there!"

Hettie smiles. "He's a good boy. Elsie's mad about him." She lowers her voice. "Although I'm not so sure about Miss May."

Loretta leans over the chaise. "What Hettie is trying to tell you, Miss Lane, is that I don't especially care for children. Although I will admit that little Thomas is rather adorable—and utterly ruined by his mother. He'll never marry and leave home if she keeps being so nice to him."

Hettie blushes at being overheard. "She's right. We do spoil him. Poor little mite. He's had a tough time of it. His father died suddenly last year."

"I'm sorry to hear that."

"Thomas is named after him. He misses his daddy terribly. We all do. My sister especially. She clings to little Thomas like her life depended on him."

"He isn't yours, then?"

"No. He's my sister's boy. I mind him sometimes to help her out, although she can hardly bear to let him out of her sight." She wraps a measuring tape around my hips and waist. I try to resist the urge to suck my stomach in. "Do you have children?"

The question hangs over me like lead. "No. No, I don't."

"Well, maybe one day. When you meet the right man—although that's easier said than done these days."

She chuckles to herself and asks me to turn around. I gaze out of the window, looking at nothing in particular, my thoughts a million miles away.

When Hettie finishes she leaves me with Miss May to practice my do-re-mi's and my dance steps. I tell her about the latest shows I've seen, and how I've been watching the girls in lead chorus, noticing how they outshine the others.

"Good. You're beginning to understand," she says, drifting across the room like a wisp of smoke. "There is far more to a performance than learning steps by rote and fixing a grin on your face. It comes from here," she says, placing her hands over her chest. "From deep inside. You can move your feet and hit all the steps in all the right places, but if you don't feel the music in your heart, you'll never truly shine. There is dancing and there is moving in time to the music. They are as different as a couture dress from a shop-bought one."

"You really don't care for shop-bought dresses, do you?"

She pulls a face as if she's sucking a lemon. "Vulgar things. I'd rather walk around naked." She lights a cigarette and blows perfect circles of smoke as she wafts around the room. She seems distracted today, unable to settle on anything. "You like to read, don't you, Miss Lane?"

"Yes. I've always loved reading."

"Did you ever read a book that captivated you so much you didn't notice the sun setting or the fire going out?"

I think of *The Adventure Book for Girls*, how I would sit by the fire and forget all about my chores or the hours passing by. "Yes. It was like everything else melted away. As if the stories became part of me."

She grabs my hands and looks into my eyes. "Exactly! And that's precisely what performing should feel like. You shouldn't think about where your feet are or where your hands are or who might be in the audience. Dancing should be as natural to you as breathing in and out. It should be like reading a book; not spelling out each individual word, but becoming lost among the sentences and paragraphs and chapters until you are transported to another place entirely."

I look at this amazing woman whose velvet-soft hands I'm holding in mine. Her green eyes carry something of sadness in them as well as beauty. Like I did the first time I met her in the Embankment Gardens, I see her as a real woman, not the theater star whose face I've admired on so many posters, but a real person with hopes and fears and flaws. She seems suddenly fragile beside me.

"You are a beautiful young woman," she says, pushing a loose hair back from my forehead. "Look at you. So perfect. Like the first flower of spring." She holds my face in her hands for a moment and I see the glisten of tears in her eyes.

"Miss May? What's wrong?"

She drops my hands and turns away. "Nothing. Take no notice of me. I'm a silly old fool."

She pours us both a drink and perches on the edge of the window seat, the afternoon light falling around her. I sip my drink. Gin. I've never really cared for it, but I don't like to say.

"Have you ever been loved, Miss Lane?" She is in one of her thoughtful moods. It happens every now and then. Something in her changes, as if she is going over her entire life. "Truly loved?"

I think about Teddy. "Yes. Yes, I have."

She walks to the writing bureau, picks up a scrapbook, and passes it to me before returning to the window seat. "I was loved once. Take a look."

I flick through the pages of cuttings, each one labeled and dated. So much love and admiration written in the press notices, but it is a single scrap of paper, lying loose among the pages, that she asks me to look at. It is a small press cutting, an image of a younger Loretta May. I have the very same cutting in my own scrapbook.

"Turn it over," she says.

I turn the paper over in my hands. On the back are the words *Now, you are mine! Always, Roger xx*

"I loved him with all my heart," she says. "I loved him so much that I was physically sick from the pain of watching him leave." I think about Teddy at the train station, about how I felt as I left him in the hospital and walked away. I understand that pain. "Roger wasn't good enough for me," she continues. "Not the titled gentleman I should have met during my Season. We wrote to each other for eighteen months and spent three blissful days together one summer. We were married in secret before he sailed back to France. It was the most reckless, most fabulous thing I'd ever done, and I told nobody."

"What happened?"

"He was killed by a shell explosion. We'd been married exactly one week."

"I'm so sorry."

She turns to look at me. "I have never loved anyone since. No one else will ever come close. Roger looked at me as though the world was made endlessly better, simply because I existed. Do you know that feeling, Miss Lane?"

I see Teddy grinning. I hear him telling me he is happy, just because I am there, beside him. I do know that feeling. And I know what it is like to be without it.

We sit in silence, watching the blossoms that dance on the trees outside the window, until Miss May sweeps across the room and places a record on the gramophone. The scratch of the needle blends into a waltz.

" 'The Merry Widow Waltz,' " she says. "Our favorite. Roger was a wonderful dancer. We danced to this very song at The Savoy beneath a starlit sky."

I smile. "Teddy was a wonderful dancer too."

"Teddy? You haven't mentioned him before."

I look at my feet. "I don't talk about him."

"I don't talk about Roger either." She looks at

me with a softness I haven't seen before. "Did he die?"

I listen to the music, the rise and fall of the piano and violin, trumpet and clarinet. "No. He survived. He suffered very badly from shell shock. I tried to help him, but he didn't remember me." I stare at my hands in my lap. "I left him and came to London. I abandoned him when he needed me the most."

The relief of saying the words I have carried in my heart for so many years prompts a sudden rush of tears. Miss May passes me a handkerchief and I weep into it, apologizing as I dab at my cheeks and wipe my nose. "I'm so sorry. I shouldn't be troubling you with these things."

She sits beside me. "We all have a past, Miss Lane. We've all done things we regret. Sometimes it is easier to ignore the truth. Pour a drink. Take a shot of morphine. Run away. Dance."

We listen to the music until it scratches to a stop. She takes another record from its sleeve. A jazz number. More upbeat.

I dry my tears and look at her. "Can I ask you something?"

"You are in my apartment drinking my best gin. You can ask me anything you wish, dear girl."

"Why are you helping me? Why me?"

She leans back against the chaise and thinks for a moment. "Why not you, Miss Lane? You and Perry stumbled into each other for some inexplicable reason. I am helping you because you are helping him, and you are both, in turn, helping me." She takes a long swig of her drink. "It occurs to me that while we may come from very different beginnings, in the end we are all looking for the same thing. To love and to be loved. Isn't that all that matters?" She stands up. "And after all, every leading lady needs a great understudy. What better than for someone I have taught myself to step into my shoes?" Her face lights up. "Talking of which, what size are you?"

"A five."

"Perfect!" She rushes from the room and reappears a moment later with a pair of silver Rayne's dance shoes in her hands. "Here. Try them on."

"But, I couldn't. They're . . ."

She sighs and puts her hands on her hips. "I may be in a benevolent mood, Miss Lane, but I have no time for silly notions of unworthiness. Put them on."

I do as I am told. The shoes slip on like silk. I think about Larry Snyder's hand against my ankle and brush the memory aside. I don't need to look over my shoulder here. I don't need to explain or apologize. These shoes come with an invitation.

"They're perfect," I say.

"Marvelous! Keep them. They can be your lucky shoes, just as they were always lucky for me. Now, Miss Lane. Show me what you've got."

I laugh as she begins to twirl around the room. I follow her steps, the shoes so light on my feet. It is like dancing on a cloud. I close my eyes, allowing myself to get lost in the music as I think of something Perry once said. *"There is a moment when you're writing a song when the lyrics and the melody begin to meld into one glorious thing and it settles across you like a gentle summer rain. That is when you know you have written something special. That is the music people will carry in their hearts. That is when their feet will truly dance."*

For the first time, I really believe that I can do this. I feel it in my heels and my toes, in my fingertips and the fine hairs that prickle at the back of my neck. For the first time, I sense that the adventure isn't waiting for me. It is here. Right now. I am in the middle of it.

I shout above the music. "I'm ready, Miss May. I'm ready to audition."

She glides and twirls around me. "I know," she laughs. "You've been ready for weeks, darling. The only person who didn't know it was you." She grabs my hands and spins me around. "You're going to be glorious, Miss Lane. Glorious! Loretta's Little Star. My very own shining star!"

Neither of us notice Perry walk into the apartment. We don't see him lean against the doorframe and watch us dance over the boards where we've rolled up the Turkey rug. Only when the gramophone record stops playing and we fall onto the chaise in an exhausted heap do I see him standing there, looking at me with those gray eyes, a gentle gaze that hints of something like love, and I wonder. I wonder if I can ever truly let Teddy go, and if I did, I wonder if a girl like me could ever find love with a man like Perry Clements.

I wonder.

36
LORETTA

"That's the beauty of a life on the stage,
one can be whomever one chooses to be."

The spring I longed for arrives with so much color
and life that it is almost impossible to think about
dying. I have confounded the doctors with my
ability to fight this disease and my stubborn
refusal to die. Whenever my thoughts do wander
to such dark places as my eventual demise, I
distract myself with the girl. It gives me such
immense pleasure to watch her bloom. Miss Lane
has become quite a marvel under my watchful
eye. She is that rare kind of girl Charlot spoke of;
the kind of girl one discovers perhaps once in a
decade, a rough diamond waiting to be polished
and brought out to dazzle for all the world to see.
It was in her all along; that indescribable magical
something that sets an ordinary girl above the
rest. She may not be the best dancer or the greatest
beauty, but she has lived—my goodness she has
lived. Miss Lane has overcome heartache and
disappointment, she has struggled and suffered,
loved and lost, and all of that sorrow and anger
blends with such determination and hope until it

shines out from her in the way she moves and sings and the way she looks at you. It excites me. *She* excites me as I watch her transform from the dowdy young girl who first walked into my apartment to the determined young woman I see now.

Perry is also transformed as the fogs of winter lift. He is less prone to the mood swings and erratic behavior that have blighted his life since the war and he is writing with more passion and enthusiasm than I've seen for a long time. His muse is certainly living up to her billing. Miss Lane makes him laugh, while he encourages her to believe in herself. They are good for each other. It is a comfortable partnership, punctuated occasionally with a hesitation, a flush to the cheek, a sense of something other than companionship that I observe between them, but such moments are fleeting and neither of them acts on whatever it is they might feel. I'm not entirely sure they should. They are happy enough without the messy complications of love, so I do nothing to encourage them. Besides, darling Bea is still waiting in the wings and she and Perry seem to be getting on rather well recently, much to my delight. I can't help but worry that everyone will become horribly unstuck if a romance were to blossom between Perry and Miss Lane, despite his claims to have fallen in love with her from the moment he first saw her. My hope is that the first flush of attraction has calmed into something less dramatic, something more akin to the love between a brother and sister than the passion between lovers.

Invigorated by Miss Lane's wry sense of humor and wonderfully down-to-earth outlook on life, Perry already has a score of delightful numbers for Charlot. He insists that I visit his apartment to hear him play each number when he is happy with it and I no longer have the energy to refuse. I drag myself up the stairs, lie on his battered old sofa, close my eyes, and listen, imagining how the numbers will sound in a theater. I can only delight in what he has produced. One number in particular that he has called "The Girl from The Savoy" is certain to be a big hit when it finally gets onto the stage.

"It's wonderful, darling. Truly, it is. When will the revue play?"

"Charlot wants to put it on at the Shaftesbury as soon as possible. Jack Buchanan and Binnie Hale are already signed up. Gertie Lawrence is a possibility. He's planning a short run in London, and if the notices are kind and the audiences enthusiastic, he'll take the entire company to Broadway. Lee Shubert has heard most of the score and loves it. He thinks it will especially appeal to American audiences. Archie Selwyn's name was mentioned too. This is going to be big, Etta. Very big. And the perfect opportunity for

Miss Lane to find her feet in the chorus. Some of the numbers are based on her story, after all. When will she audition?"

"Charlot wants to see her next week."

"Next week? Is she ready?"

"She's been ready for weeks, darling."

"Then why haven't you arranged for him to see her sooner?"

"Because *she* needed to be ready. Only she could truly know."

He looks at me with so much hope in his eyes it is almost painful to see. "I hope she impresses him, Etta. I hope she shines."

"She will do more than shine, darling. I have taught Miss Lane to dazzle."

But among all that is so new and wonderful with the onset of spring, my fears have also been realized and the routine of afternoon tea at Claridge's has begun to drift away from Perry and me. With each week that passes, one or the other of us has somewhere to go or someone to see. For him, it is usually Miss Lane, or a theatrical producer. For me, it is appointments with doctors. They are increasingly concerned. Their medication is stronger, their insistence that I must tell close family and friends more and more urgent. I have fought it well, but my illness is a truth that I cannot hide much longer. I have to regularly pull out of performances, the pain too much to drag myself from my bed. I feign a dose of laryngitis or a migraine. I claim exhaustion and nerves. The press are onto me like an owl to a mouse. They sense something stirring; a story building.

LORETTA MAY INDISPOSED AGAIN
FANS DISTRAUGHT AS UNDERSTUDY
STEPS IN DURING INTERVAL
CONCERNS RAISED FOR THE DARLING
OF THE WEST END

I'll give them a headline soon enough. For now, I must put on my best clothes and my bravest smile and meet Perry as agreed.

I keep my head down as my car pulls up outside Claridge's. I walk quickly to my usual table in the Winter Garden. I no longer dally and preen. I rush and hide, reluctant for people to see the dark shadows beneath my eyes and the sunken hollows of my once rounded cheeks, the telltale signs of a woman on the edge, a woman who seeks solace from her invisible pain in morphine and gin and any number of other drugs to get through the next hour, day, and week.

Perry is late, as usual. He finds me tired and irritable. I find him perky and annoying. We talk around in circles, about anything and everything, but not about the fact that he might have fallen in love with Miss Lane, or that he still has feelings for Bea, and never about the fact that I am dying.

I watch him push a sandwich around his plate until I cannot bear it anymore. "When are you going to tell her, Perry?"

"Tell who what?"

"You know perfectly well who and what. Don't be coy. It isn't becoming in a man."

He picks at a sprig of tarragon and fusses with a slice of cucumber as waiters dance around us like partners in a quadrille. "We've been here before, haven't we, Etta? We're getting along so well I'm afraid it might spoil things if I broach the subject of love. What if she doesn't feel the same?"

"And what if she does?" *What if you were dying, Perry? What would you do then?* I narrow my eyes and peer at him. "We are talking about the same person, aren't we? We are talking about Bea?"

He falters and takes a long sip of coffee. "Yes. Yes, of course we're talking about Bea."

I lean back in my chair and close my eyes, listening to the pianist, to the sound of people laughing and chatting. I adore this place. I drink it into my soul.

"What are you doing?"

"I'm listening, Perry. Feeling the life of this place." I open my eyes. "Isn't it marvelous? If there is a heaven I hope it is exactly like the Winter Garden at Claridge's."

He laughs. "Have you been at the gin again?"

I lean forward and grab his hand, squeezing it tight. "Look around, Perry. Look and listen. We're always rushing to be somewhere, thinking of what's next without ever noticing what's now. Life doesn't happen *to* us, darling, we must *make* it happen. Don't sit there wondering what if. Tell Bea how you feel. Tell her you love her. Ask her to marry you, if that's what you truly want. And if you're fibbing, and you really want to tell Miss Lane all those things, then do. Be brave, darling. Be reckless. There's no duller quality than caution."

I take a long drag of my cigarette. My hands tremble. I know I'm going to tell him.

"But how can I be sure?" he asks. "How can I know I'm making the right decision?"

"You can't. Nobody can ever be sure. We take risks. We close our eyes and jump. Nobody would ever fail if they didn't try. The only things we ever value in life inevitably lead us to failure. Parents fail. Actresses fail. Productions fail. How do I know that my performance was good? Because somebody else's was terrible. That's how I know." I look at him across the table. "I think you're afraid of being happy, Perry. I think you've become so used to dragging guilt and misery around that you're afraid of what life might be like if you let them go."

He stirs his coffee, first one way, then the other. His indecision apparent in everything. "I have these blissful moments when I'm writing music and I almost forget the war. It all gets lost in the melody. But then I remember." He looks at me. Those gray eyes of his forever haunted by his memories. "The men I shot will never hear music again. They'll never fall in love. Or dance. I can't help feeling that I don't deserve to be happy, Etta."

"Nobody will ever know what it was like for you to pull the trigger. Cowards. Deserters. Whatever they called them, we know they were brothers and fathers, sons and lovers. You were playing a part, my darling, following a script. None of us wanted to be involved in a war, but it happened. Roles were cast, direction given by those in command. You did only what was asked of you." I want to shake him; shake all this remorse from him. "You are not Officer Clements anymore. Not part of this battalion or that battalion. You're Peregrine Clements. That's all. A young man trying to find his way in life. It is perfectly all right to allow yourself to be happy."

He smiles and squeezes my hand. "Thank you. You really can be incredibly wise at times, Etta. Just when I think I know you, I see a side to your personality that takes me by surprise. It's like a different person has taken over for a while."

"That's the beauty of a life on the stage, one can be whomever one chooses to be. A different role each season, a new life to inhabit for a while. I've learned a lot from the women I've become on the stage. They've taught me how to love, how to laugh, how to survive . . . some have even taught me how to die."

The word hangs in the air.

Now. Now is the time.

I take my letter from my purse and place it on the table between us. I hold both his hands in mine. "I'm so sorry, Perry. I'm so sorry to have to tell you."

"Tell me what?"

I push the page toward him. "This explains everything."

He opens the folded page and starts to read the words I have agonized over for months. His face turns to stone as I lift my cigarette holder to my lips and draw in a deep lingering breath of nicotine. I hold it for a while, savoring the rush to my head before I exhale and watch the smoke dissipate around us. I read silently along with him, remembering every carefully chosen terrible word.

My darling Perry,

There is no easy way to tell you this, so I will simply set out the facts.

The doctors tell me that I have a cancer and that I am dying. It is incurable—too established for them to treat. It is this that has been the cause of my episodes and increasing withdrawal from performing over the past months.

Like a fool I thought I could beat it, but there are some battles one can never hope to win, no matter how determined one might be to fight.

Don't pity me, Perry. For God's sake, don't pity me. Let me live my life to the very end. Let me be Loretta May, not a dying actress.

I am so sorry to have to tell you this. I wish, with all my heart that it wasn't so. But it is, and we must somehow try to bear it.

Your sister, always.
Virginia
XX

He looks up at me, the color drained from his cheeks. "It can't be true."

"It is. I am dying, Perry. I'm so very sorry."

The words drift about in the space between us, not yet real, not yet understood. The pianist plays a waltz. The sun streams through the skylights, casting rainbows at my feet.

Perry holds tight to my hands. "How long have you known?"

I feel strangely calm as I find the words that have eluded me for so long. "Six months. Longer.

I can't remember. I have a cancer in my lung, darling. There is nothing they can do for me. I've kept up the performance for as long as I could, but I'm tired now."

His hands shake in mine. His face as pale as milk. "Why didn't you tell me? I could have helped."

"I've tried, Perry. I've tried to tell you so many times, but I could never find the right moment, the right words."

"But there must be something they can do. Surely. Can we get a second opinion?"

"I've been through all that. Doctors, consultants, specialists. They all tell me the same thing. The prognosis isn't good." I take a sip of tea and let out a long sigh as the burden of my secret lifts from my shoulders. I feel as though I can breathe properly for the first time in months. "I didn't know for a long while. I put it down to exhaustion, late nights, winter fogs, the usual ailments. But it worsened. It worsened quickly."

"But . . . when?" He hesitates to ask the question. "How long?"

"How long have I got?" He nods. "Not very. A couple of months, perhaps. I've told Cockie that tonight will be my last performance. Tomorrow, I'm going to Nine Elms."

"Nine Elms?"

"The doctors say the sea air will help to ease the pain in my chest. Rest and care is what I need now. From there I'll go to Cousin Freddie's place in Devon."

He grips my hands as the tears begin to fall. "Have you told Mother and Father? Aubrey?"

"Not yet. I've sent a telegram to inform Mother I'll be there tomorrow. I want to tell them in person—although I'm not expecting too much sympathy from her. The less time she has to fuss, the better. And it's the spring ball next week, so I have the perfect excuse to visit. She won't suspect anything and she'll be too distracted by canapés and sleeping arrangements to worry about her daughter dying."

"Loretta! That's a dreadful thing to say."

I smile. "Oh, come on, Perry. Let me have a little fun. This is why I've waited so long to tell anyone. I can't stand the thought of being pitied and fussed over. I want to carry on as normal for as long as possible. Go out with a bang rather than fade away. Perhaps Ada will invent a new cocktail in my honor at the American Bar at The Savoy. Although her Corpse Reviver would probably be appropriate."

Perry looks at his hands. "Please, Loretta. Don't."

I lean back in my chair. "I'm sorry, darling. One has to poke a little fun at such a ludicrous situation."

"So you'll go to the ball as if nothing is wrong?"

"Absolutely. I'll tell Mother and Father afterward—and everyone else. I'll dress to the nines and drink and dance and be merry, the same as I am every year. In fact, I was thinking that you should bring Miss Lane. It will be the perfect social outing for her. Her very own debut. It's exactly what she needs. What you need. What I need."

"But she'll never be able to take time away from the hotel."

"Of course she will. Leave that to me. Even chambermaids deserve a little holiday every now and again. I'll have a discreet word with Reeves-Smith. Invent a sick aunt, or something."

The waiter stops at our table to refill the water jug and asks if we'd like more tea.

Perry looks at me and then at the waiter. "Yes please. More tea. More cakes. More of those ridiculous little sandwiches, and a bottle of your best champagne." The waiter looks surprised. "We are extremely thirsty and desperately hungry. Hurry along now. There's a good chap."

I whisper a thank you.

"Actually," he says, "I never told you, but I really quite enjoy this whole afternoon tea business. Once a week is hardly enough. I think we should do it more often."

I laugh and squeeze his hand. "I'm glad to have told you, Perry."

"And I'm glad you have told me. I just wish you'd done so sooner. And I wish there was something I could do to help."

I look at him. "Actually, there is. There is something you can do that would give a dying lady immense joy."

I talk and he listens, and by the time we've enjoyed the entire bottle of champagne, I have finally made him see sense on the matter of his future happiness.

And that is how one announces that one is dying, over strawberry tartlets and salmon sandwiches, accompanied by the background music of a Viennese waltz, surrounded by strangers. No histrionics. No weeping and wailing and clinging to people like limpets. No stark interior of a doctor's room or a hospital corridor. Here, in my favorite place in the whole of London, with the brother I am lucky to call my friend.

My final performance is one of my very best. Cockie is utterly devastated when I tell him, but he promises not to tell anybody until I've had some time with my family. As far as the cast and the audience and the gossip columnists are concerned, it is just another splendid performance of *HOLD TIGHT!* I drink in the atmosphere, the adulation, the adoring cries from the gallery, so that I am full to the brim of love and life, a champagne glass overflowing. As I deliver my final line and sink to my knees and weep with joy for the happy conclusion of my turbulent onstage love life, the lights go out and the curtain drops, plunging me into the dark silence of a dead blackout for the final time.

I don't rush from the stage. I don't move. I stay where I am and listen to the rapturous applause and the cries for "more, more," and the stamping of appreciative feet.

I am humbled and grateful. I am the little girl who dreamed of this very moment. I am Virginia Clements, the woman who fell in love with a soldier and nursed so many others back to health. I am everybody's darling, Loretta May, and all the roles she has ever played. And here, on my knees in the pitch dark, as I finally accept the fact that I am dying, I have never felt more alive.

37
DOLLY

The words I have dreamed of. The words
I have imagined in my darkest moments.

The one constant since my life took such a curious
turn is Clover. Dear Clover. As dependable as
sunrise. We meet as often as we can at the Palais,
but I'm often too exhausted or distracted to
give her my full attention. She tells me bits of
news from Grosvenor Square—how she took a
tumble down the stairs, some trouble with the
kitchen maid, a marriage proposal for Madam's
daughter—but her words drift over me like
passing clouds.

And it's not just me. Clover's thoughts often
seem to be elsewhere as we twirl around the dance
floor or share a cigarette and a pot of tea at the
teashop. She always seems to have a headache or
a reason to head back to Grosvenor Square well
before the ten o'clock curfew, so I often find
myself back at the hotel long before the others. I
take the opportunity to practice my high kicks
and dance routines, but I can't take much joy from
my time alone. Much as I hate to admit it, a
distance is growing between Clover and me. Even

our trips to the theater aren't as much fun as they once were. I'm too busy concentrating on the chorus girls to gossip with her. I watch every move, talking through their steps, nodding my head up and down in time to the music until Clover digs me in the ribs and shushes me. We don't giggle and laugh like we used to. Clover rarely even smiles.

On the morning of my audition for Charlot, I wake early, giddy with excitement and nerves. The rehearsed steps and routines spin through my mind until they become a confusing jumble and all I can do is trip and stumble over them. I try not to think about it as I clutch little Edward's photograph beneath the bedcovers. I say a silent prayer: that he is safe and loved, wherever he is, and that I will be blessed with light feet and a voice like a blackbird.

As soon as my morning's work is done, I rush from the hotel and take the omnibus to Bond Street. I want to catch Clover before she leaves. I want to tell her about the audition and promise that I'll make it up to her and go dancing at the Palais next week. If there is a next week. I haven't even thought beyond the audition or what it will mean if I am engaged to Charlot's production. There certainly won't be time for a sixpenny dance at the Palais. How will I ever tell Clover that?

When I arrive at the Grosvenor Square house, a

maid I don't recognize answers the door. She is small and mean-looking.

"Is Clover Parker here?" I ask.

Her eyes scrunch together into a deep scowl. "Who wants to know?"

"Dolly. I used to work here. She's a friend of mine."

The maid leans against the doorframe and folds her arms across her chest. "She don't work here no more. Left last night."

"Left?"

She glances over her shoulder, steps forward, and pulls the door to behind her. "Given her marching orders after she was found out."

"Found out about what?"

"Well, I'm not one to talk out of turn, but word is that she's been earning extra money on the side." She winks at me. "You know. Hanging around on street corners. Waiting for . . . customers."

I can't believe what I'm hearing. "I'm looking for Clover *Parker*. You must have the wrong person."

"Same person. Only one Clover Parker worked here. We was wondering how she was affording all them new hats and dresses. Told us the ladies had been passing them on to her. Told us she'd got them bruises taking a tumble down the back stairs. Now we know the truth of it, don't we?" She shakes her head and tuts.

My mind whirls. All those new dresses I'd admired. The plum velvet hat. The silk stockings she bought me for Christmas. The makeup. "I don't understand. Why would she do that?"

"Don't ask me. But she did. Madam got wind of it and now she don't work here no more. That's all I know about it."

I feel panicked. How did I not notice? Why didn't she tell me? "Do you know where she went?"

"Ain't got the foggiest." She steps back inside the doorway. "Maybe you should try the corner of Tottenham Court Road."

She laughs as she closes the door and I walk away with my head spinning. I've been so wrapped up in myself I hadn't noticed the signs. All the nice things. All the excuses to leave early. The occasional bruise where she'd obviously been handled too roughly. I wince at the thought. I should have paid more attention; should have been a better friend. I rack my brain to think of all the places she might go if she was in trouble.

The tearooms. She'll be in the A.B.C. at Piccadilly Circus.

I have an hour before my audition. I run back to the omnibus stop and take the number forty-three to Piccadilly. Please be there, Clover. Please let me help you.

I find her sitting at a table beside the window, stirring a cup of cold tea. She bursts into tears when she sees me and I throw my arms around her.

"Oh, Clover. What have you done, you silly old sod."

She buries her face in my neck. "Secret's out, then. I'm such a bloody idiot, Dolly."

"I went to the house. The maid told me." I hold her cheeks with my hands. "Why, Clover? Why? I'm so cross with you. Why didn't you tell me? All those things—dresses and hats and silk stockings—nothing can be worth *that*. Surely."

She blows her nose and wipes the tears from her eyes as I sit down beside her and light us both a cigarette. Through her tears and her shame she tells me everything.

"I stopped caring, Dolly. I flirted with Tommy Mullins 'cause it made me feel good about myself, made me feel like a woman again. He started calling to the house and asked to walk out with me. I never said nothing 'cause I know you don't care for him, and I knew I'd get into trouble with Madam for having followers calling to the house, so I brushed him off. But he kept coming back and I was flattered by the attention. I agreed to go dancing with him one night." She pauses and takes a long drag on her cigarette. "He took me to a boardinghouse afterward and, well, you know. Things happened."

I grab her hand. "Oh, Clover."

"I thought I would enjoy it, but I felt numb

afterward. Cold and numb. Still, it was better than being alone. We started to meet more regularly and then he asked if I would go dancing with a friend of his. An ex-serviceman. Told me he hadn't been with a girl since the war; that nobody would look at him 'cause of his scars. You know me, Dolly. I feel sorry for everyone. So I met him—the poor bugger—and we danced and he took me back to that same boardinghouse, and when it was over he got dressed and left some money on the table. I thought I was doing him a favor. He thought I was earning a living. That's how it started. After that, Tommy told me he knew a woman who could help me earn better money if I was prepared to help other soldiers and go to boardinghouses like that more often. That's why I started to head off early from our afternoons off."

I sit and listen and hold her hand, and I cannot believe that all this time, while I've been dancing in a Mayfair apartment, my oldest friend has been going through this alone. I feel awful. Awful, and ashamed of myself.

"I'm so sorry, Clover. I let you down. I should have noticed. I've been so wrapped up in myself . . ."

"It's not your fault, Doll. It's mine. I got greedy. I had my eye on a hat in Selfridges—you know the one. I contacted Tommy's friend and she made the necessary arrangements. I bought the hat with the first bit of money I made. It seemed so easy. The number of times that hat was admired made it all seem worthwhile. I felt special when I wore it. And it was the soldiers too. Poor buggers. Some of them stuttering and muttering and most of them with a leg missing or a mask over their face to hide the scars. I felt sorry for them. Convinced myself I was helping them."

"I wish you'd told me. Maybe I could have talked some sense into you."

"I couldn't tell anyone. I was too ashamed. When I was with them, I thought of other things and just waited for it to be over. Most of them were decent enough sorts. Only a few got a bit out of hand."

"The bruises?"

She nods. "Most of them just did the business, buttoned themselves up, and went home. Didn't even know their names. But then I was set up with a friend of one of the valets and word got back to Madam and that was that. Marching orders. Told me to pack my things and leave immediately. Said she wouldn't be associated with such things. She could hardly bear to look at me."

"Oh, Clover. Where did you stay last night?"

"At the boardinghouse." She sees the question in my eyes. "Don't worry. I was alone."

I can't think of anything to say to help, so I give her a hug and let her sniffle on my shoulder, just as she did all those months ago when we sat in this very same tearoom and I told her I had a new position at The Savoy.

"Perhaps we're not so different after all," she says, as if she can read my thoughts. "Maybe we're all searching for something to cling to, something to make us feel important."

I feel guilt in every bone of my body for not being there for her. Worst of all, when my best friend in the world needs me more than ever, I am painfully aware of the minutes passing by. My audition starts in twenty minutes.

"I want you to come somewhere with me, Clover."

"Where?"

"A theater. I've an audition. A big one. Come with me and we'll go for something to eat afterward. Promise."

"But . . . I can't. Look at the state of me."

"Never mind about that. Anyway, it'll be dark inside. Come on. I'm not leaving you here. If you won't come, I'm not going either." I stand up and fold my arms across my chest to show her I mean it.

She doesn't need much persuading. We leave the tearooms and head for the Shaftesbury Theatre. I can't think of anybody I would rather have beside me right now and I link my arm through Clover's and rest my head on her shoulder.

"Who are you auditioning for anyway?" she asks as we hurry along.

"Oh, nobody special. Only one of the biggest theater producers in the business."

"You'd better be bloody good, then."

I laugh. "I suppose I'd better."

The stage-door manager, Jimmy Jones, sees us inside. Miss May has told me all about him. He's a kind man, and while I change in the dressing room he settles Clover into the auditorium with a tot of brandy. I change quickly and make my way to the wings along with a dozen other girls. We are told to assemble behind the safety curtain and wait.

After what feels like an age, a young gentleman with rolled-up shirtsleeves steps around the curtain and tells us they're ready. We file out onto the stage, our heels clattering against the boards.

André Charlot stands at the front of the stage. He's dressed in a smart tweed suit. A cigar smolders in his right hand. He has a gentle face and a round belly. I like him instantly.

"Come along, then. Two straight lines, girls. Come along, please." His voice is firm yet kind, laced with the lilt of his French accent.

As we all shuffle into position I think of everything Miss May has taught me; all the hours spent in her apartment. I pull my shoulders back. *"Walk tall, with poise and confidence, no matter how much your legs shake."* Her words ring in my ears. *"Make him notice you from the very first moment he sets eyes on you. Stand out before you even dance one step."*

He catches my eye. I hold his gaze, willing him to remember me.

"Now, girls. Miss Williams will show you the steps and then you will all dance together. It's no use to me if you can dance wonderfully on your own. The magic of the chorus is in dancing together. Understand?"

We all nod and mutter a collective yes as the dance mistress, Miss Williams, steps forward.

"Right, girls. This is a simple one. You place your feet apart, hands on your shoulders, and take a little kick out to the side with alternate feet with a little hop in between. Light on your feet. Toes pointed and a lovely flick with the ankle. Like this." She shows us the step, counting out the beat herself. "One and two and one and two and. I want you to all keep in time, without any mistakes. Concentrate on following the music and hitting the beat."

She assembles us all into a perfectly straight line and gives the pianist the cue. We all dance the step perfectly, our shoes stamping against the boards. We repeat the same step a dozen times until my calves burn. When she is satisfied, she shows us a more complicated step, following the same pattern and rhythm but using the steps to move herself around in a circle. The pianist starts the music and we dance again. One of the girls gets muddled in the middle of the step. The dance mistress pulls her to the front of the line and looks at me.

"You. What's your name?"

"Dorothy, miss. Dolly, for short."

"Come here. Show this girl the step again."

I step forward from the line and repeat the steps, kicking and flicking my feet to the side and turning myself in a perfect circle. The other girl follows and gets it right. We both fall back into line.

We continue like this for thirty minutes. Step after step. High-kicking. Moving in a line to the left. Moving in a line to the right. Linking arms and kicking our way around in a circle without breaking the line. It's exhausting. We each sing a verse of "Pack Up Your Troubles" and read a line of script from *The Dancers*. I mimic Tallulah Bankhead, affecting her slow southern drawl. Charlot smiles. Our final dance is a high-kicking routine that seems to last forever.

When he has seen enough he calls for the pianist to stop and for us to stop dancing. Our feet fall gratefully still and silent against the boards as he walks along the line, taking a moment to pause and look at each of us in turn. I think about my first morning at The Savoy and O'Hara scolding me for my vermillion lips. I almost smile at the memory. Walking back the other way, Charlot taps two girls on the shoulder and asks them to step forward. He walks past the others and comes back to me, at the very end of the line.

"Dorothy, isn't it?"

My heart bursts with hope. Restless wings flutter, longing to beat furiously. I nod. "Yes, sir." I cross my fingers on both hands and squeeze them tight together. I see little Edward's face. I see Teddy silhouetted against the setting sun. I see Perry smiling at me as he watches me dance with Miss May. Everything has come to this.

"Step forward, please."

I can hardly move, my legs are shaking so much. I hear a little squeak from the darkness of the auditorium. Clover.

"The rest of you may leave. Thank you for your time."

I stand apart from the other two girls. We look straight ahead into the pitch black as the heels of the other girls' dance shoes trudge disappointedly from the stage. I can barely breathe. *Step forward, please.* In those words are everything I've ever hoped for. All the rejections and the failures, all the pain and the heartache melt away like snow in a thaw.

Charlot stands center stage and addresses us. "Thank you, girls. You impressed me. You are not the most conventional chorus girls I have ever auditioned—two of you are two inches too short for a start—but that is precisely what I'm looking for. Something different. And I see that in each of you. A spark of something that with a little care and attention might become something extraordinary." He steps back a little to admire his selection. "Congratulations, girls. Welcome to the chorus of *Charlot's Revue*. We start rehearsals in a week."

The words I have dreamed of. The words I have imagined in my darkest moments. And now they are here, swirling around in front of me, lit by the spotlight, and they are mine to keep, to hear forever more.

Wonderful adventures await for those who dare to find them.

A wingbeat stirs in my heart and I urge it to fly. To grow stronger. To soar. I can't wait to tell Miss May and Perry.

Clover is beside herself when I eventually join her at the stage door. "I've never seen you dance like that in your life! You were terrific. I couldn't take my eyes off you. Who knew, eh! Who knew our Dolly Lane had *that* in those little legs of hers?"

"Little legs but ever such shapely ankles, you know!"

I treat us both to a supper of poached eggs and toast and we talk properly for the first time in weeks. We listen to each other. Laugh. Cry. Just like we used to. It is one of the nicest suppers we've ever had. After seeing her safely back to the boardinghouse, and promising I'll make inquiries about a position for her at The Savoy, I run all the way back to the hotel.

The evening is pleasantly still and warm and I take my time, following my preferred route along the Embankment. With the return of warmer weather, the pavement artists have also returned to brighten the gray flagstones with their drawings. I walk slowly to admire their work. At the end of the railings are several images of a beautiful young girl. I lean forward to take a closer look. In colored chalks around the images are three words, written in beautiful looping script. *Hope. Love. Adventure.*

A coffee seller walks past, pushing his cart. He stops to look at the drawings beside me. "Dead ringer for her," he says, looking at me and then back at the drawings.

"I'm sorry?"

"You. You're a dead ringer for the girl in the drawings. See? Same eyes. Same lips. The very same. Funny, eh!"

He is right. The resemblance is striking. I look around for the artist, but everyone has packed up for the day. I stare at the images. They are so like me I could almost be looking into a mirror.

The coffee seller walks on, leaving me alone, staring at the drawings on the pavement; alone, surrounded by memories; alone with the echoes of my past that whisper in the leaves that dance in the breeze.

Alone, and yet I know that he is here. Only one person could have drawn such a remarkable likeness of me.

"Teddy?" I whisper. "Where are you?"

38
TEDDY

London
April 1924

Sometimes she is a daffodil. Sometimes a
butterfly. And always, always she is surrounded
by hope and love and adventure.

I left Mawdesley on a frost-dusted November
morning. No big announcement. No dramatic
good-bye. I packed a bag, told Mam I'd be
popping out for a while, and walked away.

I hadn't planned to go. I hadn't planned
anything after returning from the hospital.

Slowly, I felt myself coming back together, as if
all the lost pieces of me scattered around those
muddy French fields gradually found their way
back home. Piece by piece, I felt myself fitting
back together. And yet peacetime came with a
hesitant step and a frequent backward glance.
We all wondered if we'd really seen the end to
the horrors of war. But somehow we found a
way to move forward. We all learned to walk
again and talk again. Some even learned to love
again.

I was making tea when I realized I had to find her. I was spooning the leaves carefully into the pot, watching a blackbird on the fence while I waited for the kettle to boil. It struck me how beautiful his song was, and I instinctively wanted Dolly to hear it too. It was as simple as that. In a moment, while the blackbird sang and the kettle whistled on the stove, I knew I had to be where she was. In London.

I never expected to find her. Her mam wasn't even sure where she was. She told me she used a poste restante address at Cambridge Circus and that she only wrote home occasionally. I went anyway. It was enough to know that I would be closer to her, that we might walk the same footpaths, see the same view, breathe the same air. Only briefly did I think about what I would do or say if I found her. What if she was happily married? What if she was horrified to discover that a piece of her past had jumped into her present? What if I unsettled her, caused her pain and sadness? What then?

I went about my business and made something of a life for myself. I found work in factories and restaurant kitchens, anything to earn a living. It was a far cry from the life I'd once imagined, but I was alive and I was over the worst of my condition and there was a lot to be said for that. And when my day's work was over I found a patch of pavement and drew my pictures on to the flagstones. I used the talent the nurses had nurtured in the hospital.

They call us screevers: pavement artists. I like to work at night, leaving my drawings as a small gift to those who wake early to watch the dawn and catch the best of the day. I draw pictures of Dolly mostly, although I have no image to work from. I use the one I imprinted onto my mind the last time I saw her. It is as clear as any photograph.

I draw her every day. Sometimes she is a daffodil. Sometimes a butterfly. And always, always she is surrounded by the things she wanted her life to be filled with: hope and love and adventure.

ACT III

⊁ Adventure ⊁

LONDON
1924

The phrase "Cochran has done it again"
is becoming hackneyed, but it describes exactly
the scenes at the first night of *Nymph Errant*
at the Adelphi Theatre. The foyer was invaded
by autograph hunters who burst through
the strong cordon of police and mingled
with the audience. Late arrivals almost had
their dresses torn from their backs.

—"Mr. Gossip" newspaper review,
V&A Museum Theatre Archive

39

DOLLY

I am wide-awake and I am right in the middle of my dreams.

Nine Elms appears above the tree line, the high turrets and chimneys offering a tantalizing glimpse of the house that I will stay in for the next few days. I edge forward on the leather seat of the motorcar—sent to collect me from the train station—craning my neck awkwardly to get a better view. Wispy clouds hang like feathers in a perfectly blue sky, reminding me of the day I left Mawdesley. As I admire my beautiful peach chiffon day dress and shoes—gifts from Miss May and which I adore so much I might never take off—I reflect on how far I have come.

Everything happened so quickly after the audition. When I told Perry that Charlot had appointed me, he lifted me off the ground and spun me around until I felt dizzy and wild and wonderful. He said he couldn't be happier for me, that I deserved it, and then he told me that he and Loretta would like to invite me to their annual spring ball. When I protested about not being able to take time away from the hotel, he told me that Loretta had already spoken with the governor, who had agreed to give me special leave so that I could visit my sick aunt. "But I don't have a sick aunt," I'd said, confused. And then the penny dropped and I laughed. "Loretta May gets what Loretta May wants," Perry said. "And she wants you to come to Nine Elms. If that means an unexpected addition to your family, then so be it."

And here I am.

My cheeks are flushed with excitement and the warmth of the sun streaming through the motor-car window. My stomach somersaults as the driver makes a sharp turn through dramatic stone pillars that mark the entrance to the house, where we continue along a perfectly straight driveway lined with nine elm trees. I count them. The tires crunch over gravel as we round a final bend and I see the house for the first time. It is beautiful. Ivy-clad red brick. A dozen lattice windows glint in the sun. Several pristine motorcars are already parked on the carriage circle in front of the house, a steady stream of valets and butlers attending to luggage and travel-weary guests, all of whom are astonishingly attractive and elegant and all of whom seem to know each other. I grip the edge of the seat as the car pulls to a stop and a valet opens the door.

Taking a deep breath, I step out onto the driveway, relieved to see Perry waiting on the steps of the house, a broad smile spreading across his lips as he sees me.

I tug at my gloves, flexing my fingers against the light cotton fabric, and smooth the creases from my dress. It's a warm day and the breeze is refreshing after the long journey. The sea is just distant on the horizon; the tang of salt in the air a welcome change from London's soot.

Perry greets me with a kiss on the cheek and stands beside me.

"So this is where you grew up," I say, gazing up at the impressive building and holding my hand over the top of my straw cloche to stop it blowing away. "No wonder."

"No wonder what?"

"No wonder you prefer your little apartment above the theater. It must have been awful living somewhere so grand."

He laughs and puts his hands in his pockets. "Great houses don't always make for great homes, Miss Lane. Nice to look at. Not always so nice to live in. Full of rules and regulations. Houses like Nine Elms are for grown-ups. A childhood can easily be lost in these vast rooms."

I sense there is more he would like to say, and there is a lot more I would like to ask, but now is ot the right time.

"How are you feeling?" he asks, turning to look at me. "Nervous? Excited?"

"Honestly?"

"Honestly."

"I'm terrified."

He smiles. "Don't be. You're our guest, just the same as everyone else. Don't forget that."

But I am not the same as everyone else. However I might blend in on the outside, I will never be the same on the inside.

As the valets busy themselves around us, Perry and I stand together, talking of this and that, and all the while sharing that now familiar gaze, searching for something behind each other's eyes, floundering in a sea of emotions we can't understand. Lover? Friend? Muse? What am I to him? And he to me? I long for him to tell me I look wonderful. I long for him to take my hand and lead me inside. I long to know what he feels when he looks at me that way, but we are interrupted as more friends arrive and rush over to Perry, the women smothering him with kisses and shrieks of excitement, the men slapping him on the back and urging him to join them in a game of cricket. He introduces me but I can't remember anyone's name.

"You'll be terrific," he says as he guides me toward the house. "Just remember everything my sister taught you and you'll be perfectly fine." He pats me lightly on the shoulder, an act of reassurance. It is an oddly cold gesture that leaves me feeling more anxious than assured.

Taking a deep breath and thinking of all the girls

who would give anything to be standing in my shoes right now, I force a smile and follow Perry up the steps and into an impressive entrance hall, Loretta's words tumbling through my mind as I walk. *"Stand taller. Pull your shoulders back. Tilt your neck, just so, and you'll immediately look less like a maid and more like a lady. Impressions are just that—impressions. We can be whomever we want to be if we act accordingly."*

Maids and footmen rush past with trays of drinks and fresh flowers, hatboxes and sewing boxes. I try not to appear too impressed by my surroundings as my eye is drawn to a painting at the foot of the stairs: yellow swirls in an inky-blue sky above a sleepy village. I recognize it immediately. The same painting hung in the drawing room at Mawdesley Hall. It was the only one I didn't mind dusting. Looking at it was like looking at my dreams.

Perry catches my eye. "Wonderful, isn't it? Van Gogh. He called it *Starry Night. 'The sight of the stars makes me dream.'* You know he chopped off his own ear after drinking too much absinthe?"

"You're teasing me," I say, walking over to look at the painting more closely.

"He honestly did! The madness of art. I suppose we must all be a little afflicted in order to create."

Miss May appears from a side room and rushes over to greet us. "Darlings. You made it!" She kisses us both on the cheek. Perry embraces her warmly. In all the time I have spent with them both, I've never seen any real affection between them. Cool indifference, at most. Now his arms engulf her and I notice how thin she's become. "I was worried the train strike would keep you trapped in London and I'd have to manage Mother and Father and all their dreadful guests on my own."

Perry laughs and fusses with a small Pekingese dog that leaps up at his knees. A maid rushes by, dropping a lady's scarf as she passes. I almost bend down to pick it up but check myself. Old habits die hard.

Miss Lane takes me to one side. "You look divine, darling. I'm so eager to show you off to everyone. How are you feeling?"

"Nervous. Terrified. Sick to my stomach."

She smiles and takes hold of my hand. "You'll be wonderful. This is your chance to shine. Look at you. How could they not adore you? And you collected the evening dress from Hettie for the ball tomorrow?"

"Yes. It's beautiful." I think about the little house in Shoreditch, the cramped sewing room at the back, so at odds with the beautiful dresses that emerge from it. I think about little Thomas, hiding behind Hettie's skirts as he peered out at me. Such a sweet, shy little boy. "She did a wonderful job. I hardly dare wear it."

Miss May frowns in mock annoyance. "You *will*

wear it and you will be the talk of the party. If you are not the subject of intense speculation by tomorrow evening, I will consider myself to have failed abysmally. Now, off with you. Madeline will show you to your room so you can freshen up. Drinks will be served on the lawn from three. There's talk of a game of hide-and-seek later, and a treasure hunt tomorrow." She rolls her eyes dramatically. "I'm exhausted just thinking about it."

I follow Madeline up a wide staircase and along a long corridor to my room on the first floor. It feels strange being one of "Them"; to be on the other side of the divide. Strange but thrilling. My bags have already been delivered to my room. My dresses hung in the wardrobe. The curtains flutter in a pleasant breeze at the open window. Madeline leaves me, and for a rare moment in my life, I have absolutely nothing to do.

I strip down to my undergarments, collapse onto the bed, and breathe. For once, my mind is as unruffled as the smooth damask pillow slip against my cheek, and with nothing to do and nothing to worry about, I soon fall into a deep asleep.

I wake to the sound of jazz and laughter and the cheery clink of glasses. I've slept longer than I intended.

I stand up and check myself in the looking glass.

My face is flushed from sleep. Pillow-slip creases mark my cheeks. I press my palms against the window and then to my face, absorbing the lovely cool of the glass against my skin. Music drifts across the landscaped gardens and meadows beyond. The afternoon sun glints off the sea on the horizon. It really is beautiful here. I wish I could go for a walk to feel the sand between my toes and the wind in my hair, but people are waiting for me. Expecting me. And there haven't been many times in my life when I could say that.

I wash and dress as quickly as I can, fix my hair, and take a deep breath. I check my posture one last time before leaving the room and make my way downstairs. Despite my apprehension, I can't help smiling to know that I am here, among these people. I am not scurrying along behind hidden corridors. I am not fetching or carrying anything. I am not apologizing for setting a tea tray down in the wrong place. I am just a young woman, beautifully dressed; the guest of a famous actress in her beautiful home. I am wide-awake and I am right in the middle of my dreams.

Crossing the marble entrance hall, I follow the sound of music toward the library, through French doors, and out onto the terrace, grateful for the waiter who passes with a tray of champagne. I take a glass, savoring the sweet cool of the liquid as I drink it quickly. I take another. The waiter looks at me, astonished.

"Dutch courage," I say. "Don't tell anyone."

He nods and rushes away.

I hesitate on the top step, scanning the sea of faces for Perry or Miss May. I can't see either of them, only beautiful people and fabulous dresses and the flutter of feather fans. I feel awkward and out of place, like a flea-market ornament among a shelf of priceless antiques. I drink the second glass of champagne too quickly and am relieved when I finally spot Perry on the lawn. He catches my eye and waves over to me enthusiastically.

Threading my way through the guests, I try to remember my posture, *"remember to glide rather than walk."* I already regret the two glasses of champagne I've drunk in as many minutes.

"Sorry I'm late," I whisper when I reach him. "I fell asleep."

"You didn't miss much. Only Father's annual speech, which very nearly sent us *all* to sleep." He turns to the group gathered around him and introduces me. "Everyone, this is Miss Dorothy Lane, who I was telling you about. She's been helping me write my new musical score and will be performing in *Charlot's Revue* this summer. Miss Lane is going to be a huge star."

I blush under his compliment as I'm introduced to a glittering array of beautiful young things: Elizabeth Ponsonby, Nancy Mitford, Cecil Beaton, Bea Balfour, Stephen Tennant, and half a dozen others; people I have known only as names in the gossip columns. Perry has often spoken about the Bloomsbury set—the "Bright Young People," as they have become known in society circles—an eccentric collection of Oxford and Cambridge graduates, writers, artists, and poets. Their lifestyle is generally considered to be extravagant; their behavior improper. They are wild and daring and exciting. I find them alluring and strange.

I shake hands and smile politely but I can't help staring at the ladies' beautiful dresses, at their headdresses and fans, and at the gentlemen's oddly effeminate faces. I notice the obvious connection between Perry and Miss Balfour, a playful familiarity, and I sense a stab of jealousy as I see how enchanted he is by her. She's extremely beautiful and perfectly lovely. Why would he not be enchanted by her?

Everyone is pleasant and polite but I soon feel lost in their conversation, unable to keep up with their shared jokes and increasingly intellectual debate. I excuse myself to fetch another drink. As I walk away, I hear the women teasing Perry.

"She's quite delightful, Perry. Wherever have you been hiding her?"

"Didn't have you down as a stage-door Johnny! Is it true that Loretta set you up?"

I can't hear Perry's reply over the sound of the band.

• • •

As the afternoon progresses, the Bloomsbury set insist on a game of hide-and-seek. Their enthusiasm is infectious. As soon as we are organized into hiders and seekers, I rush off toward the walled garden, becoming a child again, the little girl who squealed with excitement as her sisters chased her around the house and out into the fields beyond. They could never find me. I was always the best at hiding, finding the smallest gaps to crawl into, blending into the fabric of the rooms. I would press myself against a wall and stand completely motionless so that even when they burst in, calling my name, they wouldn't see me. Tess always accused me of cheating, insisting that I must have changed hiding place in the middle of the game. But I never did. I simply disappeared. Became invisible. I was always good at that.

I run among the ornamental privet hedges and birdbaths as a whistle blows to let the hiders know that the seekers are on the hunt. I find a dark nook behind a gazebo adorned with amber roses and a screen of delphinium that matches the color of my dress. Stepping as carefully as I can among the flower beds so as not to damage the plants, I crouch down and wait, listening to the squeals and roars of jubilation when the hiders are found. I hold my breath as a gentleman dashes among the gravel pathways in the garden, but he runs straight past, never seeing me.

Gradually the excitement of hiders and seekers fades along with the afternoon sun as most of the guests make their way back to the cocktail waiters and the music. I stay where I am, a childish stubbornness insisting that I hold out a little longer. And then I hear women's voices approaching and I freeze as Bea Balfour and a friend settle on a seat directly in front of my hiding place.

"She's very striking," Bea remarks as she lights a cigarette. "Unconventionally beautiful. And he does seem awfully fond of her. Always looking for her across the room. Talking about how marvelous she is. I'm afraid he has fallen in love with her, Violet."

Her companion reassures her that this is not the case as I wonder who it is they are talking about. "Don't be silly. He only has eyes for you, Bea. You know that very well. What if she's secretly an *escort*? Gosh, how delightfully improper." They giggle at the prospect of such scandal. "Still, I wonder where he found this Miss Lane."

Me? It is me they're talking about. I screw my eyes up tight and force myself to remain motionless, hardly daring to breathe.

"I heard Perry telling Geoffrey that he met her at an audition," Bea explains. "He was playing the piano. She was dancing. They started talking. She has apparently become something of a muse for him. Miss Lane is the inspiration behind the new music he's writing for *Charlot's Revue*."

"A muse?"

"Yes. Loretta encouraged it by all accounts. You know what she's like, always wanting the best for Perry. She told me that she felt he needed someone to inspire him. It would seem that Miss Lane is that someone."

"But surely if anyone was to be Perry's muse it would be you, Bea. He's been besotted with you since you were a young girl dashing about on these very lawns."

"And that's precisely the problem. There's too much history between Perry and me. Too many 'what-ifs' and distractions for me to be his muse. And there's something else. Something I can never quite put my finger on. I think it has something to do with Oscar. They were very close, you know. They were in the same battalion. I think he misses him terribly."

"Well, I don't know what you're worrying about. He is clearly dotty about you. Always was. Always will be."

Bea sighs. "Still, I find myself anxious and my tummy is all in knots. Everyone always presumed Perry would ask me to marry him after Oscar died. But he hasn't, Vi. And with this Miss Lane on the scene, he might never ask me. I haven't exactly encouraged him in his affections, have I?"

"No, darling. You have rather played him like a fish, I'm afraid. Let's just hope he doesn't turn out to be the one that got away."

I try not to move, although my legs are cramping and I long to stand up and stretch them. I can't reveal myself now.

"And what would you say if he were to ask you?" the woman called Violet asks.

To my relief Bea stands up and stretches her arms high above her head. She is like a prima ballerina dressed in raspberry pink. "I would say yes, of course. Perhaps I needed to feel him slip away from me to know how much I care for him. I do love him, Violet. Very much. Part of me always has—since I was a little girl. And I know how happy it would make Loretta to see us married. She talks of nothing else lately. It's as if she's suddenly in a hurry to see us all settled and living our happily ever after." She pulls her friend up from the seat. "Anyway, I wouldn't hold your breath. I've been waiting seven years. Why would he change his mind now? Let's go back to the house. I'm dying for a cocktail."

I let out a long breath as they link arms and walk away, the scent of their perfume lingering in the air around me. Their silk shoes crunch along the gravel as they disappear toward the house. Only when they are out of sight do I dare to stand up and brush down my skirt.

Most of the guests are already back in the house but I don't feel like dancing. I walk around to the side entrance, passing a maid and a valet kissing near the stables. They giggle and pull apart as they see me, but I'm not interested in their little romance. I'm relieved to find the service door ajar and step inside, following the corridors toward the back stairs before I realize what I am doing. I hurry on then, until I reach the door to the breakfast room, from where I cross the entrance hall toward the main staircase. But my attention is caught as I pass the library. The door is ajar and I can hear someone sobbing. I stop for a moment and listen.

I falter, unsure of what to do, and then I knock lightly on the door and peer into the room. It is dark, the shutters pulled across the windows, but as my eyes adjust to the gloom I see him, crouched on the floor, his head in his hands, his sobs choking him.

Perry.

It is Perry. And my heart breaks for him.

40
DOLLY

"Where's the honesty, Miss Lane?
Where's the love? Where's the truth of it all?"

He is sitting on the floor surrounded by photographs, his shirtsleeves rolled to the elbow, his hair disheveled. He doesn't hear me knock or step into the room and it is only when I turn to leave that a creaky floorboard gives me away.

"Miss Lane?" He looks up; his eyes are red and swollen.

"I'm sorry. I didn't mean to disturb you. I'll go."

"Don't go. Please. Stay with me for a moment."

Reluctantly, I step into the room. It bothers me to see men cry. I never know what to say. As I walk over to him, I see an assortment of photographs strewn around him on the floor. They are all of men in uniform, some laughing, some kicking a football, others lying on their backs, heads resting on backpacks, smokes dangling from the corners of mouths. I sit down on the Oriental rug beside him, my legs tucked beneath my skirt.

"I took them all myself," he says. "I was so proud of my little Kodak. It was small enough to fit in a vest pocket. The Vest Pocket Kodak, they called it. VPK. The men were impressed with the foldout lens and the different settings for the aperture. I was like a child with a toy, always snapping away, catching them off guard." He lifts up several photographs and looks at them. "It's hard to believe that a little five-shilling camera survived when all these men didn't. I should have handed it in when the War Office banned cameras at the front. They were worried they might fall into enemy hands, but I was an arrogant officer. I thought the rules didn't apply to me."

He wipes his cheek with a handkerchief. I feel useless and awkward beside him and reach for some words of comfort but none will come. "Teddy had a VPK too." I blurt out the words, desperate to say something; anything. "He sent it back to me when they were banned. I kept it."

"Teddy?" Perry looks up at me, his eyes questioning.

"A friend of mine. Private Teddy Cooper."

"Did you get the pictures developed?"

I think about little Edward's face, how my hands shook as I pressed the shutter on the final exposure. "Yes. They were mostly of the men at sea on the crossing to France. Smiling and laughing. There were none of him."

"I don't think you've mentioned Teddy before."

"No. No, I haven't." I have wanted to talk

about him so often, but there was never the right moment, not with Perry.

"I remember them all," he continues, pushing the images about on the rug. "Every single one of them. My men. My brothers-in-arms. All gone. Archie Brummell, Tom Allinson, Pete Wright, Sam Markham, Billy Greenwood—always grinning like a fool. And Oscar, of course." He sighs and sits back on his heels. "We shared such strange moments of tenderness amid all the depravity and horror. I'd never fully understood what it felt like to love another human being before I went to war. I loved them all like brothers, Miss Lane. In fact, I loved them more than I loved my own brother. Every single one of them."

"I'm sorry," I whisper. "If only we could bring them back."

"If only." Putting the photographs back into a box, Perry walks to the piano and lifts the lid. "Would you mind if I played? Sometimes I find only music can comfort me."

"Not at all."

I move over to a chair and he starts to play. I recognize the melody immediately—it is the music I rescued from the litter bin, but this time he sings lyrics to accompany the notes, words I've never heard.

" 'When autumn rests upon my soul, I still will hear you calling, You'll sing to me of happier times, When golden leaves were falling.' "

It brings tears to my eyes and I suddenly know who the song was written for. "You wrote it for them, didn't you? For your men. The men in the photographs."

He nods. "Yes. I wrote it for the only true friends I've ever had. The people out there on the terrace call themselves my friends, but they're not. Not really. They don't really know me at all. I unfurled among the trampled wildflowers in those French fields, Miss Lane. I shared a smoke with a chap by the light of a candle and told him my darkest thoughts, my greatest fears, my wildest hopes and dreams. I spoke of love and loss and regret with men I'd known only a few weeks. I can't talk of such things with the friends I surround myself with now. It is all backslapping tomfoolery, and loud guffawing and Scotch-fueled dares. Where's the honesty, Miss Lane? Where's the love? Where's the truth of it all?"

I sit and I listen and then I walk to him, and without any hesitation I wrap my arms around him and rest my head on his shoulder. There is no searching glance. No quickening of my heart. No thoughts of love. I simply want to comfort him as my friend. I place his own hand on his heart. "It is here, Perry. Here is the honesty and the love and the truth. It is here, in your heart. It was always here."

We stay like this, in silence, thinking, feeling,

hoping, both of us drowning in the past as we hold on to each other for support.

After a while he closes the piano lid and pours us both a brandy. We sit and talk as the last traces of sun dip below the horizon and the stars come out. He tells me how he had intended to propose to Bea Balfour before the war, but that he had waited too long and missed his chance. He explains how his friend Oscar had proposed to her on the very night he had planned to do it himself.

"Oscar didn't know how strong my feelings were for her. I was always very private about such things. He thought we were just childhood friends because I'd never given him any reason to believe otherwise—nor Bea for that matter. Only my sister knew the true depth of my love for her." He sighs and swirls the amber liquid around in his glass. "I thought I'd lost her for good, but then war intervened and the unimaginable happened. We fought in the same battalion, Oscar and me. He was a brave soldier, the man you would always want by your side. But then he simply fell apart. Like ice on a frozen pond, he cracked, suddenly and without warning."

"What happened?"

"He deserted his post, Miss Lane. Laid down his arms. He was sent to the firing squad." I wait patiently for him to find the words. To tell me his darkest secret. "I was one of the officers who pulled the trigger." I sit in silence, not questioning, not judging, just allowing him to share his past with me. "How could I expect Bea to ever love the man who had shot her fiancé and robbed her of her future? How could anyone love a man like that? Like me? Too afraid to stand up to his superiors; for his principles. A coward, that's what I am. A coward."

I say nothing for a while, troubled by the dilemma of whether I should betray Miss Balfour's confidence. I heard things that were not intended for my ears, and if I tell Perry, I will be sending him straight into Bea's arms and away from any hope I might have of drawing him into mine.

I look deep into those gray puddles and see my reflection suspended there among all his hurt and his loss and despair. I thought I saw my future there once, within those eyes. Now, I'm not sure where my future lies.

I stand up and walk toward the fireplace. "She loves you, you know."

"Who does?"

"Miss Balfour. Bea. I overheard her confiding in a friend. She believes you have feelings for me and is anxious about your feelings for her."

"She is?"

"Yes." I pause, part of me wondering if he might take the opportunity to confess his feelings for me, part of me wondering how I will feel if he does.

"What else did she say?"

I hesitate for just a moment, and then I tell him. "She said that if you were to ask her to marry you, she would say yes."

His eyes light up. "Really? Bea said that?"

"Yes. She loves you, Perry. Whatever has happened in the past, she loves you. I think you should tell her everything you have told me."

He stands up and walks to the window. "I couldn't tell her. She would never be able to forgive me."

"I think she would. War gave us all a past we wish we could bury. I also loved someone from childhood, and I loved a little boy named for him. I loved them both and I lost them both because I was a coward too."

Like the black feather fan in my hands, I open up and tell him everything. About Teddy, about the Scottish nephew, about the shame of the Mothers' Hospital. I tell him about my abandoned child and how I am trying to find him. My shame and my guilt pour out of me like spilled wine until there is nothing left.

Perry listens, understands, comforts. "What will you do?" he asks. "If you find the child."

I think for a moment, and for the first time I know the answer. "Just to know that he is loved and safe will be enough for me. As long as he is loved, I can find a way to let go again. I can make peace with that."

"And what about Teddy?"

"What about him?"

"Have you let him go? Have you made peace with that too?"

I hesitate. I think about the drawings on the paving stones; the sense of Teddy somewhere nearby. I thought I had let him go, made peace with our circumstances, but when faced with the question I realize that I do not have an answer after all.

The sound of motorcars and laughter below my bedroom window wakes me the next morning. My head is fogged from champagne. All I want to do is sleep on. I pull the covers over my head, but it is too hot and my head thumps. I push the covers away and roll onto my back, listening to the sounds of this vast, unfamiliar house. Doors opening and closing, clipped heels on polished marble floors, echoes of laughter, and the ebb and flow of distant conversations. Another step farther away from the rooster and the wonky table leg back in Mawdesley. Another step farther away from the life I was born into. Another step farther away from everyone and everything I have known and loved.

Dragging myself upright, I see a breakfast tray has been placed beside my bed. I prop myself up against the multitude of pillows and pull the tray across my lap. The tea is still warm in the pot.

I force myself to eat the toast, although it sticks to the roof of my mouth and threatens to choke me with every morsel I swallow. My head pounds. It feels as if every champagne bubble is still popping inside my brain.

Reluctantly, I wash and dress and make my way downstairs. I hesitate at the bottom of the stairs, unsure of where to go, and am relieved to see Miss May appear from a room to the right and spare me further embarrassment.

"Miss Lane! Darling! You're up! I thought you might have passed away in the night. Cause of death: champagne." She laughs, leans forward, and grabs my hands. Hers are cold and so terribly thin. "Are you feeling absolutely dreadful, darling? Because I have the perfect cure for a hangover."

"I'm a bit groggy. Tired more than anything."

"Yes, it was rather a late night. Although you seemed to disappear in a hurry." She links her arm through mine and guides me toward the breakfast room. "Tell me, darling, was it Bertie Balfour? I saw him making eyes at you all afternoon. He's a notorious flirt. Did he say something vulgar?"

"Gosh, no. Not at all. He was perfectly pleasant. He was as drunk as a lord and kept telling me how pretty my eyes are and that he was sure he remembered talking to me at the Latymers' garden party last summer. I played along, of course."

Miss May laughs. "Good girl! We'll make an

476

actress of you yet. What you need is strong coffee and a hearty breakfast. That will set you up to do it all again later."

I groan at the thought as we enter the breakfast room. I gladly take a cup of coffee and sit down. We are the only people in the room and I notice that the house is quiet. "Where is everyone else?"

"Most are still sleeping off the excesses. Didn't get to bed until dawn. A few had to make their way back to London. I think you and I have the best of it here. Nowhere to go. Nothing to do except nurse our hangovers. I've always thought there is something pleasurable in the daylight dissection of the night before. Who wore what? Who spoke to whom? Who disappeared with whom? Who was a dreadful bore and who provided all the entertainment?"

"I suppose I missed most of the scandal."

"There wasn't any really. Everyone was ridiculously well behaved. If anyone, it was you who proved to be the revelation of the evening."

"Me?"

"Yes. You were the cause of much speculation. They all wanted to know about the intriguing girl who had disappeared after the game of hide-and-seek. Perry went looking for you, you know. Where on earth where you?"

I sip my coffee. "I was in the garden. I hid a little too well. We found each other in the end."

"Well, you must stop hiding yourself away. You

are not the invisible working class now, dear girl. You must be the *most* visible. The *most* dazzling. My very own Little Star!"

It is another glorious spring day that feels more like summer. The heat lingers long into the afternoon and early evening. As I dress for the ball, I stand at the window of my room and observe the guests already assembled on the lawns at the back of the house. Dandelion seeds drift lazily on the lightest of breezes while bees buzz idly around the honeysuckle and lavender. The women dazzle like a jeweler's shop window in Hatton Garden, flitting about like the butterflies that dance among the flower beds. Extravagant ostrich-feather and marabou fans in all the colors of the rainbow flutter and sway as ladies in the most fashionable evening dresses attempt to cool themselves under the unseasonably balmy evening.

Hettie has done the most wonderful job with my new dress, but the beading is heavy and my shoulders droop when I don't remember to pull them back. I am hot and clammy; the borrowed string of beads irritating the skin at my neck. After delaying as long as possible, I gather my thoughts and my confidence and make my way downstairs. One more evening to impress. One more evening to shine and then I can return to London and . . . what? Everything has happened so quickly: the audition, getting leave from the hotel, coming here. I haven't had a chance to properly think about what it all means, or what I will do when I return to London. I'll have to hand in my notice at the hotel if I'm to have any chance of keeping up with Charlot's rehearsal schedule. Where will I stay? I try not to think about it and focus on the evening ahead.

Thankfully, the ball passes without incident. With the assistance of champagne, the warm breeze, and the thrilling sounds of the jazz band, I soon relax and enjoy being twirled around the dance floor by handsome gentlemen and admired by the women who watch. I shimmer as brightly as the beads on my dress, relishing the attention and the opulence of it all, and yet there are moments when I feel out of place and overwhelmed by the turn of conversation. While the others drink and dance ever more wildly inside, I seek solace in the cool of the evening to clear my head and try to make some sense of everything that is happening to me.

Perry finds me sitting on the steps that lead down to the ornamental garden.

"Would you mind if I join you?"

I look up at him and smile. "I would very much like you to join me, Mr. Clements," I say, deliberately exaggerating my newly rounded vowels.

He tells me I sound like royalty and settles beside me. "How is your evening going?"

"Very well. Everyone has been very pleasant

and I haven't offered to turn down anyone's beds yet, so I think I'm convincing enough."

He smiles. "You've made quite an impression. Everyone wants to know who you are."

"I hope you didn't tell them the truth!"

"I tell them you're a bright new star on the rise. A protégée of Loretta's. It is, after all, the truth."

I smile. "Mostly."

We sit in silence for a while, watching the inky-blue sky as the first stars appear. It reminds me of the Van Gogh painting inside. *"The sight of the stars makes me dream."*

"Did you know, Miss Lane, that there are more stars in the sky than there are grains of sand on all the beaches in the world."

"Really?"

"Yes! It's unfathomable, isn't it?"

I rest my palms on the cool stone behind me, leaning back so that my head tilts skyward. "I've always loved the stars. When I was little I used to pretend that the sky was a piece of black velvet. I imagined the stars were tiny pinpricks, little holes punctuating the material. Do you think we all have our own star to guide us, like they say?"

"Perhaps. It would be nice to think so." Perry leans back beside me. *" 'When he shall die, take him and cut him out in little stars, and he will make the face of Heaven so fine that all the world will be in love with night, and pay no worship to the garish sun.' "*

"That's beautiful. Did you write it?"

"If only I could write anything as beautiful. It's Shakespeare. *Romeo and Juliet*. The eternal star-crossed lovers."

We sit in silence for a while, watching the stars. I fiddle with the beading on my dress while he picks at a loose thread on his sock.

"Miss Lane, I wanted to thank you for listening to me last night, and for being so honest about . . . well . . . everything." He turns to look at me. "And there's something else. Something I wanted to say to you . . ."

The band strikes up on the terrace, interrupting him. Voices and laughter move closer toward us.

"There you are, Peregrine. What are you doing hiding out here? Come and dance with me, you rotten man. The band is killing!"

It is Bea and several others. Perry stands up, brushes down his trousers, and holds out his hand to help me up. "Miss Lane, did I introduce you to a very good friend of mine, Miss Bea Balfour?"

She smiles graciously and takes my hand. "We already met, Perry. You really are a dreadful host! It is a pleasure to meet you—again—Miss Lane. I've heard so much about you."

I am again struck by her beauty and her relaxed manner around Perry. I manage a smile and mumble a thank you, trying to ignore the overheard conversation between herself and Violet that dances about in my mind.

481

Perry hesitates, floundering between us. "Would you like to come up to the house to dance, Miss Lane?"

I decline as graciously as I can. "You go ahead. I'll come up in a minute. I'd like to look at the stars a little longer."

His questioning eyes meet mine. "Are you sure?"

"Of course. It feels like a night for watching shooting stars."

"But do come in soon," Bea adds, grabbing Perry's hand. "The band really is fabulous."

I watch them walk back together toward the lights and the music, her arm looped through his, her head resting on his shoulder. They look for all the world like a happily married couple. I try to imagine that it is me walking so easily alongside him, but the image doesn't quite fit.

I think of how I used to rest my head on Teddy's shoulder.

Dear Teddy.

Don't forget me, Dolly. Look for me in the stars.

I think about the drawings on the Embankment pavements. I think about the last time I saw him. I think about everything that awaits when I return to London, and I sit alone in this beautiful place, with a million stars and the velvet sky and my thoughts and dreams and the sound of jazz drifting through the warm night. And it is enough.

It is more than enough.

For a girl like me, it is perfect.

41
DOLLY

"Perhaps we all become
more colorful, more fascinating
as we reach our autumn months."

After a while I wander away from the house toward the gardens, where I'm surprised to find Loretta sitting alone on a bench.

"Miss May? What are you doing here? I thought you'd be up there showing them all how to dance!"

She smiles. "They don't need *me*. They'll make their own amusement now the cocktails are flowing. I wanted a little peace and quiet." She pats the empty bench beside her. "Sit with me. I've been watching the leaves on the trees. Look at them, dancing in the breeze. Perfectly in time to the music. It's quite enchanting."

I settle down beside her and watch the nod of the branches and the sway of the leaves, illuminated by a string of lights between the branches. She is right. They do seem to be dancing to the music. I notice she is holding a crimson leaf in her hand.

"It's a little early for autumn leaves, isn't it?"

She twirls the leaf by its stem. "This is my lucky leaf. When I was a little girl my father taught me to catch falling autumn leaves and make a wish," she says. "I couldn't believe the stiff and starchy man I usually only saw in the parlor was leaping around, chasing leaves as the breeze blew them just out of his reach. I was mesmerized by him. I'll never forget it. Leaves and shooting stars. That's what I remember most about my father."

"Shooting stars?"

"He told me that a shooting star is a dying star. They always held a sadness for me after he'd told me that." She sighs and closes her eyes. She looks tired beneath the lights. "It's curious, isn't it, Miss Lane, how things are often at their most beautiful when they are at the end of their life. Shooting stars, autumn leaves. Nobody notices the leaves when they're all green and lush in the summer—only when they turn crimson and golden in the autumn. Perhaps we all become more colorful, more fascinating as we reach our autumn months."

A tear slips down her cheek as she speaks. "Miss May? What is it?"

She turns to face me and grasps my hand. "I am an autumn leaf, Miss Lane. A shooting star. My time to shine is coming to an end."

An uncomfortable feeling stirs in my stomach. "What do you mean?"

"I am not well, dear girl. I'm afraid I'm not well at all."

I sit beside this great beauty who has become so much more to me than a famous theater star, and only now do I feel her bones, like sticks, through her skin. Only now do I see the gray shadows under her eyes, the sickly pallor of her skin. I think of the past few months, how she has reduced her performance schedule, how she has become tired more quickly, her increasing episodes, taking to her bed, drinking heavily.

I swallow hard. "How bad is it?"

"I am afraid it is the worst, Miss Lane. The very worst."

I cannot move. Cannot respond other than to say how sorry I am. "I don't know what to say."

"Then don't say anything."

The laughter and music from the house drifts around us. The sky is alight with stars. I think again of the Van Gogh painting—*"The sight of the stars makes me dream"*—and let the tears fall silently.

"What will you do?" I ask when I've composed myself a little.

"What can anyone do? I must accept it and embrace the time I have left. I have lived a most wonderful life, Miss Lane, but now I must take my bow. My cousin has a delightful little place in Devon. Quiet. Private. The perfect place to slip away."

"But what about your family? And friends. Won't you want them with you . . . at the end?"

"What for? So we can all feel miserable together and weep into our brandy? I'd prefer to say my good-byes while I can still hold my head up high. Who needs to watch me dribbling onto a pillow? I can't think of anything worse. I shall say my farewells and then it will just be me, a nurse, and the sea to witness my demise."

I dare hardly ask the question. "When will you go?"

"The end of the week. And I shall leave safe in the knowledge that I have taught you well and that in you, my star will shine ever on."

Her words brush against my skin, sending goose bumps rippling along my arms, each tiny hair standing up, reaching toward her to take notice, to remember. I grasp her hands in mine and we watch the leaves dancing on their branches.

"I will be wonderful, Miss May. I *will* be a shining star because you have taught me. You will be the breeze that keeps me dancing. I won't let you down. I will never let you down."

She rubs my arm affectionately. "And would you do me a small favor?"

"Of course. Anything."

"Would you meet Perry for afternoon tea at Claridge's every now and again? It's become a thing of his. I think he rather likes it there."

• • •

On my final morning at Nine Elms, I wake to a lovely sense of calm. Most of the guests have left and there is a wonderful stillness about the place, like a long exhale after a held breath.

On my breakfast tray, I find an envelope. I sit up in bed and take the page from inside.

My dear Miss Lane,

You once said that real life is full of kinks and creases. That nobody is perfect. That people are very good at messing things up, but not so good at setting things right, and that is why being a chambermaid was the most important job in the world. Do you remember? You made me laugh so much that I nearly choked on my tea!

You have always made me laugh, Miss Lane, and for that I will be forever in your debt.

You turned my world upside down when you bumped into me in the rain all those months ago. I always insisted you knocked me down, but I now know that you helped me up. I was adrift long before I met you. You offered me your hand, and I took it without a moment's hesitation. Something changed in that moment, and like a drowning man, I have clung to it ever since.

And now there is something I must tell you. I would be grateful if you would meet me by the pond this morning.

I will be waiting.

Perry

I eat scraps of breakfast and dress in a hurry. The early-morning sun dazzles as I make my way to the pond. He is sitting on his jacket, threading daisies into a chain.

I spread my shawl onto the grass and sit beside him.

The lawns roll away from us like velvet, peppered here and there with a birdbath or a privet hedge or a poplar tree. Beyond the formal gardens the fields dip and roll. Cotton-wool sheep graze idly, their backs illuminated by the strengthening sun. A blackbird settles in a bush behind us and takes up his song. It reminds me of the military hospital in Maghull, of the blackbird that always sang beyond the window, of the butterfly that refused to fly away.

"Thank you for coming. I'd intended to write everything in a letter, but I couldn't find the words. I hope I can find them now."

My heart beats wildly. I'm not sure what I want him to say.

"The thing is, Miss Lane, that I've spent my entire life trying to live up to other people's expectations—my father's, my lieutenant's, my so-called friends'. I jump to others' commands. I take aim and pull the trigger when they tell me to. Instructions, rules, expectations. Always singing to someone else's tune." He pulls a daisy from the lawn and sighs a long deep sigh. "And then you came along and I remembered who I am. You helped me to find the man I want to be. You helped me more than you can ever know. And for that, I thank you, Miss Lane. I have grown to care for you deeply."

I pick a daisy, pulling the tiny petals off one by one, remembering the innocent game my sisters and I used to play. *He loves me. He loves me not.* I pick at the petals in turn as Perry continues to speak.

"In fact, there was a time when I thought I was falling in love with you, Miss Lane. I am not ashamed to admit it, and I am certain you have sensed it, or seen it in my face." I think of all those lost moments and held breaths. All the times I have wondered. "But there has always been someone else. No matter how often I have tried to deny it or ignore it, she has always been there; an inescapable part of my life. A part of me. I presume it is the same for you with Teddy? Always thinking about him. Always wondering, even when he is far away."

I pull my knees up to my chest and rest my cheek against them. "Yes. That's exactly what it is like."

"You see, Miss Lane, I am not the boy who fell in love with Bea Balfour all those years ago. Neither am I the shy young man who knew it would please my parents if I were to marry her. I am a man who has done unspeakable things, and in my reluctance to tell her the truth about Oscar, I've forgotten the biggest truth of all."

"And what is that, Mr. Clements?"

He looks at me with those eyes. Gray puddles to drown in. "The truth is that I have always loved Bea, and always will. And that is why I have asked her to marry me."

I feel light-headed. "You have?"

"Yes. And I have you and my sister to thank for making me see sense."

"Your sister?"

"Loretta has always wanted to see the two of us married. It is her dying wish. My only regret is that I didn't ask Bea years ago."

His delight is clear to see, etched onto his cheeks in the warmth of the sun. I pull the last petal from the daisy. *He loves me not.* And in that moment, I know. I know that a girl like me could never truly love a man like Perry. Although the fabrics we are dressed in come from the same London fashion houses, the fabrics of our souls are stitched from very different things. I have imagined being in love with Perry Clements. I became as fascinated with him as he was with me. I've dreamed about him, wondered about him, but there was always a doubt and there was always a question. What about Teddy?

"Then I am very happy for you both," I say. "She is very lovely, and you are clearly the happiest man in England."

He can't deny it. "Thank you, Miss Lane. For understanding and for encouraging me to open my heart."

"You have nothing to thank me for, Perry. What else would a friend do?"

He stalls. "You called me Perry."

"Yes, I did. You're not my employer anymore. This isn't a business arrangement, is it? We are just two friends, sharing happy news on a lovely morning."

He stands up and helps me to my feet.

"Do you remember when we first met in the tearooms?" I ask.

He nods. "Please don't remind me. I have been such a fool around you."

"We spoke about neither of us being a very good swimmer. You said we should keep our feet on terra firma since we would be no good at rescuing each other."

He smiles. "Yes, I remember. And it's true. I'm a terrible swimmer. I never even liked paddling in this pond."

"But there are other ways to rescue a person, aren't there? People can be saved in all sorts of ways."

He lifts my shawl and wraps it around my shoulders, and as the sun bathes the lawns in a soft golden light, we stand together, side by side, and my heart soars, not with the sensation of desire or infatuation, but with the gentle caress of affection, of being truly cared for; of being someone who matters.

42

DOLLY

Her "last season's clothes" become my brand-new, and I am thrilled with them.

There was much that changed during the few days I spent at Nine Elms. While Perry and I danced the first hesitant steps of a newfound friendship, Miss May began to fade away, like a breath on glass. We couldn't bear to leave her, but we also knew she couldn't bear to see our pity, so we held back our tears. "You all look beastly when you cry," she said. "I want to remember you as beautiful young things, not sniveling wretches." Perry said she was the only person he knew who could become more formidable as they were dying. We all laughed. We laughed a lot. We laughed with her in public, and we cried for her in private.

I can't believe I will never see her again.

When I return to The Savoy, I discover that much has changed there too.

"Gladys left!" Sissy explains. "Packed her things and off she's gone to Hollywood. Heading off on a steamer to take a part in a talking movie."

I can't believe it. "Really?"

"Yes. She impressed Larry Snyder just like she

told us she would. Turns out she wasn't cracked in the head after all! And she asked me to give you this."

She passes me a small paper packet. Inside, wrapped in tissue paper, is the scallop-edged powder compact and a note.

Dear Dolly,

I'm going to America! Larry Snyder thinks I have the perfect face for the movies and I sail tomorrow. I hoped to see you before I go, but it has all happened so suddenly. O'Hara is most put out!

Before I go, I owe you an apology. It was me who put the hair comb beneath your pillow. I did a dreadful thing, Dolly, and I'm so sorry for it. Snyder wanted to get your attention. He asked me to help. I would never have done it, only he promised me that he would intervene and make sure you weren't dismissed. My judgment was clouded by my dreams and desires. I wanted to impress him. I was flattered by his attention. I would have done anything for him, and I was a silly fool.

Thankfully, it all worked out. You kept your job and my audition was a success. Even so, I am ashamed of what I did. When you want something badly enough you will risk anything for it—even friendship.

I have left you the powder compact you always admired. It was my absolute favorite and I hope that by my giving it to you, you will know how truly sorry I am.

Perhaps I will see you across the pond sometime? Wish me luck!

Gladys

X

Suddenly everything makes sense.

"What does she say?" Sissy asks.

"It was Gladys who put the hair comb under my pillow. Snyder asked her to do it to get my attention."

"Well, he did that all right."

I sigh and place the letter back inside the envelope. "You don't know the half of it."

We sit together on my bed and I tell Sissy all about my private audition for Snyder and Mademoiselle's silver shoes and how he had intimidated and threatened me. I feel better for telling her. She's shocked, but not surprised.

"What did I tell you? This place is no different from any other. There's us and there's them and that's the way it will always be. I can't believe he went so far, though. You poor thing. You must have been terrified wondering what he was going to do next."

"I was, but I was lucky. Do you remember he left suddenly after Mademoiselle Delysia was taken ill and had to return to France? I thought I'd seen the last of him, but he came back. Thankfully, he was accommodated on a different floor. I made sure I kept well away from him. His attentions had obviously turned to Gladys by then anyway."

"Well, thank God he's gone. And good riddance to bad rubbish. So, where were you the past few days anyway? O'Hara said you'd been called away suddenly on family business, but if I know you there was more to it than that."

I can't stop the grin that spreads across my face. "Oh, Sissy! You'll never believe me when I tell you!"

After lunch, I ask to speak with O'Hara on a matter of some urgency. Although she's in a terrific hurry as usual, she takes me into her office, tells me to close the door and to take a seat.

"I'm glad to see you back, Dorothy. I hope your aunt is feeling better?"

"My aunt?"

She peers over the top of her spectacles. "Yes. Your aunt who took a sudden turn for the worse last week?"

Clearly she knows there was no such thing as a sick aunt. "Oh, yes. My aunt. She is much better. Thank you."

"Good. So, what is it you wish to speak with me about as a matter of such urgency? Another sick relative perhaps?"

I start at the beginning and I don't stop talking until I have told her everything. My life in Mawdesley. My scrapbooks. The notice in *The Stage*. Mr. Clements. Miss May. My trip to Nine Elms. She sits quietly opposite me, never flinching, never moving. I tell her about my audition for Charlot and the upcoming revue and my rehearsal schedule.

"And I presume the conclusion of all this is that you will be ending your employment at the hotel?"

I nod. "I've tried to fit everything in as long as I could, but it isn't possible with the rehearsal schedule and two performances a day. And I expect the revue will tour around the country if it's a success."

She is surprisingly understanding in her own stiff way. "Very well, then. I will make the necessary arrangements. It is like spring fever here. I won't have any maids left if you all keep abandoning me for a life on the stage."

"I know it is very short notice," I say. She raises her eyebrows at this. "But I know someone looking for work and she's available immediately. A very good friend of mine. It would mean the world to me—and to her—if you would consider her."

I tell her about Clover and how she has fallen on bad times. There is an understanding in O'Hara's eyes that I haven't seen before.

"Very well. Tell her to come and see me this afternoon. If she really is as reliable and hard-working as you say she is, then I might have to take her on. Either that or have the guests returning to unmade beds and goodness knows what else."

"Thank you. You won't regret it."

She raises an eyebrow. "I think *I* will be the judge of that." She scribbles something on a pad of paper in front of her. "I must say, Dorothy, with all that has been going on outside the hotel, your work has been remarkably consistent."

"I've enjoyed working here, miss—most of the time. I took pride in it, and no matter what's going on in a person's life, we all need a home and a family to return to, don't we?"

"Yes. I suppose we do."

I wish I could tell her how I've come to understand the governor's sentiments about the hotel; how I've come to think of The Savoy as my home. I wish I could tell her so many things, but despite everything, she is still O'Hara and I am just a maid.

"Where will you stay once you leave here?" she asks.

"At the Theatre Girls' Club in Soho. It's where lots of the chorus girls stay." I'm grateful to Miss May for making the arrangements, or rather, I'm grateful to Hettie, who made the arrangements on Miss May's behalf.

"The Theatre Girls' Club," she remarks, a distant look in her eyes. "Yes. I know it well."

I work a week's notice and have never known seven days to pass so slowly.

On my last day I wake early, and just as I have on so many mornings, I lie still and listen. I smile at the familiar snores coming from Clover, who O'Hara hired immediately and who now sleeps in Gladys's old bed. I listen to the pop of the mattress springs as Sissy and Mildred shuffle in their sleep. I listen to the patter of rain against the window—rain to arrive in, rain to leave in—and I clutch little Edward's photograph tight to my chest. My heart brightens at the prospect of dancing in Charlot's chorus. It is lightened by the understanding I have reached with Perry. And yet it aches for the warmth of my child in my arms. If only I could hear word of him. If only I could hear that he was safe and well.

I dress in a pretty plum-pink rayon day dress—one of Hettie's designs—and matching T-strap shoes. My outfit is all thanks to Miss May's overflowing wardrobe. Her "last season's clothes" become my brand-new, and I am thrilled with them. The ill-fitting borrowed brown garments I arrived in have been happily sent to the Salvation Army. I promise myself that I will always dress colorfully now, and never again in the drab shades of a life in service.

"You must dress and think and act like a star— even before you become one. It is the first rule of show business. Never forget it." I recall Miss May's words as I take a last walk along the hotel corridors. I remember the bewilderment I felt on my first day; O'Hara's words snapping at me like crabs, Sissy and Gladys and Mildred bursting into the room and into my life. I remember the governor and all his wisdom. I walk past suite 401—Snyder's room—and make myself stop and stand outside for a moment. Nothing bad can happen to me now. He is gone. It is only a room. I push the memories away and fill my mind with the sound of Mr. Somers's Orpheans band and the laughter of the girls in the maids' bathroom. I choose to remember the things that have made me smile, not the things that have made me feel invisible and unimportant.

As I say my good-byes to the girls we all cry. Even Mildred seems sorry to see me leave. Sissy gives me a little package in a Woolworth's bag. "Vermillion," she says. "It always suited you." Mildred passes me a letter, which she asks me to open later, when I have a quiet moment. Clover flings her arms around me and makes me promise on my mam's life that I won't forget her when I'm famous. "I knew you'd get onto that stage, Dolly. I felt it in my waters."

Before I leave, O'Hara asks if she might have a word in her office. It seems fitting that I should go there on my last day, having spent so many occasions in it during my employment here.

She fidgets and pulls at the buttons at the top of her dress as I sit in a chair across the desk from her. "You have done very well here, Dorothy. I'm not afraid to admit that I was certain you would amount to nothing when I first saw you. I was sure that you would be another of life's failures, but despite the occasional misdemeanor, you have worked hard and have done everything asked of you."

I feel my cheeks redden. I wasn't expecting this. Praise from O'Hara is not easily given, and even harder to take.

"It has been heartening to watch you flourish here," she continues, "and I can only admire you for what you have achieved." She fiddles with a menu card on her desk and tugs at the collar of her dress. "I was a dancer too once. A chorus girl for three seasons. I understand the pull of a life on the stage."

I don't tell her that I know about Mildred. I don't tell her that I already know our lives are not so different after all. She is still my superior. There are lines that cannot be crossed.

"Now, I'm sure you have places to go," she says, standing up and walking briskly to her office door. She offers me her hand, as stiff and formal as ever. "I wish you the very best of luck, Dolly. I wish you the very best."

She called me Dolly! I almost throw my arms around her, but stop myself in time. I simply nod and thank her and walk away from her office along the long dark corridors, away from a life of servitude, away from my past, until I emerge into the sunlight outside. The rain has stopped. The sun dazzles as it glistens off the wet roads and pavements.

With my bag in my hand, I walk around to the front of the hotel and stand beside the florist's shop window. I watch the front doors as they swing open, taking glittering guests inside this incredible place. I watch the ladies in their beautiful shoes and elegant dresses and coats, and I smile, because I know. I know what it feels like to walk in soft Parisian leather. I know what it feels like to be twirled around a dance floor in chiffon and silk. I know what it feels like to be one of them.

I hold my head high and walk away from this place that I have called home, and as I go I sense the hotel watching me. Like a hundred searching eyes, I feel every glinting window watching me leave, and my heart dances at the prospect of my triumphant return.

43
DOLLY

"Take a breath. Sense the ending.
Prepare for the beginning."

Summer rolls up the Thames and London bursts into life. The magnolia trees infuse Green Park with their sweet perfume, the floral candles lighting up the great horse chestnuts that sway in the breeze. The streets are filled with the lilting sounds of the organ grinders and the Negro bands that pop up on street corners. London excites me on days like these. I can think of nowhere else I would rather be.

Weeks of exhausting rehearsals and last-minute adjustments to scripts and score and costumes have finally resulted in a production that Charlot is proud of. Perry's musical score is full of heart and humor and the principal actors and actresses fall in love with it as much as I did as I watched it take shape. I feel privileged to have heard these numbers as the first tentative chords and possibly-maybe harmonies, and to hear them played now by a full orchestra. Of course no production reaches opening night without its share of despair and frustration. I've seen it all: slammed piano lids, scrunched-up sheets of music, wearyingly late nights and horribly early mornings, but somehow opening night arrives. *Charlot's Revue of 1924*, a production in which Dolly Lane appears on the billing as a chorus girl, arrives at the Shaftesbury Theatre, and we are due to open to a packed house.

The call for five minutes to curtain up sends a collective shiver through the two dozen excited girls crammed like sardines into the small dressing room at the top of the theater. The stagehands tell us about the distinguished guests who have already arrived, describing all the glitz and glamour out front. Backstage it is all frantic noise and chaos, last-minute nerves and panic about lost costumes and mismatched shoes and forgotten lines. The excitement and tension is like nothing I have ever felt before. It is exhilarating.

As the girls rush ahead, their heels click-clacking like castanets down the stairs, I linger behind to snatch a few seconds alone. I want to savor the moment. This is what I have dreamed of for so many years, this is what I have imagined over and over in my mind as I scrubbed steps and blacked fires and listened to conversations and gramophone records through open doors. I look around the dressing room. It is a muddle of glistening stockings and shimmering shoes, feathers and fans in all the colors of the rainbow, spilled face powder, blunted kohl pencils, combs and bobby pins, curling irons and buttons, needles and thread. It is everything I had hoped it would be.

I take the letter from my makeup bag and quickly read it once more.

> There is a peculiar moment, Miss Lane, between the end of one thing and the start of another. Like that strange light between night and dawn—not quite dark and not yet light—a sense of something other, something in between. Brides sense it on their wedding day. Actresses sense it on opening night. For weeks, there is only anticipation and then the day arrives and the moment takes over so that you can't remember a time when this thing, this feeling, wasn't a part of you.
>
> Take a breath. Sense the ending. Prepare for the beginning.
>
> You will be marvelous. You will be my shining star.
>
> Loretta

I wish she could be here. She'd sent the letter, accompanied by a single pink peony and a perfect crimson leaf and the newspaper cutting that Roger had fallen in love with in the dugout all those years ago. She has written on the back, her words to me written beside his words to her. *You are my shining star. Always, L. X.*

I close my eyes and breathe in deep and allow myself to let go of all the hurtful rejections, all the failed auditions, all the loss and the sadness in my life. It lifts from me like a shadow erased by the sun.

"There you are, Dolly! Bloody hell! Nearly gave us all a heart attack." I jump as Aggie, one of the chorus girls, bursts into the dressing room. "Come on. They're about to raise the curtain. Quick!"

Giggling, I run after her, the sequins on my skirt swishing at my knees, both of us up on our tiptoes so our heels don't make a sound against the floor. We rush up the small wooden steps at the wings and into position. I adjust my beaded skullcap and pull at the elastic on my knickers.

"Stand still," Aggie hisses. "You're as jittery as a fish."

The murmur of the audience beyond the safety curtain dissipates to a final *shhhh* and then silence.

"Here we go, girls," Aggie whispers. "Remember: teeth, tits, and turns."

The curtain parts in a dramatic swoop, the spotlights dazzle, the orchestra booms into life, and our well-rehearsed routine begins.

For a second I am so mesmerized by the lights and the moment that I almost forget to dance and then everything else fades into the background and all I can hear is the music. All I can feel is the reverberation through my calves as we stamp our feet against the wooden boards in perfect time. I kick and flick, twirl and dance as I have never danced before until my thighs burn and my arms shake under the strain of holding them aloft and my cheeks ache with smiling. On we go, number after number, off at stage left, back on at stage right. A whirl of breathless girls and sweat-beaded limbs and pure, pure exhilaration.

In a brief scene change, the dance manager pulls me to one side. I don't care that I'm half undressed, wriggling into my new costume, pulling the straps over my shoulders, and tugging at the fabric as it sticks to my clammy skin.

"You're doing very well," she says. "What's your name?"

"Dolly. Dolly Lane."

"This your first show?"

"Yes."

"Well, it certainly won't be your last. Come and see me after."

"Yes. Yes, I will." I'm in such a rush to button my shoes that I can't even process what she's saying. Hoisting up my stockings, I run after the others to take my position again. Now the nerves have settled. Now I am reveling in the performance. My limbs ache but my mind won't allow me to think about that. I look for faces in the audience, my eyes adjusting to the glare of the footlights. I see them in the front row, beaming up at me: Perry. Bea. Charlot. And farther back I see Sissy and Clover, who waves every time I look in her direction. Even Mildred and O'Hara have come to show their support.

I dance on and on, hopping and quickstepping and high-kicking, always in perfect time with the other girls. We move as one, so that I feel like an extension of the girls on both sides of me and not a separate person at all. I move in time with the music, my body taking over, responding to the rhythm. *"It comes from here . . . from deep inside. You can move your feet and hit all the steps in all the right places, but if you don't feel the music in your heart you'll never shine. Dancing should be as natural to you as breathing in and out."*

As the orchestra plays the final crescendo, the curtain falls and the lights go out and we run off into the wings as the auditorium erupts in applause.

Immediately we run around the back of the stage and line up to take our bow. The curtains part and we move forward, my ears deafened by the stamping and cheering from the gallery and the emphatic applause from the stalls and dress circle. We, in turn, applaud the principals, the applause and the stamping increasing to a level that shakes the boards I am standing on, and then the curtain falls for the final time, the house-lights go up, and it is over.

· · ·

The first night notices are generous. I scour the morning papers and devour the words.

André Charlot has finally followed the lead of Ziegfeld and others and lent his name to a revue, and he can be rightly proud to do so. If you want to hold your own in small talk, it will quite simply require you to have seen Miss Binnie Hale in *Charlot's Revue of 1924*. Despite the fact that the out-of-town air was noticeable in the stalls, where the only celebrities of note were resting theater stars, opening night was a resounding success. The chorus were particularly enchanting.

Of course, the most helpful item in building up a part is the clothes, and Miss Hale's costumes, partly designed by Miss May's personal dresser, Miss Hettie Bennett, did not disappoint. The frocks are up-to-the-minute—short, just below the knee. The necklines are round and moderately low, and cunningly introduced draperies and flutterings add to the charm.

In my room at the Theatre Girls' Club, I cut them carefully from the newspapers, dozens and dozens of them, and stick them into my new scrapbook. I write the date at the top of the page and add the billing from the program. I draw a little star next to my name.

The daily matinees and evening performances come and go in a blur of costume changes and aching legs; a continuous cycle of excitement and nerves. It is an exhausting schedule and I've never known hunger like it. Between acts, we tuck into great chunks of bread and pickled onions, begging the dresser to run out for more when the cup runs empty. Some of the girls gripe and moan about their blisters and corns, but I never do. I never will. Blisters and corns on my toes are a blessing after years of chilblains on my hands.

We train from noon until four every day and I work hard on my dance steps and my fitness, determined to get better and better, to become the shining star I promised Miss May I would be. She sends occasional letters and telegrams from Devon to tell me how she's doing. She tells me she is following the show's success in the papers. My only regret is that she cannot see me perform.

On Wednesdays, during my short afternoon break between training and performing, Clover meets me for a cup of tea and we chatter ten to the dozen about her life at The Savoy and my life at the Theatre Girls' Club. She has settled in well at the hotel. We laugh about O'Hara's funny ways and she tells me Mildred is becoming much friendlier. I think of the letter she wrote to me on my final day. A few short words to thank me for listening to her and to tell me that she will pray that I find little Edward and that I will find peace when I do. A few short words that meant so much to me.

My hard work and dedication pay off and I quickly progress from the second line of the chorus to the front line and then to the coveted position of lead chorus, where I take a few precious moments alone in the limelight to dazzle and amuse. The gallery-ites hoot and cheer when I do my tumbles and turns. I look to them especially as I take my applause. The press notices flood in, my name picked out again and again.

Each sketch and musical number is packed with verve, vivacity, and vim, skillfully choreographed by Max Rivers to the musical arrangements of Perry Clements, whose music has undergone something of a remarkable transformation. What a way to make a comeback! His numbers rival anything written by Coward or Porter or Berlin of late. As the audience left the theater, the words to the most popular numbers, "Dolly Daydream" and "The Girl from The Savoy," were on everyone's lips. I suspect we will hear much more of these particular numbers, such was their originality and impact. Each number and comedy turn leads to a frenetic climax that made the audience jazz in their seats. As the leading lady, Miss Binnie Hale had a total of fifteen costume changes, with only ninety seconds for each change. A special mention must be made of Dolly Lane, who amazes and amuses as the perfect lead chorus."

When one of the actresses playing a supporting role is struck down with laryngitis, I am asked to step in. Despite my nerves, I fill her shoes admirably. My name moves farther up the billing.

As usual, Charlot's Chorus was irresistible, but what especially caught this reviewer's attention was Miss Dorothy Lane, a late replacement for Kitty Ellis in the role of Eleanor. Miss Lane dazzled each time she took to the stage. She is most definitely someone to watch. An ordinary girl with an extraordinary talent to charm an audience. I'll wager that Miss Lane is going to become a very important person in the English theater.

It is everything I have ever dreamed of, right there in black and white. *An ordinary girl with an extraordinary talent to charm an audience. I'll wager that Miss Lane is going to become a very important person in the English theater.*

My name is on everyone's lips and I am center stage at the after-show parties, attracting admiring glances and attention wherever I go. The cry of "Miss Lane! Miss Lane! Over here!" from the press photographers is a sound I am becoming accustomed to.

With the revue causing such a stir, Charlot asks Perry to work on a full score for a musical comedy based on the Act Two sketches and the song "The Girl from The Savoy." Perry tells me Charlot has me in mind for the lead role when the production opens in America.

"America?" I flop down into my chair at the dressing table.

"Yes. America! For a seven-week run, starting in Baltimore and ending up goodness knows where. Broadway, maybe!" I don't even know where Baltimore is. "And he wants me to write more numbers, especially for you. You're to have your own billing, Dolly. Isn't it wonderful?"

"Yes. Yes, it is, but . . . America. It sounds so far away."

Perry laughs. "It *is* far away! We'll travel on the SS *Caronia*. What an adventure it will be!"

"When do we leave?"

"Three weeks. After the London run." He senses the hesitation in my eyes. "This is everything you ever wanted, isn't it? Your name at the top of the billing. Your name in lights out front! Just imagine it."

I have imagined it so often. "I didn't think I would ever leave London. It's all so sudden. So exciting. I was folding bed linen just a few months ago."

He takes my hands in his. "I know this is all happening quickly, Dolly, and I know how much you love London, but what do you have to lose? What is there here for you?"

I think about Teddy and the drawings on the paving stones on the Embankment. Was I imagining the likeness after all? I think about little Edward. Is he lost to me, forever? Endless questions without any answers, always waiting, always wondering: what if?

The question to ask isn't why . . . it is why not?

I stand up. "You're right. There's nothing for me here. Why not go to America?"

His gray eyes smile. "Start to say your good-byes, Dolly. If America falls in love with you as quickly as London has, it may be some time before you're back. You may never come back at all!"

But there is one final question on my mind.

How will I ever tell Clover?

44
LORETTA

Some might say that I have lived my life recklessly. I say only that I have lived, in every sense of the word.

I lie in my bed and watch the curtains fluttering at the open window as broad leaves sway in two-four time on the horse-chestnut trees beyond. When the sun fades and darkness falls, I see shooting stars.

Life dances on.

When I close my eyes I hear the waves rolling in to shore, the endless ebb and flow of the tide. Sometimes my breathing matches the sound—in and out, in and out, in and out—so that I feel I could never die as long as the tide comes and goes.

There are days, hours, moments when I feel myself slipping away and I cling desperately on, refusing to give in. Other times I will myself to fall asleep and welcome whatever awaits beyond.

Some might say that I have lived my life recklessly. I say only that I have lived, in every sense of the word. I have loved and laughed, I have felt the darkest sadness and the brightest joy.

I have affected people, left a mark, an imprint in the sand. Isn't that what matters after all? To know that even when you are no longer there, your words, your face, your story will be remembered. Your star will shine on.

But every performance must come to an end.

The lights are fading.

The curtain is falling.

The spotlight flickers and goes out.

I take my final bow and wait in the silence of a dead blackout before I turn and make my exit to the fading applause.

And there he is, waiting in the wings. His uniform pristine. A pink peony in his buttonhole. His hands outstretched.

I run to him and we fall into each other's arms and everything is wonderful as we commence our eternal waltz beneath the stars.

45
DOLLY

My heart folds in on itself as all my life comes rushing toward me . . .

The news we have all been dreading arrives on a misty July morning and the houselights are dimmed across London's theaters.

She is gone and we are left with only our memories and Elsie's scrapbook and the empty spaces she leaves behind: rooms without the scent of her perfume, dinner parties without her caustic tongue and infectious laughter, dresses hanging limp in the cupboard, shoes unworn, theaters without her name blazing out front.

Loretta May. The darling of the West End. The actress who gave joy to so many. The woman who I was fortunate to know as more than her stage persona. Loretta May was a performance. Virginia Clements was a daughter, a sister, a friend, a nurse, a lover. The most important roles she ever played were those she played behind the curtain, away from the public's adoring gaze.

Arrangements are made and the sudden heartache of death becomes an endless series of things to organize. She is buried in her favorite

Poiret gown with a posy of pink peonies in her hands. The funeral brings Londoners out in the thousands, lining the streets to watch the procession as we say our final good-byes and she is laid to rest.

Our star has fallen.

To cheer ourselves up, Perry and Bea insist on taking me to Claridge's for afternoon tea in the Winter Garden. "Loretta loved to come here," Perry explains, and I can understand why. I am instantly charmed by it. "We met here every Wednesday. I complained about it rather a lot, but I think I will rather miss it now she's gone."

"Then we must keep coming, darling," Bea suggests as the waiter shows us to our table. "When we get back from America we will keep up the tradition. I think Loretta would rather like that."

And so it is settled.

Just as she did when she was alive, Miss May is to have the last word. She leaves strict instructions that after a reasonably dignified period of somber reflection, we must all dress in our finest and celebrate her life. Charlot arranges for the entire cast to gather at The Savoy for an after-show party.

We arrive in an entourage of motorcars, the principal stars stepping out into the hotel courtyard to a volley of flashbulbs. Jack Buchanan, Gertie

Lawrence, and Binnie Hale stand together, relishing the limelight. And then Perry and I step out of our car to the same pop and fizz of the bulbs and calls for us to look this way and that way.

I take a deep breath. *"You, Dorothy Lane, are a prime example of someone who will never get on in life. You will never become anything."*

Perry takes my hand and leads me toward the door. And there's Bert the doorman, and the smart young page boys.

"Front entrances are of no concern to a maid, other than when she is scrubbing the steps or polishing the handle."

I see myself standing beside the florist's shop window not so many months ago, shoulders back, head held high, my hands scrunched into tight determined balls. I hear my words. *"One day, Dorothy Mary Lane, you'll walk through that door. And when you do, you'll be dressed so beautifully and be so famous that* everybody *will notice you."*

I place the palm of my hand against the glass of the swing door, turn around, and smile my brightest smile. The cameras click and whir frantically behind me and everybody stares, everybody notices as the door opens and transports me into the Front Hall.

I am instantly surrounded by an oasis of calm and elegance. Polite chatter, the clink of glasses, the lilt of the piano as liveried footmen, valets, porters, lift attendants, and cloakroom attendants all take their turn in a carefully orchestrated dance across the chessboard floor. I think about Cutler steering me away from the guests. *"Back-of-house staff must not be seen. As far as our guests are concerned, they are invisible. You, Miss Lane, do not exist."* I see the smirk on Snyder's face; feel his hand against my stocking. I see O'Hara's starchy gaze and Mademoiselle Delysia, moving like silk around her suite. So many memories come rushing back.

As my cape is taken from me, the governor appears, shaking Perry's hand enthusiastically and kissing my cheek.

"Miss Lane. Mr. Clements. You are both very welcome. We were desperately sorry to hear of Miss May's passing."

Perry thanks him. "She was a wonderful sister to me and a wonderful friend to Miss Lane."

Reeves-Smith turns to me. "And any friend of Miss May's is always welcome at The Savoy."

"And a friend of yours?" I prompt. "Would *she* be welcome here too?"

He clears his throat, adjusts his bow tie, and lowers his voice. "It isn't often one exits by the back door and returns through the front, Miss Lane. It is a most unusual turn of events. Most unusual indeed. You are an extraordinary young woman. You are welcome here anytime."

As the others make their way to the Ballroom, I

excuse myself for a moment. Being careful not to be seen, I rush toward the back stairs, run up to the second floor, knock at the bedroom door, and push it open.

There they are, as if I had never left. Sissy reading a magazine on her bed, legs sticking up in the air. Mildred's pen scratching across the surface of a page. Clover, leaning over her sewing. At the click of the door, she looks up.

"Well, would you look what the cat dragged in. It's only Dolly bloody Daydream!"

We look at each other and burst out laughing as she bounds toward me and I throw my arms around her. Dear Clover. Always the same, although she looks happier and healthier than I've seen her look in months.

"Well, would you look at you!" she exclaims, turning me around. "Quite the little flapper."

"Oh, hush. I had a haircut. That's all." I put my fingers self-consciously to the nape of my neck. I still haven't got used to my shingled bob.

"Well, I feel like a pantomime horse with you all turned out so nice and proper. Come on, then. Tell us everything."

I sit on Clover's bed and tell them about the show and life on the stage. I tell them about Loretta's last wishes and the party we are having to celebrate her life and the photographers all shouting my name outside. It pours out of me like good champagne. When I tell them I'm leaving for America in two days, Clover bursts into tears. I laugh and hug her close to me and in my thickest Lancashire accent I tell her she's a silly old sod and that I love her.

"Promise me you'll never change, Clover Parker."

"What would I be changing for? You don't need to worry about me. This is it for me now. I like it here. Posh hotels suit me!"

Sissy laughs. "She likes the porter she's walking out with, more like."

Clover blushes and admits she's sweet on one of the porters. I know him and I approve entirely.

We talk for a while, remembering, laughing, until I have to go, and for the last time I leave the little room I once called home and head back down the stairs. The passing porters and maids gawp at me as if they've seen a ghost.

When I return to the Front Hall, the governor escorts me to the Grand Ballroom, where the music is already in full swing under the expert guidance of Debroy Somers. Taking my hand, Perry guides me to the dance floor. My companion. My dance partner. It is easy to be around him now, to let our friendship blossom without the nagging uncertainties of love. When we switch partners, I watch him and Bea together and feel nothing but happiness for them. With a little direction, we have all found the roles we were destined to play.

It is a perfect night, just as Loretta would have wanted, everyone laughing and dancing and sparkling beneath the crystal chandeliers as we foxtrot and tango our way past midnight and into a new day, a new scene, a new Act in this play of life.

We leave for America in two days. All the arrangements have been made. Our tickets for the SS *Caronia* to New York have been booked. Trunks and cases are stuffed full of shoes and dresses, costumes and hope. *Charlot's Revue* will play its opening night to an American audience in just over a fortnight's time. The thought of leaving London excites and troubles me. Questions linger. Doubts and uncertainties remain. I dream of Teddy and little Edward, whose photograph I still keep beneath my pillow. I try to put him from my mind and focus on the future.

Hettie is working on costumes for the new numbers. She can hardly keep up with Charlot's demands, but the columnists are delighted by her creations and she is establishing quite a name for herself. She's been working on a dress especially for me and I have a final fitting to attend before we sail.

As I open the latch on the little gate at her house in Shoreditch, I see young Thomas standing at an upstairs window. He blows hot breaths onto the glass and draws pictures into the mist with his fingertips. He presses his nose and lips against the windowpane until they are completely squashed. I smile as I watch and wave up at him when he sees me, but he ducks down, too shy to wave back. I walk down the narrow path toward the front door.

Hettie greets me, half-moon spectacles perched on the end of her nose and a tape measure snaking around her neck, as always. I step inside the house. It is small, but neat and simply furnished.

"Come through. The dress is all ready for you. I hope you like it."

"I'm sure I'll love it."

I follow her along a narrow hallway into a small room at the back of the house, behind the scullery. A sewing machine sits on a little table, surrounded by swatches of fabric. Pincushions, pins, needles, and bobbins of multicolored cotton are spread over a narrow workbench and much of the floor.

"It's always so colorful in here," I say, setting my purse down on a wooden stool. "It's like walking into a rainbow!"

"Like walking into a very messy rainbow, maybe."

She shows me some sketches she's been working on for the new costumes and some of the materials she's chosen. They're all beautiful.

"Let me get the dress and you can try it on. I can make a few last-minute adjustments if they're needed."

I wriggle out of my dress and into the new one,

ivory chiffon with beautiful beading and a handkerchief hem. I'm still surprised by the slim feel of my hips and stomach, the fabric slipping easily across my dance-toned body. No doughy flesh to pinch now. All my training has paid off. It fits perfectly.

"It's beautiful, Hettie. Thank you."

She brushes my compliments aside. "Don't thank me. Thank Miss May for choosing such wonderful material."

"She chose it?"

"A while ago. She told me to use it when the right opportunity came about. It looks beautiful on you."

I smile and turn my shoulder to admire the back in the looking glass.

"I miss her terribly, Dolly."

"Me too. I only knew her for a short while, but she became everything to me: a mother, a teacher, a sister, a friend. I still can't believe she's gone."

Hettie rests her hand on mine and we both try not to think about our loss.

We talk for a while as she makes a few small adjustments to the dress, pinning it here and there. "I'll have it ready for you tomorrow. I can drop it to the theater if you like."

"Don't trouble yourself. I'll call by. You've enough on your plate with little Thomas to mind. How is your sister?"

"She's doing much better. She's up and about

again. She'll be here to collect him soon. I still take him the odd morning until she gets back to full health. To be honest, I love having him around. Gives me a bit of company."

As she sees me back through into the hallway Thomas bounds down the stairs. He stands and looks at me, his fingers stuck into his mouth.

"Well, hello there, Thomas," I say.

He looks at his feet as Hettie ruffles his hair. "I thought I told you to wait upstairs while the lady was with me," she whispers. He looks up at her with big brown eyes. She can't be cross with him and scoops him up into her arms.

"It's all right," I say. "I don't mind a bit. It's always lovely to see you, Thomas." I hold out my hand to shake his but he hides in Hettie's hair.

"If only he was this quiet all the time," she laughs, rubbing his back.

"He's adorable. Such gorgeous brown eyes. Does he get them from your sister?"

She hesitates. Lowers her voice. "We're not sure who he gets them from. Thomas was adopted."

"Oh. I'm sorry. I just assumed . . ."

"No need to apologize. Most people assume." She lets him down from her arms and he runs through to the scullery. "My brother-in-law was left badly injured after the war and unable to father a child. Thomas was abandoned at a Mothers' Hospital. He was only a few weeks old when Helen took him. He's never known anyone but her as his mother. She loves him with all her heart."

I feel dizzy as she speaks. *Thomas was abandoned* . . . It sounds so harsh. So thoughtless and cruel.

"I'd better get going. Thank you again, Hettie. The dress is perfect."

She smiles and takes my coat from the stand as there's a knock at the door. "That'll be your mother, Thomas! Come along now."

She opens the door and I watch as little Thomas squeals with excitement and runs into his mother's arms.

Like a pause between breathing in and breathing out, everything is suspended.

She is standing in front of me, like spring in a daffodil-yellow coat.

Thomas buries his face in her red hair as he perches so naturally on her hip. I almost fall sideways with the need to feel him on mine. I look at him and I look at her. *"Thomas was adopted."* His eyes so brown, like mine, when hers are so blue. *"Thomas was abandoned at a Mothers' Hospital."* I stall on the doorstep and I stare at them both. *"He was only a few weeks old when Helen took him. He's never known anyone but her as his mother. She loves him with all her heart."*

Her name is Helen. And I wished for her.

My heart folds in on itself as all my life comes

rushing toward me in this single moment. I stare at this doting mother and her happy child, his fat little legs wrapped around her daffodil-yellow coat, and my arms feel crushed by the absence of him.

And then he jumps down and stands on the path and I am saying good-bye and he turns to me and waves. "Bye bye, pretty lady." He is dressed in powder blue and he is waving good-bye.

I sink to my knees and throw my arms around him, holding him there for a perfect wonderful moment. I feel the warmth of him, breathe in the smell of him. I feel the rapid beat of his butterfly heart and I know him. I know him. Little Edward, my child.

Too quickly, he wriggles free and rushes back to his mother, back to the arms he feels secure in, loved in, burying himself in her skirts.

Somehow I walk away from him, down the narrow path. Somehow I open the latch on the gate and let it click shut behind me. Somehow I put one foot in front of the other. Somehow I breathe. Somehow, I find the strength to accept that in the very moment I find my little boy, I must lose him all over again.

Like the girls in the gallery, I must watch from a distance and cheer and applaud and stamp my feet in admiration. I must be content to know that he is loved and happy. I must put down my net and set him free. I must let him spread his wings and fly.

46
DOLLY

*. . . he has always been a part of me,
something I do to keep myself afloat.*

What a send-off London gives us! Our final
performance is blessed with a perfect summer's
evening. London glows beneath the generous sun
as I make my way to the theater. The Thames
glistens. The Houses of Parliament dazzle, bathed
in rose gold. It is truly beautiful. I will miss this
skyline; these familiar buildings and landmarks.

Fans flock to the theater in their hundreds.
Police constables are brought in to control the
crush; the gallery girls causing a stampede when
the doors are opened. The lobby is filled with
autograph hunters and reporters, society ladies
and gentlemen. I try to take it all in; try to
understand how it is possible that I am now part of
this, that I am the one signing the autographs, not
the one pleading for them.

In the dressing room, I go through the usual
routine: warm-up, makeup, costume, and a silent
prayer for a good performance. Charlot pokes
his head around the door just before the five-
minute curtain call, making us all scream as we

throw coats and wrappers over our exposed limbs.

"Let's make it a good one, girls," he says. "Let's leave London begging for us to return and America salivating at the prospect of our arrival!"

The fizz of excitement passes among us like electricity. I take Loretta's picture from my coat pocket. "I am ready, Miss May," I whisper. "I am ready to shine."

The show is our best yet. The audience's enthusiasm is infectious and everyone lifts their performance in response. The principal actors and actresses ad-lib and improvise brilliantly, sending the audience into raptures.

As we reach the grand finale, my eyes are drawn to a man in the second row of the stalls, his head held high, his eyes fixed only on me. A familiar broad chin. A dimple in the cheek. It can't be. My heart races faster and faster as I move in and out of the spotlight, trying to find him again, but the glare of the footlights blinds me so that I can't be sure, and then the curtain falls and the place erupts to thunderous applause and incessant cries for more.

I run to the wings waiting for my curtain call, and as I step out onto the stage, again I search for him, able to see a little more clearly now that more of the houselights are up. I take my bow and throw grateful smiles at our adoring audience and I search for him in the twilight as the curtain rises and falls, rises and falls. I scour the rows and rows of faces, but all I find is an empty seat. He isn't there. It wasn't him.

As I rush to the dressing room, one of the stagehands gives me a package.

"This was delivered for you, Miss Lane. The gentleman said it was urgent."

I've become so used to gifts from admirers that I hardly give the package a moment's notice. I take it from him and carry on along the corridor, eager to be in the privacy of the dressing room. I close the door behind me and lean my back against it, taking a long deep breath.

I have done it. I have danced and performed in the most talked-about show of the season. I have risen from the gray obscurity of a chambermaid at The Savoy to the dazzling spotlight of an actress on the West End stage, my name in large print on the program. I have walked into my very own dream and I am wonderfully awake.

Perspiration peppers my skin. The dresser wraps a robe around me to prevent a chill as my skin cools. I place the package among all the other gifts from fans and would-be lovers and settle at the dressing table, peering at myself in the mirror. I sip a glass of water and wish it were something stronger. Miss May was right. *Gin is an acquired taste, and once acquired, it is rarely lost.* I smile to myself, remembering her wonderful turn of phrase as I rub cold cream into my face, carefully removing the heavy stage makeup. I follow my usual routine: cold cream and Vaseline followed by pancake and rouge. A sweep of mascara, kohl, and lipstick and I am ready to face the world again.

As I leave the dressing room, my eye is drawn to the package. I pick it up and look at it properly as I close the door behind me and stand in the corridor.

To Little Thing.

My heart tilts at the sight of the words, written so carefully onto the brown paper in neat looping script. I pull roughly at the string and tear open the careful wrappings. Every nerve, every part of me jolts at the sight. A chalk drawing. A young woman with butterfly wings, surrounded by the words *Love, Hope,* and *Adventure.* A shiver runs across my skin as I brush my fingers lightly across the page. I have admired the same image so often among the work of the Embankment screevers.

"I remembered you, Dolly."

His voice, a million fragments of ice slipping down my back. The drawing tumbles from my hands and falls at my feet as I turn around.

He is here.

He is here.

He is here.

"Teddy?"

He smiles and I cannot speak, cannot breathe. I grasp the edge of the doorframe, my knees trembling like leaves shaken by a tempest.

"Teddy?" His name the faintest whisper on my lips, a distant echo of the thousands of times I have said it, longing for him to hear me, to reply, to remember.

He walks slowly toward me and takes my hands in his. "Dear Little Thing. Dear Dolly. Look at you. Even more beautiful beneath the spotlights. Who would have thought it possible?"

His voice, his words, tumble and swirl in my mind, and I cannot grasp them. I stand perfectly still while all my life rushes forward to this moment, to this man—my hopes, my life, my past, my onetime future.

"But . . . how? Why? I don't understand." My tears fall in quiet, confused ribbons.

"I saw your name in the newspaper. MISS DOLLY LANE. Right there, in black and white. Right here in London. I always knew you were destined for a bigger stage than Mawdesley village hall. I always said I would come and watch you perform and clap and cheer . . ."

". . . and blow me kisses and throw roses at my feet." I finish the sentence for him. I remember the words so clearly.

"I forgot the roses."

We both smile; shy and hesitant, and yet so comfortable and familiar. It is like finding the missing piece of a jigsaw puzzle. We fit. It feels right.

His eyes search deep into my soul, looking for the part of me he remembers. Lost words and years stretch between us, while all around us doors slam, scenery clunks and thuds, stagehands curse and shout to one another. All is chaos here. All is chaos in my mind; my heart.

"Is there somewhere quieter we can go?" he asks. "To talk?

"Yes. Yes, of course."

"Miss Lane, I wondered if . . ." Perry rushes along the corridor, stalling when he sees us. He looks at me and I look from him to Teddy and I am drowning and I don't know what to cling to.

"This is Teddy. He came to see the show." My words are clipped, suffocated by my confusion. Perry doesn't move. His eyes searching; understanding. "I can't come to the after party. I'm sorry, Perry. Will you explain? I have to go."

I take Teddy's arm and we walk together, through the stage door and out to the waiting car.

Everything around me is a blur—the reporters, the gallery girls—they all shout my name and the magnesium bulbs pop and fizz, but I am underwater and I cannot hear clearly. As we step into the car and drive away, I cannot speak; cannot catch my breath. The man I have loved since I was a little girl is sitting beside me, and I am terrified and exhilarated because I do not know him, and yet I know him better than I have ever known anyone. All my life has been about Teddy Cooper. Thinking about him, writing to him, loving him, waiting for him, praying for him to remember. Like breathing and blinking, sleeping and walking, he has always been a part of me, something I do to keep myself afloat.

We travel in silence as a thousand questions and unspoken words fill the air between us. It isn't a hesitant or an awkward silence. It is patient and understanding. Necessary.

I take him to Miss May's home in Belgravia. She'd left instructions that I was to think of it as my own home; that I was to use it whenever I needed to, whenever I needed to escape from things. I need it now more than ever.

Elsie answers the door and doesn't say a word as I explain that I need a little time alone with Mr. Cooper. I show Teddy into the drawing room. I pour myself a martini and him a Scotch. We sit at opposite ends of the sofa and try to make sense of the lost years and all those that came before.

"I want you to know that I forgive you," he says, as he passes me a sheet of paper. I recognize my writing, my words. It is my final letter to him.

> You are a good, good man, Teddy Cooper, and I wish you nothing but happiness. My only hope is that one day these words will mean something to you,

and that you will remember me and all that we once had. And when you remember, I hope that you will find it in your heart to forgive me. More than anything, I can't bear the thought of bringing you any more pain.

"I remembered you at the hospital," he says. "You sat beside me and read your letters to me. For months, I thought you were a nurse; a dream. And then there you were, sitting beside me. My Dolly. My Little Thing. It was like a fog had lifted, and I knew you."

"You remembered?"

He nods. Smiles. "And then I watched you leave. I watched you walk away."

"Oh, Teddy. I'm so sorry." I throw my arms around him and I am ten years old, and we are dangling our legs over the stone bridge and all is warmth and peace in the world. "I couldn't bear to leave you, but I had to. I had to go."

I remember the conversation I'd had with his mother and mine, fabricating a story about how it was breaking my heart to see Teddy suffer in the hospital and that it was kinder for us both if I left.

"I don't blame you for leaving, Dolly. I never did and I never will." He takes my hands in his and I can't believe he is sitting here, in front of me. That he is talking to me, looking at me, touching me, forgiving me. "Do you remember in my hospital room there was a butterfly always at the window?"

I smile through my tears. "Yes! It would never fly away, and whenever it did it always came back. I often wondered if it ever left."

"It did. It flew on the same day that you did, Dolly. You both needed to stretch your wings."

"I wanted to stay, Teddy. I wanted to help you get better, but things . . . things had happened while you were away. Terrible things."

And I tell him. I somehow find the courage to revisit those dark moments and tell him everything, and as I do, I feel the cracks in my heart coming back together. I feel myself heal.

He listens and wipes the tears from my cheeks. He never questions or judges. "I wish you had told me," he whispers. "I wish I could have helped you."

He tells me that when he left the hospital he tried to settle back into life in Mawdesley, but everything had changed. "I hadn't appreciated how far the war had reached. Not one person was unaffected. Not one person hadn't lost someone they loved. Mam got me back. I lost you. That's what war does. It breaks things apart. Tears things up."

"I should have stayed. I was a coward to run away."

"You were right to leave, Dolly. I watched so many couples struggle on after the war, trying to find the passion they'd once felt for each other. The men couldn't explain how they felt. The women could never understand. We all changed, Dolly. You loved the man who went to war. It wasn't fair to expect you to love the stranger who came back."

"But I *did* love you. I did."

I did.

The words hang in the air between us. What about now? What do I feel when I look at him now? Love? Pity? Hope? What?

He stands up and walks to the window. "I'm so sorry for the reason that took you away, Dolly. I wish things could have been different for us, I really do, but you helped me more by leaving than you could ever have done by staying. What use would I have been to you and your child? I could barely look after myself. Your absence gave me a purpose, Dolly; a reason to keep living, to keep searching. And I had your letters. You gave me words when I had none. You showed me who I had been—a person who had loved and laughed and hoped. Because of your words, I wasn't just a recovering soldier, I was Teddy Cooper, and I had loved a girl called Dorothy Lane. To know that I had been someone so full of life meant everything to me. It made me want to be that person again."

We talk for a long time, finding our way slowly back to each other across all the years we have been apart.

"Why did you come looking for me, Teddy? Why now?"

"Because I wanted you to know that I remembered. I wanted you to know that I didn't blame you for leaving. And I wanted to know that you were happy." He looks around the room. "And look what I found! If you hadn't left Mawdesley you wouldn't be sitting here in this house wearing that beautiful dress. You wouldn't have your name on a poster outside one of London's finest theaters. You would have sat beside me, miserable and incomplete and unfulfilled, working at Mawdesley Hall for the rest of your days, and that would have damaged me more than any heavy artillery ever could."

We talk until the gray light of dawn creeps through the windows. He tells me about the work he has been doing in the factories and the drawings he does on the streets, and as he talks the eager young girl who loved the very bones of him throws her arms around his neck and reaches up onto her tiptoes to plant kisses all over his weather-reddened cheeks. But I am not that eager young girl. I am a young woman, and I am leaving for America. I can hardly bear to tell him, but I must.

I walk to the window and watch London wake up. "I'm leaving, Teddy. We are taking the revue to America."

"When do you leave?"

"Tomorrow." I watch the lamplighter extinguish the lights on the street below and correct myself. "Today."

He smiles as he walks over to me. "So I must lose you twice in one lifetime." He takes my hands and holds them in his. "When I left Mawdesley, I made myself a promise that to find you would be enough. I didn't allow myself to imagine anything more. I would find you, and with or without you I would go back to Lancashire." He squeezes my hands so tight. "What if I asked you to stay, Dolly. What if I asked you to give up your dream, and come home with me? What would you say?"

So many times I have imagined what I would do if I saw Teddy again. I've pictured myself running into his arms, everything swept away in his warm embrace. I have pictured us sitting by the fire as an old couple in love, grandchildren playing at our feet. But this is not the end of a picture, or the end of a novel, or the final act of a play. This is real life, and when faced with the question, I don't have an answer.

He rests his fingers against my lips. "I would never ask that of you. Never. I'll be on the three o'clock train to Liverpool, and I will go with peace in my heart to know that you are sailing toward your future."

There are times when words are inadequate. He wraps his arms around me and I close my eyes, allowing myself to walk with him, back across the years to a small village hall in Lancashire. He is an awkward young boy. I am an excitable young girl in search of adventures. Our eyes meet and we feel something stir within our hearts; something we will later come to understand as love. I blow at a dandelion clock, the seeds drifting between us, whispering of a future we cannot yet imagine.

I stand in silence as he picks up his coat and hat.

I hear his soft footfall on the stairs. I hear the door gently close and I am torn apart—half my heart in the past, half my heart in the future.

I sit quietly at the window and watch him leave, hands in his pockets, the rising sun at his back. Teddy Cooper. The man I would once have followed all the way to the end of the earth, the man I would once have run to across all the endless miles.

I don't follow, or run. I watch him walk farther and farther away from me until he is a distant dot and then nothing.

"And what about Teddy? . . . Have you let him go? Have you made peace with that too?"

Peach and lavender clouds bloom over London as the chimes of Big Ben strike six. The wagons rumble toward the markets. Hawkers drag heavy handcarts. A milk float rattles past. A bread van crunches its brakes as it pulls up in the street. Life goes on as the turmoil in my heart gradually calms.

Only then do I know what I must do.

47

DOLLY

". . . the stars will always shine and I will always be looking up, Dolly: looking for you, thinking of you, loving you."

The warm summer breeze tugs at my hat and skirt as I step out of the bookshop on Charing Cross Road. There is a wild recklessness in the air as I prepare to say farewell to this city I have grown to love. I let it swirl around me, pulling the dark shadows of my past away from me, blowing them over the rooftops and far away to some distant place beyond the horizon. I am liberated from the guilt that has trailed behind me all these years. Teddy is recovered and content with his life. My child is much loved and well cared for.

And yet there are still creases to smooth, frayed edges to neaten.

From Charing Cross Road, I travel to Shoreditch, to Hettie's house. As I open the latch on the gate, my eyes glance toward the upper windows in the hope that he will be there. But there is no movement at the curtains today, no face pressed against the glass. My heart is restless as I knock on the door.

Hettie invites me in for tea but I decline, explaining that I don't have time.

"Of course, of course. Lots to do! Steamships to board! I'll fetch the dress. Come in. I won't be a minute."

I step into the hallway as she rushes through to the workroom. I listen keenly, hoping to catch the sound of him. Little footsteps. A small voice. But the house is quiet today. Too quiet.

While I wait for Hettie, I study a collection of photographs on the wall. A happy young couple with a baby. A happy boy cuddling a teddy bear. I take my own photograph from my coat pocket. He came from such a dark and troubled place, the memory of which will always cause me sorrow, but I gave him life and I gave a mother and father a son to love, and by that thought I will always be comforted.

Hettie reappears with my finished dress wrapped in tissue paper. I take it from her and give her something in return.

"It's for little Thomas," I explain. "I was hoping he might be here. Would you give it to him?"

Hettie looks a little surprised. "Of course."

"I just . . . well . . . it's a book. You told me how much he likes to read. I hope he'll like it."

I was so pleased to find *The Adventure Book for Boys*. Before the shopkeeper wrapped it for me, I wrote an inscription inside: *To dear Thomas, Wonderful adventures await for those who dare to find them. Be brave. Be daring. With much love, Auntie Dolly. X.*

Hettie smiles. "You're very kind, Miss Lane. I'll be sure to give it to him."

"Perhaps I could write to him occasionally. I'm sure it would be very exciting to receive a letter all the way from America."

"He would like that. Thank you. But only if you have time."

I look into her eyes, knowing that I can never tell her, that I can never explain why I will always have time for Thomas; that there will never be enough time for all I want to say to him and give to him.

I take her hand. "Thank you for all your incredible work, Hettie. We will wow America with your costumes. Soon everyone will want a Hettie Bennett!"

She blushes. "Well, I don't know about that. But I hope the tour is a roaring success. I wouldn't be surprised if you never come back. I have a feeling America will suit you, Miss Lane."

"I hope so, Hettie. I hope so very much."

From Shoreditch, I take a motor cab to Liverpool Street station. The driver weaves laboriously through the heavy weekday traffic. I fidget with my gloves, opening and closing my purse and drumming my fingers on the empty seat beside me. I huff and sigh like a piston engine. "How much farther?" I ask, again and again, my heartbeat quickening with each new line of traffic we become obstructed by.

"Not long now, miss. I'll get you there as quick as I can."

But it isn't quick enough. I urge the wind to blow us along.

Eventually we arrive. The station concourse hums to the sound of harried travelers and the cry of porters. Great trollies of luggage rumble past as the shrill whistle of a departing train sends a shiver right through me. It is so final. So beseeching. I think of the many hearts that will lurch as the wheels set in motion, men, women, and children leaning through the windows to wave their farewells, some with joy at what lies ahead down the tracks, some with the deepest sorrow at what they leave behind.

I look up at the departures board, searching desperately for the train to Liverpool. The three o'clock train is preparing to depart. I make a dash for platform five, dodging mothers who stop suddenly to fuss over their children, stepping around elderly gentlemen who seem to purposely block my way. The stationmaster checks his pocket watch and looks up at the station clock hanging from the great iron brackets above the platform. As he lifts a whistle to his lips, I urge him not to blow.

"Teddy!"

I run through the gate as the whistle is blown. Someone is running behind me, calling for the train to wait. I turn. "Teddy?" but it isn't him, it isn't him. Steam hisses from the brakes as the train creaks and groans, the carriages jolting to attention as the locomotive pulls away with a great yawning effort, as if it would pull every bit of my heart along with it. I run along the platform, stretching up onto my tiptoes to see inside the carriage windows as they begin to rumble slowly past.

"Teddy!" I cry. "Teddy Cooper!"

For a moment, I am a young girl again, weeping on the station platform as he presses a bunch of daffodils into my hands. *"We'll be married in the spring and we'll have little 'uns running around our feet and everything will be back to normal, Dolly. Just you and me and a quiet simple life. Just like we've always wanted."* The life I know in one hand. The life I dream of in the other.

Lovers' hands are torn apart, fingers out-stretched in the void. Windows are pulled shut. Hands stop waving. I cannot see him.

"Teddy!"

I glance desperately up and down the platform but he is not there.

"Teddy!"

He has gone.

He has gone.

And I am the fool that let him go.

I watch the last of the carriages disappear amid the clouds of smoke before I turn and walk back along the platform, slumping down onto a bench like a bundle of washday rags, my tears blurring my vision. "I wanted to say good-bye, Teddy. I just wanted to say a proper good-bye."

And then I see it. A brown paper package on the seat beside me.

I pick it up.

To Little Thing.

I look around me, but the platform is empty.

I pull the string and fold back the paper and I gasp when I see it. My book. *The Adventure Book for Girls.* Tears spill onto the pages as I lift the book from its wrapping and open the cover, and there they are, the words I have heard so often as a gentle whisper, a reminder: *Wonderful adventures await for those who dare to find them. With much love, Auntie Gert.* But there are new words written beneath. A new inscription. *I always knew you would find those adventures. Fly, my Little Butterfly. Spread your wings and soar. Always, Teddy. X*

And there's a letter. I unfold the page and start to read.

My dear Little Thing,
We have shared so many words, you and I, and yet when it comes to saying good-bye it is as if the world has no words at all.

I took the two o'clock train, Dolly. I had always planned to take the two o'clock train. I didn't want to confuse you or muddle your thoughts. We have shared too many good-byes, you and me. It is better this way.

Life has been strangely cruel to us in many ways, but it has also been extraordinarily generous and kind and that is what I choose to remember. Those are the memories I will care for as if they were the most precious jewels. From the very first time I saw you, you drew me into your soul and held me there, before blowing me gently back out as you puffed at a dandelion clock. You were eight years old and I was ten. I still don't know how I spent ten whole years of my life without you in it.

When I was in France I would look at the stars every night and think of you, knowing that you would be looking too. I didn't know what life had in store for us then, and I don't know now. But I do know this: that after everything we have been through, and all that we might lament and regret, the sun will always rise and the stars will always shine and I will always be looking up, Dolly: looking for you, thinking of you, loving you.

Don't be sad for us. Don't mourn what we might have had or what might have been. Embrace what is. Go to America and find your adventures. Go and live the life you were meant to live. Set your dreams free and see where they take you.

Your wings were always restless, Dolly. I knew you would fly away. Like the butterfly at my window you were never mine to keep, and you are both more beautiful in your freedom.

Don't forget me, Dolly. Look for me in the stars.

Always, and forever.

Teddy

X

I place the letter back inside the book and clutch it to my chest as the clatter and chaos of life goes on around me. In the middle of it all, I am perfectly still.

"There is a moment, Miss Lane, between the end of one thing and the start of another. It is a most peculiar thing, like that strange light between night and dawn: not dark and not yet light. A sense of something other—something in between . . . Sense the ending. Prepare for the new beginning."

I stand up, hold my head high, and walk along the platform, away from my past, one foot in front of the other. Sometimes our dreams come true.

Sometimes they frighten us and break our hearts. Sometimes we must let them go. That is the way of things. That is the path the adventurer takes.

As I walk, I feel my wings unfold behind me. They start to beat, strong and steady.

"Thank you, Teddy," I whisper. "Thank you."

I am ready.

I am ready to fly.

I am ready for adventures.

EPILOGUE

The soothing lilt of the piano drifts around the Foyer at Claridge's, the pleasing medley of old-time jazz captivating us all, the music mingling with polite chatter and the jangle of silver teaspoons against fine china cups. The sound of afternoon tea. The sound of luxury.

The annual tradition of afternoon tea at Claridge's began as Perry's idea. Once a year, on Loretta's birthday. He felt it was a fitting tribute to the sister he had loved so dearly and the woman who had touched all our hearts. She loved this place and we continue to love it for her. The truth is, I am as enchanted by it now as I was the first time I came here as a rising young star of the theater.

I sit at our usual table for two, seated behind a huge date palm while I wait for him to arrive. He is late, as usual. At least I have a little privacy while I wait—a little, but not too much. The spaces between the foliage afford the guests an occasional glimpse, sending whispered speculations racing across the crisp white tablecloths.

"Is it her?" "I thought she was still in America." "Yes, I'm certain it's her."

I smile. Let them whisper. Let them wonder. It is, after all, part of the performance.

I sip my coffee and watch the raindrops slip down the windowpane. It reminds me of the day I first chased adventures along the Strand and bumped into dear Perry. I smile at the memory: sagging cotton stockings splashed with dirt. Borrowed coat. Thirdhand shoes. Unpunctual. Untidy. A girl who would never get on in life.

Except she did.

She got on remarkably well.

I check the time on my wristwatch and then I see him crossing the road, dressed to the nines, a walking stick at his side. After all this time, after all these years, my heart still jumps a little at the sight of him.

I stand to greet him as he limps toward the table and I cannot stop the smile that spreads across my lips as my arms open wide to embrace him. I rest my head on his shoulder, absorbing the familiar feel of him.

"Look at you!" he says, his eyes smiling. "America is treating you well, I see!"

"Dear Teddy. It has been too long."

"It has been exactly a year, Dolly. It is always exactly a year."

We are old friends, Teddy and me, separated by an ocean and a lifetime of memories, and we are always so very delighted to see each other. I squeeze his hands. He squeezes mine in return. Our hands may be frail and lined with age, yet when I close my eyes I am a girl of just eight years beneath his gentle touch, and he is a boy of ten. We sit beside each other, dangling our legs over the stone bridge, and all is wonderful with the world.

Teddy once said that life is as fragile as a butterfly wing and we must carry it lightly. Sometimes it will sit happily in our hands, sometimes it will fly away from us, but in the end—no matter the distance or the complications in between—the things we truly care for will always come back to us.

Like our greatest hopes and dreams, they will be a part of us.

Always.

Acknowledgments

As with any production where the spotlight shines on the principal actor, there is always an incredible supporting cast and crew in the wings. A book is no different, and I must now stand aside and drum up frenzied applause for all of the following.

Firstly, my leading ladies: agent of wonders, Michelle Brower—a rock of sense, great judgment, and endlessly sound advice—and my editor at William Morrow, Lucia Macro, for mentioning the 1920s in the first place, and for your unerring calmness and wisdom, which kept this book on course and added extra sparkle where I'd missed a bit.

To my publisher, Liate Stehlik, and the wonderful team at William Morrow in New York—Nicole Fischer, Megan Schumann, Molly Waxman, Jennifer Hart—and the production and copy editors who spare my blushes. Thank you all for your endless support and hard work. Special thanks to Rhea Braunstein for the beautiful interior design and Mumtaz Mustafa for the stunning U.S. cover.

In writing this book, I completed a journey I started way back in 2013 when I was first introduced to Kate Bradley, senior editor at

HarperCollins UK. I am so excited to now be working with Kate and the fabulous team at HarperFiction. To stand on the 16th floor of the News Building in London and see my books lined up along the shelves is a moment I will never forget. Thank you so much, Kate, for your belief in me, and your patience! Special thanks also to Charlotte Abrams-Simpson for the beautiful UK and Ireland cover.

Huge thanks to Tony Purdue, Mary Byrne, and Ann-Marie Dolan at Team HarperCollins Ireland. It has been great fun getting to know you over the last year and I'm so happy to be working with you all. Go raibh maith agaibh!

A very special thank you to Susan Scott, archivist at The Savoy. From my first tentative email in the summer of 2014, you answered my questions with patience and fascinating detail. In particular, the two books you recommended—*Imperial Palace* and *Madeleine Grown Up*—were absolute jewels to research. I must also thank you for recommending the lavender éclairs from the Melba patisserie outside the hotel! Thanks also to Orla Hickey at Claridge's for helping with historical matters of afternoon tea!

Also joining me on stage are my fabulous family and friends who continue to tolerate my incessant need for reassurance, advice, and gin while I write. In Ireland, special thanks to Sheena Lambert for reading early drafts and, along with

Catherine Ryan Howard, supplying regular doses of coffee, cocktails, and sanity. To writing friends Carmel Harrington and Fionnuala Kearney, thank you for the laughs and the kebabs! To Carol Longeran and Gillian Comiskey, thank you for corrupting me on various very long lunches. To Ciara Morgan, Angela Legg, and Tanya Flanagan, thank you for all your support and the camping! Huge thanks to my big sister, Helen, for enthusiastically reading everything I send and finding appropriate emojis to express your reactions. The cocktail glass was definitely overused on this one! A special hello to the newest additions to the family, Cian, Rosie, and Berry, who are *The Girl from The Savoy* book babies (and book dog!).

Thanks are also due to Taraya Middleton, for offering the highest bid to be mentioned in my acknowledgments as part of the Authors for Nepal fund-raiser, organized by Julia Williams to help the communities affected by the devastating earthquake in April 2015.

Thank you, always, to Damien, Max, and Sam for giving me the attic and keeping me sane and suggesting endless ideas for titles. I love you all. And thank you, Puffin the cat, for rearranging my Post-it note plot layout. Several chapters would possibly have remained in the wrong place if they hadn't stuck to your fur.

And finally, to you, my readers. Your support

and kind words mean absolutely everything. Thank you for letting me continue to write for you. I am the luckiest girl in the world and I applaud you all.

X

Center Point Large Print
600 Brooks Road / PO Box 1
Thorndike, ME 04986-0001 USA

(207) 568-3717

US & Canada:
1 800 929-9108
www.centerpointlargeprint.com

8-16